LISA WINGATE

Drenched in Light

BERKLEY
NEW YORK

BERKLEY
An imprint of Penguin Random House LLC
penguinrandomhouse.com

Copyright © 2006 by Wingate Media, LLC
Conversation guide copyright © 2006 by Penguin Random House LLC
Excerpt from *The Book of Lost Friends* copyright © 2020 by Wingate Media, LLC

ISBN: 9781984804211

The Library of Congress has cataloged the NAL Accent edition as follows:

Wingate, Lisa.
Drenched in light/Lisa Wingate.
p. cm.
ISBN 0-451-21848-5 (trade pbk.)
1. Ballerinas—Fiction.   2. Student counselors—Fiction.
3. Performing arts high schools—Fiction.
I. Title.
PS3573.I53165D74 2006
813'.6—dc22   2005035659

NAL Accent trade paperback edition / July 2006
Berkley trade paperback edition / April 2021

Printed in the United States of America
1   3   5   7   9   10   8   6   4   2

Book design by Elke Sigal

This is a work of fiction. Names, characters, places, and incidents either
are the product of the author's imagination or are used fictitiously, and any
resemblance to actual persons, living or dead, business establishments,
events, or locales is entirely coincidental.

"A feisty, flirtatious, homegrown Texas tale."
—Dixie Cash, author of *My Heart May Be Broken,
But My Hair Still Looks Great*

Lone Star Café

"A charmingly nostalgic treat. . . . Wingate handles the book's strong spiritual element deftly, creating a novel that is sweetly inspirational but not saccharine."
—*Publishers Weekly*

"A beautifully written, heartwarming tale about finding love where you least expect it."
—Barbara Freethy

"Leaves you feeling like you've danced the two-step across Texas."
—Jodi Thomas

"A remarkably talented and innovative writer, with a real feel for human emotion."
—Linda Lael Miller

Texas Cooking

"A delightful love story as heartwarming and vivid as its setting in the beautiful Texas hill country."
—Janice Woods Windle

"*Texas Cooking* . . . will have readers drooling for the next installment . . . [a] beautifully written mix of comedy, drama, cooking, and journalism."
—*Dallas Morning News*

"Takes the reader on a delightful journey into the most secret places of every woman's heart."
—Catherine Anderson

"The story is a treasure. You will be swept along, refreshed, and amused. . . . Give yourself a treat and read this tender, unusual story."
—Dorothy Garlock

Praise for Lisa Wingate's Novels

Done

The Book of Lost Friends

"Enthralling and ultimately heartening."   —*Library Journal*

"Wingate makes history come alive."   —*Booklist*

Before We Were Yours

"A poignant, engrossing tale about sibling love."   —*People*

"Sure to be one of the most compelling books you pick up this year."
—*Parade*

"Take note: This may be the best book of the year."
—*The Times* (Shreveport, LA)

"A tale of enduring power . . . vivid and affecting."
—Paula McLain, *New York Times* bestselling author of
Love and Ruin

The Tending Roses Series

The Language of Sycamores

"Heartfelt, honest, and entirely entertaining . . . this poignant story will
touch your heart from the first page to the last."   —Kristin Hannah

"Wingate's smoothly flowing prose fills the pages with emotional drama."
—*Romantic Times* (top pick)

Good Hope Road

"A novel bursting with joy amidst crisis: Small-town life is painted with scope and detail in the capable hands of a writer who understands longing, grief, and the landscape of a woman's heart."

—Adrian Trigiani, author of the Big Stone Gap trilogy

"Wingate has written a genuinely heartwarming story about how a sense of possibility can be awakened in the aftermath of a tragedy to bring a community together and demonstrate the true American spirit."

—*Booklist*

Tending Roses

"A story at once gentle and powerful about the very old and the very young, and about the young woman who loves them all. Richly emotional and spiritual, *Tending Roses* affected me from the first page."

—Luanne Rice, *New York Times* bestselling author of *Silver Bells*

"You can't put it down without . . . taking a good look at your own life and how misplaced priorities might have led to missed opportunities. *Tending Roses* is an excellent read for any season, a celebration of the power of love."

—*El Paso Times*

The Texas Hill Country Series

Over the Moon at the Big Lizard Diner

"A beautifully crafted and insightfully drawn page-turner . . . this is storytelling at its best. . . . Wingate delivers an insightful, heartfelt, and sometimes crazy novel of romance, redemption, and personal change. A journey you simply must not miss."

—Julie Cannon, author of the
Homegrown series and *Those Pearly Gates*

"A warmhearted tale of love and longing, grits and cowboys, horse psychology and dinosaur tracks."

—Claire Cook, author of *Multiple Choice* and *Must Love Dogs*

To my mom
For letting me drop out of piano lessons
And ballet school,
For saying yes when I wanted to try gymnastics,
Then sitting through countless hours of lessons and competitions

To my dad
For letting me have a pony,
Which led to years of horse shows, here, there, and everywhere

You never pushed
Or criticized, or seemed disappointed
You gave me the dreams of my childhood
While you cheered from the bleachers

Acknowledgments

Anyone who's ever remodeled a home knows that you start out thinking you have the project under control, and things go downhill from there. Eventually you realize you're going to need help. Lots of help. From people who know things you don't know, people who can do things you can't do, and friendly neighbors who come by with baskets of cookies or pots of coffee, to tell you they think the place is coming along wonderfully, and they can't wait to see the finished product.

Story writing is a fairly similar process. Few authors journey from *Once Upon a Time* to *The End* alone. The final product becomes a combined effort of friends, neighbors, and benevolent strangers gracious enough to share their time and expertise. Many friends, neighbors, and benevolent strangers have contributed to the creation of *Drenched in Light* and have encouraged me along the path. In particular, my thanks go out to Dr. Sharon Mannion, for sharing details from her many years of experience in school administration; Jan Lassiter, for sharing her knowledge of magnet schools; Kaye Johnson, English teacher par excellence, for helping me with literary selections for Dell's English class; Trooper Steve Adcock, for sharing valuable information about school drug prevention programs and adolescent substance abuse issues; Maria Salas, for contributing descriptions of traditional dances and customs in her hometown of Mexico City, so that the Jumpkids in the story could properly enjoy their pretend trip to La Fiesta; and Cathy Campbell, for contributing those hard-to-research details about Kansas City.

My gratitude also goes out to those who contributed knowledge of the worlds of both professional and amateur ballet, including Shaelyne Robertson, teacher to would-be ballerinas, and Mandy Koger, super Web site designer, former ballet dancer, and priceless friend. A special thanks goes to Madeline Lively, for sharing her son Michael (How often, I ask you, does a writer desperately needing ballet research just happen to be seated at a luncheon right next to the mother of a professional ballet dancer?). A full cup of thank-yous also goes to Michael Lively, for spending hours with me on the phone, discussing the intricate details of ballet with a dance-school dropout who appreciates the art but knew little about it.

On the publishing side of things, I would like to thank my agent, Claudia Cross of Sterling Lord Literistic, my editor, Ellen Edwards, and everyone at New American Library. Thanks also to the many bookstore owners and media personnel who have supported the books, and to friends and readers far and wide who take time to share my books with friends and family, and to send so many wonderful letters and e-mails. You can't imagine how blessed I feel to be sharing these journeys with each of you. You are the friendly neighbors stopping by my latest construction project with coffee and cookies, shoring me up with words of encouragement when I need them most, tipping up the coffeepot and filling my cup to overflowing.

Last of all, thank you to my family. You are, as always, the treasures of my heart.

Chapter 1

M^{e.}

Not much of a topic for an essay. There's nothing to me that anyone would want to read about.

The books I read in English class last semester.

Not much of a topic, either.

How those books are like my life.

None of those books are like my life. How could they be? Grandma Rose always said that two folks might go along the same path, but how they walk it depends a lot on the shoes they're in. There's an old Indian saying she had hanging on her kitchen wall. I can't remember it exactly, but it means that if we all had the same shoes, we'd understand each other better. But we don't.

I don't like to wear shoes, so I'm a little like Huckleberry Finn. Of course, I have to wear shoes most of the time, now that I live in Kansas City with Karen and James. Good shoes, and nice clothes, and my hair combed back in a pretty silver clip most of the time, so it doesn't hang dark and stringy over my face—that's how I have to look here. That's how all the students look at Harrington Academy. I don't mind wearing the same shoes as everybody else. It's easy. It makes you fit in, and no-body questions where you've been or what you've done. When you have the right shoes, everyone takes you in without a second glance. I'm not used to that. It feels strange, like I'm moving around in someone else's body.

In my mind, I'm barefoot like Huckleberry Finn, but I don't tell anybody that. Not my music teachers, not Karen and James, not the kids at school, not my caseworker, not that reporter from Kansas City Artweek who interviewed me about our spring concert with the symphonic. *They'd think I was ungrateful. Grandma Rose always said that an ungrateful heart makes an unhappy life. I want to be happy.*

Of course I'm thankful for these new shoes. Who wouldn't be?

But deep in my heart, a part of me will always be barefoot, running through the shallows of Mulberry Creek, with my eyes closed and my arms stretched out like I could fly.

That girl doesn't wear the right shoes, but she's lighter than air. The sun pushes hard through the trees, and she's soaked in it until it's deep down inside her. She stops and stands with her feet in the water. The glow reflects all around and the sycamore leaves whisper, then hush. She holds her breath, afraid to move. She can feel God in everything. He touches her with His fingertip, and her heart is drenched in light.

"Pick me up and take me away," she says in her mind, and she waits. But it doesn't happen. The answer is always no. She wishes the river would rise and sweep her off, carry her to someplace where it's easier to be.

But the river doesn't listen. . . .

I set down the handwritten essay and looked across the desk at the thirteen-year-old girl on the other side. She seemed small sitting there, caramel-colored fingers fiddling nervously between her knees, body huddled against the office chair like she was trying to disappear into it. Her long, straight dark hair fell around her face like a shield, making her look like a Native American girl in some turn-of-the-century photo, afraid the camera would steal her soul.

"Everything OK, Dell?" Leaning back in my chair, I tried to appear empathic, nonthreatening.

She flicked the mistrusting glance they all use for social workers, counselors, court advocates, teachers—anyone with the power to interfere in their lives, to ferret out the adult truths they hide behind their childhood faces.

"Uh-huh." She shrugged noncommittally.

"Do you know why you're here?"

"Yes." No further comment.

I chuckled, and she glanced up, surprised. "Not much of a talker, huh?" The joke lightened her up for an instant before the shields rose again. My mind flashed back to an adolescent counseling course last year in grad school—*ask only open-ended questions*. So far, I hadn't had many occasions to actually counsel anyone at Harrington Arts Academy. Mostly my job consisted of arranging class schedules, writing grant applications and press releases, maintaining attendance sheets, calling substitute teachers, giving parent tours, and resolving spats among kids. If any real counseling was needed, families with kids at Harrington could afford private-practice psychologists.

Which was why Dell Jordan seemed like such an enigma, sitting there in my office. Foster kids from backwater towns like Hindsville, Missouri, didn't get into schools like Harrington—not these days, anyway. Harrington may have once been conceived as a magnet school for talented kids from all sectors of society, but where competition is stiff and prestige is high, those who can afford the private lessons and the expensive instruments and the high-profile letters of recommendation win out. In the seven weeks I'd been middle school counselor, I hadn't seen many needy-but-talented kids walking the halls. Harrington students came in bright packages with designer labels. They glittered with the glow of self-confidence, wore easy smiles that said, *Look at me; I'm someone special. I'm a star.*

But not Dell Jordan. I'd caught only a few glimpses of her these past weeks. She was a slim shadow on the fringes, adept at getting lost in the crowd—not a hard thing to accomplish in a large student population.

"Can you tell me why you're here?"

"Because I'm stupid." It was a flat statement. No sarcasm or teenage attitude.

"What makes you say that?"

Picking at a fingernail, she twisted her full lips to one side, then finally answered. "Because it's true. I can't pass English because I'm stupid. That's why I had to write that essay. For extra credit, or else I'd flunk."

"Well, Mrs. Morris's English class is tough." That much was true. Mrs. Morris was old, grim-faced, a stickler for the rules, even when the rules needed to be bent. "I didn't do so well in there, myself."

Blinking, she jerked her head up, and I could see the wheels turning. *How could the blond-headed grown-up lady in the pantsuit have ever been in Mrs. Morris's English class?* No doubt at twenty-seven, sitting behind the counselor's desk, I looked ancient to her, which meant that Mrs. Morris was right up there with the Crypt Keeper.

Dell sank back miserably. "I hate English."

"Yeah, I did, too," I admitted, focusing on the papers as I jotted some notes in her file.

Shifting in her chair, she leaned closer to see what I was writing. "Am I gonna get kicked out?"

"Of course not." I didn't look up, but continued writing. Kids usually found it easier to talk to the top of a head. "Did you want to get kicked out?"

"Huh-uh." The answer came without hesitation, the first definitive thing she'd said, other than, *Because I'm stupid.* "I want to stay. I like music. I *love* music."

Glancing up, I caught a glitter of enthusiasm in her dark eyes. She scooted forward in the chair and the thick brown-black hair fell away from her face, which was suddenly bright and animated. This was not the same kid who hated English. "I see you're good at it." I motioned to the notes in the file. "What do you play?"

"Oh, lots of stuff." She was remarkably talkative now that we were entering territory outside Mrs. Morris's English class. "Piano, guitar, the flute some, and I want to learn violin, but, gosh, that's hard. I do vocal, too."

"Wow. That's quite a laundry list." Between that and the notes in her file, I could see why a foster kid from Hindsville had been accepted into the seventh-grade program at Harrington in her first year of application. She had an incredible talent in music. Unfortunately, her first-semester report card showed that she was behind in every other subject.

"Did *you* do music here?" Her preemptive question surprised me. Normally, kids in my office were primarily interested in my ability to solve their problems with class schedules, or summer grant applications, or attendance paperwork.

Resting an elbow on my desk, I twirled the pencil in my fingers like a tiny baton, until I caught myself doing it; then I set the pencil down. Fidgeting. Unattractive nervous habit. Showed lack of confidence. "I did. Vocal, theater, and dance. Dance was really my thing."

She frowned, and I saw the question on her face—the one they all wanted to ask: *If you were such a good dancer, how did you end up sitting behind the counselor's desk? Loser.*

Kids didn't understand that fairy tales sometimes end unhappily. In a place like Harrington, where the atmosphere was so thick with high expectations that you could choke on it, nothing but one hundred percent success seemed like a possibility.

Dell, however, looked like she already knew that life isn't fair, and you do the best you can with the result. Her eyes met mine, dark and liquid, and I had a sense that she understood my story without my ever telling it. I turned away, caught off guard by the power of that sympathetic glance.

Silence fell on us, and I found myself studying the old beadboard wainscot and the plaster walls with the fan-shaped sponge pattern that made it look like giant butterflies had been decoupaged to the school walls. I'd spent hours staring at their lifeless wings as a student, but I'd never been inside the counselor's office. Anything that needed to be taken up with the administration, my parents handled for me. Mostly, I worked hard to be perfect, so that my mom would stay away from the school.

"I wasn't gonna turn it in, you know." Dell spoke up, and I focused on her again, aware of my sudden lapse. "The essay," she explained. "I wasn't gonna turn it in. Mrs. Morris wasn't supposed to see it. I was gon . . . going to write another one that didn't say . . ." Cheeks twitching, she arrested the comment, pulled her hands inside her sweatshirt sleeves, then finished with, ". . . that stuff."

"What stuff?" *What stuff, indeed?* What stuff this kid had inside her,

I couldn't imagine. She was a well so deep that the bottom was hidden in a quiet, inky darkness. No telling what was down there. The girl in the river was down there, wishing God would pluck her off the face of the Earth.

Why?

Pinching her lip between her thumb and forefinger, she muttered behind her hand, "That stuff about shoes and Karen and James and all." Her lashes darted upward with alarm, and her hand fell away from her mouth. "Karen and James didn't see that paper, did they? Mrs. Morris didn't send it to them?"

Her earnest expression of panic raised the barometer of concern in my mind. I'd done my final college internship in social work. When kids are genuinely frightened of their parents' responses to things, it's a red flag. "No. Mrs. Morris brought it to me. Are you afraid of what your foster parents would think of it?"

Scuffing her red tennis shoes back and forth under the chair, she studied the floor. "No. But I don't want them to see it."

"Are you afraid it would hurt their feelings?" Looking at the file, I noted that there were several pages of information behind the admissions form—a letter from the foster mother, a report from a social worker in Hindsville, transcripts from her former school. Information haphazardly added by the previous counselor at Harrington, who had retired unexpectedly after the fall semester, creating the job opening I had filled. On the corner of Dell's admissions form, a tiny yellow dot indicated that there was additional information in a confidential folder. I wished I'd taken time to look it over, rather than letting Mrs. Morris bring her directly into my office.

Dell nodded. "Yes."

"And what would happen if you hurt their feelings?"

"I don't know."

"Are you afraid to find out?" She responded with a questioning glance, and I added, "Are you afraid to find out what would happen if you hurt your foster parents' feelings? Do you worry about it?"

Lacing her fingers in her lap, she tightened her grip until her knuckles turned white. "I just don't want them to see that stuff I wrote, OK?

Nobody was supposed to read it. Mrs. Morris shouldn't of brought it to you. She hates me and she wants to get me kicked out."

"On the contrary, Mrs. Morris brought the essay to me because she was concerned about you." Though knowing Mrs. Morris, I figured Dell was probably correct. Mrs. Morris liked only the *right* kind of kids, the bound-for-the-philharmonic kids from good families. I couldn't, of course, admit that to a student. "She was worried about some of the things you wrote."

Squirming in her chair, Dell cast her gaze toward the door like an animal in a trap. "That was private stuff. It don't mean"—pausing, she gave a frustrated jerk of her chin and corrected—"doesn't mean anything."

"Sometimes the things we write for ourselves mean the most of all." I handed the essay across the desk to her. "When we don't think anybody's going to read it, we can say what we really mean. We don't have to be a certain way to make other people happy."

Taking the paper with a sigh of relief, she folded it into the smallest possible cube and tucked it into her pocket. Clearly, it was headed for the nearest trash can.

"There's nothing wrong with writing down what you feel, Dell," I said. "It's a good idea to get those things out on paper."

"Yeah, unless you do it in Mrs. Morris's class." The observation made me chuckle, and her lips twitched upward.

"True enough. Sometimes it helps to talk about those issues with someone, though." Her eyes met mine, and I again had the feeling I'd only skimmed the surface of a lake. There were things she didn't share with anybody, and probably not even with herself. She had a sense of desperation, an obvious need to keep everything tamped down. "I'd like to know about the girl in the river. If you decide to write more of her story, I'd like to read it. . . . We could talk about her—the girl in the river, I mean—maybe understand what she's feeling a little better. But it's your choice. Nobody's going to force you to do anything, all right?"

" 'Kay," she answered, blinking at me, first surprised, then doubtful. "Are you gonna call James and Karen?"

"No." I folded my hands on the desk. "Did you want me to?"

Her expression said that I was nuts. "Huh-uh." She started to get up, then sat down again, crossed and uncrossed her thin arms. "Are you gonna call anybody?"

"I wasn't planning to. Do you think I need to call somebody?"

She eyed me narrowly again, trying to figure things out. Like most kids I'd met during my short stint with the foster care system, she was accustomed to being powerless in the world of adults—a pawn, a case study, a number and a file. Turning her head to one side, she watched me from the corner of her eye, trying to discern the catch. *There's always a catch,* her look said. "If I don't come back here, are you gonna call somebody?"

"If you don't come back to my office, you mean?"

"Yeah, if I don't write more of the story, are you gonna call somebody?"

"No."

"If I write some more, are you gonna tell people what it says?"

"No, Dell. As long as no one is in imminent danger, what's said in this office is between you and me. If we both decide, at some point, that there's someone else we need to talk to—say, a teacher you're having trouble with, or another student, or your foster parents—we'll do that together. You and I together, all right?"

Considering it momentarily, she said, "All right," then stood up, walked to the door, and hovered there with her fingers on the handle. "Can I go now?"

I checked my watch. "Yes, you may. You should be just in time to catch your ride home."

"My foster mom picks me up." She brightened with an affection that was obvious. Clearly, she looked forward to being out of school for the day and back with her foster family. "She runs the Jumpkids after-school arts program, so I have to help her with the little kids. We go to a different elementary school every day of the week." Suddenly there was no sign of the girl who had been sulking about Mrs. Morris's English class. This kid, the after-school arts helper, didn't seem anything like the girl in the river.

"I've heard of Jumpkids," I commented. "Sometime, I'd like to see how it works."

Her mouth lifted into a wide smile that was dazzling in its contrast to her former gloom. "That'd be cool." Then she bit her lip, losing the enthusiasm, worried, no doubt, because I'd learned things she didn't want her foster parents to know.

"What's said in this office stays in this office."

Her posture relaxed. " 'Kay." Opening the door, she let in the sounds of the hallway—lockers slamming, kids talking, clothes rustling, shoes squealing on the old wooden floors. "Thanks," she muttered, then disappeared into the fray, leaving the door ajar.

Watching her go, I took out her confidential file and started reading it. There was an unusual amount of information—as if quite a few people were invested in the fate of this one girl. Looking at her application forms, I could see why. She was musically talented to a degree that caused even the stodgy curmudgeons on the admissions committee to use words like "gifted" and "prodigy."

> . . . *extremely gifted musically* . . .
> . . . *talented, particularly for a low-socioeconomic child* . . .
> . . . *in my opinion, a prodigy heretofore thwarted by a disadvantaged environment.*
> *I recommend admission be granted, despite the child's obvious lack of past academic achievement. Given the quality of instruction at Harrington, she will no doubt* . . .

Only one committee member expressed any reservations.

> . . . *my concern is that Dell appeared extremely stressed during the interview process. Certainly this is normal for children in such a demanding situation, but Dell was very inanimate, overly focused on silently and continually checking the reactions of her foster parents, who seem genuinely interested in her welfare, but perhaps unaware of the obvious social difficulties mentioned in the report from her former school and apparent during her interview. Given this child's difficult and isolative history, I wonder if consideration should be given to tabling her application until next year. I have no doubt that Har-*

*rington is the best place for her musically, but I wonder if, consider-
ing her recent placement in foster care and other issues, Harrington,
with its inherent demands, is the best place for her as a person . . .*

The door squeaked, and I looked up to find Mrs. Morris entering
my office. Out of habit, I covered the papers on my desk, then reminded myself that I wasn't a kid writing contraband notes in her English class anymore. "Yes, Mrs. Morris?" I felt fourteen again, despite
my determination not to. Something about my former English teacher's
withering glare was ingrained in my psyche, like one of those horror
movies you never forget. "May I help you?"

"The essay." She fanned her fingers back and forth against her palm,
as if she were confiscating chewing gum from a student. The disgusting
thing was that my heart jumped into my throat. Her nasal voice
scratched up and down my spine like one of her thick, yellow fingernails, leaving an itchy trail of chalk dust.

"I returned it to Dell." The comment sounded amazingly calm and self-
assured, considering that I was confronting my worst teenage nightmare.

Mrs. Morris's face went pale, then flushed red again, her eyes widening and her mouth squeezing into a thin downward line. "You did *what?*"

"I returned her essay to her," I repeated, struggling to appear pleasant. I was rapidly moving from intimidated to angry and insulted. "We
talked about it, and she assured me that she never intended to hand in
that essay, and she would write another one for you."

Ramming her fists onto her coat-hanger hip bones, Mrs. Morris
flared her nostrils. "How dare you!" she screeched, and three kids passing in the hallway stopped to look. "I intended for you to . . ."

Motioning for the teenage audience to move on, I waited until the
coast was clear before standing up. Even at five foot six, I towered over
my former nemesis. "Mrs. Morris." I came around the desk to assert my
territory. "I am the counselor here. You brought the matter to me, and
I took care of it as I thought best."

Incensed, she sucked in air through a tight, lipless "O," flailing a
hand toward the hallway. "That girl is *disturbed,* suicidal, on top of
her *obvious* academic problems. She doesn't *belong* here." Her voice

echoed through the open door, and I tried not to imagine who might be listening outside.

"Fortunately, Mrs. Morris"—my composure flew out the window, and I clenched the desktop behind me to keep from saying something I would later regret—"neither you nor I choose who belongs here. I will, however, do my level best to help the children who *are* here, and I hope you will, too."

Lowering her chin, she delivered a disdainful glare over the top of her reading glasses. "We can best help Harrington kids by removing those"—she blinked in a pointed way that let me know we were now talking about me, not about Dell—"who don't have *what it takes* to live up to this school's *standard* of *excellence*. Our mission is to produce artists here, Ms. Costell, not middle school *guidance* counselors."

I was momentarily stunned, at a loss as to how to respond. My nemesis looked pleased. She'd tapped into an old wound, and she knew it. Something inside me twisted and ached, and tears prickled in the back of my nose. Swallowing hard, I dug my fingernails into the desk and answered in the flattest tone I could muster, "Fortunately, Mrs. Morris, the world needs both."

Hissing through her teeth, she spun around. "Not from this school, it doesn't." With a furious yank on the front of her sweater, she disappeared through the door.

I kicked it shut, listening as her squeaky grandma shoes stalked around the corner toward the principal's office. Now there would be trouble. The evil queen of English was on a roll, and I was standing in the road.

Sinking into a chair by the wall, I let my head fall into my hand, the argument replaying in my mind.

"I am the counselor here. . . ."

"Fortunately, Mrs. Morris, the world needs both. . . ."

Who was I trying to fool?

Oh, yes, the lifelong quest of professional ballet means nothing to me. I'm happy to have become a guidance counselor, serving up the next generation of Harrington hopes and dreams. . . .

What a crock.

Chapter 2

*M*y cell phone rang just as I was putting away files and preparing to leave the office. It was my father, of course. His daily four-forty-five p.m. call.

"Just called to check on you, Julia. See if you'd be home soon." His voice sent me rocketing back to adolescence, and I pictured the stern-faced father of my childhood, sitting at his desk in his business suit, white shirt, conservative tie, brown hair cut short and neatly combed with a dash of greasy kid stuff. My stomach sank like a stone thrown into the ocean, then swayed back and forth on invisible currents of emotion.

"Sure, Dad. I was just packing up." There's something inherently pathetic about moving back in with your parents at twenty-seven years old. Even more so when they seem happy about it. All those years of struggling to break free and form my own identity, down the drain.

There was a pregnant pause on the other end of the line. "Good . . . Well, listen, Mom and I have a charity event tonight with Bethany and Jason. We're going to meet Jason's parents at this thing, so there's not much chance of slipping out early. Probably be gone the whole evening."

"Sounds like fun, Dad." This, at least, was progress. "You two need to get out more. You haven't been anywhere since"—*since I got out of the hospital and moved home*—"well, for a long time, anyway." Guilt needled me for a dozen different reasons, not the least of which was that, for the last three months, my parents had surrendered their active social schedule to stay home and babysit me. "It's good timing," I added, to reassure him that I could be left home alone and the world would not come to an end. "I have a lot of work to do tonight." Reaching into the file cabinet, I pulled out a federal grant application booklet and Dell Jordan's file.

"But you are coming home?" Trepidation rose in his voice. "Mom and I were hoping you'd sit with Joujou. You know, her bladder isn't good. She wets all over when she's left by herself."

Great. Just me and Mom's neurotic Pekingese, spending Thursday night together in front of Dad's new plasma TV. "Yes, Dad. I'm on my way home."

"Good. Great." The words conveyed obvious relief. "Just a minute, sugar." He paused while someone came into his office and asked a question about an upcoming Microsoft stock split. "So, you get some rest this evening," he said finally. "Mom made dinner for you there at the house. Chicken Florentine, I think."

Food. Of course, it always came down to food, and whether I was eating it, and how much I was eating, and when. "Dad." The word ended in a sigh. "She didn't have to—"

"It's Joujou's favorite," he defended, clearly realizing that we'd slipped into the tenuous territory of my required daily intake.

Well, as long as she made it for the dog, OK. "Tell Mom thanks," I said meekly. How could I blame them for hovering? After finding your daughter passed out in a pool of blood, it's probably hard to let go. "Joujou will enjoy the chicken Florentine, I'm sure."

"And you?"

"Yes, Dad, and me. Tell the food police to relax. I'm not going to give it all to the dog." As soon as the words were out, I wished I could take them back. I sounded immature and ungrateful. Glancing toward the doorway, I checked the hall, making sure no one was lingering nearby.

"Don't be flip, young lady." That was more like the father I remembered—the man who ran the family as confidently as he did his brokerage company. This kinder, gentler dad, who called me at the end of each school day, was a new creation, a product of the hours when no one knew whether I would live or die, and of counselors at St. Francis Hospital's eating-disorders unit, who warned that we needed to keep the family communication lines open. "Your mother is doing her best to help."

Mom was doing her best to control the situation, as always. To make it neat and clean. Mop up all the stains and bleach everything white again, add some starch, and press out the wrinkles to perfection. "I know she is." I slid the folders into my new briefcase—classy taupe leather with brown trim, a getting-on-with-life gift from my incredibly fashionable little sister, Bethany, whose new job as buyer for a chain of women's boutiques allowed her way too much time to shop the trade shows for trendy attaché cases. Every time I put the butter-soft leather bag under my arm, I felt like I had Bett tucked right there close to me, propping me up and pushing me onward. No doubt, she was responsible for getting my parents to leave the house for an evening. "I don't want Mom feeling that she has to cook for me all the time, Dad, that's all. I can pick up McDonald's, or Pizza Hut, Wendy's, Taco Bell, Meals-On-Wheels, you name it. There are a dozen restaurants within two blocks of the school. I'll even order something for the dog. Just tell Mom not to wear herself out. I'm all right. Really."

Someone came into Dad's office again, and I busied myself with putting on my coat, while he said something about SQLI, earnings, and ten thousand shares, then came back on the line. "That's another thing. Mom and I don't want you making stops in that part of town. It isn't like it was when Grandma Rice lived down there. That neighborhood's gone downhill. Remember, once you're off the school grounds, there's no chain-link fence, no campus security officer. Anything can happen. Especially this time of day."

Backing out of my office, I pulled the door shut behind me, then headed for the exit, hoping I wouldn't run into Mr. Stafford, the principal, or Mrs. Morris, who was still lingering in her room. As usual, the other teachers in the main hall had already closed their doors and gone home. "Dad, it's *rush hour*. I doubt I'm in much danger at the Mc-Donald's drive-through. There are people everywhere. The street is full of cars."

"Be careful in the traffic. The downtown streets are a madhouse," he warned, and I slapped my hand over my forehead. *I give up. I just . . . give up.* No matter what I did, my parents were never going to get over my taking this job so soon after being released from the hospital. They would never again trust me to run my own life.

Mrs. Jorgenson, the school secretary, exited the administration door just in time to catch my look of dismay. Pointing at the cell phone, she mouthed, *Dad?* I nodded, rolling my eyes. Mrs. Jorgenson knew that my father called regularly at four forty-five, and that my mother often phoned more than once a day. She was kind enough not to ask why, and considerate in discreetly tucking the Mom messages under my Day-Minder, so everyone wouldn't see that Julia Costell's parents called with an obsessive frequency.

"OK, Dad." There was no point arguing with him. "Listen, I'm walking out the door now, so I'll sign off. Traffic looks thick today. I'll probably be close to an hour getting home. You and Mom go on with your evening, and have a great time, all right? Don't wait for me to get there. I'm going to swing by Riverside Square on the way. I need to stop off for some feminine necessities."

Dad coughed and sputtered into the phone. "Oh . . . well . . . uh . . . all, all right, honey. Bye now."

"Bye, Dad." I closed the phone with a silly sense of satisfaction at having finally found an excuse my father wouldn't question. Normally, when I mentioned shopping, he and Mom got anxious—worried, no doubt, that I'd be buying secret supplies of diet pills, or guzzling laxatives in the store restroom.

God, how had my life come to this?

Pausing to button my coat on the ancient, ivy-covered steps of Harrington, I tried to plot the path from where I had been to where I was now. It seemed an impossible distance from rising teenage protégée, Harrington student with talent and a real chance at professional ballet, to college kid drifting through an education degree while dancing in the

University Ballet, to grad student throwing up every meal I ate, and finally to new member of the corps de ballet at the Kansas City Metro Ballet Company, convinced that if I got just a little thinner, if the body line were a bit cleaner, I could break through the glass ceiling to a leading role.

Soloist. Principal dancer. If it doesn't happen by the time you're out of your twenties, it never will. If they find you lying on the dressing room floor with your stomach hemorrhaging up your throat, you can forget the dream altogether. They won't even speak to you after that.

Stop. Stop it. The voice in my head was philosophical, emotionless. *That was then. This is now. You were there; now you're here.*

Everything happens for a reason. The portly, round-faced nun at St. Francis Hospital told me that. Every day, during the initial deprogramming phase in the eating-disorders unit, when I was isolated from my family and all visitors, Sister Margaret stopped by to ask how I was doing. We talked about the weather, or the Kansas City Chiefs, and then she'd pat my hand and say, *"Have faith. Everything happens for a reason,"* as if, behind the conversation, she could read all the things I wasn't saying.

She knew I didn't believe that any of this was happening for a reason. . . .

A slice of February wind slid under my collar, pushing the questions away. In spite of the unusually springlike day, it was going to be cold tonight. Hurrying down the steps, I got in my car and left Harrington behind, cutting through the side streets out of downtown, rather than squeezing into the bumper-to-bumper traffic on the main thoroughfare. The decaying row houses and businesses made me feel at home, despite what my father had said about the degeneration of the neighborhood. The streets were lined with memories of my grandmother, whose tall, art deco brick house stood less than two miles from the school. It never occurred to me, growing up, that there was anything unusual about living with her during the week and with my parents on weekends. It seemed perfectly normal that Bethany, focused on being a cheerleader, lived at home full-time while I took the separate path of staying at Grandma Rice's house so I could participate in Harrington's dance program. For me, nothing mattered more than ballet.

Passing by my grandmother's neighborhood, I gazed down the street, but didn't turn in. Things weren't the same there anymore. The grand old homes that had once housed the families of Kansas City's high society were slipping into disrepair and being divided into apartments. Overgrown iris beds and winter-bare forsythia bushes lingered as the only reminders of what were once neatly landscaped yards. Antique stained-glass windows were covered with plywood and tinfoil, and portable air conditioners hung crooked in their rotting frames. Here and there, yuppies had moved in, taken over the old mansions, renovated them to their former beauty, and reclaimed neglected yards and goldfish ponds. There was hope for rebirth, but still far to go. The neighborhood hung suspended in a search for identity, caught between past glory and future potential, in need of vision and elbow grease.

It seemed an appropriate metaphor for my life. Each night as I left Harrington and traveled toward my parents' house in Overland Park, my mind slid into analysis mode. On a good day, I could confine myself to the here and now—focus on some problem with conflicting class schedules or unexcused absences, and avoid the larger questions of the past year. Tonight, Mrs. Morris and Dell Jordan rode with me to the other side of town, through the grocery store, and back home to the neighborhood of new redbrick minimansions with tiny lots and manicured flower beds, where Mom and Dad had moved after selling the house in which Bett and I grew up.

Joujou had lost her battle with incontinence by the time I walked in the door. Carrying in my grocery bag, I stepped in a puddle in the entryway. At the end of the hall, Joujou wagged her tail and smiled with her lips drawn back from the underbite in her little pug snout.

"Geez, Joujou."

She whined, then growled, as I kicked off my wet shoe and stepped around Lake Joujou. Mom and Dad might have been happy to have me back home, but Joujou was not. In her view, I was the competition. There was room for only one prima donna in this house, and as far as Joujou was concerned, she was it.

Setting down my grocery bag, I scooped her up and carried her, growling and squirming, past two more puddles to the sliding glass door. She yipped as I put her out on the patio.

"Out here to potty."

If she felt scolded, it didn't show. Wagging her tail like a propeller, she ran to the flower bed to start digging. Mom wouldn't care. Everything in the patio existed for Joujou's pleasure. The problem of the dog wetting in the house could have been solved easily enough, if Joujou spent more time on the patio. She even had a doggie dream palace, a tiny replica of Mom and Dad's house that Mom had commissioned as a canine Christmas present. Joujou loved to run in the front door, dash up the stairs, and scramble down the ramp from the second-story window. She did it over and over again. She probably would have kept at it all day, but Mom allowed only short, supervised trips outside, for fear that dastardly Pekingese kidnappers would scale the fence and make off with her in all her rhinestone-studded glory. One could never be certain a hyperactive, incontinent house dog was safe.

Mom was as obsessive about the dog as she'd always been about us. With me *and* Joujou to focus on, Mom was more content than she'd been since Bethany graduated from design school, found Jason, and moved into her own apartment. Even with a bad case of empty-nest syndrome, Mom was surprisingly supportive of Bethany's traveling the path to grown-up independence. Until I moved home, Mom had contented herself by joining Bett on her trips to trade shows and the Market District down in Dallas. All of that stopped as soon as my eating disorder came to light. Now, Mom had me to worry about, and my sister was on her own.

But that was all right, because Bett was the sensible, competent one. The *real* daughter, I had begun to understand when I was seven and my grandmother made a perfectly innocent comment about family resemblances and the possible origins of my talent for dance. Suddenly, I fully comprehended why there were no baby pictures of me with my father, why Bethany had his dark hair and brown eyes, his short fingers and stubby toes, and I didn't. Life came into focus with a bang.

I wasn't his. I came into my mother's world before my dad did. It wasn't a family secret, really. It was just something they never brought up and I never asked about. I was too afraid that if I did, Dad would say, *"Well, no need to continue that sham anymore,"* and suddenly, he wouldn't love me.

But deep inside, I'd always wondered if he loved me as much as he loved Bett, and how he possibly could. She was his, and I was . . . I couldn't even imagine who I was. In my mind, my real father was everything from a touring member of the Imperial Russian Ballet, for whom my mom may have repaired costumes when she worked for the wardrobe mistress at the KC Metro Ballet, to a stranger who had grabbed her in a dark alley as she left the studio late at night.

There was no way to know . . .

Without asking.

Leaning against the sliding door, I pressed my face to the cold glass and tried to decide whether that was where my identity crisis began. Or was it at auditions for sixth-grade spring repertory, when the guest instructor, an excommunicated artistic director from St. Petersburg, made some comment about aesthetics and body line? The dancers he cast were tall and slim—*"like the willow,"* he said. I was sure that if I lost a few pounds, I could achieve that line, as well.

The counselor at St. Francis thought my crisis was caused by a combination of factors, including a tendency toward compulsiveness and a family history of mild depression.

Sister Margaret thought it was because I didn't have enough faith in God's plan. *"Be patient,"* she said. *"God makes all things known in His own time."*

Lately, my life was playing out as if someone had failed to give God the script, and the cast had gone haywire due to lack of direction. I was supposed to be in New York by now, dancing, all my little secrets neatly hidden behind brilliant performances and a perfect aesthetic. Instead, the cat was out of the bag, and I was in Kansas City, living with my parents, trapped in the body of a guidance counselor.

In the meantime, the dog puddles were spreading across the tile, and the frozen food I'd bought was melting.

I cleaned up Joujou's mess, hurried upstairs and put on my sweats, then carried the grocery bag to the kitchen and started emptying it. The next thing I knew, I was standing at the bar, halfway through a quart of Häagen-Dazs. Gazing into the container, I awakened like a sleepwalker. My stomach rolled over, my head whirled through a mental calorie count, and I wanted to be sick. Popping the cap on the container, I found myself searching frantically for a place to hide it. The food police would go ballistic. Mom would never believe I hadn't immediately rushed to the bathroom and thrown it up.

I wanted to throw it up. . . .

"Whatever you do, Julia, never let yourself cross the line into purging again." The parting words of Dr. Leland at St. Francis Hospital. He looked me straight in the eyes, laid his hands on my shoulders, and said, "There's no room here for halfway. If you start again, Julia, you'll be dead."

I heard his voice every time I felt myself sliding—his and Sister Margaret's. This time, they stopped me from eating more ice cream, and from purging what I'd consumed. Instead, I tucked the half-empty container inside a Wal-Mart sack, grabbed a jacket, put Joujou on a leash, and headed out jogging. As we passed the public Dumpster at the park, I tossed in the ice-cream container, treating it like the evidence of a crime.

By the time we returned to the house, my lungs were burning from taking in frigid air, my legs felt like rubber, and Joujou was exhausted. She searched the rooms for my parents, then flopped down on the kitchen tile, too tired to consider making protest puddles. She'd worked up an appetite, and was happy to eat her portion of chicken Florentine, and mine too.

I put two plates in the sink, even though only one was used. The ice-cream spoon I washed and tucked away. The fork I left with chicken strings on it, beside a glass with milk dribbled inside, a perfectly placed display.

I did not purge the ice cream.

Grabbing my briefcase from the dining table, I walked to the entertainment room and sat on the sofa, feeling triumphant. Left alone for an entire evening, and the worst I'd done was binge on some ice cream and jog until my legs gave out.

Not bad. This was progress.

Joujou limped into the room, jumped onto the sofa, and curled into a ball by my thigh, then yawned a breath that smelled of chicken Florentine. Rolling her bug eyes upward, she smiled at me with her protruding bottom teeth, like we'd just been through a bonding experience—a couple of dingy dishwater blondes, partners in crime.

Neurotic sisters in Mom's button-down world.

I worked on a federal grant application for the school's new performance hall for half an hour, then set the application booklet aside and opened Dell Jordan's cumulative folder and the confidential file. Thumbing through her paperwork, I pictured her sitting in my office, doe-eyed and silent like one of those sad, soulful Indian maidens painted on T-shirts and coffee mugs in roadside tourist traps.

Maybe I shouldn't have let her off the hook so easily. She needed support, someone to talk to. I should have set up a regular schedule of appointments, kept the essay as leverage, and insisted she come back. I probably wasn't handling her situation correctly. I was undoubtedly failing, and Mrs. Morris, as awful as she was, was correct in insisting that I shouldn't have returned the essay.

What if the girl in the river really did have a death wish? Did I know enough to distinguish a serious emotional problem from normal teenage angst?

I should have paid more attention in my psychology classes, back when I never intended to become a guidance counselor, back when I thought grad school was just a way to avoid getting a real job. My part-time teaching position with the college's high school outreach program had paid for my apartment and basic necessities. Most important, it had allowed me to focus on dancing in the college ballet and traveling to auditions for professional companies, until I could finally get into the corps somewhere. Who knew that the break into full-time professional ballet would almost be the death of me, and the counseling degree would turn out to be what really mattered?

Sister Margaret would have said, *"Life happens according to a plan."*

The problem is that when you don't know the plan, you can't adequately prepare.

Looking at the file in my lap, I couldn't imagine what the plan might be for Dell Jordan. Half Choctaw Indian, no father in the picture, mother a habitual drug user who abandoned her child to be raised in the small town of Hindsville by a grandmother—now deceased. Finally taken in by foster parents, Karen and James Sommerfield, who enrolled Dell in Harrington, where she could pursue her gift for music. Now she was having difficulty adjusting.

Her story made my overly controlling parents, eating disorder, and failed ballet career seem like a minor speed bump in the road of life. Suddenly, feeling sorry for myself rated as a pathetic waste of time. Compared to Dell, I was like Joujou, wetting on the floor because my mommy left me home alone.

When I returned to school tomorrow, I was going to find some way to get Dell back into my office—maybe call her in and ask more questions about the after-school arts program run by her foster mother. Anything to start up a conversation and dig a little deeper.

I spent the rest of the evening combing through her file with a new passion, a revitalized interest in my job. By the time I finished reading, I had a glimmer of hope that I might have learned enough about Dell to help.

Resting my head against the sofa pillow, I closed my eyes and pictured the place she came from—a tiny house in a row of decaying shacks squatting along the river bottom near a rural farming town. A grandmother who wasn't equipped to raise a little girl, a small-town school where teachers tried to intervene, then found it easier to look the other way. A life that slipped from one year to the next, untended, unstructured, unprotected, unrestricted, in which Dell spent her time roaming the woods in solitude, stayed home from school when she felt like it, and largely kept to herself.

Compared to that, Harrington was the other side of the moon. All the fuss about her instrumental and vocal abilities, the constant scrutiny of teachers and instructors in the music department, undoubtedly felt like suffocation. In a place like Harrington, there was no breathing room, only pressure and expectations. . . .

My thoughts drifted away from the social worker's report, away from memories of Dell in my office, away from my parents' living room and Joujou snoring beside me, far from the half quart of Häagen-Dazs sitting like lead in my stomach. Miles from all that was real.

Shedding the weight of everything, I soared through a cloudless summer sky, gliding southward, where the Ozarks lay like folds in a thick green blanket. Nestled in a valley, the river wound through the shade of the sycamores, carrying glints of sunlight that sailed past the girl in the water, travelers on a journey even she could not predict. Stretching out her arms, she closed her eyes, let her head fall back, and floated on the surface.

I was the girl in the river, dancing the part of the Black Swan from KC Metro's season opening performance of *Swan Lake*. Stretching out my arms, I sailed through the sunbeams, whirling like a floating leaf, lighter than air. . . .

The sound of the front door opening pulled me from my dream. Beside me, Joujou yipped and jumped up, then dashed from the room, spinning out on the tile as she screeched around the corner to the entry-way.

"It's just us," Mom called, the way she used to when I was home alone as a teenager. "Anyone awake in here?" She came into the room carrying Joujou, who was happily slathering her face with kisses.

"Hi, Mom," I said, and stretched, slipping the files back into my briefcase.

"Did you girls have a good time?" It was hard to tell whether she was talking to me or Joujou. "How did your evening go?" Her gaze gravitated toward the kitchen. What she really wanted to do was check the plates, then weigh and measure the leftovers.

"Where's Dad?" I asked.

"Oh, he ran over to the store for some milk." Setting Joujou down, she blinked in surprise when the dog hopped onto the sofa with me. "Didn't want to be out of milk at breakfast."

"We should call his cell and tell him not to bother. I picked some up on the way home."

Mom gave me a panicked look, no doubt imagining a shopping cart full of binge food and laxatives. She glanced toward the kitchen again. "Oh, he'll be back in a minute." Instead of finding an excuse to check for leftovers, she sat down on the sofa next to me.

I sensed an old parental tactic—the one in which Dad conveniently left the house so Mom could tell me something, or discuss a girls-only subject, or, lately, question me about food. "So, I have some news." Twining her hands together in her lap, she plastered on a broad smile obviously meant to bolster me. "Bethany and Jason made a little announcement tonight. They're getting married. Next month, if you can believe it. Jason just got word that he's to be transferred out of state, and . . . well . . ." Mom leaned close to me, holding a hand beside her mouth, whispering, "They're expecting."

I sat blinking at her, the words spinning around me. My little sister was getting married, moving out of state, and having a baby? Where was I when all that was taking shape?

"Of course, they didn't intend for it to happen—in that order, I mean," Mom continued on, still whispering, as if Joujou shouldn't hear. "But, you know, times change. These days, it's not nearly the issue it used to be, way back when."

The sentence ended there, but I mentally finished it with, *When you had me. It's not the big issue it was when you had me.* "That's big news," I heard myself say. "I'll call her tomorrow and tell her congratulations. I'm kind of wiped out tonight." Suddenly, my body felt five hundred pounds too heavy. "I think I'll go to bed."

Mom felt my forehead. "Sure. Are you OK? I could make you some herbal tea."

"No . . . no, that's all right." My feet were in quicksand. "I'm fine. I just need to get some rest." Not trusting myself to say anything else, I hugged Mom good night, climbed the stairs to my bedroom, and locked the door. Below, I heard my father come home and their voices vibrating in a low hum—no words, just muffled tones of concern.

Joujou scratched at my door, and I let her in. We curled up on the bed together, and I hugged my body around hers, wishing I could slip out the second-story window, run down the street, fish the other half quart of ice cream from the Dumpster, and eat until the lost feeling went away.

Instead, I closed my eyes, hoping I could fall asleep and dream of the girl in the river, dancing *Swan Lake*.

Chapter 3

I awoke to a wintery wind howling outside the window and Mom tapping on my door, asking if she should call the school to tell them I was home sick this morning.

My thoughts floated between past and present as I opened my eyes, bringing into focus the white jewelry box beside the dresser mirror, its tiny plastic ballerina frozen in time. Around me, a dream of dancing hung suspended, luring me to close my eyes and go back to sleep.

Rolling over, I checked the alarm clock, and everything snapped into focus. Friday, six-o-one a.m. It was a workday, and if I didn't get moving, I would be late.

"No, Mom, I'm fine." Scrambling from the bed, I scooped up Jou-jou and handed her out the door. "Thanks for waking me up. I forgot to set my alarm."

"You don't look well this morning." Mom's brows knotted. "Why don't you stay home and go have lunch with Bethany and me? We're going to talk about wedding plans." She looked exhausted, as if she'd been up all night worrying. "I don't know how we're going to put together a wedding in less than a month, but I guess we will."

My burst of adrenaline drained away as reality solidified in my mind. My little sister was moving on in life, which made my failures seem that much more monumental. "I can't," I rushed out. "I'm in the middle of some things at work. I'd better get going. I have hall duty this morning."

Mom smacked her lips in disgust, the lines deepening on her forehead. "They shouldn't be asking you to perform hall duty when you live all the way across town."

I had a vision of her calling the principal to complain. "It's all right, Mom. It's a good way for me to get to know the students." Kissing her on the cheek, I backed away. "When I left St. Francis, Dr. Leland said the best thing was to keep busy, remember?" Anytime I couldn't win a debate with Mom, I could fall back on Dr. Leland's advice.

"All right," she muttered, starting down the hall with Joujou under her arm. "I'll hurry down and fix some breakfast for you."

"No. Don't bother. No time." Every morning, we repeated the same painful ritual in which Mom produced a June Cleaver breakfast, and the three of us sat down together. Mom silently counted every bite of food going into my mouth, and Dad hid behind his *Wall Street Journal*, trying to remain neutral, the Switzerland of food wars. This morning, we'd have to do that *and* talk about Bett's wedding and unexpected pregnancy.

"It won't take a minute," Mom called back as she disappeared. "I'll have it ready in a jiffy. The weather's turned cold and nasty this morning. You'll need something solid in your stomach." On the way downstairs, she cooed to Joujou, probably asking what she wanted for breakfast.

I hurried through showering, then put on makeup and combed my hair back, twisted it upward and secured it with a clip, so that little blond shoots stuck out the top. *Not great,* I thought, looking at the woman in the mirror in her bra and panties, studying herself with a hollow blue gaze.

I hated the way her eyes were rimmed with dark circles and sunken in around the cheekbones. She looked older than twenty-seven—sallow and weary, like the homeless people who lived under bridges and pushed shopping carts on downtown streets.

The body line could be more refined—slimmer. That ice cream is showing. . . . I'd turned sideways and started to examine myself before I awakened to what was happening. *Stop it. Stop it. You're not going to do this.* Moving away from the mirror, I stepped on the scale. When I had those thoughts, it helped to get on the scale, think of my target weight range, and see how far off I was. One hundred and two pounds was too low for someone five-foot-six, but not dangerously thin.

Also not fat.

Leaving the scale behind, I rushed to the closet and slipped on a flowered dress, then remembered the change in the weather and grabbed a blazer. Outside, the moaning wind was testifying to the fact that, in spite of an unseasonably warm February so far, spring wasn't here yet.

By the time I'd gathered my things and arrived downstairs, Mom was setting the kitchen table.

"Mom, I don't have time," I said, looking at the clock. Six forty-five. If I didn't leave now, I would definitely be late. Mrs. Morris would probably be standing at the door, taking notes.

"You have to eat." Mom stacked toast on a napkin, then scooped scrambled eggs onto a plate.

Grabbing a piece of toast, I piled some eggs onto it, folded it over, and took a Diet Dr Pepper from the refrigerator. "Mom, I love you, but I have to leave. Now." She pointed the spatula at me like a weapon, and I took a bite of my sandwich. "I'm eating—look, this is me, eating. Mmmmm."

"Don't be sassy. You should have some milk. And a heavy coat. It's cold."

Grabbing the glass from the table, I downed a swig of milk, then set it in the refrigerator, said, "I'll save it for later," snatched up my briefcase, and rushed out the door.

Fortunately, the traffic was light for a Friday, and the seven-thirty bell had just starting ringing as I jogged up the side steps at Harrington, and blew through the doorway on a stiff north wind. Mrs. Morris was already patroling by her classroom door. Checking her watch, she frowned as I passed by, her hawkish gaze following my rush to drop my things at my office, then take my duty station before the principal unlocked the front doors so that early arrivals could start coming in.

Mr. Stafford shook his keys at me as he walked by. "You're giving me gray hairs, Costell." It was one of his standard jokes, since he didn't have any hair.

"Sorry." I ducked my head, embarrassed about skating in at the last minute. "Bad commute today." Excuses, excuses. If Mr. Stafford hadn't been an easygoing guy coasting toward retirement, he probably would have fired me already for being woefully underqualified as a guidance counselor. I was learning on the job, and he was extraordinarily patient with that. Then again, the former guidance counselor had been an old battle-axe like Mrs. Morris. Stafford was probably relieved not to have two vipers denned up near his office.

"Watch out for Morris. She's hot about yesterday," Mr. Stafford muttered from the corner of his mouth as he paused by the administration office across the hall. "She's got friends on the school board." He sighed wearily, no doubt counting the months until he could spend his mornings on the golf course. "Would have been easier to just give her the essay."

"It wasn't the right thing to do," I replied, and he made a *tsk-tsk* sound, frowning in a way that said, *Great. Just great. Another hopeless idealist who's never held down a real job and doesn't have a clue how the world works. When will she learn?*

"Just . . . watch out." Opening the administration door, he stepped partway in, then added, "She wants something to come of this."

"I didn't do anything wrong." At the end of the hall, Mrs. Morris was busy forcing a half dozen kids to about-face at the side door, so that they could walk around the building and come in the front as the rules prescribed. She looked disturbingly pleased about sending them out in the cold. "It was a judgment call, that's all. In my opinion, returning the paper was in the best interest of the student involved. Morris'll just have to tear the wings off some ladybugs for fun." The school was notorious for its prespring hatching of ladybugs, for which there seemed to be no cure. The bugs gathered in corners, marched in lines up and down the walls, and sailed down the corridors, landing like ornaments in students' hair. They were probably smart enough to stay away from Mrs. Morris.

Rubbing the side of his face, Stafford stretched his sagging cheek skin, his tired sigh saying, *I don't need this. What have I done to deserve this?* "It's Say No to Drugs Day." He shrugged over his shoulder toward the huge banner that announced a special Kansas City Drug Task Force assembly after roll call. "You're supposed to be wearing red." Without another word, he disappeared into his office, and I stood reading the banner—FRIDAY: WEAR RED INSTEAD.

Crossing my arms over my pastel flowered dress and peach blazer, I stepped back against the wall, watching as the hall became a shifting sea of color coordination. Mrs. Morris, of course, had on red. Later, maybe she'd pop out her devil's horns and complete the outfit.

"Hey, Ms. Costell," one of the kids—an eighth grader I'd helped with a summer music scholarship application—called, "it's Red Day."

Groaning in my throat, I chirped out, "It's OK, Colton. I like to be different." What else was there to say?

Twenty minutes later, when we filed into assembly, I ended up in the front row, looking like a party pooper at the antidrug extravaganza. Even the police officers seemed to notice, or maybe that was my own paranoia. Across the aisle, Mrs. Morris was whispering to another teacher and glaring at me. It looked like she was pantomiming yesterday's disagreement over Dell Jordan.

I searched for Dell in the crowd of students and teachers, but couldn't find her. *Maybe she's absent.* The thought brought a pang of disappointment as I settled back into my seat, listening with one ear to the drug task force's spiel about teenage substance abuse: the effects on the body; tragic stories of kids who'd died or screwed up their lives by smoking, snorting, huffing; graphic tales of drug arrests and junkies; and neighborhoods where dealers had taken over the streets. It was too much information for middle schoolers, and I fidgeted uncomfortably in my chair, anxious for the assembly to be over. When it finally was, I slipped to the exit, watching for Dell as the students filed out, jostling among themselves and making jokes about the assembly with immature bravado, while teachers ordered them to stop visiting and proceed to class. Dell wasn't in the crowd, and I walked back to my office feeling that I'd missed the mark the day before. She was probably ducking me and avoiding my suggestion that she write down more of her story so we could talk about it. My first real counseling opportunity, and I had no idea what I should have done.

The corridor cleared as students filed into their classrooms, and teachers stood in the doorways, urging kids on and breaking up lingering conversations. Outside the seventh-grade science room, the science teacher was holding a test tube with something smoking inside it, and the literature teacher was loudly quoting a Shakespeare passage about haste.

As the halls emptied, Mr. Stafford escorted the officers from the police task force toward the front door, so that they could walk over to the high school building and repeat their assembly for the older kids. "Down the front steps, follow the covered walkway around the middle school building to the right, through the parking lot, past the performance hall, the maintenance building, and the tennis courts, to the three-story brick building with the glass doors. The newer building." It had always chafed at Mr. Stafford that the high school facility was years newer than the middle school building, which had originated in the thirties. After closing as a public school, the building had become an arts magnet high school, then finally a magnet middle school, as the program grew and a new high school was constructed. "The administration office is just inside the double doors, and . . ." He glanced at his watch, frowning. "I thought someone from the other building was coming to walk you over." Spying me, he angled his guests my way. "Ms. Costell can escort you over there and check you in at the office."

He paused to introduce me. Shaking hands, I thanked the officers, politely complimenting the assembly and saying that it was beneficial for the kids. But what did I know, really? I was no expert on kids and drugs. I was just the dork in the sherbet-colored dress on Red Day.

The police officers weren't aware of that, of course. They assumed that, as my staff name tag indicated, I was an actual guidance counselor. The sergeant, a fifty-something seen-it-all type whose badge read REUPER, delivered some stats about marijuana, crack, meth, Ecstasy, and huffing common household substances among area teens. Giving me a list of Web sites that offered good information, he suggested follow-up techniques I might use to develop a cooperative home- and school-based prevention program.

I tried to imagine actually calling some Harrington kid into my office and questioning him or her about drug use. The parents would have a fit. Harrington kids were above such interrogation.

"It can happen anywhere. It's not just gang kids from the wrong side of town." Sergeant Reuper appeared to be reading my mind. "High expectations and performance pressure can cause kids to look for an escape hatch. These days, marijuana and methamphetamine are inexpensive and relatively easy for young people to procure. They can buy just about anything they want on street corners not four blocks from here. Then there's the entire class of commonly available household products we talked about during the assembly. Kids don't think that inhaling butane, correction fluid, or aerosol propellants is drug use, but it is. It's pervasive, and it's deadly." His eyes narrowed toward the hallway, as if he could feel the demanding culture in the atmosphere. "Addiction is an equal opportunity killer. It's a tough thing to beat, and the only effective solution is a coordinated effort between home and school. There's no room for denial, in either place."

In that instant, I could relate to what the kids in our classrooms might be going through. I knew about addiction and denial. Not drug addiction, but I knew about keeping secrets and hiding who you really were. Even in middle school, I realized I had a problem with food, but I didn't think anyone would understand, so I kept dabbling with binging and purging until I had an addiction I couldn't control. "You're right," I said. "I'll get busy putting together some awareness programs and parent information."

Mr. Stafford blinked in surprise. Clearly, he didn't think I was capable of constructing an awareness program. He couldn't imagine how much I really knew about hitting rock bottom, admitting the truth to your family, and climbing the twelve steps out of the pit.

"Call us if we can help," the sergeant said, chewing his lip as he surveyed the ceiling, where a line of ladybugs was marching in a lazy circle around the art deco light fixture. "You'd be surprised, even in a place like this, where the kids come from higher socioeconomic families, how many children go days at a time without anybody really talking to them. The thing about a smart kid with some resources is, he can keep up appearances for a long time. Combine that with parents, or schools, or teachers with reputations to uphold, and sometimes the reputation is more important than the truth, or the kid." Turning back, he held my gaze for a moment, and I felt my focus narrow until it was just him and me in the corridor. I got it. He wasn't talking in generalities. He was talking about Harrington.

Breaking the connection, Sergeant Reuper glanced at the principal and said, "No offense intended, of course, but in this business it's essential to be proactive."

"Oh, of course, of course. No offense taken. Children are always our first priority here," Mr. Stafford answered, but he was starting to bristle. His short, round body had stretched to its full height, and his arms were stiff at his sides. He was ready to have the *Say No to Drugs* crew proceed to the high school building. They'd stepped on his toes, and worse yet, now they'd noticed the ladybugs. All four police officers were gaping at the ceiling in amazement.

"Well, we thank you all for coming." Clapping his hands together, Mr. Stafford wrung his fingers roughly like he was trying to compact a ball of rubbish before pitching it into the wastebasket.

He reminded me of Dell, folding her essay into a paper wad and stuffing it into her pocket.

"Guess we'd better get going," the sergeant said. "We can find our way. No need to walk us around. It's cold out this morning. Norther blowing in." He pulled a couple of business cards from his pocket and handed them to Mr. Stafford and me. "Call us if you need anything."

"Absolutely," Mr. Stafford replied as the front doors opened and the high school principal entered with his guidance counselor at his side. "Well, there are your escorts now. Dr. Lee, Mr. Fortier, this is Sergeant Reuper and his staff. They've just given our students a real eye-opener, and I'm sure they'll do the same for yours."

Dr. Lee and Mr. Fortier made quick introductions, seeming only slightly more sincere than Mr. Stafford. I felt sorry for the police officers. They could probably tell that their hard work was falling largely on deaf ears. They undoubtedly got this reception at a lot of places. No school, no family, no adult, no kid wanted to admit to an ongoing problem with addiction.

As he turned to leave, Sergeant Reuper caught my gaze again and squinted thoughtfully, as if he could see the wheels turning in my mind. Then we said our farewells, all shook hands again, and he headed out the door with his crew, as Dr. Lee and Mr. Fortier made pleasant conversation about the wintry turn in the weather.

Clapping his hands together again, Mr. Stafford rocked back on his heels, as in, *Mission accomplished; now let's get back to the bond elections and the federal grant applications for the new performance hall.* He checked his watch, as if time were critical. "Well, that takes care of our Drug Education Prevention hours for the semester." His shoulders sagged as he headed toward his office. "I don't know when we're supposed to educate these kids, between the DEP hours to keep them off drugs, and the character ed programs to make them good citizens, and the phys ed classes because they're too fat, and the sex ed classes so they won't get AIDS, and that idiotic mandatory achievement test. You'd think they don't have any parents at home."

These days a lot of them don't, I thought, but I didn't say it. Mr. Stafford wasn't in the mood. He wouldn't have understood, anyway. But I knew how easy it was for a kid in a perfectly normal family to hide a problem for years. Even though I always knew my parents loved me, they never had a clue about my eating disorder. The fact was that they were both busy, and as long as everything appeared to be under control, they assumed it was.

Family enablement trap number one, I'd learned in rehab at St. Francis: *convenient assumptions. A smooth surface often hides a deadly undertow.*

Still standing in the hallway, I planned my day while watching the ladybugs, now marching single file down the center of the ceiling. First, read the rest of the grant application booklet, then spend some time looking over the Web sites the sergeant had mentioned. See if I could come up with ideas that would be viable at Harrington, then figure out how to get Stafford to agree. In the past, he'd backhandedly made it clear that I wasn't to delve into the private lives of students, because, after all, their parents might complain to the superintendent or the school board. Heaven forbid.

Flipping on the lights in my office, I realized that it was almost ten, and I hadn't done a thing except attend the drug education program. In a way, I could see Mr. Stafford's point. There were only so many hours in a school day. Trying to do anything more than process all the required paperwork seemed impossible, and probably not worth the effort. Who was I to think I could change the tightly woven fabric of Harrington? The place was what it was, and I had to learn to operate within the confines that existed, not butt my head against them. Getting into a snit with Mrs. Morris about Dell Jordan's essay hadn't been a smart move, either. I was only making trouble for myself, and probably for Dell.

When I picked up my briefcase from my desk, something fluttered underneath it—two pieces of lined paper, torn out of a spiral notebook. I recognized the handwriting. A ladybug was sitting in the center of the page. I blew on it, and it flew away as I sat down and started reading.

>It's Say No to Drugs assembly, but I'm sitting in the storeroom behind the instrumental music hall. I think Mr. Verhaden knows I come in here sometimes, but he pretends like he doesn't. He never says anything about it. Anything is fine with Mr. Verhaden, as long as when it's time for music, my mind is on music. Other than that, he doesn't care if I go in the storeroom where it's quiet. Maybe he understands, or maybe he only cares about the music. I don't know.

>I didn't want to go to the assembly today, so I hung around until everyone left, and then I slipped into the storeroom while Verhaden was locking his office. I almost thought he saw me, but he didn't turn around. My heart was in my neck, because I couldn't stand it if he made me go to the Red Day assembly. I forgot to wear red today. I'd be the only one there in a lime-green sweatshirt.

>That isn't why I didn't want to go. I hate those assemblies, because I know what they'll say. They'll talk about drugs, and all the bad things they can do to your body, and they'll show some pictures of messed-up

brain slices and lungs that are all rotted from huffing, or crack, or smoking weed. They'll show some babies that scream day and night and will never be normal because their mamas did drugs.

I'll look at those babies and wonder if that's me. Is my brain messed up like that? Was I like those babies? Did I cry, and twitch, and look all shrunk up and pale? Is that why Mama brought me home to my granny and didn't stay six months before she went away again? Did she leave me there because she figured I was messed up and always would be? Is that why my daddy didn't want me, either?

Did he even know there was a me?

I'll go through the questions in my mind—why did Mama straighten herself out for more than a year when she had my baby brother? She wouldn't do that for me. She was in love with Angelo's daddy. Maybe that was the difference. He used to come around Granny's house sometimes, when Angelo was tiny. Mama said that after she got straight, they would get married and move off and get a real house. If I was good, maybe she'd take me.

I used to hear them fight sometimes in the other bedroom. Granny's old house had walls thin as paper. I'd get Angelo and wrap him in a blanket, and take him out to the woods or down by the river. We'd sit where it was quiet, me propped up against a tree, and Angelo resting on my knees. He'd kick little baby kicks, and giggle, and stare up at the sky. His eyes were clear and blue, just like a mirror of what was above. I'd ruffle his hair, and he'd smile at me, and I knew how it was to really love somebody. I thought, if Mama left again, I'd take care of Angelo and I'd never be alone.

By the time he got big enough to walk, I was sure that was how it would be. Angelo's daddy had quit coming around. I knew sooner or later Mama would be gone, too. Some guy with long black hair was coming by the house a lot, and they'd go off in his pickup for a few hours, or all night, and she'd come back messed up. Even when you're only eight years old, you know what messed up looks like. Angelo knew it, too. He'd cry when Mama would hold him and stumble around. Once, she almost dropped him off the front steps, and Granny said she wasn't to pick him up anymore. They had a big fight, and Granny said Mama needed to stay home, that it wasn't right for Mama to dump her kids on Granny. Granny was too old to raise another baby.

I felt like someone yanked the floor out from under me, and I was just hanging there in space. I started walking down the river and stayed gone all day until after dark, thinking I wouldn't come back. When I did, Granny was asleep, and Mama was in the front yard talking to somebody in a car.

The next morning, Angelo was gone. Mama said she gave him to his daddy because she was afraid, now that he was walking, he'd drown in the river.

Granny said I wasn't to talk about it anymore. That was that.

I told them I could watch after Angelo and they should bring him back. But there's no point fussing about things, because nobody hears you.

I went down to the river and sat for a long time. Just sat right in the water, and felt it sweep around me. The light went behind clouds, sending a shadow skimming over the surface like a water strider. I closed my eyes and felt it start to rain, quiet and soft.

I dreamed that Angelo was someplace dry, in a baby bed with little ruffles around the edges, in a big house somewhere. Angelo's daddy would pick him up from the crib, and bounce him, and laugh with him. Maybe sometimes, they'd go out into the woods, and Angelo would remember when the two of us did that. Maybe he'd remember.

Mostly, I thought he'd be happy, even though he was someplace else. Because he was someplace else.

A lot of what happens to you depends on who your daddy is.

I always wondered why my daddy didn't want me.

And now sometimes I think, if he knew I could play the piano like I do, would he feel any different?

I can hear the Red Instead assembly through the wall. It's so loud, I can even understand the words. Say no to drugs! Wear red instead. Say no to drugs! Wear red instead.

Just say no. . . .

If it's that easy, I think to myself, why didn't my mama do it?

Chapter 4

I read the essay again before writing a hall pass so that Dell could come to my office. The third-period office aid, a chubby, baby-faced saxophone player named Barry, frowned disdainfully when I asked him to find Dell and give her the note. Apparently, even Barry was too cool for Dell Jordan.

"Tell her not to come if she's in the middle of something," I instructed, and Barry blinked slowly, silently protesting, *Now you want me to actually talk to her? My social standing as a chubby saxophone player will never survive this.* "You know what . . ." Retrieving the note, I propped it against my office door. "I'll just write that on here myself. That way you won't be disturbing Mr. Campbell's class as much."

Barry looked relieved. "Sure," he replied in the straitjacketed way of an adolescent terrified of any potential uncoolness.

"Thank you, Barry."

His plump lips parted in a smile, revealing several thousand dollars' worth of ongoing orthodontic work. Blushing, he ducked his head, and muttered, "Nice red shirt, Ms. C." Walking away, he glanced back over his shoulder, smirking like he'd really gotten in a clever one that time.

"Well, what can I say?" I held up my hands. "I'm a hopeless nerd."

His eyes widened in surprise at the idea that painful feelings of nerdiness were not limited to teenagers. With a look of empathy, he shook his head and said, "You look OK, Ms. C," and slouched off down the hall, his oversize pants swishing against the floor.

Slipping back into my office, I closed the door, took a deep breath, and dialed Bethany's number. I couldn't put it off any longer. If I didn't call soon, her feelings would be hurt, and she'd know I was having an emotional meltdown about her unexpected wedding-and-baby news.

Closing my eyes, I pursed my lips and blew out, trying to practice the guided-meditation techniques I'd learned from Dr. Leland. I pictured a clear blue sky.

Thunderheads were roiling on the horizon.

"Hello, this is Bethany . . ."

The storm swelled around me. "Hi, Bett," I choked out, and completely without warning, a sob fell on the heels of the words. A rush of tears filled my eyes, and panic tightened my throat.

Bett kept right on talking. ". . . I can't answer the phone right now, but if you'll leave a message on my voice mail, I'll call you back as soon as I can."

Relief spiraled through me.

"Have a great day," she said, and I hung up before the tone beeped. If I left a message sounding like this, Bett would know I was a basket case. Then she would be worrying about me, and right now she had enough to worry about. I couldn't do that to her. I wouldn't. Everything had been about *me* these past few months. Now it was Bett's time.

I'd get my head together and call back in a little while, put on a happy voice and talk about bridesmaids' dresses, tell her that even though the baby was a surprise, she and Jason would be wonderful parents, and I was really happy for them. . . .

This problem, *my* problem, wasn't going to ruin one more relationship in my life. . . .

Through the blur, I stared at my fingers, remembering when Jonathan's ring had been there. At twenty-four, when I was Bett's age, that ring seemed like the perfect accessory. Just out of a five-year undergrad program, double major in education and dance, engaged, starting grad school, teaching part-time with the outreach gifted and talented program, still dancing. Getting married . . . eventually, sometime down the road when we were both out of grad school and life was stable. Maybe in New York, where I would be dancing with the New York City Ballet.

By the time I was twenty-six, the engagement ring felt like a weight. Jonathan was finished with grad school, signing on as a chemist with a small pharmaceutical company, talking about buying a house with room for a family.

After I'd suffered a minor ankle injury, a round of tendonitis, and two on-again-off-again seasons with the university dance company, the New York Ballet seemed a million miles away, completely off the map. I told Jonathan I wanted to concentrate on dancing first, think about children later. I didn't admit that the idea of gaining all that weight made me sick, but eventually he began to figure it out. He started studying my body when I wasn't looking, complaining about the hours I spent jogging and on the exercise bike. I passed it off as pushing hard to get in shape for the KC Metro's spring auditions. Now that I was finishing my final grad school internships, and my college dance career was over, I wanted to put everything I had into making the cut with a professional ballet company.

When I was chosen for the corps at the KC Metro, Jonathan's ring became a noose. He was concerned that I was pushing myself too hard, trying to compete with dancers who were five and six years younger than I was, in my quest to move up to a soloist position. He wanted me to quit, to be realistic about the fact that, at twenty-six with a history of injuries, it was unlikely that I'd ever achieve the dream of being a soloist or a lead dancer with a large professional company. He thought I should "see someone" about all the weight I'd lost. He wanted to set a wedding date and move on with our lives. In July, I gave him back the ring and told him I thought we should take some time apart.

He found someone else within two months. It was love at first sight. They ran off to Cancún in October and got married while I was in rehearsals for *Swan Lake*. I was so consumed with the upcoming performance, I found it easy to push aside lingering thoughts of Jonathan. I was understudying the Dance of the Four Little Swans, and one of the dancers was nursing an inflamed ligament. The evening of spacing rehearsal, I was to stand in for her. Then my parents, who always came to watch spacing rehearsal, found me on the dressing room floor in a pool of blood.

I woke up in the hospital two days later, a monitor hooked to my finger and IVs pumping glucose and electrolytes into my veins. My secret was out, and there was plenty of time to think about what I'd done to myself, to my career, and to Jonathan. I felt as if someone had yanked the floor out from under me, and I was floating in space, just like Dell in her essay. . . .

I looked up from my desk, and Dell was standing in the doorway, watching me through soft, contemplative eyes. I felt myself being drawn into the steadiness of her gaze before my mind kicked into gear, causing me to motion her in. Grabbing a Kleenex, I pretended to reach for something on the floor as I wiped my eyes.

"Allergies," I said, when I sat back up. Pulling the door closed, she moved along the wall and slid into the same chair she'd occupied the day before.

"Oh," she muttered, ready to accept the excuse for the fact that I was crying in my office in the middle of a school day. *Whatever,* her look said.

"So . . ." I tried not to imagine my appearance from her point of view: bedraggled and off-kilter. "I guess you missed the Red Day assembly."

She winced, her attention darting around my office as if she were looking for a hole to crawl into. "Am I in trouble?"

"No."

"Are you gonna tell anyone?"

"No. I guess Mr. Verhaden didn't see you, and you made it to your next class on time?"

Sagging with relief, she nodded. "I don't think Mr. Verhaden cares. If I go in the storage room, I mean. Sometimes I go there during lunch. He doesn't say anything."

"You spend lunch in the instrument closet?" I said it with a little more shock than I meant to, not because the idea surprised me, but because I'd done the same thing myself during my years at Harrington—

not for the same reasons Dell probably did. For me, hanging out in the instrument closet and sometimes the practice room or the library was a way of avoiding the cafeteria. I ate with my friends just often enough to keep anyone from becoming suspicious, but when I could get away with it, I slipped off to someplace quiet, where there were no food issues to deal with.

Crossing her slender arms defensively, Dell drew back. "Sometimes. Not all the time. Just when I have a sack lunch with me, and when . . ." Sighing hard, she focused out the window. "Some days there's too many people. They're all around and it's too loud."

I thought about the girl in the river, standing silent in the sunlight, or curled tightly into a ball against the rain, always alone. I realized again how different it was for her here.

"Sometimes I need it quiet, that's all," she added. "They're always watching me here."

"The other students?" I interpreted, and she nodded.

"And the teachers. I'm not used to it. I worry what they're thinking when they look at me." A ladybug crawled across her shoe, and she paused to watch it, looking peaceful for a moment before the arch of her dark brows straightened again, and she slid her foot to the file cabinet so the ladybug could crawl to safety. "My mind says it's bad stuff— like I'm stupid and ugly and I shouldn't be here. Karen—ummm, my foster mom—tells me I shouldn't listen to that stuff when I hear it in my mind. I know she's right. Grandma Rose says just ignore it and go on. She says you can't know what anybody else is thinking, and anyway, ugly thoughts come from ugly minds."

I chuckled. "It sounds like Grandma Rose gives some good advice."

She fluttered a smile. "Grandma Rose don't"—a quick shake of her head faded the smile—"doesn't put up with much from people. I wish she was here to talk to Mrs. Morris."

"I imagine that would be quite a conversation." I pictured the evil Frau of English getting a no-nonsense lesson in kindness, civility, and treating other people the way she'd like to be treated. Then I remembered that, according to the paperwork, Dell's biological grandmother was deceased. "Grandma Rose isn't the grandmother you lived with in Hindsville?"

"Huh-uh," she replied, focusing out the window again, seeming as far away as the wispy white clouds over the Kansas City skyline. "She's my foster mom's grandma. She lived across the river from my real granny's house. Grandma Rose is how I met my foster parents in the first place. They knew me because I'd stay at Grandma Rose's farm a lot when my real granny was sick and stuff. I think Grandma Rose was the reason James and Karen wanted to be my parents after my real granny died. Grandma Rose is more like a grandma than my real granny was. She understands stuff, you know?"

I nodded, thinking of my grandma Rice, and how close we were during the years I was staying with her and going to Harrington. Of all the people I lied to about my eating disorder, she was the one I felt the most guilty about deceiving. Grandma Rice was closest to my heart. She sat through hours of rehearsals, never missed a dance performance, helped me with my homework, and fixed the four-course lunches I threw in the trash every day. In some ways I was glad she'd passed away before the truth came out. "Grandmas are good that way, sometimes," I agreed.

"She told me I ought to write it down when I think things that bother me." With a shrug, Dell indicated the notebook papers on the desk.

Pulling them closer, I pretended to read the words again, but they were already etched in my head. "So, if Grandma Rose were here, what do you think she'd say about your skipping the Red Day assembly today?"

Dell considered the floor under my desk for a moment. "I dunno."

"How do you feel about it?"

"About what?"

"Skipping the assembly. How do you feel about it?"

Brows knitted, she shrugged, as if she couldn't imagine that her feelings would matter. "I just couldn't go, you know? It makes me think about . . . things."

"About your mother?"

"My real mom, you mean?"

"Yes."

"I don't like to talk about her." Her lips trembled, and she pulled them into a firm line. Focusing on her hands, she picked mercilessly at her short fingernails. "Karen wants me to talk about her sometimes, and I tell her I can't remember anything. My granny took all the pictures of Mama and burned them after Mama gave Angelo to his daddy. They had a big fight, and then the guy with the long black hair came to pick Mama up. Mama wanted to take me with them, but Granny said no. Mama just loaded her stuff in the truck, and before she left, she picked me up like I was a baby, like Angelo. She was all sweaty and shaking, and I just wanted her to let me go, and leave. Then she did, and I was sorry I thought that, because then she did drugs until she died from it. When I was a kid, I always figured maybe I made it happen with all those mean thoughts."

The sentence ended with a silent question mark that found me wanting to cross the space between us, fold Dell into my arms, replay and recast that embrace from her mother. I couldn't, of course. No one could, but I understood the yearning. Even after all these years, and as much as I loved my dad, I still wondered about my biological father. I wondered why he didn't want me, or if he ever knew I existed.

"But now that you're older," I said, hiding my own thoughts behind the therapist's mask, "you know that you were not the cause of what happened. Your mother's choices were her own. We all have to take ownership of our decisions." A textbook psychologist's phrase. Something Dr. Phil might use on his show. Small comfort to a kid abandoned by both of her biological parents.

"I know." Obviously, she'd heard that line before. Slanting a glance upward, she checked my reaction. "She decided to leave and go do drugs again. It's not as easy as Just Say No."

"No, it isn't," I agreed, and I knew we understood each other.

The bell rang, and Dell jerked in her seat, glancing over her shoulder as the corridor filled with students and staff members. "Great, now they're gonna see me in here. Everyone's gonna think I'm a suck-up."

"Why don't you wait a minute until after the halls clear, and I'll give you an admit for class," I suggested, picking up my pad.

"I better not." Standing up, she straightened her body, taking a fortifying breath, bracing for the tide of people outside the door. "I've got Mrs. Morris next hour. If I'm late, she'll make me read out loud and everybody'll laugh."

"I see." I had the strongest urge to walk down the hall and wrap my hands around Mrs. Morris's bony neck—a fantasy I'd entertained many times back in middle school.

"I'm gonna flunk her class anyway," Dell added, looking glum. "All we do is read stupid books, and I hate reading."

"Really?" I motioned to the papers on my desk. "I would think you'd love reading. You write so beautifully."

She rolled her eyes.

"Seriously," I said.

With a shrug, she started toward the door. "Reading's different. You don't already know the words. When you write, you can use the words you already know. I read that stuff in Mrs. Morris's class, and it doesn't make any sense."

Reading comprehension problems, I thought. *That could explain a lot of things.* Kids who didn't read well had trouble in every subject, and kids who grew up in homes without books often didn't read well.

I was surprised to find myself actually thinking like a real guidance counselor. Apparently, I had learned something in graduate school. For the first time in a long while I had a sense of being useful, rather than just a burden to everyone else. It felt good. "What book are you reading in class now?"

"Today we're gonna start *The Grapes of Wrath,*" Dell said with an obvious lack of enthusiasm. "Mrs. Morris said the school board put it on the list, and she doesn't even like it. It's got bad grammar in it, and she doesn't see how we're gonna diagram the sentences, like we usually do."

"You diagram the sentences from what you read?" The words came out with more disbelief than I meant to show. Criticizing a teacher in front of a student was strictly unprofessional, but nobody diagrammed sentences anymore.

"Yes." Huffing a breath, Dell glanced nervously toward the hall clock. "And I can't do that part, either. We have to do fifteen sentences every day from what we read."

Drumming my fingers on the desk, I stood up to walk her to the door. No sense making her late for Mrs. Morris's house of linguistic horrors. An idea struck me as I rounded the corner of my desk. "Dell, what would you think if I set up some daily tutoring sessions for you?"

"With you?" she asked hopefully, and I found myself nodding, even though what I'd actually intended was to find her a tutor—maybe a high school student. The National Honor Society kids were required to do school service hours, and tutoring would fit the bill.

Pulling her bottom lip between her teeth, she surveyed the office with a pained look. "Would I have to come here? Because everyone would see." She ducked her head, seeming worried that she'd said the wrong thing. "Y'know?"

"I'll work something out." Though I couldn't imagine how, exactly. I couldn't start tutoring every academically challenged kid in Harrington middle school.

" 'Kay," she replied doubtfully, then hovered in the doorway, looking toward Mrs. Morris's room like a prisoner heading down death row. Pausing, she vacillated in place, as if there were something more she wanted to say but was uncertain.

"Anything else?"

She turned halfway toward the door. "We've got Jumpkids after school near here," she mumbled, pulling a slim brown foot out of her clogs, curling her toes, then slipping them back in. "You said I should . . . I don't know . . . tell you when we did. On Fridays we're at Simmons-Haley Elementary. We feed the kids a snack, and do singing and dance class with them until five, and then they get dinner at the school cafeteria before they go home." She pointed vaguely toward the window. "It's over that way a few blocks by that big old Catholic church with the tall bell thing."

I was momentarily blindsided by the invitation. I had no idea she'd remember, much less care, that I'd expressed interest in her foster mother's after-school arts program. "Sounds great." I felt an unexpected rush of warmth for the shy teenager in the doorway. "What time?"

"Three thirty. Right after school."

"Hmmm," I mused out loud. "I'm on duty until four thirty."

Dell's shoulders went up, then slumped. "It's OK," she muttered, surrendering like a kid who was accustomed to being brushed off. Stepping backward into the hallway, she turned toward her English class. "See ya later."

"Well . . . wait." I followed her into the corridor. "What if I come by after four thirty? Will I be interrupting anything?"

Walking backward into the fray of students, she grinned, tucking loose strands of hair behind her ears. "No, that'd be cool." An eighth grader brushed past her, knocking her off balance with his backpack, and reminding her that she was in the hallway, where other kids might see her making nice with the counselor. Holding her hand near her waist, she gave a quick, covert wave, then hurried away.

I went back to my desk and made notes to myself. *Tutoring—find location, get copy of seventh-grade textbooks, check out* The Grapes of Wrath *from library. . . .*

Research drug education programs. . . .

When I looked up, the principal was hovering in my doorway. "Got that matching-funds app for the new PAC ready yet?" he asked, snapping his fingers and holding his hand palm out, as if I could make the thirty-page grant application materialize by magic.

Write enormous grant application for fancy new performing arts center. . . .

"Not yet," I said, pulling the application booklet from under the stack of attendance papers that had coagulated on my desk.

Finish checking daily attendance records. . . .

Suddenly, the job that had seemed boring and pointless yesterday was crammed full of demands and activities. Some of which actually mattered.

"I'll get right on it." Opening the booklet, I folded my elbows on my desk and waited for him to move on, but he didn't. "Anything else?"

Tapping his pen against the wooden door frame, he gazed at the trim board, following the sound, then regarding me solemnly. "Don't get too involved with the Jordan girl." He crossed his arms above the bubble of his stomach, drummed the pen on his chest. I had the sense that he hadn't stopped by to ask me about the grant application, but to talk to me about Dell. Or more specifically, to warn me off.

"I'm not sure I know what you mean." But I was afraid I did. He was telling me to let Mrs. Morris have her way—that he agreed with her point of view. "It *is* my job to help these kids." My reply came out sounding surprisingly territorial.

Mr. Stafford drew back, eyeing me down his bulbous nose. Clearly, the burst of attitude surprised him, too. "Play the crusader here, and you'll end up getting your head cut off, Julia." His use of my first name told me that we were down to bare knuckles now. "Some admissions committee members stuck their feet in it, getting that kid in here, and when it doesn't work out, they're going to be looking for a scapegoat. You don't want to be the one they blame."

I gaped at him in complete mortification and disbelief. "So, it's better if I don't get involved. Is that what you're saying? I should look the other way and let a kid fail?"

If the question bothered him, he didn't show it. "I'm saying it's a high-profile issue, especially now that Morris has her nose in it. And if it comes down to her or you . . ." He looked me over in a way that made me feel two inches tall and hopelessly blond. "They aren't going to side with you."

Blood rushed to my face, and I felt my back stiffen. His expression, his tone of voice, and the way he continued calmly tapping the pen against his fleshy chest told me much more than I wanted to know. Suddenly, I understood why a failed dancer with lackluster grad school grades could get a counselor's job, even one that had come up unexpectedly during semester break, at a school like Harrington. I was supposed to be the cute, blond patsy who would complacently fill out forms and write grant applications month after month, while happily accepting the status quo.

"Well, it won't be an issue if Dell's grades come up to a passing level," I said, turning my attention to my papers to hide the fact that I was fuming.

"She can't make the grades," he replied flatly. "She's got an unusual talent in music. That's it. Other than that, she doesn't have the stuff."

"I guess time will tell." I pretended not to catch his meaning. Stabbing my pen into the grant application, I started writing, determined not to look up as he shuffled away, his shadow receding slowly from my desk until finally it disappeared.

Chapter 5

During lunch break I went to the teachers' lounge, where, as usual, I picked at a cafeteria salad while listening to teachers talk about their trials and triumphs of the day. Halfway through the period, Mrs. Morris walked past the door, headed for the cafeteria line with her cronies. Tossing my salad in the trash, I went back to my office and started surfing the Web sites Sergeant Reuper had recommended.

After lunch, one of the math teachers went home sick, and I taught algebra for two periods, which was largely a joke, and the kids knew it. When they asked questions, all I could say was, "Well, let's look in the book," which, as far as I could tell, was written in Greek. Whatever math I'd taken in college had long since left me.

I noticed some things while I was in the classroom—small details I'd never picked up on before. Even though it was unusually warm in the classroom, kids in the back had sweatshirt hoods pulled over their heads—a sign to watch for, the drug prevention Web sites said. Kids could lay their heads on the desks and use the hood as a tent to trap the vapors of Magic Marker ink, glue, an open bottle of correction fluid, a rag or cotton ball soaked in dry-cleaning solution or electronic-contact cleaner. They carried the rags hidden in Ziploc bags, candy containers, plastic pencil boxes, lipstick tubes. Hard to believe, but apparently true.

Halfway through class, one of my students asked to go to the bathroom to blow his nose and became agitated when I suggested he grab a Kleenex off the bookshelf and wait until after class. Again, signs of possible drug use—runny noses and kids who desperately wanted to hang out in the restroom, where they could light up a joint, snort a powdered form of meth, or huff solvents from deodorant or hair spray cans. Sometimes they'd even smoke meth or crack through tiny pipes disguised as ink pens, belt buckles, or eyeliner pencils.

In the back, two girls were covertly investigating the scent of a flavored lip gloss. Probably innocent, but possibly the tube contained more than makeup. When I walked by, they quickly hid the lip gloss; then one of them grabbed her purse and pulled it into her lap—another sign, hyperpossessiveness toward personal belongings.

"If I see that lip gloss again, it's mine," I said, and they looked surprised, then denied having it.

In the front row, the middle school student council vice president, Cameron Ansler, had a zoned-out look and an unusual case of the sniffles.

Passing by his desk, I tapped his notebook to get him back on task. "Everything all right, Cameron?" I asked, and he nodded, hunching over his paper.

"Yes, ma'am." He was, as usual, polite but distant. "I'm just tired."

"Don't stay up so late," I advised, and he laughed.

"Sure, Ms. C," he replied, then started back to work, his cheek resting on his free hand, and his eyes drifting closed until he jerked, woke up, then tried to refocus on his paper.

"You sure you're all right?" I asked, passing by again.

"Sure." He smiled, as if falling asleep at his desk were perfectly normal.

Maybe it was. Adolescents didn't keep regular hours, especially these days, when they had cable TV, Internet service, and video games in their rooms. Teenage behavior was unpredictable at best: mood swings, sullenness, fatigue, withdrawal, strange fashion choices, like wearing a hood in a warm room, were all perfectly normal.

Or maybe not. How would I know? How would I ever separate everyday teenage behavior from warning signs? If I started questioning kids, parents would find out, there would be complaints, and Mr. Stafford would have a conniption.

If I left things alone, some of these kids might end up where I had—in the hospital, or worse, tangled in a web of guilt and lies, saddled with a lifetime addiction.

Sitting on the edge of the desk, I watched them, wondering what was going on in their minds, what their lives were like. They were here at Harrington because they were exceptional, because they had extraordinary potential in art, music, theater, dance.

Yet being extraordinary didn't stop them from having ordinary problems.

They deserved a real counselor, one who knew how to read the signs. The only experience I had with teenagers was with students in the university's college-bound gifted and talented program, where the kids were high school juniors and seniors, mature beyond their years, serious about their futures, working to rack up college credits before they finished high school. The classes were small. The students were studious, competitive about grades and potential scholarships. They didn't have time to chitchat over lip gloss or fall asleep at their desks. But here at Harrington, among kids who were still trying to navigate the pitfalls of adolescence, and years away from worrying about college, things were different, and I was woefully unprepared.

By the time the substitute teacher finally arrived, and I turned over the classroom, I had a sense that, in taking the position at Harrington, I'd stepped into quicksand up to my neck. My parents were right—I wasn't ready to handle such a complicated and demanding job. I could barely keep my own life on an even keel.

Sister Margaret's voice was in my head as I walked back to my office. *"When life provides mountains, God provides the strength to climb."*

If God had anything to do with my getting the counselor's job at Harrington, He certainly had a fine sense of humor, or irony, or both.

Back in my office, I closed the door and spent the rest of the afternoon working on the matching-funds application for the new performing arts center. Suddenly, the tedium of writing grants seemed refreshingly manageable and predictable, a part of my job I could handle. Even if I wasn't much of a drug prevention czar, I was a pretty good writer.

If the grant application was successful, I'd be a hero. Mr. Stafford would be overjoyed. The superintendent, the central administration, and the school board would be pleased. Everyone would be content with my job performance for the semester, and I wouldn't have to do a single thing about the possible drug problem at Harrington.

Except turn my head.

My cell phone rang, and I glanced at the clock. Four forty already. Dad's daily babysitting-Julia call. He was a few minutes early this afternoon.

We went through the usual niceties; then Dad got down to business. "Mom wanted me to ask how your day went. She's worried that you haven't called Bett."

Ohhhh . . . my sister's wedding and pregnancy. Hard to believe, but I'd completely forgotten about it in the rush of the day.

Dad went on talking. "Mom thought maybe we'd all go out to dinner at the club, or down in Westport. I could circle by the school and pick you up. We can get your car later on this weekend. They'll lock it up in the school parking lot, won't they?" He didn't mention that neither the country club nor Westport was anywhere close to Harrington. Apparently, Mom and Dad were worried that I was too distraught over Bett's news to drive myself home tonight.

"No, that's all right. . . ." I paused, searching for an excuse that, without hurting anyone's feelings, would prevent Dad from coming over to pick me up. Shifting my DayMinder on the desk, I unearthed several messages from Mom, as well as Dell's torn spiral notebook papers. *The Jumpkids program tonight . . .* I started putting things in my briefcase. "You know what, Dad, I can't. I . . . I already made a commitment for this afternoon. But, listen, we can all do dinner this weekend. I'll call Bett right now, I promise. I tried earlier, but the day got busy and I just forgot about it. Tell Mom I'm sorry." I imagined her at home, pacing the floor, calling Bett every little while, trying to find out whether I had checked in.

"A commitment . . ." Dad, now suspicious, fished discreetly for an explanation. Had it been Mom on the phone, she would have come right out and demanded answers. "Well . . . how long will it take? We could have dinner after—"

"I'm not sure how long," I admitted, "but I think supper's included." *Might as well go ahead and explain. You'll never get off the phone otherwise.* "I'm going by an after-school arts program a few blocks from here. One of my students invited me, and it sounds like it lasts through supper."

"You're going to stay down in *that* neighborhood until after dark?" The tone was just right for, *Now listen here, young lady, we'll have no more of this nonsense.*

Slipping on my blazer and grabbing my briefcase, I started toward the door. A ladybug was roosting on the jamb, in exactly the right position to be compacted by the latch. I urged it onto my finger and carried it into the hall. My random act of kindness for the afternoon. Sister Margaret's instructions were never to let a day go by without at least one.

"Dad, until a few years ago, *Grandma* lived in this neighborhood," I pointed out, as I hurried past the administration office and out the front door. As was typical on Friday afternoon, the place was a ghost town. Everyone, including Mr. Stafford, hit the door at four twenty-nine, so as to be at their cars and driving off the lot at four thirty, quitting time, officially.

Sensing the fresh air from the front doors, the ladybug fanned its red wings, showing the diaphanous black skirt underneath before it flew away as I exited the building and hurried down the steps.

"That neighborhood's not what it used to be." Dad's voice disappeared into static, then cleared again. For a moment, I thought he was going to insist on accompanying me to wherever I was going.

"Dad, I'll be fine." The tone was more petulant than I'd intended, and with a sigh, I added, "Thanks for worrying about me, but it's OK. I won't be by myself. The mother of one of my students runs this program. They're at this school every Friday. I'm sure it's perfectly safe." Call waiting beeped as I climbed into my car and cranked the engine to get the heater started. "Listen, Dad, that's my call waiting. It's probably

Bett, so I'm going to sign off. I'll see you later on. Don't wait around for me, all right? You and Mom go out if you want to. I'll be fine."

"Call us when you start for home."

"All right," I replied, relieved that the conversation was finally over. "Love you." Then I hit the button to answer the other line.

"Julia?" Bett said quietly, like an explosives expert hovering near a bomb, trying to decide which wire to cut. "Everything OK?"

If one more person asked me that one more time, I was going to explode. Everyone acted like I was made of glass lately. "Everything's fine. Bett, I'm so sorry I forgot to call you. I tried earlier this morning and got your voice mail. I meant to call again, but it's been crazy at work today."

"Really? What happened?" As usual, Bethany was happy to let the conversation focus on me. If there was a selfish, jealous, or unkind bone in Bett's body, I hadn't found it yet. She was going to be a terrific mother. Jason was getting a wonderful wife.

"Long story. I'll tell you all about it this weekend." Buckling my seat belt, I coasted out of the parking lot. "So, let's talk about you, and the wedding, and the baby. How in the world can you get married, move away, have a baby, and leave me here with Mom and Dad? I'm sorry, but you're not allowed. You'll have to tell Jason no."

Bett sniffed. "It wasn't supposed to happen this way. . . ."

"Bethany"—I chuckled—"I was just kidding. I'm happy for you. I really am."

She choked and coughed on the other end of the phone, then sobbed out, "I know." The word ended in a trembling gurgle. "But it wasn't supposed to happen this way. We were going to have a big wedding next summer, and . . ." She sniffed and coughed again. "But the baby, and Jason's job transfer . . . with the economy the way it is, he doesn't dare say no, and th-then . . ." The torrent of words faded into tears.

"Beth-a-*nee*," I scolded. "I know this isn't what you planned, but it's OK. You and Jason are going to be fantastic parents. Did Mom say something that upset you?"

"N-no-oh-oh," she sobbed out. "I can tell she and Dad are disappointed in us, but she just . . . she just . . . said it's not such a big deal like it used to be . . . the baby, I mean . . . that it's different."

Different from when she was pregnant with me. The thought stabbed unexpectedly. I pictured my mother in Bethany's position. Did she cry when she learned that I was coming?

Weaving through the downtown streets, I pushed the images from my mind. "Bett, it's all right," I soothed. "This is a good thing. Jason is a great guy. You two are wonderful together. He lights up whenever you come into a room. You both knew you wanted kids—maybe not right now, but you knew you wanted them. You two are going to have a perfect life." Doubtless, no such promises were made to my mother when she was pregnant with me. Whoever my real father was, he was gone by the time I came into the world—Grandma Rice had let that slip, as well. My mother was living with her and Grandpa when I was born. Theirs was the house she brought me home to. In the photos, she was neither smiling nor frowning. She just looked worried.

Within a year, she had met and married my dad, and his name officially became mine.

Bett's voice snapped me back to the present. "You're right. I'm sorry. I think I'm just hormonal."

"Well, OK, you're allowed to be hormonal." I won a stuffy-nosed laugh from my sister as I pulled into the parking lot of Simmons-Haley Elementary. "And, if it's absolutely necessary, you're even allowed to get married and move hundreds of miles away. I'll forgive you, I promise."

Bett forced another strangled chuckle, then fell silent, drawing a long, shuddering breath. "I just wanted to be here for you, you know? Sisters are supposed to be there."

Tears prickled in my nose, and my insides twisted as if someone were wringing me out like an old rag. *Sisters are supposed to be there. . . .* How was I ever *there* for Bett when I was sneaking around, purging food, letting her think that I could magically stay wafer-thin while binging with her on Girl Scout Cookies, Häagen-Dazs, movie-theater popcorn, and deep-fried restaurant appetizers? All her life, Bett had worried about her weight, and the comparison to me didn't help. If I were her, I would have felt betrayed and angry when the truth came out. Instead, Bett felt guilty for having a life of her own.

Swallowing hard, I drained the tears from my throat. "Now, you listen here, Bethany Costell, you are not allowed to waste one minute worrying, do you hear me? We're always going to be there for each other." *But you'll be hundreds of miles away.* "We'll call; we'll instant message. You'll e-mail me sonograms. We'll trade pictures from decorating magazines, and I'll send you articles about how to have the perfect baby, the perfect marriage—" Pressing the tremors from my lips, I swallowed another rush of painful emotions, and added, "But don't count on me for recipes, because you know I can't cook."

The irony of that statement was clear as soon as I said it. Bethany didn't answer at first, and when she did, her voice was low and serious. "I just want you to be OK. I need you to be OK."

"I am." No matter what it took, I was going to be the sister Bett deserved—this time. "Really." Dabbing my eyes, I looked toward the school door, where a Jumpkids banner was waving in the wind. "Listen, Bett, I'd better go. I promised one of my students I'd stop by this after-school arts program on my way home. I already told Dad I couldn't do dinner tonight, but we'll get together this weekend, all right? Dad wasn't happy that I won't be reporting home immediately after work today, and Mom will probably hit the roof, so I'm going to leave the cell phone in the car. Call me in the morning if you want to canvass the bridal shops and stuff, OK?" The invitation came out sounding genuine enough, but the thought made me feel like I couldn't breathe. How was I going to put on a happy face while my sister moved on in life and left me behind?

"I'll take care of Mom and Dad." As usual, Bethany was resigned to acting as the family peacemaker. "Don't worry about it; just enjoy your evening. We'll see about the bridal shopping. Mom wants this big to-do at the country club, and, really, if it were up to me, we'd just go to the courthouse and get it over with."

"Bethany," I snapped, because I knew better. My little sister had been dreaming of herself as a bride for as long as I could remember.

"You're not getting married at the courthouse. You deserve the whole fairy tale—like one of those Malibu Barbie weddings you used to stage in the dollhouse, remember? It's not like Mom and Dad can't afford it. Mom's been waiting for years to plan a wedding."

"I guess," she acquiesced reluctantly. "There's just so much going on right now. . . ." The sentence trailed off in a way that was filled with issues unspoken. The "so much going on" was about me—my problems, my eating disorder, my brush with death last October. Bethany didn't want to have a wedding because she was afraid I couldn't handle it—that her joy would somehow cast a deeper shadow over my pathetic life.

"Not for the next few weeks, there's not. There's nothing else going on. It's the Bethany-Jason wedding month, and that's it." My level of enthusiasm was almost convincing, but undoubtedly Bett knew I was putting on a show for her benefit. "Gotta go now, sis. I'll talk to you tomorrow."

"All right." She hung on the line for a moment. "Hey, call me tonight and tell me how the after-school arts thing was. Sounds intriguing."

"I'll see what time I get done." Bett wasn't the least bit interested in after-school arts. She was just worried, like everyone else, that I couldn't be trusted to spend an evening on my own, unsupervised. "Talk to you later. Love you."

"You too. Night, Ju-ju."

I groaned. "Ackh. Don't call me that anymore. That's the dog's name now."

"Night, Ju-lia," she rephrased, and we hung up the phone laughing at our own private joke. Mom had named her precious Pekingese in honor of Bethany's childhood pet name for me.

"Night," I said, then set the phone down and got out of the car. The cool air was bracing, and I drew it in, clearing my mind as I entered the school through a door where the Jumpkids banner was posted. The hum of children's voices drifted from somewhere near the center of the building, guiding me down a long corridor of classrooms framed with plain cement-block walls and low ceilings. Paint was chipping on the walls, and the overhead tiles were bowed and stained with odd-shaped patterns of dirt and mildew. On a rainy day, water probably dripped through in places.

The classrooms were equally spartan—rows of desks with sagging tabletops and graffiti scratched into the wood. No cheerful bulletin boards, just a few posters here and there. In one room, a collage of children's pictures provided a splash of color beneath a hand-lettered banner that said, *In My World . . .* With crayon on manila paper, the kids had drawn places that were bright and beautiful, people who were happy, smiling, holding hands.

> *In my world, there's five prizes in every cereal box.*
> *In my world, it only rains when you're sleeping.*
> *In my world, nobody has fights.*
> *In my world, there's no school.*
> *In my world, everyone's got a coat in the winter.*
> *In my world, nobody's in jail.*
> *In my world, there's no wars.*
> *In my world, nobody's hungry.*
> *In my world, everyone laughs.*
> *In my world, nobody hits anybody or shoots anybody.*
> *In my world, Mom and Dad are in my house.*
> *In my world, there's no gangs. Nobody uses drugs. There's no bullies.*
> *In my world, everyone is beautiful.*
> *In my world, everybody dances.*
> *In my world, everyone loves.*

I stood in the doorway until I'd read them all—dozens of visions of a perfect Crayola world. When I was finished, I couldn't wait to meet the children who had created the images.

I found the Jumpkids in the cafeteria finishing up a snack of cheese crackers and juice, then heading across the hall to the gymnasium, where what sounded like yoga music was playing. Standing in the hallway, I looked into one room and then the other, finally choosing the cafeteria, where an attractive forty-something woman with shoulder-length brown hair was directing kids as they cleaned up paper plates and cups. She didn't notice me by the door, but continued helping young-sters pack their leftovers into brown paper bags with names on them. As the kids passed by the door, they set their bags on a table. Studying me inquisitively, a few of them placed their bags on the corner farthest from me, like they thought I might eat their leftover crackers. A Hispanic girl with bouncing pigtails, perhaps six or seven years old, deposited her sack next to me, smiled with eight teeth missing in front, and gave me a bear hug. I supposed I looked like I needed it.

"Ooof," I grunted as the air rushed from my lungs. "Thanks."

Still smiling, she let go and skipped out the door, motioning for me to follow. Since the woman in the cafeteria was busy, I crossed the hall to the gymnasium. Inside, the gym floor was covered with kids sitting on old towels, carefully imitating the yoga movements of a middle-aged African-American woman with her hair pulled back in a headband of folk-art tapestry. Her eyes were closed as she slid through the yoga po-sitions with catlike grace, seeming oblivious to the sea of small bodies around her and the rustle of new kids coming in. The latecomers en-tered with amazing reverence, quietly slipping off their shoes at the door, picking up their towels with determined, sober faces, and moving to empty places. There was no jostling, no giggling, no talking, just the quiet whisper of breath and motion.

My mind raced back to the rehearsal room, in the moments before a performance, when everyone was silent, stretching, each of us in our own quiet sanctuary, already living the magic of stepping onstage to dance. My lungs constricted with the yearning I had struggled so hard to banish. In spite of everything that had happened to make it come crashing down, I missed my old life in a way that ached in every fiber of my body.

You should go, I thought, *before anyone sees you here.* There was a rea-son I avoided the Harrington dance classes, the performance hall, the practice studios each day as I went about my job. They were too stark a reminder of the past. Even the innocuous sounds of *Giselle* or *Scheherazade* in the hallways, or a dance teacher counting meter—*"and one, and two, and three, and four"*—was more than I could bear. The swish of pointe shoes, the rustle of costumes, the elastic snap of a dancer adjusting a leotard, filled me with remembered sensations.

I turned toward the door, but Dell was there. I realized I was standing in first position with my arms in rounded *devant*—a function of old habits and muscle memory. *Once a dancer, always a dancer,* my childhood madame used to say.

"Hey," Dell whispered, smiling and waving as she grabbed a towel and jogged toward me.

"Hey," I replied softly, sensing that she had been wondering if I would come. By making an appearance here, I had passed some sort of reliability test. "This is really something." I waved toward the children, perhaps fifty or sixty in all. "I can't believe the kids are so quiet."

"Mrs. Mindia *makes* everyone be quiet." Holding her towel beside her mouth as a shield, Dell motioned to the front of the room, and I noticed that the yoga instructor was watching us through one disapproving eye. "If you're not quiet, you don't get to dance."

Oh, I mouthed.

Dell shrugged toward the door. "Come meet Karen." Turning, she started toward the hallway, crossing the floor in her soft, pink ballet shoes. She moved like a dancer—confident, graceful, in command. She didn't look like the same kid I'd seen slinking down the hallways at Harrington, trying to achieve invisibility. This girl, with her dark hair twisted neatly back in a clip, her chin up and her shoulders square, her eyes bright and lively, was a different person entirely.

I was interested in getting to know her.

Chapter 6

*I*n the cafeteria, the dark-haired woman in the Jumpkids sweat-shirt—Dell's foster mother, I assumed—was ushering a few remaining kids off to the gym while a couple of elderly women cleaned and wiped tables. The kids hugged the workers with obvious affection as they passed. The last child, a little African-American boy with his hair shaved short, stood up in his seat, bounded from chair to chair until he reached Dell's foster mother, and launched himself at her. She caught him and he wrapped his arms and legs around her like an octopus.

"I wub Dumpkids day!" he bubbled, a speech impediment making the words hard to understand.

"Me, too, Justin." Stumbling backward, she collided lightly with the furniture. "But Jumpkids only walk on the floor. Never on tables or chairs, right?"

"Www-wite!" he exclaimed with a smile that overtook his face.

"Ohhhkay, then." Peeling him off, she set him on the ground. "Now"—laying a hand atop his head, she spun him around like a puppet—"you'd better get over to the gym. Mrs. Mindia's doing stretching exercises, and you want to do that. Today, we're going to try some Latin dancing and learn some things about the mandolin and the mariachis. You don't want to miss that, right?"

Justin twisted back and forth beneath her hand, swinging his arms at his sides like tiny pendulums. "Nope."

Drawing back, she made a quick *tsk-tsk* through her teeth, looking shocked. "I just know you haven't forgotten how Jumpkids answer a question. Remember, we talked about that a few weeks ago? When we speak to people, it's important to show that we have respect for the other person, and for ourselves. We don't want people to think we're just any old kids. We want them to know we're Jumpkids, right?" Justin nodded, and she prompted, "I bet you can show me how a Jumpkid answers a question, can't you?"

Snapping to attention, Justin cleared his throat and said, "Yes, ma'am." Then he grinned again, puffed his chest out, and added, "Dat's how a Dumpkid does it."

"You are right, sir." She smiled back. "See, I can tell just by the way you answered that you are no regular old kid. I bet I'll also be able to tell you're a Jumpkid by how quietly you go across the hall to Mrs. Mindia."

"Yes, ma'am," Justin said again, then spun around and marched toward the door like a soldier. When he came to Dell and me, he stopped, gave Dell a hug, then stuck his hand out to me with great formality. "Good mo-wning, I'm Dus-tin."

It wasn't morning, of course, but the introduction was charming. "Good afternoon, Justin." I shook his hand, which was sticky from something I didn't want to think about. "I'm Julia Costell. It is a pleasure to make your acquaintance."

Narrowing one eye, Justin considered all those big words, then shrugged and said, "You a pretty wady. Bye." He trotted off, and Dell and I laughed together as Dell's foster mother crossed the room and introduced herself.

"Karen Sommerfield." Her bemused expression told me she had no idea who I was or why I was there.

"Julia Costell," I said as we shook hands. "I'm Dell's guidance counselor at school." Her confusion turned to worry, and she cast a concerned glance at Dell, so I quickly added, "Dell mentioned the Jumpkids program to me the other day, and she invited me to come by and see how it works. I hope I'm not disturbing anything."

"Oh, gosh, no. We're thrilled to have you." Cocking her head to one side, she squinted at me. "You're the guidance counselor at Harrington?"

I wondered if she thought I was too young or too blond to hold such an esteemed position, then realized that she was probably confused because until seven weeks ago, the guidance counselor had been old Mrs. Kazinski, Mrs. Morris's evil twin. "Mrs. Kazinski retired at the end of fall semester." Since taking over, I'd done a woefully poor job of getting out and meeting parents, or anyone else. I'd been completely overwhelmed with my own problems, the grant application, and the mess of incomplete student records Mrs. Kazinski had piled up during her last few months before retirement. I suspected that she had been combing through files, removing things she didn't want anyone to see. I couldn't imagine what—maybe evil spells and recipes for witch's brew.

"Oh . . ." The wheels were turning in Karen's mind. Scratching her head, she pushed strands of hair behind her ear. "I'm sorry. You must think I'm incredibly rude. It's just that when Dell enrolled at the first of the year, I explained her situation and particularly asked that the school keep in touch. Since then, not one person has contacted me, except her music teacher. When we went in to ask about grades and things, Mr. Stafford and Mrs. Kazinski assured me that we shouldn't worry, that all students are given only a pass/fail grade their first semester at Harrington, and that Dell was passing. Am I correct in assuming that at the end of this nine-week grading period, she'll be receiving an actual report card with letter grades?"

My stomach tensed up. I was terribly uninformed as to the current grading system, except that I knew the school was now operating under nine-week grading periods, rather than the traditional six-week blocks. There were grades for Dell in my folder, and they were not good. Why would Stafford or Kazinski have kept that from her foster parents? When the next report card came home two weeks from now, Karen would be in for a shock.

Dell's gaze darted back and forth between her foster mother and me with genuine terror. Right now, in front of her, wasn't the time to be talking about problems with the school's grading system or lack of parent communication. "Yes, she should be receiving a regular report card at the end of this nine weeks." My mind was racing through grades and percentages—trying to determine whether it was possible to bring Dell's grades up to passing in two weeks. Tutoring? Extra credit? Divine intervention?

Oh, God.

"Good. We just want to be sure everything's OK." Karen was clearly relieved. Slipping an arm around Dell's slim shoulders, she pulled her close and kissed the top of her head. "Dell's had such a big transition this year. We want to be there for her in whatever ways we need to be. She's a pretty special kid." Her love for Dell was obvious, and so was the fact that, so far this year, she'd been given a snow job with whipped cream and a cherry on top.

Laying her head on her foster mother's shoulder, Dell cast a pained, pleading gaze my way. The message was clear: *Please don't say anything and mess this up.*

Now I knew why she had returned to my office with another essay today, why she'd invited me here this afternoon, and why she'd insisted on confidentiality between us. She was desperate. She needed help. She couldn't tell her foster parents that things weren't wonderful at Harrington, because she was afraid that if she couldn't be perfect, she wouldn't be wanted.

I felt a stab of understanding in the part of me that had always been empty, uncertain. The messy, hollow space marked BIOLOGICAL FATHER, where questions roiled endlessly, simmering like a volcanic pool beneath a cooled surface. No amount of love could ever completely rescue you from the scars of being abandoned by someone who was supposed to love you. No matter who else came along, or how devoted they were, there was always a part that feared everyone else would eventually discover the reasons you were left behind in the first place, and they'd leave too.

My dad had loved me unwaveringly for twenty-seven years, and still, I didn't trust it. Because of a man I'd never met, and was afraid to ask about. I'd seen his name on my original birth certificate when I started college, punched it into Yahoo! search, then closed the window before the results came up, worried that somehow Dad would find out. I'd even erased the history screen, as if going to Yahoo! People Search were a crime.

I understood exactly how Dell felt. If I caved on her now, the fragile connection between us would be severed. There wouldn't be anyone she could trust with the truth. "Well, listen, I don't want to hold you up," I said to Karen, in hopes of smoothly breaking out of the conversation. "My door's always open at the school. But today, I'm just here to watch."

Karen smiled pleasantly. "The first rule of Jumpkids," she said as we started across the hall, "is nobody just watches."

"Ms. Costell's a dancer," Dell chimed in, regarding me with admiration and no small measure of gratitude. "She went to Harrington."

Karen blinked in surprise, the way everyone did when they found out I went to Harrington and ended up back there as a counselor.

"Oh . . . well . . . I don't dance anymore," I stammered.

"It's a cinch that you won't get outclassed around here," Karen said, just before we reached the quiet zone in the gym-slash–yoga studio. "Although some of our kids are taking a pretty serious interest in dance and voice, and a few in instrumental music. Instrumental is harder for us to accomplish, because we only have enough instruments to teach a few kids each week. Right now we're offering piano and guitar, but I'd like to expand, if we can get equipment and teachers." She shrugged apologetically. "I'm sorry. I'm giving you the full tour, whether you want it or not, aren't I? I've only been with Jumpkids since last fall, so it's all new and exciting to me."

"Oh, no, it's interesting," I whispered as Mrs. Mindia moved the kids into a downward-dog position, then had them slowly stretch upward. "Like trees," she said, "rising toward the sun."

Karen handed me a towel from a basket near the door. She and Dell kicked off their shoes, and I stood awkwardly looking at my pastel print dress with the flowing fluttery skirt. "I didn't exactly come dressed for this. . . ." I felt like the nerd who'd forgotten her gym suit in PE class.

"I don't know." Lifting her hands, Karen grinned, pretending to spread an imaginary skirt. "As soon as the kids finish their ballet positions, we're doing flamenco. Looks like you're the only one with the right dress on."

Dell butted me playfully in the shoulder, something I couldn't imagine her doing at school. "Come on, Ms. Costell, nobody just watches in Jumpkids."

I gave her a mean face, my imitation of Mrs. Morris. "You should have told me *that* before you invited me."

"If I told you that, you wouldn't of come." Fanning her towel like a Latin dance dress, she hurried across the gym.

Karen smiled after her. "It's so good to see her happy and acting like a normal kid," she said, as I took off my shoes and blazer, and we started after Dell. "She's come out of herself so much in these past few months."

You wouldn't know it if you saw her at school, I thought. Fortunately, we'd moved into the silent zone, so I didn't have to answer. I had a feeling that Dell's foster mother knew nothing about the girl in the river, and she wasn't going to find out, if Dell could help it.

As we laid our towels on the floor and began transitioning through the combination of dance stretches and yoga positions, my thoughts slowed and wound inward, like a wobbling gyroscope finding its center, finally spinning effortlessly, in motion yet silent. There was an inner joy, a poetry of muscle and mind as my body stretched, then tightened, weaving and swaying, filled with a lightness of rhythm, and air, and memory. Closing my eyes, I moved through the ballet positions, barely hearing Mrs. Mindia directing from the front of the room. I was far away, in the studio warming up before rehearsal—going through the basics like dance class students. Brian McGregor, the artistic director at KC Metro Ballet, insisted on first things first. *"No matter how great your talent,"* he said, *"without the basics, you are nothing."*

In my mind, Mrs. Mindia's voice became his as he directed the cast, rehearsing the Dance of the Four Little Swans. *"Technically correct,"* he said, *"but this is professional ballet. It is a level beyond. You must feel the magic of your art. You must think like dancers. Give me the opening sequence on three. And one, and two, and three, and . . ."*

I felt myself begin to move as one of the Four Little Swans, the dancer I was to replace on the afternoon of spacing rehearsal. Music filled every corner of my soul until it spilled out into the theater, into cavernous empty space, so that no emptiness remained. In my soul, in the theater, there was only a perfect marriage of melody and motion. No questions, no answers, no problems of the world. Only beauty, only the sense of transcending gravity and taking flight, like the swan itself . . .

Mrs. Mindia paused to help a student, and my mind rocketed back with an elastic snap. When I opened my eyes, Dell was watching me with amazement. I flushed, feeling as if I'd been caught doing something I shouldn't. Dancing. The forbidden obsession. After my stint in the hospital, I'd promised my parents I would give it up and everything that went with it. The doctors agreed that I should steer clear of *"that environment,"* as if I were a drug addict staying away from the local crack house, or a compulsive gambler avoiding proximity to a casino. A studio full of mirrors and willowy dancers with perfect body lines was no place for a woman with an eating disorder.

But then, the Simmons-Haley Elementary School gym was about as far from a professional ballet studio as possible. There were no mirrors, and none of the dancers here were over four feet tall.

Smiling, Dell gave me the thumbs-up and mouthed, *Cool!*

I fell into the rhythm of the warm-up again, enjoying the muted drumbeat of feet softly striking the floor in unison and the feel of fabric swirling around my legs. By the time we'd moved to demi plié, I realized that not only Dell but some of the other kids were watching me each time Mrs. Mindia gave an instruction.

"If you cannot see well from the back," Ms. Mindia said, "you may watch Dell, or Mrs. Karen, or the beautiful ballerina in the flowered dress." She regarded me with interest. "I don't believe I know her name."

"Ms. Costell," Dell piped up, pleased that the instructor had noticed she'd brought a friend.

"Greetings, Ms. Costell. Welcome." The teacher delivered a wise, slow smile, and everyone turned to look. "I see that we have a professional in our midst."

My heart lurched, and for a fleeting instant, I was afraid that she'd recognized me, that we'd met sometime in the past, perhaps worked together on some performance long ago. What if she knew the truth about how I'd ended up here? If word got around, Mrs. Morris would have all the ammunition she needed to bury me. When I'd applied for the job at Harrington, I hadn't mentioned my hospital stay, or the back-stage collapse that ended my dancing career. I'd simply acted as if, now that I'd obtained my master's degree, it was time to stop dancing and get a real job—as if that had been the plan all along.

Mrs. Mindia wheeled a hand gracefully in front of herself. "I can see that you are well trained," she explained, and the tension melted from my body as quickly as it had come.

"Oh, not that much," I stammered, skirting the subject so as not to pile a new lie atop old ones. Better just to offer fewer details.

"She's from *Harrington,*" Dell interjected, with a note of pride that surprised me. When she was actually *at* Harrington, she didn't seem nearly so positive about the place.

Mrs. Mindia studied me from beneath her headdress, her face stern with some hidden meaning I could only wonder at. "Well, we're glad to have someone from *Harrington* joining us. Welcome to our dance, Ms. Costell."

"Julia," I corrected, wondering if it was my imagination or if Mrs. Mindia had become less delighted with me as soon as Harrington was mentioned.

"Ms. Julia." Presenting me to the class with a queenly wave of her hand, Mrs. Mindia brought the lesson to order again. Every student fell silent, and all eyes immediately faced forward. A young dancer scooted to a boom box nearby and changed the CD, cueing up a soft, slow Latin rhythm.

"Now," said Mrs. Mindia, clapping her hands over her head, "be-cause we have all been so attentive and done such impressive work in our yoga stretches and our study of ballet, and because all of you have been so perfectly quiet . . ." She paused to look at Justin, who was vi-brating like a windup toy in the front row. Her smile widened, white against mocha-brown skin, as she went on. "We will have time to con-tinue our around-the-world tour of dance. Because we know that as dancers, it is important to study all cultures. When we understand all cultures, we understand all things, and all people, and the world becomes a smaller place. When we think of the world as a small place, we see that there is not so much difference between ourselves and other people. Not so much distance between here and there.

"So now, let's close our eyes and listen to the rhythms of Mexico. Perhaps you are a young child who lives in a tiny village where the wind is hot, and the streets are made of sand. Can you feel the warmth between your toes as you walk many miles to Mexico City for the *días de fiesta?* Or perhaps you come from a wealthy family, and you live in a big hacienda where the rooms have colorful clay tile, and wide wooden doors swing open to the courtyard. Today, you run to your balcony and listen, because it is no ordinary day. Can you hear the music of Cinco de Mayo coming from the plaza? Girls, will you put on your new *china poblana* dress or, boys, your handsome *traje y sombrero de charro,* and come with me? Can you hear the *zapatillas de baile* on your feet, tapping against the brick streets as we run along? Are you ready to join *jarabe tapatío,* the hat dance?"

On cue, the students opened their eyes and cried, "Yeeesss!"

"Then let's dance!" Picking up her yoga towel, Mrs. Mindia held it around her shoulders like a shawl and said, "But first, ladies, we must have our *rebozo,* our fancy shawl made of Spanish lace so fine we could pass it through the space of a wedding ring. *Jarabe tapatío* is about color, and movement, and fabric, as much as it is about dance. It is a feast for the eyes and the senses. Young men, you may tie yours around your waist. Perhaps later, you will use it as a cape, to face the bull in the Monumental Plaza, the bullfighting ring. But, not to worry, we will never hurt the bull. We will only join him in a fierce dance, then send him on his way to smell the flowers, like Ferdinand."

The children giggled, and Mrs. Mindia turned sideways, stomped her foot, and clapped her hands over her head. "Our *jarabe tapatío* begins like this."

Following her lead, the children began joining her in the dance, learning the basic steps slowly at first, then more rapidly as the tempo increased. Dell, Karen, and I joined in, but this time I was no fine example. The only Latin dance I knew was a smattering I'd learned while dancing in the living room with my father, and some flamenco taught to me by my grandmother's housekeeper, Carmen. Even though my Mexican hat dance left something to be desired, at least I was appropriately attired. My filmy flowered dress might not have been right for Red Day, but it was perfect for *jarabe tapatío* in the grade school gym.

When the dance lesson was finished, most of the kids went to the cafeteria to write about the day's experiences in their Jumpkids journals. A few older kids proceeded to instrumental and vocal music lessons in various rooms around the school.

"I wish we had more to offer them," Karen commented as we stood in the hall watching kids pass by. "Some of these children have real talent, and if they can't develop it in the after-school program, they can't develop it at all. School funding being what it is, the music and art programs here were cut long ago. The sad thing is that these kids need it more than most. In large part, they come from deprived home environments, and they go to underfunded schools. Music and dance and art open doors in their minds, but you can't make state legislators see that." She winced apologetically. "Sorry. I'm on my soapbox again. Coming from the corporate world, where you do what has to be done to get results, I've found the politics of public education a little shocking."

"I'm just beginning to deal with that," I said. *And it's driving me crazy.* Nothing in my formal education had prepared me for the frustration of school bureaucracy. "How did you go from a corporation to after-school arts, anyway? That seems like a huge switch." It was hard to believe Karen was new at her job. She seemed so competent with the kids, so into her work.

Lifting her palms, she shrugged, as in, *Search me.* "It just kind of happened. The company downsized in Boston. I was laid off. I came out to Missouri to visit my sister, and the next thing I knew, I was a Jumpkid." Her brown eyes twinkled in a way that told me there was more to the story, but in the cafeteria, the natives were getting restless. "Better watch out," she teased. "It's addictive."

Laughing, I rubbed the small of my back. "I don't think I could do this very often. Mrs. Mindia has me twisted up like a pretzel."

"You get used to it." Karen grinned as Mrs. Mindia came out of the gym, carrying her boom box and yoga towel–slash–flamenco skirt. "Thank you, Mrs. Mindia."

Pausing in the doorway, she nodded, seeming regal in her headband and long African-print dress. "As always, it was my pleasure. I must hurry off to rehearsal now, but I will see you again tomorrow," she said to Karen. Then, turning to me, she added, "Come again and join us, Ms. Julia. I have enjoyed dancing with you very much."

"Thank you." I felt as if I'd been invited to tea by the queen of England. "I'll try to do that."

"Some Ben-Gay will help that sore back." A wide grin spread on Mrs. Mindia's face as she turned away and started down the hall. "Ben-Gay and regular exercise. A dancer of merit should never allow her gift to wane."

I gaped after her, taking in the compliment. *A dancer of merit.* I hadn't thought of myself that way in months.

"That's high praise," Karen commented. "Mrs. Mindia directs and dances in the Kansas City Black Dance Theater. She knows what she's talking about. We're really lucky to have her as a Jumpkids volunteer."

"Wow. I guess so," I breathed as Karen and I stood transfixed, watching Mrs. Mindia walk down the hall, her disappearing figure casting the shadow of an African queen, floating through the long beams of evening light, until she finally vanished altogether.

Chapter 7

"**Y**ou know, I was just thinking about something," I mused after the door fell closed behind Mrs. Mindia. "I wonder if there would be a way to partner the Jumpkids program with Harrington. Our storage closets are full of old instruments that could probably be made usable. Maybe we could even set up some Harrington students as volunteer instructors." It was one of the ideas on the antidrug Web sites—get kids involved in the community. Give them activities that matter. Help them develop a sense of purpose.

Karen's expression said, *Oh, you poor little thing. You're adorable, but you don't have any idea what's realistic, do you?* It reminded me of Mr. Stafford. "I'll be honest," she said finally. "I've already tried the Harrington route, and I was shown the door."

"Really?" I drew back, surprised. "I can't imagine why, because part of the school charter is arts as a community service. Harrington kids are supposed to complete school and community service hours as a curriculum requirement. Back when I was a student, we did everything from concerts for famine relief to collecting school supplies for orphanages in Mexico." I sounded like a tour guide, a Stepford counselor, describing the perfect school environment, full of happy, extraordinary, high-minded kids who wanted to make the world a better place.

One of the older Jumpkids, passing by on her way to the cafeteria, stopped to ogle me. "Pppfff," she scoffed, with an in-your-face head bob that seemed far too grown-up for a girl who couldn't have been more than ten or eleven. "Harrington kids don' leave Harrington, unless they goin' by the buzz bomb stand to pick up some weed or score some bolt. And das the truth."

Karen flushed. "Shamika, that's enough. That was rude, wasn't it?"

Pressing her lips into a straight, tight line, Shamika muttered, "Yes, ma'am. Sorry," and hurried on to the cafeteria.

Karen apologized. "Naturally, the children here harbor some resentment toward Harrington. It's hard to be where they are, watching the have-everything kids drive expensive cars, wear nice clothes, and carry instruments that cost more than the household incomes of families in Simmons-Haley. I hate to sound cynical, but I did try to get Harrington involved with the Jumpkids program last fall when Dell started there. I pushed pretty hard, and finally I was afraid I might be jeopardizing Dell's situation, so I let it go. She's had enough drama in her life this past year, and she's adjusted so well, I didn't want her to start having trouble at school."

She's already having trouble at school, I thought, and my mind began sifting through a complicated web of counseling ethics, confidentiality, school rules, professional confidences, and the overriding promise I'd made to Dell: *What's said in my office stays in my office.* How far should that go? Where was the dividing line between communicating with the parent and betraying the child? The truth was that I didn't know. A few semesters in a master's degree program and a short internship don't prepare you for what awaits in the real world.

Passing through the cafeteria with an armload of notebooks, Dell eyed us warily, and started in our direction.

Karen, her back to the door, kept talking. "No offense intended, but the powers that be at Harrington only seem to be interested in a *certain*"—holding up her fingers, she encased the word in invisible quotation marks—"kind of kid. I've had the nagging feeling that there are some who resent Dell's presence there, in spite of the fact that she made it through the audition process, and she has an incredible talent. If she isn't the *kind* of kid Harrington is intended to serve, I can't imagine who is, but I get the impression some people think her being there might open up the floodgates to every underprivileged child with an uncommon talent. You'd think the admissions committee would be seeking out kids who need a leg up, but the former Jumpkids director told me she sent some talented kids through the application process, and not one of them was accepted." Face tightening with frustration, she braced her hands on her hips. "Explain that to me, will you, because I don't understand."

I didn't have an answer—not one I could share with a parent, anyway. Dell had come within earshot and was obviously listening, so I diverted the subject to something safer. "Maybe some donations of old instruments and student volunteer hours would open the lines of communication. People are afraid of what they don't understand."

Dell slipped into the hallway with us, her brows rising with interest as she propped the stack of notebooks on her hip.

"True enough," Karen acquiesced, but her expression was doubtful. Absently, she slid Dell's loose ponytail holder from her hair, smoothed the tangled strands with her fingers, and replaced the hairband. Kissing Dell on the top of her head, she leaned over to look at her. "What did you need, sweetheart?"

"Where do you want me to put the folders for the kids who aren't here today?" Dell's gaze darted toward me, making it obvious she was on a reconnaissance mission to see what her foster mom and I were talking about.

"Just put them back in the Friday box by the door. Thanks for passing them out. You're a trouper. I don't know what I'd do without you."

Flushing, Dell ducked her head, brushing off the compliment with a muttered excuse. "Guess I'd better go take care of these."

Watching her wiggle free and turn away, I recognized that lost look in her eyes. People are afraid of what they don't understand, and she couldn't understand how someone could love her just for who she was. I saw that same uncertainty every time I stood at the mirror and gazed into the hollow face of the washed-up dancer who still wondered why her real father was a family secret.

"Are you stayin' for dinner?" Dell asked, and my mind hopscotched back to the conversation. "It's Shakey's Kansas City Barbecue tonight."

"Local restaurants donate our meals so that the kids can have a hot supper before they go home," Karen explained. "Shakey's takes care of us on Friday nights—chopped-beef sandwiches, usually. You're welcome to stay."

My stomach roiled at the idea of slugging down barbecue. Fat, sugar, salt. That would cause water retention. . . .

A door opened at the end of the hall, and Karen glanced up. "Well, look who else is tromping in, just in time for dinner."

I watched a tall man in some sort of a uniform cross the narrowing stream of twilight as the door drifted shut behind him. He moved with an easy stride, whistling softly, glancing into classrooms as he passed.

"Hey, James!" Stuffing the folders hurriedly into Karen's arms, Dell ran down the hall and tackled him with an exuberant hug. I surmised that the latecomer was her foster father, as they approached us, his arm looped loosely over Dell's shoulders, her head resting near the wings on his airline pilot's uniform. The captain's hat was missing, though his salt-and-pepper hair still held the shape of one.

"Well, how are my girls?" he asked, as he stopped beside us with Dell still attached to his side.

"Good," Dell answered, looking up at him adoringly. "I got my piano music for the spring concert with the symphonic."

"Great. Think I can play it on the guitar?"

"Probably," Dell replied cheerfully, sparkling under his attention.

James smiled back, the adoration between them obvious. "Great." He chuckled. "We'll just call the symphonic and tell them to book a duet. I've got a new Ovation guitar to break in."

Dell's eyes widened until white circled the dark centers. "Cool!"

"Another one?" Karen groaned, bracing a hand on her hip. "Geez, James, when you get that urge, you're supposed to call your guitar-a-holics sponsor and talk until the need to collect more guitars goes away."

Grinning, he kissed Karen's cheek and whispered, "It was such a bargain," then turned to me and introduced himself. "James Sommerfield. Sorry, I don't think we've met."

"Julia Costell. Nice to meet you."

"Julia is Dell's new guidance counselor at Harrington," Karen interjected.

He blinked, seeming surprised, but not alarmed, at the idea of the school guidance counselor showing up unexpectedly. "Oh . . . great to meet you." He pumped my hand before letting go. I noted his cheerful, open reaction. Clearly, any problems at Harrington were completely off his radar.

Slipping away from him, Dell frowned, ready for the subject to divert from school issues.

"Staying for dinner?" James asked, leaning to look into the cafeteria, where the sounds of food preparation were now under way. "I smell Shakey's."

"I'd love to, but I can't." *Animal fat ground up and covered in brown sugar and ketchup.* "I have to head home. I live out in Overland Park." *With my parents.*

Karen seemed surprised. "Gosh, that's a bit of a commute to Harrington, especially with rush-hour traffic." Her look of parental concern made me think of my mother. "We looked at some places in Overland Park because we'd heard the schools were good, but after Dell was accepted into Harrington, we settled on a house in Prairie Village to cut down on the commute."

"I might move closer in, eventually. I haven't decided where I want to be yet." *True, so true.* As usual, I skirted the issue of the house in Overland Park being my parents' place. It was hard to gain respect from other adults when you were still living with your mom and dad. "But I don't mind the drive to Harrington. It's not that bad usually, and it gives me time to think about the school day."

"I can understand that." There was a load of unspoken commentary in Karen's face, and for a moment, I thought we were going to enter another Harrington discussion.

"Well . . ." I backed out of the circle before things could heat up again. "I'd better go. Dell, thank you so much for inviting me. I've enjoyed this. What a fantastic program."

Both Karen and Dell smiled, and Karen said, "Come back any-time." She glanced toward the cafeteria, where the two elderly women who'd cleaned the tables earlier were now helping kids finish their journals. "Volunteers are always welcome."

"I'll see what I can do about getting some student volunteers, and I'll definitely come back myself." I stretched my back from side to side. "Mrs. Mindia gives quite a workout. Tomorrow morning I'm going to wake up realizing how out of shape I am."

Karen, James, and Dell all looked at me in unison, thinking, no doubt, *She's thin as a rail; how could she possibly be out of shape?*

I was suddenly uncomfortable. The scent of food, the discussion of where I lived, their bemused expressions had knocked me off balance. Under their scrutiny, I felt like an actor in a counselor costume. "Well, thanks again. It was fun. You three have a great weekend."

"You, too, Ms. Costell," Dell said. "Thanks for coming. See you Monday."

"See you Monday. Nice meeting all of you." Waving good-bye, I headed down the hall without looking back, or forward, right, or left. My mind filled with a swirl of thoughts from the day—Dell and her foster family, Harrington, instrument donations, student volunteers, Mrs. Morris, Mrs. Mindia and the Jumpkids, Shamika, who said Harrington kids went by the "buzz bomb" stand to score some "bolt," Red Instead Day, the girl in the river sitting with her baby brother beneath the trees. My sister's wedding. Was it going to be indoors or outdoors? Day or evening? Long dresses or tea length?

Bett was getting married and moving away.

It didn't seem real. I couldn't frame the picture any more than I could imagine kids from Harrington High School hopping in their Beemers and Mustangs and making a buy on the way home. Yet Shamika seemed to know what she was talking about. She'd mentioned weed, buzz bomb, bolt—marijuana, nitrous oxide–filled balloons, and methamphetamine—three common drugs of choice for high school kids. Inexpensive, readily available, easy to use, easy to conceal. Deadly.

It was a difficult reality to reconcile, but during my time at St. Francis, I'd learned that accepting reality is important. Trying to run from it is like sprinting on water. No matter how much perpetual motion you generate, you eventually sink. I had to deal with this new reality, but what I really wanted to do was point the car in some direction, any direction, and just drive, and drive, and drive, until I'd left it all behind. I wanted to travel back to my life, my real life—the one in which I was living in my own apartment near the KC Metro studio, dancing, not dealing with my sister getting married and having a baby, or me living with my parents, or a school full of kids with potential drug problems.

But the car, of course, went home on autopilot. When I walked in the door, Mom was waiting with bridal magazines and a wedding-planner book from Dillards. Dad had disappeared upstairs to watch "one of those silly basketball games," according to Mom. No doubt, she had booted him out so we could talk. He was probably also in trouble for letting me go AWOL this evening.

Mom would want to know exactly where I'd been and what I'd been doing. Her first question: "Hi, sweetheart. Have you eaten?"

I realized I hadn't had anything since the salad at noon in the staff lounge. "Yes," I answered. "Barbecue. I told Dad I was going to eat with the kids at the after-school program." I glanced at the clock. Almost seven thirty. Surely, they'd eaten by now. "You didn't wait supper, did you?"

"Oh, no, of course not." Mom dismissed the question with a back-handed wave. *Psshaw. We're not waiting around to monitor your meals, Julia. We trust you. Honestly, we do.* "We ate take-out Chinese with Bethany and Jason over at their place. I took a bunch of bridal magazines over to Bett. There's some leftover in the fridge, if you'd like it."

"Bridal magazines?"

"No—Chinese food. Very funny." She didn't laugh, as she normally would have. In fact, she looked exhausted. "I'll fix a plate for you."

Slicing my hands back and forth in the air, I backed away. "No, no, don't get up. I can fix myself something." With a suspicious frown, she braced a hand on the sofa arm to pull herself up, so I added, "I'll bring it back in here and we can look at the bridal magazines *while I eat.*"

"All right." She scooted back into her seat, satisfied with the idea of watching me eat Chinese while perusing the pages of *Perfect Bride*.

I hoped I could stomach both.

"I don't know how we're going to plan a wedding in less than a month," she muttered as I left the room.

I wasn't sure whether she was talking to herself or to me, but I answered anyway. "Don't worry about it, Mom. Between the three of us, we'll get it done."

"I can't convince Bethany to settle on anything," Mom called as I opened the fridge and took out a half dozen full containers of take-out Chinese. Clearly, Mom had overordered to make sure I'd have plenty of choices. "She hasn't even picked out dresses."

She just told us she was getting married yesterday. "I assumed she was going to wear your dress." Ever since she was little, Bett had been pulling Mom's dress from the linen closet, putting it on, and dreaming of the day.

"Oh, that old thing?" Mom was coming down the hall. "It's in such bad shape—stained, and there's a tear under the arm. Some of the lace is moth-eaten and the seed pearls are God knows where. We'd never get it in shape in time."

Investigating the food containers, I selected fried rice and a fortune cookie before Mom could fill my plate with wontons and sweet-and-sour pork. Wa-a-ay too fattening.

"I think we could get the dress ready," I said, putting away the extra food, and quickly turning the conversation back to wedding details. "There's a cleaner's downtown that specializes in restorations and alterations. I noticed it today, when I was driving to the after-school program. I could take the dress by there Monday morning, and see what they can do."

"I don't know that it's worth it." Mom eagle-eyed my plate as I stuck it in the microwave.

"Of course it is. It's your dress. It's special. It has history." It bothered me to hear her call the dress she had worn when she married my dad, the dress she had designed and sewn herself in the wardrobe studio where she worked, *"that old thing."* Was that what she was thinking the day she wore it—that it was nothing special, that the day was nothing special? Was she merely doing something she felt she had to

do, because of me? Where was I at the time? There were no pictures
of Mom in the dress, Dad in the suit, and me. There were no dates on
any of the photographs, and in the album the wedding came first, and
then my baby pictures. But if you looked closely enough, you could
see that my baby pictures weren't taken at Mom and Dad's first house
over on Hollyhock Drive. In the pictures of the day she brought me
home, Mom's hair was long. Long blond hair, flowing over her bare
shoulders in a flowered summer maternity dress. Her hair was short
in the pictures of my first Christmas, then longer again on my first
Easter, then short in the wedding photos and in my first birthday pictures, where suddenly my dad was at the party, standing with me and
his new wife.

Hair does not grow long and short and long and short again that
quickly. Apparently, Mom never thought of that when she arranged the
album into a format that would look proper for guests, neighbors, and
other people who did not know our family secret. . . .

I realized I was standing there, staring at Mom. Stopping the microwave, I pulled out my plate, and we sat down at the breakfast table in
the kitchen. "So, let me take the dress to the cleaner downtown on
Monday," I said, stirring up the rice. "It isn't even out of the way. Just a
few blocks from Harrington, right next to the school I was at this afternoon."

"Oh, it's all right." Mom watched the food travel from the plate to
my mouth, and then somberly waited until I swallowed, as if talking
might distract me from taking in calories. "I'll find a cleaner here, if
that's what Bethany wants."

"Mom, please. Let me . . . I can handle this, all right?" I set down
the fork, and she focused on it with foreboding, no doubt thinking that
the pressure of dealing with Bethany's wedding dress might cause me to
relapse. "You have enough to do."

Putting on her Polly Sunshine face, Mom batted her lashes, like she
couldn't imagine what I meant. "Oh, goodness, no. I'm fine. Everything's under control." Her voice cracked on the last word, and she offered a pasted-on smile, trying to sell me her *fineness* like swampland.

"You're about to have a nervous breakdown," I countered, grabbing the fork and holding it up, so that she would focus on me instead of the food. "Just relax, Mom. Everything's going to be fine."

Her pale blue eyes met mine—my eyes, my color. The same eyebrows, the same hair. The same need to keep things under control. *Everything wasn't fine with you,* her gaze said. *You fell off a cliff, and I wasn't there to catch you until it was almost too late.* "Things have been a little off keel lately, that's all." It was a surprisingly honest admission, for Mom. Eyes glittering with moisture, she focused out the window. "Too many . . . unexpected changes, all at once."

Patting her hand, I took another bite of food, because I knew it would make her happy. "We'll muddle through." That was Grandma Rice's famous quote. Anything she didn't like, she muddled through. "Tell you what: I'll call Bethany in the morning, and we'll take her out shopping. We'll do the mall, look for bridesmaids' dresses, go by the flower shop—all that stuff." The idea settled in my mind, painted with a watercolor wash of dread. "We'll get everything picked out in one day—like a marathon. We'll tell her she can't go home to Jason until we do the whole checklist." Raking up another bite of rice, I stuffed it into my mouth, even though it tasted old and I didn't feel like eating anything else. "Gosh, I'm starving. This is good Chinese."

Mom was pleased. Resting her chin on her hand, she smiled and said, "I told Bethany and Dad you'd need something by the time you got home. No sense going hungry."

The comment pinched, because, unless she could monitor my eating, she was convinced that I was starving myself. I pretended to concentrate on finishing the rice. Nice to know everyone was talking about me while they were supposed to be planning Bethany's wedding.

Drumming her fingers on her chin, Mom toyed with the corner of a napkin. "So, where was it that you went this afternoon? Dad said you were working late at school? You had a barbecue there?"

My chest convulsed in an involuntary chuckle, and I snorted up rice, then coughed and grabbed a glass of water. A barbecue at school? Sometimes, I had a feeling Mom heard only half of what we said; then she filled in the blanks like pieces of a crossword puzzle. "I went by an after-school arts program at an elementary school near Harrington. One of the students I've been counseling invited me. It was nice—I ended up having a really good time. This Jumpkids program is something special, amazing really. They serve some of the most underprivileged children in the city, and they do fantastic things with them. The kids are grateful for the opportunity—not like the students at Harrington, who take it for granted that everything is going to be handed to them. It's . . ."

I stopped talking, and Mom never even noticed. She was glassed-over. "That's nice," she said, when she realized the conversational ball was back in her court. "Do you think it's safe to be hanging around that part of town at night?"

"It's fine," I muttered.

"Maybe we should do silk flowers . . ." Mom mused, squinting at a basket of fake roses on the cornice above the kitchen cabinets.

Joujou scratched at the patio door, and Mom didn't react. I glanced over, surprised. Joujou was out in the backyard *alone*. At risk of kidnapping and attack by giant rodents. What was going on?

"Joujou's outside." I waved my hand in front of Mom's face. "Joujou's outside."

Jerking upright, Mom came back to earth. Slowly rolling her attention to the sliding glass door, she walked over to let Joujou in. "Oh, I know. She's fine out there. This morning, she kept scratching at the door, and I was busy trying to book the country club for Bethany and Jason, so I just let her go out."

"This morning?" I gaped toward the door. Even though the sun had come out in the afternoon, I couldn't believe Mom had left her baby on the patio so long—especially now that it was dark, and getting nippy again. "She's been out there all day?"

Mom lifted her hands helplessly. "I had so much to do. This way, she's not underfoot. She has water, food, and her house out there. The sunshine is good for her."

Wonders never cease. Mom had finally lightened up on Joujou. Maybe there was hope for the rest of us. Slipping the remaining rice into the trash while Mom was busy asking the dog about her day, I broke my fortune cookie in half and unrolled the paper slip, first looking at the Chinese characters in red ink, then turning it over so I could read the English side.

A journey of a thousand miles begins with a single step.
—CHINESE PROVERB

Chapter 8

*I*n the morning, Mom was at my bedroom door with Bett on the phone and breakfast ready downstairs. I blinked at the ceiling, waiting for the day to come into focus. Ever since my stay at St. Francis, my dreams were sensory and tactile, more vivid than real life.

I always dreamed of dancing—in various locations, but always, I was dancing. This time, I was in the gym at Simmons-Haley Elementary School. The floor was marked with lines for basketball, but around me, the bleachers became rows and rows of theater seats, stretching toward elaborate balconies of intricate fresco and gold leaf. Sister Margaret was in a box seat, clapping and cheering, giving me a standing ovation. From somewhere overhead, in tune with the music, kids were reading aloud the lines from the "In My World" wall.

> *In my world, there's five prizes in every cereal box.*
> *In my world, it only rains when you're sleeping.*
> *In my world, nobody has fights.*
> *In my world, everyone laughs.*
> *In my world, everyone is beautiful.*
> *In my world, everybody dances.*

As they read, the drawings floated down from overhead, and I danced in the bright Crayola world. . . .

"Pumpkin, time to get up." Mom pulled me back as I was drifting into the dream again. "Breakfast is ready. I've got Bett on the phone."

"Just . . . just a minute," I mumbled as the door squeaked open and Joujou rocketed through, launching herself onto my bed.

"Heeeeere's Joujou," Mom announced, like the dog was Johnny Carson and she was Ed McMahon. Joujou started sprinkling while racing around on my bed.

"Joujou!" Scooping up the dog, I rolled off the mattress and rushed to the bathroom. Joujou yipped happily and wagged her tail as I deposited her in the bathtub, then grabbed a towel and hurried back to wipe the droplets off the comforter.

"I think Joujou needs to go outside," I said.

Mom gasped at the comforter, as though it were a surprise for Joujou to make tinkie where she wasn't supposed to. "Oh, my." Handing me the phone, she headed toward the bathroom to have a discussion with the dog, dismissing the comforter with a backhanded wave. "I'll wash that later. You go ahead and talk to Bett. You two can plan our agenda for the day."

Bett was laughing on the other end of the phone. "What's going on over there?"

"Joujou watered my bed."

Bett laughed harder, and I laughed with her. It was good to hear her sounding like her usual upbeat self. "Hey, at least she missed you this time."

"Good point. I think I'm growing on her."

"So-o-o . . ." Bett drew the word out contemplatively. "Mom said you wanted to talk about shopping today."

Squinting toward the bathroom door, I cupped a hand over my mouth and the phone receiver. "Actually, I wasn't even up yet."

"Me, either," Bett admitted. "Jason usually brings me a protein shake in bed, so I can settle my stomach before I start walking around. Morning sickness."

It hit me that Bett really was pregnant. Expecting. In a family way.

My little sister. There was a tiny person growing inside her. My niece or nephew. My parents' first grandchild. A new little someone to be added to our family. Planned or unplanned, it was a miracle.

Smoothing a hand over my own stomach, sallow and thin beneath my nightgown, I wondered if my body would ever be capable of producing life. Had I sacrificed that potential with the years of bingeing, and purging, and starving my body until the normal female cycles were off schedule, and sometimes nonexistent? The doctors said there was no way to tell. *"The body is an amazing machine,"* Dr. Leland had told me, *"with an incredible capacity to heal itself. But esophageal rupture is extremely serious, as is the depletion of electrolytes in your system. Either can be fatal and can have lasting health implications. Give your body time to recover and regain its balance; then we'll see what we're dealing with."*

At the time, I didn't want to hear what he was saying. All I cared about was finding a way to explain my absence to the artistic director, so I could regain my spot in *Swan Lake.*

Now, thinking about Bett's baby, I felt the intense burn of guilt and a hollowness over what might never be. "I can't believe you're having morning sickness already."

Bett sighed, completely unaware of the rush of thoughts in my head. "I know. Mom says she had it right away, too. Especially with you."

"I always was trouble," I joked, but it came out sounding like a whine, and I changed the subject. "So, listen—what about this shopping trip?"

Bett groaned.

I glanced toward the bathroom, where Joujou was apparently playing tug-of-war with the shower curtain while my mother tried to catch her. Leaning away from the door, I whispered into the phone, "If we don't get busy on this wedding business, Mom is going to have a nervous breakdown."

Bett moaned again. "I just don't feel like it. I think I'm still in shock over everything."

"Come on; we'll make it a girl day. We haven't done that since . . ." *Since before I went to the hospital.* "In a long time, anyway. We'll make it fun. I'll hold your hand all the way."

"Mom's driving me crazy," Bett ground out. "I know she's got a lot on her mind, and she's just trying to help, but she won't let up. She has to be in control of everything. I'm hormonal, I know I am, but I'll end up saying something I shouldn't and hurting her feelings."

"Then I'll hold your mouth." The joke won a rueful laugh from Bett.

"Promise?"

"Yeah, I prom—" Something smashed against the tile in the bathroom and shattered. Bolting upright, I ran to the door in time to see Mom trap Joujou behind the toilet and try to pry her mouth open.

"Mom, what . . . What's going on?"

Her face was ashen. "What were those pills you had on the counter?"

"Pills?" I muttered. "Wha . . ."

"Julia?" Bett said on the phone.

"Just a minute, Bett." I held the receiver against my chest as Mom stood up, cradling Joujou, who shook her head and sneezed, then smiled with her overbite.

"What were those pills on the counter?" Pulling drawers open frantically, Mom raked through the contents. "Those pills, Julia. The two pills in the dish right there. I set Joujou on the counter, and she ate them. What were they?"

"An antidepressant and an aspirin." Popping open the medicine cabinet, I handed her the bottles before I thought about the fact that the antidepressant container was practically full, and it wasn't supposed to be.

Frustrated, panicked, Mom held it up, shaking it at me, momentarily forgetting about Joujou. "Julia Ann, why is this bottle full? You are supposed to be taking these twice daily."

I refilled it. That's a new bottle, almost rolled off my tongue. In the old days, that would have been my first reaction—deny, defend, divert, evade. Anything to keep the facts from coming out. Which only created bigger problems later on, so this time I admitted the truth with a resigned sigh. "I don't like the way they make me feel. I'm so mellow on that stuff, I can't function, and I don't get anything done at work."

"Pppfff. Work," Mom spat, with a disgusted sneer that outlined the network of wrinkles around her eyes. "That job isn't worth risking your health, and certainly not worth skipping your prescriptions."

I pressed the phone harder against my chest, hoping Bethany couldn't hear. "I don't need pills, Mom. I'm fine. I can handle it."

You can't handle it, her face said. *If I don't handle everything for you, things will fall apart.* "If the medication wasn't working for you, you should have told us. We can ask Dr. Leland to prescribe something else."

"I don't need anything else." The words shot out in a commanding tone that surprised even me. "I'm fine. I'm sorry I left the pills lying around and Joujou got into them, but I don't think it'll hurt her. I've heard they use aspirin and antidepressants for dogs, but Joujou's not very big, so it might be best to call the vet. I'll call, if you want."

Mom glanced from the prescription bottle to the dog and back. With a sigh, Joujou rolled her eyes upward and blinked contentedly. Tucking the bottle in her pocket, Mom squeezed past me, her face turned away. I could tell she was hurt. "I'd better take her in. You and Bett go shopping."

"Mom . . ."

Without waiting for an answer, she rushed out the door and down the stairs.

I put the phone to my ear again. "Well, I hurt her feelings. Joujou ate one of my antidepressants, and Mom found out I haven't been taking them. Now she's upset. She's taking Joujou to the vet and she wants us to go on with the shopping trip."

"That's probably best," Bett said gingerly. "We all need some time to decompress, especially Mom. All of us going wedding shopping together would probably cause a total Costell family meltdown. Why don't you take your time with breakfast and whatever, then come get me when you're ready?"

I checked the clock, just now blinking eight a.m. "All right. I'll be by your place at nine, and we'll head to the mall. We can look at dresses, and pick out bridal registry stuff at Dillards, and anything else you want to do. Sound good?"

"Sounds great." Her voice held a new enthusiasm. "This'll be fun."

"All right, get out your shopping shoes," I said, feeling more positive about the day. Bett and I needed sister time, especially now. "See you at nine. Bye."

By nine a.m., I was pulling up in front of Bett's apartment. Jason walked her to my car. "Take it easy on her," he said as he opened the passenger door for her. "She's kind of woogedie this morning." "Woogedie" was one of my mother's synonyms for generally under the weather. Where the word came from, no one knew, but when we were peaked, depressed, or slightly ill, Mom would check our foreheads and say, "Oh, are we feeling a little woogedie today?" Joujou felt woogedie a lot, and usually the cure was extra doggie treats.

"I'm fine," Bett said with a sigh.

Leaning through the passenger window, Jason kissed her, then flashed me a smile and mouthed, *Woogedie*.

I nodded and his blue eyes twinkled beneath a mop of dark hair that was already neatly combed at nine a.m. Jason was adorable at any hour, always charming, always perfectly groomed and dressed, and cheerful. No wonder he was such a great salesman and moving up in his career—it was impossible not to like him. He even had a way of making light of Mom that was sweet, rather than cruel. It was cute that he'd adopted "woogedie."

"I saw that," Bett complained, sounding uncharacteristically petulant.

Her bad mood rolled off Jason like water off a mallard. "I love you." He kissed her again, not so quickly this time.

Leaning away, I raised a hand to shield myself from the PDA. "Eeewww, I can leave if you need me to."

Bethany giggled and Jason drew back sheepishly. "No way. Because then I'd have to go on the wedding shopping extravaganza. By the way, anything's fine with me. Silk flowers, real flowers, long dress, short dress, no dress." Snapping his lips shut, he grinned at Bett, and she flushed. "Oops, did I say that out loud? Anyway, I'll take care of the tuxes and the rest is up to you two. All I want to do is marry my girl."

Bethany started to tear up, and I sighed wistfully. Jason was incredibly sweet, completely smitten. He and Bett were a perfect match. She deserved him, and all the happiness they could find. Even when Jonathan and I were engaged, he never looked at me the way Jason looked at Bett.

Jason closed the door and we watched him walk back up the sidewalk as I put the car in gear. Hands in his jacket pockets, he strolled along, looking up at the clear February sky like he hadn't a care in the world.

"You know you're incredibly lucky," I told Bett as we backed out of the parking space.

"I know." She sighed through her tears. "He's amazing."

"And he loves you like crazy."

"I know," she said again, her lips trembling into a wan smile.

"Then stop crying."

Pulling a leftover napkin from the console, she wiped her eyes. "Oh, all right," she huffed playfully, choking on the tears. "It's just the hormones. He knows that. This morning I had a breakdown because I knocked over a glass of soda. I cried for twenty minutes. Dad says Mom was like this when she was pregnant."

When she was pregnant with you. I felt the familiar pang of alienation, like a splinter wedged between my ribs.

Blowing her nose, Bett wadded up the napkin and tucked it in a discarded bank envelope in the door pocket. "Jason says as long as I'm not like this after the pregnancy, it's OK."

We laughed and talked about the wedding as we headed to the mall. It felt good to be with Bett, shopping, giggling, talking, finally spending time together doing normal things. We discussed baby nurseries as we passed the infants' and children's departments at Dillards. In the bridal department, I made a joke about maternity clothes, and Bett blushed and shushed me. By the time we moved on to the mall's bridal registry, Bett was tired of discussing her life and wanted to talk about mine. Telling her about the strange turn of events last week at my job, I was struck by how reassuring it was to have someone listen with interest, rather than tell me I couldn't handle having a job.

"It sounds like you've really stepped into the middle of something,"

Bett observed with a wry smile. "Those stuffed shirts at Harrington had better watch out. They don't know who they're dealing with."

I hugged her around the shoulders as we stood near the mall's gift registry computer, waiting at a polite distance as a young couple used the touch screen to sign up for baby gifts. "Maybe we should sign you up for baby gifts, too, while we're here," I whispered, and Bethany hip-butted me sideways a few steps. "It was just a thought."

"Miss Manners would have a cow," she joked. The phone rang, as if on cue, and both of us descended into gales of laughter. Giggling and sputtering, Bethany answered. It was Mom, of course. When Bett told her we had selected a maid-of-honor dress at Dillards, Mom wanted a complete description. Snatching it out of the basket, I held it in front of me as if I were Vanna White, modeling the periwinkle creation complete with its protective plastic covering.

Bethany proceeded to describe the dress the way a newspaper article about the wedding would read. "Julia Costell was seen looking lovely in a strapless gown of periwinkle organza, with a sky blue satin underlayer and coordinating organza shawl in periwinkle blue, fading to delicate summer sky around the edges, and showing the faintest hint of tasteful iridescence, so as to . . ." Bethany must have caught the surprised, horrified look on my face, because she stopped talking midsentence. Following my line of vision, she turned slowly toward the touch screen center, and realized what I had comprehended only a second earlier. The people standing arm in arm at the computer weren't just any couple. It was Jonathan and his new wife, the one he fell in love with at first sight, only a couple of months after we broke up. They looked blissfully happy, registering for baby gifts.

We stood staring at each other, frozen in place, before Jonathan spoke. "Hi, Julia." His voice was soft, sympathetic, the careful tone people use when they see a cancer survivor out and about after chemo. Obviously, he knew what had happened. His sister had probably heard about it, since she was a dancer as well. Jonathan and I had first met through her.

I stood there, still clutching the dress against myself, feeling thin and lifeless, like a scarecrow with hollow eyes and a knobby body lightly stuffed with dry grass.

"Hi, Jonathan." My voice seemed to come from somewhere outside. I tried to force a smile, but nothing happened.

Bethany jumped to the rescue. Slipping the dress out of my hands, she set it in the shopping basket, saying, "Let's put this down until we get done with the computer."

Jonathan glanced speculatively from the computer to me. "Wedding registry?"

"Bett's getting married the seventeeth of March," I choked out, wishing I could shrink down to the size of one of Harrington's ladybugs and fly away. I looked at Jonathan's wife, cuddled happily on his arm, and my life flashed before my eyes. *That could be me. Married, settled, one half of a whole. . . .*

"We're expecting," she bubbled, and Jonathan winced, as if she shouldn't say that in front of me.

Expecting a baby, completed the list in my mind. Regret stabbed hard, and I wanted to cry. Jonathan met my eyes in a way that told me he saw every pathetic thought. His face filled with sadness and sympathy. His wife, the future mother of his child, tightened her grasp on his arm.

"You look good," he said, and she blinked up at him, holding her eyes wide afterward.

I suddenly felt sorry for her, sorry for myself, sorry for all of us. One minute, you're happily registering for baby gifts, and the next, you're face-to-face with your husband's anorexic/bulimic ex-fiancée, modeling a maid-of-honor dress. And then, the first thing he says to her is, *"You look good."*

Irony didn't come any more twisted than that. "You do too." I pasted on a smile. The performance was under way. Time to shut out all the personal issues and dance. "Both of you. Congratulations. I know you must be really excited."

"We are." Jonathan's wife smiled, and he smiled with her, feeling free to glow about the baby news, now that it was obvious I wouldn't collapse into a sobbing heap on the floor.

"It was good seeing you guys," Bethany added, with a nervous little wave that said, *Nice knowing you, but move along now. Enough of this uncomfortable reunion.*

Jonathan took advantage of the opportunity to exit. "Take care," he said, catching my gaze with an earnest look, the one he always used when he said, *"I love you."*

Had he? I wondered. Had he really loved me? If he had, how could he have found someone else so quickly? Eight months ago, we were engaged. "I will," I said quietly, as they started away. "You too."

I stood watching Jonathan walk out of the store with his arm around his wife, the soon-to-be mother of his child. The farther away he got, the more his step lightened, as if my presence were a weight he was throwing off, piece by piece.

The pieces landed all around me, and I stood in a circle of the wreckage I'd created—trapped on an ordinary day in the mall.

Chapter 9

✦

After a weekend of serious shopping and an intense powwow with all wedding-involved parties, including the parents of the groom, the wedding plans were starting to solidify. I entered everything on the computer, so that Mom could track every detail of the wedding process via spreadsheet on cyberweddingplanner.com. Before heading off for my Monday-morning commute, I showed her how to use the Web site.

Mom was impressed that nuptials had moved into the electronic age. "I had no idea you knew how to do this kind of thing," she said, standing over my shoulder in Dad's cluttered home office.

"Do what?" I asked.

"Put things on the Internet. You know, all of this computer business."

Everyone knows how to use the Internet these days, I thought, but I said, "We did Web pages and PowerPoint presentations all the time in college. It's part of the curriculum. In fact, we even teach Web design and basic programming at Harrington." Just for fun, I brought the Harrington Web site up on the screen. "The students in the Web-design class actually create and maintain the school home page as part of their coursework."

"Really?" Leaning close, Mom investigated the photo collage of dancers, musicians, theater performers, and student artwork. "Well, isn't that lovely?"

I felt a note of pride—not because I'd had anything to do with the Web site, but because for the first time Mom was showing some interest in my job. "The kids do good work," I went on. "I'm thinking of having them help me put up a Counselor's Corner, with some parent information pages, family counseling and communication suggestions, drug prevention information—things like that. Drugs are, apparently, a bigger issue at Harrington than anyone realizes."

"Well, that's nice." Once again Mom was zoned out. She was staring wistfully at the picture of a young ballerina dancing as the Sugar Plum Fairy in the top right-hand corner of the screen. "Isn't she lovely?" Leaning forward, she traced the dancer's outline with her finger. "I wonder who she is."

Obviously, she'd forgotten I was anywhere in the room. These days she would never have intentionally admired anything dance-related in front of me. "Don't know," I muttered, and she jerked away from the screen.

"The costume, I mean." She tried to cover up her moment of guilty reminiscence. "It's lovely. I wonder who designed it." As if her interest were merely from a design perspective—unrelated to the fact that her daughter, the dancer she was so proud of, was now a middle school counselor and recovering bulimic.

"No telling. The kids get those pictures from the yearbook archives. It could be anybody." I bit my lip, clicking the back button to return the screen to cyberweddingplanner.com. "So, you see how to enter the dates and times in here, right? When you're finished, click *create* over in the left-hand corner, and it will put everything into a spreadsheet for you. You can print daily or weekly time lines, have the computer give you pop-up reminders of appointments, generate to-do lists, things like that. It's really simple." Pushing back from the desk, I stood up, purposely turning toward the door and away from her. I was afraid that if she saw my face, she would read something into it and one or both of us would end up with hurt feelings again.

"I'd better head for work, if I'm going to take the dress by the cleaner this morning." During our Saturday-evening wedding powwow, my sister had admitted that her dream really was to wear Mom's wedding gown. Bett had even tried it on so that Mom could mark it for fitting and hemming to accommodate Bett's shorter stature. It fit surprisingly well, but was in desperate need of restoration. The next order of business was to have it cleaned and altered, assuming we could find someone who could do the work in time.

"Oh, honey, I can take care of that." Mom was right behind me now. "Joujou's feeling better, and I have plenty of time." In the corner, Joujou lifted her head and perked her ears.

"I've got it, Mom," I said, trying to sound cheerful. "It's no problem. I really think the cleaner by Harrington will do a good job. All their work is done on-site, and they have a big sign out that says they specialize in vintage-clothing restoration and alterations. There are even old wedding dresses hanging in the window. If we take it to some drive-through place around here, they might send it out for cleaning, and who knows what could happen." I headed for the guest bedroom, where Bett had left the dress after our impromptu modeling session.

Mom stood in the doorway as I scooped it off the bed. "I don't get many occasions to go downtown anymore." Frowning, she inspected the torn, yellowed lace around the hem. "I could save you having to go by the cleaner's, and we could meet for lunch, maybe drive by Grandma Rice's old house. That would be fun."

I scooted past her, unable to imagine why we were playing tug-of-war with the dress. Did she really think I couldn't handle taking laundry to the cleaner? "Mom, you don't want to go by Grandma's place. It's depressing. The neighborhood has gone way downhill, and all those gorgeous old homes are being divided up into low-rent apartments."

A flash of emotion crossed her face at the mention of Grandma Rice's house. "I know. The Realtor's been telling me that whenever this renter moves out, we'll have to either section the house into upstairs and downstairs apartments, or sell it. No one in that neighborhood can afford to heat and air-condition that much space." Pressing her lips together sorrowfully, she shook her head. "Grandma Rice would turn over in her grave."

I patted her on the shoulder and moved into the hallway. "Try not to worry about it, all right?" Once again, she looked exhausted, as if she hadn't slept at all last night. "I'll ask around at Harrington. Maybe one of the teachers would be interested." But I knew that no one who taught at Harrington would live in that neighborhood. Shamika at Jumpkids was right—"Harrington people" didn't leave the chain-link enclosure of the school.

Mom brightened. "That would be nice." Forcing a smile, she followed me into the hallway. "So how about lunch? I thought, after this weekend, maybe you could use a little companionship today."

"Mom, I have several hundred little companions at Harrington. Loneliness is not a problem."

Chewing her lip, she touched the lacy sleeve of the dress. "I just thought that after this weekend—" She cut off the sentence abruptly, trying to decide how much to say.

"What about this weekend?"

Her fingers nervously picked at a loose seed pearl, then tried to press it back into place. Joujou, sensing signs of stress, trotted across the room and whined at Mom's feet until she picked her up. "Well, that little surprise at the mall. I know that must have been hard for you. I just thought that . . . I was afraid that . . . with all of the ongoing wedding plans, and then running into Jonathan and Carrie, and finding them registering for baby gifts . . ." Tipping her head to one side, she gave me a sympathetic look.

Carrie. Her name is Carrie. I'd forgotten that. *Jonathan and Carrie.* "Bett told you that we ran into them?" How could Bett do that? The idea of her and Mom talking about the scene with Jonathan and his wife was horrifying.

"Bett didn't tell me about it." Trapped between her desire to shelter me and the need to protect Bett, Mom fidgeted with Joujou's collar, then finally said, "Jonathan called Saturday while you were still out with Bett."

My mouth fell open in disbelief. "He *called* here? *Jonathan* called here?" Why would Jonathan call my mother? What was he thinking?

Mom must have seen me speeding toward an explosive meltdown, because she laid a hand on my arm. "He was worried about you."

"I'll bet."

She set Joujou on the floor, out of harm's way. "He was concerned. He thought you looked upset. He just wanted to make sure you were . . . OK after . . . after everything that's happened. He still loves you, Julia. Just because you marry someone else, it doesn't mean you lose those old feelings."

A hot flush rushed over my body as Mom's words crashed carelessly through the most fragile part of my psyche—the part that wondered if, by choosing dance instead of Jonathan, I had given up my chance at a happy, normal life. The kind of life Bethany was going to have with Jason.

He still loves you, Julia. What if he really did? It was too late now. He was married to someone else. Having babies with someone else. Moving on with life, while I watched from this bizarre limbo of almost-but-not-quite adulthood.

I put on what I hoped was an impassive mask. "You told him I was fine, right?"

"I told him you're trying."

Blood boiled into my ears, and my heart did a furious flip against my chest. I felt betrayed in every possible way. Mom had spilled details to Jonathan, of all people. Whatever pride I'd managed to salvage at our surprise meeting was now thoroughly destroyed.

"Thank you *so* much," I spat, my voice reverberating against the walls. Jumping up from her spot under a plant stand, Joujou disappeared down the hall. Nobody yelled like that in my mother's house. Ever. In Mother's house, anger was kept firmly corked beneath a surface that stayed smooth, like frosting on a cake.

Eyes wide, Mom drew back, laying a hand splay-fingered on her chest. "There is *no* need for *that* tone of voice. I was not trying to hurt your feelings. Jonathan was concerned about you. Certainly, I wasn't going to lie to him."

"I have to get to work," I ground out, then swept from the room, grabbed my coat, purse, and briefcase from the stairway, and headed for the garage, leaving Mom dumbstruck in my wake. For the first time in a long time, I'd worked up the guts to take back my life. *My* life. Mine.

I collided with Dad in the doorway. Still in his sweat suit after his morning jog, he looked flushed and chipper. "Good morning, sweet-heart."

"Good morning." Stuffing the dress in the car, I slammed the door.

"How are you this . . ." Craning to see around me, he noticed Mom. His gaze ping-ponged back and forth between us for a moment, and fi-nally, quite wisely, he sighed, said, "Guess I'd better go cool down," then walked out the door.

Climbing into my car without another word to Mom, I headed for work, the normal sights and sounds of Overland Park lost in a blur of anger and frustration. I wished I could rewind all the way back to Sat-urday morning. This time, I would stay away from the mall's gift reg-istry, and the past and present wouldn't collide. Threading my way through the morning traffic, I replayed the scene over and over in my mind—tweaking it to make it less painful, less humiliating. In rerun, I came up with something clever to say. I flashed a dazzling smile, intro-duced myself to Jonathan's wife, made friendly chitchat.

In the edited version, Jonathan didn't regard me as if I were a wounded animal, a bird flopping around on the grass with a broken wing. . . .

I was so occupied with mentally recasting the encounter that I al-most forgot to take the wedding dress to the cleaner. At the last minute, I bypassed the Harrington parking lot and continued down the block. Mr. Stafford, who was just getting out of his car by the gate, watched me with mild curiosity, rocking back on his heels with his hands in his pockets. Maybe he thought I'd finally reached the breaking point and decided to go AWOL. I just waved and pointed to indicate that I had somewhere to go, then proceeded to the cleaner's parking lot. I pulled in just as the neon signs in the windows were coming on.

An elderly African-American woman unlocked the burglar bars on the door as I climbed out of the car, slipped on my coat, and reached in for the dress. Oblivious to my presence, the woman stood in the doorway, squinting toward a row of decaying two-story buildings that had once been a thriving business district. Some now sat empty, while others had been taken over by hole-in-the-wall restaurants offering *menudo* and homemade tamales, bars advertising *cerveza*, pawnshops, and various other businesses. The sidewalk was dotted with vendors' carts selling tacos and breakfast burritos. Unlike the cleaners, the taco stands and restaurants were already open and doing a brisk morning business. Cars were zipping up to the curbs or the drive-through windows along narrow alleyways, picking up bags of breakfast burritos and other specialties.

Amid the chaos of traffic, children trudged off to Simmons-Haley Elementary School, lugging their backpacks. A few of them I recognized from the Jumpkids class, but they didn't look like dancers today. They jostled along the crowded street, passing the bars and taco stands with unhurried steps that lacked the expectation of anything good around the corner.

"Looks like the taco business is brisk," I commented when the woman opening the cleaner's looked my way.

Scoffing, she cut a narrow-eyed glare down the street, "Oh, honey, they ain't there for tacos." Turning sideways, she ushered two children onto the stoop. I recognized them from Jumpkids: Shamika, who told me Harrington kids didn't leave the school compound, except to buy drugs, and Justin, who crossed the cafeteria by jumping from chair to chair.

Shamika gave me a quick double take. "She a Jumpkids lady. She a dancer." Studying me and the wedding dress with curiosity, she added, "What're you doin' here? You gettin' married?"

Justin bounded forward and wrapped his arms around my waist in a hug that pushed a chuckle from my compressed lungs. "No, but my sister is. I saw that the cleaner here does vintage-clothing restorations." My hands were trapped under Justin and the dress, so I just stood there while he bear-wrestled me.

Grabbing his arm, the woman pulled him off. "OK, that's enough," she said, standing him on his feet. "Justin, you gonna be the death of Granmae. This poor woman didn't come here to be wallowed on by no seven-year-old little boy."

"Actually, I needed a hug this morning," I interjected, and both Justin and his grandmother smiled at me.

"Oh, Lordy, don't tell him that," she said. "This the huggin'est boy that ever lived." Twisting him around like a tin soldier, she pointed him down the street. "Now, you two get on off to school. Don't give Granmae no trouble today." Pausing, she checked them over, lovingly zipping Justin's jacket and straightening Shamika's braids before gazing sternly into their eyes. "Don't look right nor left. Don't talk to none of them people on the street. Stay together." She pretended to pluck something out of the air and drop it on Shamika's coat; then she repeated the process with Justin. "There. I put a little angel on each of your shoulders. You keep good care a' them all day. Stay on the straight path. Angels don't like no strayin' off the path now, y'hear?"

Shamika nodded with a veiled look of understanding. "Yes, ma'am."

"The sta-waight path," Justin echoed, his face surprisingly somber. "Did I det a boy angewl today?"

Studying his shoulder, his grandmother considered the question. "Nope. This is a shiny little white one with long yella hair. She don't know the neighborhood, so you take special care a' her, you hear? Now, git on off." With slaps on their rear ends, she sent them both bolting down the street like racehorses out of a starting gate. She watched until they disappeared behind a sidewalk taco cart, then turned to me. "Now, let's see what we can do about that dress."

"Sure," I said, but I was still thinking about Shamika and Justin, dashing off down the busy street with angels on their shoulders. "*Stay on the straight path. Don't look right nor left. She don't know the neighborhood. Honey, they ain't there for the tacos. . . .*"

I was beginning to get an inkling of what it all meant. On the street, cars came and went. Old cars, new cars, cars way too fancy for the neighborhood. A few cars I was fairly sure I recognized from the Harrington parking lot. No wonder Shamika knew that Harrington students left the campus to "score some bolt." She passed right by it every day on her way to school.

"I think we can fix this." Shamika's grandmother was examining the dress.

"It's pretty much a mess," I muttered, still studying the street, trying to decide which cars I recognized, straining to peer through windshields and spot Harrington parking decals. My chest slowly tensed into a painful knot.

"Oh, honey, we do magic here," the woman said. "We been fixin' wedding dresses for over sixty years. My daddy opened this shop. He learnt all his cleanin' secrets on a ship in the navy." She chuckled in her throat. "Mighty odd for a black man to know how to wash things white as snow, but he did. Folks send us weddin' dresses from all over. Always have, and . . ." Pausing, she followed my line of vision, then slipped an arm around my shoulders, whispering, "Don' look too long," as she guided me in the door.

As my eyes adjusted to the dim store interior, I tried to concentrate on the dress and Bett's wedding, but my mind was still outside. Could it really be that Harrington kids—kids I saw every day at school, kids from good families, kids with talent, potential, all the advantages—drove by seedy taco stands to pick up breakfast tacos and God knew what? Was it possible?

"Here, hand that dress over to Granmae." Taking the gown from my arms, the laundress traversed the narrow, chair-lined waiting area to the end of an old oak counter. She paused as an elderly woman in faded sweats and a striped Nike jacket hobbled in the side door, pushing an old-fashioned two-wheeled shopping cart with buckets of long-stemmed roses. Brushing flyaway strands of gray hair from her face, the visitor surveyed the room through blue eyes.

"You here already this mornin'?" Granmae asked, acknowledging the newcomer with a quick nod, then sweeping around the end of the counter.

"My feet were tired." The woman hobbled across the lobby, bent over her cart like one of Tolkien's hobbits. "Time for a rest."

"No rest fo' the wicked," Granmae joked, then motioned to a small table in the corner. "They's coffee there, and some doughnuts. Yesterday's, but they still good."

"I'll have some in a minute." The woman with the flowers continued toward me, smiling, her eyes like bright blue marbles tucked among folds of weathered cloth. "I'm trying to watch my figure." She winked, and I laughed. Something about her reminded me of Sister Margaret.

The blue eyes, maybe, or the quick sense of humor. Sister Margaret could always make me laugh.

"How's business this morning, Mim?" Granmae called from behind the counter.

Sighing, Mim, parked her cart, slipped off her jacket, then lowered herself into a chair. "Not so good." Her lips kneaded like she was chewing on a thought. "They're all in a hurry this morning. No one has time."

"It'll pick up," Granmae assured her. "Maybe this lady might be needin' some flowers." Motioning to me, she fluffed my mother's dress out on the counter. "She got a weddin' to plan."

"That so?" Mim turned to me with interest.

"My sister's," I told her. "I'm just helping with getting the dress ready, and things like that."

"I see," Mim said. "Well, perhaps a rose to take with you today?"

Nodding, I pulled out my wallet, out of habit. Since taking the job at Harrington, it seemed like all I did was buy student fund-raising cookies, coupon books, and candles I didn't want. "Sure. I'll take three. I can carry a couple home to my mother and sister." It would be good to bring a peace offering tonight, considering this morning's blowup about the dress. "Do they cure prewedding hysteria?"

Mim rose from her chair with surprising agility, now that a sale was at hand. "Oh, certainly. There's no better pick-me-up for a weary heart than fresh flowers." Tilting her chin upward, she winked at me. "Good way to clear up a spat, too."

"Wonderful. I'd like the spat-clearing variety, please." There was more lingering frustration in the comment than I'd intended.

Mim shook her head, muttering a regretful, "Umm-mmm-mmm."

I rolled my eyes in silent admission of this morning's eruption.

"That's weddin's. Lord a-mercy," Granmae muttered from behind the counter as Mim selected two pink roses and a yellow one.

"How much?" I asked, thumbing through the bills in my wallet.

"No charge." Patting my hands, Mim slipped the stems into my fingers. "The first ones are free."

I instantly felt guilty. "No, really. Thank you, but I'm happy to pay for them."

Lowering herself back into her chair, Mim waved me away. "They're already paid for."

"I can't take your flowers," I said, trying to hand them back.

At the counter, Granmae made a *tsk-tsk* under her breath. "Oh, honey, God makes the flowers; Mim just scatters them around."

"Well said, Granmae." Mim pushed away my hands and the flowers. "You take the roses, and if you want to pay me back, do someone else a kindness today." Meeting my gaze, she crossed her arms over her chest in a wise, unhurried motion. "When you need more flowers, you come back to me. Mine are of the highest quality. I grow them myself. I water only from the rainwater in my cistern. The chlorine in this municipal water is too harsh on their little bodies. Probably not good for the rest of us, either."

"Probably not," I said, trying to imagine where anyone would have a cistern and a sizable greenhouse around here. It was too early in the year for the roses to have been grown outdoors. She was right that the roses were exquisite—large and full, with not a blemish or torn petal anywhere. Holding them up, I closed my eyes and drank in the soothing fragrance, the scent reminding me of my grandmother's flower beds. "Do you do wedding flowers?" What was I saying? There was no way Bett would let me buy wedding flowers from a lady with a shopping cart downtown.

"I might." When I opened my eyes, Mim was studying me, looking pleased.

"Do you have a business card? Or a phone number? I'll talk to my sister about it." Had I lost my mind? Bett was never going to go for this, and if she did, Mom would have a conniption that even spat-curing roses couldn't fix.

Glancing toward the counter, Mim gave Granmae a knowing look, then said simply, "You can find me here."

Granmae chuckled, clucking her tongue against her teeth, her full lips popping open with every sound, then pursing with concern as she looked over the wedding dress. "Honey, you better save yo' money for this weddin' dress. This is gonna be one expensive job. When did you say you needed it?"

"March ninth?" The words came out sounding like a plea, which, indeed, they were. "That would give us a week before the wedding, in case any last-minute alterations are needed."

Dropping her chin against her ample chest, Granmae stared at me from beneath heavy eyelids. "What'd you say? You gotta be kiddin'."

I groaned inwardly, trying to imagine how, after arguing with Mom about it, I could possibly take the dress to the corner cleaner in Overland Park. "Is there any chance? It's really important to my sister. She's always wanted to wear this dress, and we only have three weeks to plan the wedding. Her fiancé's been transferred, and they're moving away. It's an emotional time, and I just want to make everything perfect for her. The wedding isn't until March seventeenth. I could even pick the dress up that week, if you're sure it will be ready."

From behind the counter, Granmae grimaced as if I were causing her pain.

"Please?" I added. "We'll pay extra."

Mim's hand fluttered into the air impatiently. "Oh, for heaven's sake, take the girl's dress. I'll help you get it finished. You know I'm good with a needle."

Granmae continued shaking her head, thumbing reluctantly through the yards and yards of discolored cloth. "Lord, oh, Lord, oh, Lord," she muttered. "Lord, have mercy. I don' know. Are these pins marking where you want the hem?"

"Yes." I nodded hopefully. "And my mother marked a few small alterations to the bodice, as well. She used to be a seamstress, so when we get the dress back, if there are any other minor changes needed, she can take care of it." *I hope.*

"*Lord,* have mercy," Granmae said again, shaking her head. "You gonna git me in trouble with some folks who been waitin' a lot longer than this for dresses to be ready."

"I won't tell *anyone.*"

Her nostrils flared with a long breath as she braced her hands on the counter. "You realize this gown ain't gonna be white when I get through. It'll be antique, a warm ivory color. That all right?" I nodded, and she returned to the dress. "I'll have to dig through my scraps and find some lace to match this that's missin' here. That costs extra."

"Just let me know how much." I stopped short of saying, *Anything, anything you want, it's yours. . . .*

Silence enveloped us as I stood holding my roses, waiting for—breathless for—Granmae's verdict. Why it seemed like such a big deal, I couldn't say. Perhaps it was the antique dresses in the window that gave me such confidence she could make my mother's gown perfect for Bethany.

"All right," she acquiesced finally. "You come by at the end a' the day, and I'll have a list with everything it'll need and what it's gonna cost."

"Great," I said, bouncing in place like I'd been picked for contestants' row on *The Price Is Right.* I felt as if I'd just won the lotto, as if I should pump a hand in the air and scream, *Yes, yes, yes! I've just accomplished something my mother thought I couldn't handle. Woo-hoo!*

Checking my watch, I realized that if I didn't get going, I would be late for work. Even though I didn't have hall duty this week, I still had to be there before the second bell rang. Mrs. Morris would, no doubt, be watching. "I'd better go," I said, turning toward the door. "I work right down the road at Harrington, so I'll come by after school and look at the estimate." Granmae stiffened slightly at the mention of Harrington, and I sensed that, if I'd divulged that information earlier, she wouldn't have taken the dress. As it was, she swept it off the counter less than carefully.

"Thanks," I added, fishing for my keys. "Really. This means a lot."

"Welcome," she called, as she headed for the back room and I turned toward the door.

Mim craned her chin upward with a wicked twinkle in her eye. "She was going to take the dress all along," she whispered behind her fingers. "She just likes to make sure her work will be properly appreciated."

"It will be," I promised, waving with the roses in my hand. "And thanks for the flowers."

"My pleasure."

"I'll talk to my sister about the bouquets for the wedding." The scent of the roses was all around me just before I opened the door and let in the cool morning air. I imagined that fragrance enveloping Bett's wedding, saturating everyone and everything with the promise of something incredible and beautiful and new. "These flowers are absolutely lovely."

Mim patted her bucket benevolently. "They know when someone loves them. Mine are sturdy flowers. Not like the ones that are grown in hothouses. I protect my plants, but not too much. A little adversity makes them strong."

I wondered again where she grew the plants, but there was no time to ask, so I thanked her again and went on. The sounds and smells of the street assaulted me in a gust of brisk February air, chasing away the comfortable silence of the old shop, the scent of aging fabric, and the aroma of roses. Gazing down the street, I studied the bars and taco stands, watching vehicles come and go as I slipped into my car. Undoubtedly, some of them were from Harrington. But how deep did the problem go, and what was I going to do about it?

Chapter 10

The faculty parking lot was crowded by the time I pulled into an empty space by the back fence next to the student parking area. By seven forty-five, most of the staff members had already reported. The parent drop-off lane in front of the middle school was crowded bumper-to-bumper, and a steady stream of cars was headed around back to the high school building, as well. In the student parking area, the middle school music director, Mr. Verhaden, was trying to hustle sluggish kids toward the building. Obviously, he had been given the dreaded parking lot duty, an honor that, fortunately, I had missed out on this week. Standing in a cold parking lot watching for fights, stopping kids from making out in backseats, and chasing loiterers from the bushes was everyone's least favorite assignment.

Buttoning up my coat as I climbed out of my car, I studied the high school students' vehicles, watching kids amble toward the building, girls in tight jeans, formfitting T-shirts, and bare feet with flip-flops, despite the fact that it was a typically chilly late-winter morning. The boys presented an opposite picture, their bodies draped in wrinkled T-shirts and oversize jeans hiked to just the right height—drooping, but not quite falling off. Both boys and girls struggled up the stairs carrying backpacks, instrument cases, art portfolios, and athletic bags.

Now I wondered what else they were carrying. What might be hidden among the paraphernalia they came and went with every day, and how would anyone know?

A silver Lexus whipped into the parking lot, and Mr. Verhaden wagged a finger, homing in on the car as if he were tracking it with a radar gun. The driver, a high school boy with shaggy dyed-black hair, hit the brakes, then lifted his hands in apology. Rolling down the window, he stuck his head out, grinning.

"Sorry, Mr. Verhaden."

Verhaden glanced skeptically at his watch. "Working on another tardy today, Sebastian?"

"No, sir," Sebastian replied, leaning farther out the window as Mr. Verhaden peered at the backseat passengers, then reached down and opened the back door.

"Boys, you'd better hop out here and hustle to class," he commanded, ushering out the passengers, a couple of my eighth-grade students from last Friday's algebra class. Cameron, the student council vice president who couldn't stay awake in algebra, seemed plenty chipper this morning. Stuffing breakfast in his mouth while grabbing his backpack, saxophone, and lunch bag, he posed for a moment with his hand on the car door, glancing around to make sure his middle school friends noticed that he'd arrived in an ultracool high schooler's car, rather than with his mom or dad, as was usually the case.

"All right, get moving," Verhaden insisted, pointing sternly toward the steps. Cameron and his friend backed away from the car.

"OK, Mr. Verhaden," Cameron mumbled with part of a tortilla hanging down his chin.

Breakfast tacos, I thought, studying the car. Had the boys gone by the taco stands this morning? Was Sebastian's silver Lexus one of the cars I'd seen driving down Division Street?

Cameron noticed me watching as he jogged toward the building. "Hey, Ms. C. You teaching algebra today?"

"I hope not," I called back, glancing toward the high schooler's car a second time.

"You're missing your parking permit again," Verhaden was telling the driver. "Sebastian, you get one more ticket from the security officer, you're going to be parking off campus. Get going. One more tardy and you'll be on probation during the district contest."

Sebastian ducked back in the window. "Yes, sir!" With an overzealous salute, he piloted the car around the corner while hanging his parking pass on the rearview mirror.

Had he taken it down so that it wouldn't be noticed at some taco stand on Division Street? When I was in high school, the parking decals were huge and permanently affixed to the car windows. Everywhere we went, we were marked as Harrington students, whether we wanted to be or not. When had the school changed to removable parking permits, and why?

Turning the questions over in my head, I hurried up the side stairs and through the entrance next to Mrs. Morris's classroom. Fortunately, she was busy haranguing some student about chewing gum. Halfway down the hall, Cameron was stuffing his things into his locker, laughing and flirting with a couple of girls as he squirted breath freshener in his mouth, then offered it around.

"Hey, Barry," he called, as my third-period office assistant frumped by in his oversize clothes, which did nothing to hide the spare tire his mom had been in to talk to me about already. She wanted us to regulate what Barry ate in the cafeteria, which, of course, we couldn't.

Barry glanced up just as Cameron tossed a grease-stained paper sack at him. "Here, have some breakfast." Cameron laughed, and the girls giggled. "You look hungry."

Dropping his binder, Barry caught the sack, then bent over to pick up his belongings, his pants sliding down to show the fleshy roll at the top of his rear end.

"Hey, dude, say no to crack," Cameron quipped.

The girls laughed maliciously.

Barry hiked up his pants and pretended to laugh along with them. Shifting the breakfast sack to the other hand, he pitched it into the trash, muttering, "No, thanks," as he slouched off to his first-period class.

"He-hey!" Cameron complained, jogging toward the trash can. "Dude, that was my lunch."

I strode up the hall with my teeth clenched and I met up with Cameron as he tried to fish his lunch from the refuse container. "Leave it," I hissed, watching Barry disappear around the corner, hugging his notebook. "Next time, be more careful what you do with your lunch."

Grinning in a way he no doubt thought was charming, Cameron leaned over to reach into the trash can again.

"I believe you heard me, Mr. Ansler," I ground out. "Go to class. And leave Barry alone. He's my main man third hour in the office."

Cameron looked me up and down in a way that was shockingly improper, considering that he was usually a well-behaved kid, polite to the point that it was disconcerting. "You could do better, Ms. C."

One of the girls by the lockers drew an audible breath, her eyes widening. Cameron grinned impishly.

Leaning close, I pointed a finger between my face and his. "You're right there on the line, *young man,* and I am *not* in the mood today." The gravel in those words surprised even me. Where did that voice come from?

Cameron snapped his lips shut, his Adam's apple bobbing up and down. The girls stood frozen.

From somewhere nearby, Mrs. Morris's voice squawked, "*What* is going *on* out here?"

"It's under control," I snapped in my new go-ahead-make-my-day counselor voice before I turned back to Cameron. "Go to class."

"Yes, ma'am." Grabbing his books, he scooted away like a dog who'd just been bitten by a much bigger dog. Waiting until he was gone and the halls were cleared, I fished the lunch sack out of the trash and looked through it.

Nothing but soft tacos in plain paper wrappings. I dropped it back in the trash.

In my office, I pulled out the antidrug leaflets the task force had left, then logged on to the Web sites and began composing a list of things that needed to be checked into around the school. An hour later, Mrs. Jorgenson called about some problems with achievement-testing report sheets from last year, and I spent time in the basement helping her sort through boxes Mrs. Kazinski had mistakenly sent to long-term storage.

A textbook company representative was waiting in the admin office when we returned, and I was trapped into listening to a sales pitch and taking samples, because the principal was nowhere to be found. By the time I returned to my computer and logged on to the antidrug Web sites again, I'd completely lost my place. Mr. Stafford stopped by my door just as I was getting back in sync.

"That press release ready for this weekend's sidewalk jazz review?" he asked casually, giving the mess on my desk a pleasant but detached once-over.

Something I'd been about to write down flew from my head and buzzed around the room like a fly. "No, sorry," I answered, still trying to regrasp the thought. In my study of taco stands and other drug-related issues, I'd completely forgotten that press releases were due at the city desk by five p.m. Monday. Harrington sent out notices about some performance or other nearly every week. This week it was the Harrington Jazz Players giving a concert at the mall. "But I'll have it done by the end of the day, I promise." One thing I had learned in Mrs. Morris's English class was to whip up paragraphs of nice-sounding drivel in a flash.

"Good enough. I'll get Verhaden to e-mail you a few notes about the performance." Mr. Stafford nodded approvingly, as if I were the world's finest high school counselor because I could put together press releases in time to make the newspaper. Apparently, he'd had trouble getting even that much out of Mrs. Kazinski.

"Grant application coming along?" He leaned against my door, seeming content to stay there and chat awhile. Stafford was hard to figure out. One minute, he was locking everyone out of his office, too engrossed in school budgets to be bothered, and the next minute, he had all the time in the world to stand around and visit.

"It's coming along." I nodded to make it sound more convincing. "I worked on it some this weekend." *So* not true. Between Jumpkids on Friday and Bett's wedding plans the rest of the weekend, I'd spent about twenty minutes on the grant. *Mental note—take grant materials home tonight.*

"Good . . . Good." Tipping his head back, Stafford narrowed his eyes, and I realized he was ogling the materials on my desk. Luckily, it was such a mishmash of student records, attendance sheets, grants, scholarships, state achievement tests, and drug prevention information, that he probably couldn't tell I was scanning student files, trying to decide if this drug issue was real or imaginary. According to the files, there hadn't been anyone at Harrington's middle school reported, disciplined, investigated, or suspended for drug use or possession in the recent past. But, in the back of my mind, there was Shamika's comment, and also Sergeant Reuper looking at me with emphasis when he said, *"The thing about a smart kid with some resources is, he can keep up appearances for a long time. . . ."*

The thought I'd lost when Mr. Stafford came in returned, and I jotted it on my notepad: *Drug dog.*

Tapping the pen on the desk, I looked up at Mr. Stafford. "I noticed in the Harrington handbook that the school is searched regularly by a drug-sniffing dog." I tried to sound casual, not accusatory. "When does that happen? I've been here seven weeks and I've never even noticed." My tone added a ditzy, *Isn't that a funny thing?* But I was thinking, *If there's a drug dog here, it's invisible.*

Mr. Stafford shrugged. "They come through on the weekends, when the students are out of the way."

"Why on the weekends?" *Whoops, watch out. Question way too direct.*

Pushing off the door frame, Stafford shifted to a defensive posture. "Certainly, we can't have dogs and uniformed handlers wandering the halls during instructional time. How would that look if a parent or a reporter or a visitor came in?" Obviously, he'd been asked the question before, and it was a sore spot. "There's *never* been a drug problem at Harrington."

How would we know? I thought. *The drugs come and go with the kids. You have to look for them when the kids are here. Duh.*

"This is a high-profile school, Ms. Costell," he added, pulling off his glasses and using them to punctuate the air between us. "Public funding being what it is, and with support for the arts dwindling all the time, we have an image to maintain. That image brings in the grants and fellowships and private endowments we need to survive. There are plenty of important people out there who would say that the time of the arts magnet school has come and gone, that it's all about drilling kids on reading, writing, and arithmetic until they can pass some idiotic state-mandated test. There are plenty who would like to see some scandal bring this school down. It's our job to make sure that doesn't happen. Harrington comes first."

Which means the kids come second, third, or somewhere down the line. As long as they look good on the outside, nothing else matters. "Of course it does," I replied, doing a surprisingly adept job of hiding my emotions. "By the way—unrelated subject." *Not exactly so.* "I was wondering, when did the student parking passes change? I remember the old ones with the big purple sticker that took up half of the back windshield."

Stafford chuckled, relieved that we'd tacked to a safer subject. "Oh, that's been"—rolling his eyes upward, he thought for a moment—"three or four years ago now. Our kids drive nice cars, and some of the parents didn't like those big stickers junking up the windshields. There was also some discussion as to whether the display of a Harrington sticker might provoke harassment by students who attend school at Simmons-Haley High, down the block. There certainly are some latent resentments from locals. This way, our students can come and go in relative anonymity."

I wondered if Harrington parents had any clue what their kids were doing with that anonymity. "I hadn't thought of that."

In the hallway, the lunch bell rang, and the corridor began to fill up with students. Mr. Stafford took a step backward. "You'll e-mail me the press release for approval when it's finished?"

"Always do," I said, falsely cheerful.

"Good girl," he replied, turning away, and I wanted to shoot him in the back of the head with a rubber band. Pop. Right on the bald spot. *Good girl,* indeed.

I realized it was lunchtime, and I hadn't seen Dell Jordan or done anything about gathering some tutoring materials for her. With only two weeks left in the nine-week grading period, there was no time to waste.

Hurrying down the hall to the book storage room, I pulled together a set of seventh-grade teacher's guides, then headed for the cafeteria, where I stood surveying the serving lines until finally I concluded that Dell wasn't there. Since she hadn't been reported absent for the day, she was somewhere in the school. I had an inkling of where that might be. Leaving the chaos of the lunchroom behind, I walked around the corner to the instrumental music hall.

Memories assaulted me as I crossed the room. The ballet studios were nearby, rooms similar to this one. I could picture them, with their high arched windows, tall pressed-tin ceilings, and yawning wood floors. Closing my eyes, I drank in the scent, the feeling of being there again. Outside in the courtyard, the metal clips on the U.S. flag slapped against the pole—*ping, ping, ping*—and my mind raced back through the years, until I was a sixth-grade girl, standing still and silent, in the moments before the music began, listening to the flag beat against the pole, protesting its imprisonment. I knew that in a moment, the music would carry me away, and I wouldn't think about anything.

Every fiber of my body ached as I relived the anticipation of the dance. It was like remembering air, or water, or light, and realizing there was no more. There wouldn't be. Ever.

There's a time to every purpose, Sister Margaret had said as I gazed out the hospital window and wept because my ballet career was over. Sister Margaret read patiently from Ecclesiastes, or quoted it from memory, I wasn't sure, because I couldn't look at her.

> *. . . a time to break down and a time to build up;*
> *a time to weep, and a time to laugh;*
> *a time to mourn, and a time to dance;*
> *a time to cast away stones, and a time to gather stones together;*
> *a time to embrace . . .*
> *a time to end . . .*
> *. . . a time of peace . . .*
> *He hath made every thing beautiful in his time . . .*
> *. . . there is no good in them, but for a man to rejoice, and to do good in his life . . .*

She filled the room with words while I lay silent, wondering what possible good there could be in my life, ever again. . . .

The sound of a door closing somewhere in the hallway snapped me back to reality, and I opened my eyes, half expecting to find myself back in the hospital room with Sister Margaret.

Crossing the music hall with her voice still in my head, I quietly opened the storage closet door. Dell was sitting on the floor in the window light, a sack lunch spread out around her, her body curled over the pages of a book—alone, except for the ladybugs, and the dust, and dozens of decaying instruments stacked high on shelves. Around the walls, dance bars testified to the fact that, at some time, the room had been a practice studio.

Dell jerked upright as I entered. Eyes wide, she searched my face with a mixture of uncertainty and trepidation, wondering, no doubt, what I would say.

Stepping into the room, I closed the door behind me, and she stiffened.

"Studying?" I asked, and she sagged against her knees.

She held up *The Grapes of Wrath,* so that I could see the cover, then set it on the floor again, propping the book open with her slim brown feet. "We have a test on the first three chapters tomorrow morning. I read it, but Mrs. Morris always asks weird questions, and I get confused."

"Ah, the infamous Mrs. Morris literature tests." I realized I'd almost said Mrs. Bore-us, because that's what we used to call her. Mrs. Morris could make anything boring. It was her specialty.

Setting my stack of teacher's editions on a shelf, I stood reading over Dell's shoulder. "What don't you understand?"

"Everything." She clamped her hands to her head, circling her hair with her long, slim fingers and digging in. "I'm not any good at reading. I can read the words, but it takes me forever, and I don't *get* it, you know?"

Hiking up my straight, dark skirt, I lowered myself to the floor beside her. She blinked in surprise, and I groaned. "I'm not dressed for this." *Mental note—tomorrow, wear pants. Not black. Something dust-colored.* "So, let's see the book."

Happily, she handed it over, cocking her head sideways and regarding me with a bemused smile that said, *Are we really going to sit on the floor in the storage closet and read my literature book?*

I tried to act as if it were perfectly normal. After the chaos of the morning, it felt good to be in a place that was quiet, disturbed only by divided shafts of sunlight and dust dancers.

"So, let's see. . . ." Flipping back to the first page, I scanned the words, searching my memory banks for *The Grapes of Wrath*. Maybe I could get the CliffsNotes version.

Dell reached for her lunch sack. "Want something to eat? Karen always packs me a ton, in case I want a snack after school, before we go to Jumpkids."

The scent of Cheetos wafted up, and my stomach rumbled with surprising enthusiasm. Normally at lunchtime, the overwhelming smell of the cafeteria's mystery meat turned me off to the point that I was lucky if I could force down a few bites of salad. Here in the storage closet, Cheetos and Chips Ahoy! smelled good. "Sure. You know what? I am hungry," I admitted, and Dell produced another bag of chips, three cookies, and an apple juice box from the sack, then picked up her peanut butter–and–jelly sandwich and tore it in half.

"Now the thing about reading," I said, savoring a Cheeto, which at the moment tasted like heaven, "is that it's not about remembering the words. It's all about letting them paint a picture in your mind. Like you're living in the story . . ."

Chapter 11

The passages of Steinbeck's novel transported us from the storage room at Harrington to the sunbaked prairies of dust bowl–era Oklahoma. We traveled parched dirt roads with young Tom Joad, newly released from prison, trying to find his way home to the family farm, only to learn that drought and the Depression had changed the country in his absence. All the familiar reference points were gone, and home was no longer a safe haven. In a world that seemed foreign, difficult to understand, with obstacles impossible to surmount, he was struggling to find his way.

I wondered if Dell saw the similarity to her own situation. Resting her head on her knees, she stared out the window as I read. Finally, she closed her eyes and breathed in, as if she were picturing the images.

"I don't see what the turtle crossing the road has to do with anything," she said when I finished the third chapter—one of Steinbeck's famous lyrical vignettes.

I was tempted to admit that I'd long suspected the vignettes were put there just to baffle literature students. "The turtle is a metaphor." Now that we were into the story, I could remember sitting in Mrs. Morris's class all those years ago, half listening as her discussion of Steinbeck's turtle went right over my head. My grandmother had reread the chapters with me every night, explaining the symbolism and adding our family's own Depression-era stories, to get me through the arduous weeks of *The Grapes of Wrath*. "It represents the struggle of the poor farmers during that time period."

Dell squinted sideways at me. "Why doesn't he just talk about farmers, then?"

"I don't know."

"It'd be easier." I chuckled as she picked up the book and flipped through the last few pages. "Why does the one driver go around the turtle, and then the other one tries to run it over?"

"Why do you think—considering the story, what do you think that might represent?"

Contemplating the question momentarily, she flicked the pages of the book with a fingertip, then shrugged. "I dunno. I'm not good with this kind of stuff. Every time Mrs. Morris asks me, I get it wrong. If I was gonna—going to—write a book about farmers, I'd write about farmers, not turtles, you know?"

"Me too," I conceded. "But take a guess at Steinbeck's meaning here. It doesn't matter if you get it wrong. It's just the two of us. If you had to guess, what do the drivers represent?"

"Maybe other people?"

"All right, what about other people?"

"Some of them just kind of ignore people, and some of them do mean things to them, because they're poor."

"Good analysis," I commented, and she sat back, surprised.

"Really?"

"Really. The turtle on the road is thought to represent all of those things—the difficulty the characters are going to face, the drought, problems with other people like the land barons who are forcing them off their farms, and so on. Not so hard to understand, right?" Not so far, but who knew how long my remembered middle school literature knowledge would hold out? "You're good at this, even if it is about turtles."

"I like the way you read it." She brushed off my compliment. "It's easier just to listen; then I can see the story."

"Well, don't get too used to it," I said. Her look of disappointment surprised me. "I did the reading today so that we could get through as much as possible before your quiz, but tomorrow we're going to sit and read it together."

Her lip curled plaintively, showing a distinct lack of enthusiasm for anything that involved more than passive listening. "How are we gonna do that?"

"You're going to read and I'm going to read at the same time." Neurological Impress Method—I'd studied it in some long-ago education course. Who knew all of that was somewhere in my memory banks along with *The Grapes of Wrath*?

Her nose wrinkled in obvious distaste. "Out *loud*?" she asked, and I nodded. "At the same time?" Her expression added, *Lady, are you nuts?*

"Sure." I gave an encouraging nod. "That makes the words easier. When you look at them, and hear them, and say them, it helps store the information in your brain. Besides, it's fun."

Clearly, she wasn't buying my merry-sunshine act. " 'Kay . . ." she muttered reluctantly. "But I don't read fast like you."

"That's all right." Poor readers were typically resistant to reading in front of people. No doubt Dell was afraid I'd snarl and look down my long, pointy nose, like Mrs. Morris. "When we don't have so much to read all at once, we can slow down and enjoy the story." If it was possible to enjoy *The Grapes of Wrath*.

Gathering her books and the lunch leftovers, Dell stood up. "I like the part about the Joads," she admitted. "It doesn't have as many big words as some of the other chapters." Holding the sack open so that I could stuff in my Cheetos bag and used-up juice box, she added, "That's probably why Mrs. Morris doesn't like those parts."

I couldn't help it; I laughed. "Could be."

"Mrs. Morris is, like, the worst teacher I ever had. She hates me. That's why I don't do good in her class."

Pretending to be occupied with getting to my feet, I pondered what to say. *Yes, you're right—she's a lousy teacher. She always has been. She doesn't like children, and she doesn't like you.* Probably not the most professional response. On the other hand, it was ludicrous to deny it. Dell would think I was yet another Harrington staff member espousing the party line, and some amount of trust between us would be lost. "That may or may not be so," I said finally, dusting my skirt. "But it isn't Mrs. Morris who's going to fail the class. It's you. Your education is your responsibility." An artistic director had said that to me once. *"Your performance is your responsibility."* "If you can't get what you need from the teacher, you have to figure out where else you're going to get it. There are people willing to help you here and, I suspect, at home, as well."

Her face went pale, and she stopped halfway through putting on her clogs. "Please don't tell Karen and James. I don't want them to know how bad I am."

"Dell, there's nothing to—"

"Please!" Eyes welling up, she raised her hands between us in a silent plea.

"Dell, it's obvious that James and Karen love you very much." If only I could convince her that her best chance was to have tutoring both at home and at school. "They would want to help. They'll understand."

"No, they won't!" she exploded, tears spilling over and trailing down her cheeks. "They're smart, and all their families are smart. They don't know anything about someone who's too dumb to read a stupid book!" Clenching her jaw, she wiped the tears with her sleeve, then rammed her other foot into her shoe, yanking her jeans in frustration when the hem caught under the sole.

I blew out what my mother called a patience breath. This conversation was disintegrating rapidly. "Tell you what. Let's see what we can do in the next two weeks." I hoped I was doing the right thing. If I forced her to tell her foster parents about her grades, she might give up completely. Right now, keeping them from finding out the truth was her major motivation for trying to pass. "We're going to have to work really hard, though. You're right on the borderline in math and science, but social studies and English are another matter. Getting a 'C' is going to take some serious effort."

" 'Kay." She added a definitive nod. "Besides, like you said, it's my responsibility, not James and Karen's, right?"

Ouch. Nothing like having your own words thrown back at you.

"You're a smart girl. Let's start trying to work during lunch and in the afternoon during Study Buddy time, OK?"

She winced at the mention of Study Buddy time. It was supposed to be a period for kids to read, catch up on assignments, work together in peer mentoring groups, but most of the kids didn't use it that way.

"Mr. Verhaden likes for me to come in and practice during Study Buddy time. There's lots to learn for the spring symphonic concert, and I'm behind everyone else because I haven't had all the music lessons like they have. I've been coming in extra, like at the end of some of my classes, if we don't have a test or stuff, and during Study Buddy time."

No wonder there's trouble with your grades, I thought. "You're doing fine in music. It's the other subjects that need attention. No more time out of class to practice music. I'll talk to Mr. Verhaden about it, all right?"

Deflated by the pinprick of reality, she slouched toward the door. "All right."

"Same place, same time tomorrow," I said, and she looked surprised. "This is as good as anyplace," I added.

She nodded. "It's quiet, and nobody'll see."

"You're right." If I tried to tutor Dell anywhere else, Mr. Stafford would probably track me down with some all-important grant application, or Mrs. Morris would start up with her snide complaints about wasting time on the *"wrong kind"* of student. This way, neither she nor Stafford could get on my case for sticking my nose in where it didn't belong. "I'll see what I can do about getting a desk and a couple of chairs in here."

" 'Kay," she said. "I'll bring lunch."

"We'll take turns." I couldn't help feeling guilty for having eaten so much of her food today. "Tomorrow, I'll bring."

" 'Kay."

In the hall, the second lunch bell rang, warning us that any moment kids would be showing up for music class. "You'd better go." Opening the door, I shooed her into the instrumental music hall.

Halfway across the room, she stopped and glanced over her shoulder at me. "You gonna come to Jumpkids tonight? Today we're at Barger Elementary, over by the big fire station. Do you know where that is?"

"Yes, I do." I felt a surprising urge to join in for another day of yoga and dance, cheese crackers, and Kool-Aid. Unfortunately, there was the inconvenient matter of all the other work that wasn't getting done while I was sitting in the storage room reading *The Grapes of Wrath* with Dell. "But I'll have to see how the day goes. I have a pile of work on my desk." Her face fell, and I felt like a party pooper. "We'll see."

Her glum look said that she figured "we'll see" meant no. "Well . . . ummm, then Tuesday, we're at Bell Elementary, then the next day Carver, Ollie Munson, then Friday back at Simmons-Haley. This week-end, we're doing a minicamp in Hindsville at the Baptist church. You could come to that, if you wanted. It'll be really cool. Keiler's gonna come down and help. He's my friend who did Jumpkids last summer."

I couldn't help feeling charmed by her invitation and her desire to introduce me to her friend, or boyfriend, or whoever Keiler was, back in her hometown. "Well, I'll have to give that some thought, and maybe talk to your mom. It sounds like fun, though." Inside me, there was an unexpected urge to see where she came from. It seemed the only way to really understand her. Maybe there was a part of myself I was looking for, as well. The part that dreamed of dancing on the river. The part that could identify with the lost, lonely person I saw in Dell.

"I'll try," was as close to committed as I could safely go. "We're busy planning my sister's wedding at home, so things might come up."

" 'Kay," she said, jerking an ear toward the door at the sounds of kids coming in. Yanking open her notebook, she pulled out two torn sheets, thrust them at me, and said, "Here," without meeting my eyes. "I wrote down some junk last night." As I took the papers, she darted off like a stray puppy trying to stay out of reach. "Thanks, Ms. C," she called just before the door opened and a group of eighth-grade girls entered. I watched as Dell slunk past them, trying not to be no-ticed. She needn't have bothered. The girls were laughing and ogling a crumpled sheet of paper, too busy to see Dell or me. Moving through the doorway in a jostling, hair-tossing knot, they giggled and passed the note around, pointing at and reading names. I stood lis-tening until they noticed my presence—first one, then the next, until each of them jerked upright, eyes wide, lips snapping shut, bodies stiff and frozen. Like antelope having suddenly sensed a predator, they stood on high alert.

I pretended not to notice their caught-in-the-act expressions. "What's so funny?"

"Nothing," said a leggy, slim brunette with a cute, pert nose and the toned arms of a dancer. She stood at the head of the group, the apparent herd leader. I couldn't remember her name.

"I see." I surveyed the guilty body language. A few days ago, I would have laughed it off as teenage mischief, but lately I was suspicious of everything. Crossing the room, I held out my hand. "How about I have a look?"

There was an audible intake of breath from somewhere in the group, but the dark-haired girl covered perfectly.

Leaning close, she held a hand next to her mouth, like we were two grown-ups leveling with each other. "It's just something one of the boys dropped. A list—you know, like who's cool and stuff."

"Ohhh," I replied, grateful that this was normal teenage silliness. "Well, I'll tell you what—why don't you let me take it, so I'll know who's cool, and then you girls"—pausing, I slid a stern gaze across the group of mortified young faces—"won't end up being tardy for your next class."

"Sure," the herd leader agreed with an innocent flutter of lashes that probably worked at home with her daddy. Snatching the note from her redheaded companion, she handed it to me. "See? It's just, like, a list of cool girls in the eighth grade. Who's hot and who's not."

"Mmm-hmm." Tucking Dell's essay under my arm, I turned the list over in my hands, glancing at the handwritten column headings—*Hots, Nots*—with various names written below. "Did you make the cut?" I asked, and the girls giggled in a way that said they were all in the cool column, and I could be too, if only I would give back the list. "This might come in handy," I joked, and the brunette chuckled with a sneering lip that told me I was being dumped from the list. *Poof, you're outta there.* "Go on to class, now." Folding the paper, I handed it back to the pack leader.

The group breathed a collective sigh of relief as I headed out the door. Behind me, they descended into a whirlwind of chatter.

"I can't believe you let her look at the list."

"What was I supposed to do, huh? She, like, asked for it."

"Tell her it's ours."

"Yeah, right. So I can end up in detention again? My dad would, like, kill me."

"Your dad's such a Nazi."

"Well, at least she gave it back. What was she doing in here, anyway? Who was with her?"

"Some seventh grader. That weird girl that Verhaden likes so much. She's in here practicing all the time. Kiss-up."

"You know she's, like, a welfare case from back in the sticks somewhere. My mom heard it at school board. . . ."

As I passed through the second set of doors, the buzz of hallway chatter drowned out the conversation. Walking away with Dell's notebook papers tucked under my arm, I understood more than ever how difficult the Harrington social scene must be for her, and why she preferred the storage room to the cafeteria.

The vocal music teacher stopped me as I rounded the corner into the main hallway. "I'm missing a group of girls," she said, standing on her toes, trying to see through the crowd in the corridor. "About five of them. Tall, cute brunette, little redhead, a couple others. Giggle a lot. They were supposed to come directly from lunch to Spring Fling auditions. We can't start until we get everybody together. The guest director is sitting there waiting, and he is *not* happy."

"I just saw them in Verhaden's room. They didn't look like they were in a hurry to be anywhere."

Growling in her throat, she checked her clipboard. "Some of these kids can't remember things from one minute to the next, I swear. They've probably gone on to their regular class. If I didn't need those girls in the performance, I wouldn't even bother looking."

"I can understand that," I said, but I was really thinking that the girls needed to pay a visit to the school of hard knocks. Late for an audition, no audition. That was how it worked in the real world.

"Speaking of auditions, I noticed you had Dell Jordan in your office the other day." The teacher glanced down the hall, then checked her clipboard again. "Think she's going to have the grades to be available for Spring Fling? She has an amazing voice, three octaves—not the trained kind, either. It's natural. But if she's on academic probation, I can't use her."

I waited until a group of kids had passed by before I answered. "I think so." Hopefully that was true. Hopefully, I could make it true. "She's trying."

"Good." Nodding, she made a note on her clipboard, then headed off in search of the cool girls, while I continued down the main hall.

When I reached my office, Barry was sitting in a chair by the administration door, watching with wistful interest as a pair of girls walked past, oblivious to his existence. Sighing, he stood up and came across the hall.

"Hey, Ms. C." Clearly, my presence was a poor substitute for the attention of cute teenage girls. It wouldn't do any good to tell him that life is not dictated by how you look at fourteen. One of these days he'd grow out of his baby fat, develop muscles, and find that girls were interested. But promises like that are cold comfort when you *are* fourteen, chubby, and unpopular, loaded with potential no one else can see.

"What are you doing here?" I asked. It wasn't his normal period to serve as office aid.

"I'm off this hour. They're working on history projects, and I already did mine. Mr. Cantor said I could stay and help other people, or come down here. You need me to do anything?"

"I have some attendance sheets that could be alphabetized and filed." The attendance sheets weren't urgent, but Barry obviously needed a place to hang out for a while. I wondered if his glum mood had anything to do with the breakfast burrito incident in the hall this morning.

He shrugged, looking like a pathetic cartoon character in his oversize Orange County Choppers T-shirt. "OK."

I opened my door so we could go in. "There are a bunch of DAT forms on the chair in the corner. You know where they go. I need to work on a press release."

"Another one?" Picking up the stack of papers, he glanced over his shoulder. "You do one of those about every day, Ms. C."

"Seems like it." Tucking Dell's latest notebook pages under my Day-Minder, I opened an e-mail from Mr. Stafford and tried to work myself into the right frame of mind to write yet another fluffy article about next weekend's sidewalk jazz concert, during which—as Stafford put it—the Harrington Jazz Players would *go out into the community and delight crowds with refrains of fine jazz and blues music, performed by talented young musicians and vocalists.* What he really meant was that on Saturday, Harrington would bus a select group of eighth graders and their instruments to the *right* side of town to provide music for shoppers at the mall. Bingo. Community service hours completed while delighted parents and school board members looked on. Meanwhile, of course, no one would dream of holding a concert for the community in which the school was actually located.

"What's it about this time?" Sidling along the narrow space between the extra chairs and the desk, Barry peered toward the computer screen.

"Saturday's jazz concert at the mall."

He brightened instantly. "I'm in that."

I reprimanded myself for having negative thoughts. Any event that made Barry look so happy had to be a good thing. "You are? I didn't know you were in the jazz group."

"I finally made it this semester." Hiking up his pants, he expanded his chest as if he were about to breathe life into his saxophone. "I've been trying out since seventh grade, but I never got in until now." Laughing under his breath, he added, "The sax section's a bunch of stoners now, so the competition's not that tough."

I sat blinking into space as Barry ambled casually back to the file cabinet, completely unconcerned about what he'd said and whom he'd said it to. "Excuse me?" I choked. "What?"

He opened the file drawer and craned over it. "The sax section's a bunch of stoners. Everybody knows it." Muttering his ABCs, he started dropping papers into folders.

"*Who* knows it?"

Both shoulders rose and fell in a matter-of-fact shrug. "Everybody," he repeated with an amazing lack of emotion. "Why?" As in, *Why in the world would you ask that, Ms. Costell?*

I was momentarily at a loss for an answer, mentally replaying Stafford's litany about why we couldn't possibly have a drug dog come during school hours, and the fact that Harrington had *never* had a drug problem.

By contrast, there was Barry casually mentioning that the saxophone section was a bunch of stoners and everyone knew it. By *everyone*, did he mean that it was common knowledge among the students, or did he mean that faculty members knew and chose to do nothing about it?

In the lull, Barry changed the topic. "I could write that press release for you, Ms. Costell. I know all about the concert—who's got solos and all. How about you file the DAT sheets and I write the press release? I can do it in, like, twenty minutes."

"I . . . sure . . ." I stammered, abandoning my chair, still shell-shocked as we slid past each other and he settled into my desk. "I didn't know you were a writer."

"Heck, yeah." Punching up a word processor window, he began typing. "I won the KC Young Writers Award last semester. I wrote about rehab."

My jaw fell to the floor and I slowly reeled it back up. Fortunately, my back was turned to Barry. "What kind of rehab? I . . . I mean, what was the article about?"

He paused momentarily to look over Mr. Stafford's specs for the press release. "Oh, you know, like for drugs. My friend from last year got sent to rehab in Montana. One of those challenge camps. I interviewed him and wrote an article about it, what it was like for him and all. He doesn't go to Harrington anymore. His parents thought it'd be better if he didn't come back here."

"I guess you miss him, huh?" I tried to imagine Barry with a friend who ended up in drug rehab. As far as I could tell, Barry was about the cleanest kid on campus. He was into his music, worked hard in his classes, still hugged his mother good-bye every day when she dropped him at the front steps. She always watched until he got to the door. Sometimes, he'd turn and wave as he entered.

Not a kid likely to be involved with drugs.

"Yeah, some." Craning to see the screen through his glasses, he started typing again, the words flying into the blank space with amazing speed.

"Did you know he was using?" I pretended to be busy dropping forms into folders.

Stopping to read what he'd written, he drummed his fingers nervously on the keyboard. "Not at first. Then he started hanging around with—" The sentence stopped abruptly, then finished with, ". . . some other kids. I knew what the deal was. I tried to talk to him, but he didn't want to listen. We'd been friends for a long time. We went to the same school out in Prairie Village and applied for Harrington together, and all that. Then after we'd been here awhile, last year he started hanging out with some high school kids and stuff, and we just weren't friends anymore. I wrote about that in the article—how it feels to be on the other side when someone is doing the crash and burn, and there's no way you can stop it. It's like part of you is addicted, but you don't have any control over it, you know? It stinks."

A sick feeling rippled through me. I wondered if that was how my parents and Bethany felt when they learned about my eating disorder—as if I'd chosen *it* over *them*. "I'm sorry," I said.

"It's OK," Barry answered, but it wasn't him I was talking to.

Leaning on the file cabinet, I combed a hand into my hair, holding it away from my face. "Barry, what do you know about the taco stands down on Division Street?"

He studied me with the keen eye of a junior ace reporter. "Nothing, Ms. C, why?"

"Barry," I admonished. He may have been a good reporter, but he was a poor liar. "The way you threw the taco bag away this morning in the hall—I had the impression you knew something else might be in it."

Fidgeting nervously, he leaned closer to the screen. Suddenly, he needed to concentrate very hard, too hard to be talking to me. "I don't know anything about it," he rushed, checking his watch. "I better finish this. I gotta go back to history class before the period's over."

"All right." I let my disappointment show in the words. I wanted him to know I expected more from him.

"It's not a place you want to go, OK?" He fluttered a meaningful glance my way, then quickly went back to typing, suddenly in a rush to finish up and be out of my office.

Chapter 12

*B*y the time Barry completed the press release and left, it was already one o'clock, and my desk remained crowded with more attendance sheets, substitute teacher requests, and a packet of sample testing materials from the textbook rep who'd come by earlier. The modern dance instructor, Mrs. Newberg, showed up at my door with a seventh-grade girl who was having an emotional collapse because she hadn't made soloist for the upcoming Spring Fling performances.

"Ashlee doesn't really want to talk about it," Mrs. Newberg explained, depositing the girl in my doorway. "She just needs somewhere quiet to sit until she can get her emotions together." Grimacing apologetically, she mouthed, *Sorry,* then turned around and hurried back to her class.

"Come on in and have a seat, Ashlee," I said, handing her a Kleenex as she slumped into one of my chairs. "Do you need anything?"

Ashlee shook her head, curling her legs into the chair and burying her head between her arms.

"Sure you don't want to talk about how you feel?"

Another head shake.

"OK. That's fine. Let me know if I can do anything. We don't have to talk."

Drawing in a long, shuddering breath, she reached blindly for another Kleenex, and I held out the box so she could grab one. "Oh, God," she wailed, her voice coming from somewhere behind a wall of thick blond curls. "My mom's going to *kill* me. She's got a whole section booked for all her friends, and I don't have a solo. She's *chairman* of the Spring Fling committee. My *grandparents* are supposed to fly in, and I don't have a solo. Oh, God . . ."

For a girl who didn't want to talk, Ashlee ended up having a lot to say about Harrington, Spring Fling, family expectations, performance pressure from her mother, the Spring Fling guest director, the teachers at Harrington and their inability to spot real talent like hers.

We talked until after two o'clock. Ashlee finally wandered off to her next class, feeling slightly better after having vented her complaints. Watching her disappear down the hall, I saw my seventh-grade self, stressed out over things that seemed all-important at the time but wouldn't make a bit of difference in six months. I hoped in the long run Ashlee would handle the demands of Harrington better than I did.

The bell rang, testifying to the fact that, on top of everything else, she was about to rack up a tardy. Poor kid. I should have sent an admit slip so the teacher would excuse her.

Shaking my head, I turned back to my desk, still piled with things that needed to be done. No choice but to dig in, try to bring some order to the chaos, and hope there were no more Spring Fling audition meltdowns this afternoon. I wouldn't be zipping out of here at four thirty today, that was for sure. I couldn't help wondering if Mrs. Kazinski had been given so many tasks that were outside the normal scope of counseling, or if Stafford was just taking advantage of me because I was new and the school secretary was perpetually overwhelmed. Each day, it felt more like I was trying to bail out a sinking ship with a shot glass.

By the time I'd finished everything and scoured the phone list for substitute teachers, it was nearly five thirty, and the school was empty, except for the janitorial staff. Dad had called twice to check on me and warn that I'd be fighting the worst of the rush-hour traffic on the way home, and I shouldn't stay in the neighborhood after dark. He insisted I remain on the phone until I was safely in my car, even though I'd assured him that one of the maintenance men was in the parking lot, picking up trash.

The maintenance man waved to me and said, "*¿Hola, cómo estás?*" as I opened my trunk and set a box of grant-writing materials inside.

"*¿Muy bien, y tú?*" I replied, and he laughed at my Spanish.

Dad was finally satisfied that I wasn't alone, and said good-bye.

The scent of flowers swirled around me as I climbed into my car. The roses, forgotten on the passenger seat in my rush that morning, still looked amazingly fresh. They also reminded me that it was probably too late to go by the cleaner's and pick up the estimate for Bett's dress. Their sign said they closed at five thirty. A trip down the street confirmed it. The door was locked, the parking lot silent. Nearby, the taco stands were doing a brisk business, the curbside crowded with cars.

Across the street from the cleaner's, two men in a black lowrider pickup watched me as I peered through the burglar bars into the dry cleaner's lobby, just in case there was someone inside. I dreaded the idea of telling Mom I'd forgotten to pick up the restoration estimate, and that work on the dress hadn't been started yet. It would only confirm the assertion that I couldn't handle even the simplest task.

The two men watched me as I stood at the door, alternately knocking and peering through the glass. Finally, their interest and the growing twilight became uncomfortable, and I got back in my car. Pausing with my hand on the keys, I briefly considered joining what was left of the Jumpkids session, but even as I thought about it, my cell phone rang and Mom was on the other end, talking about the pasta carbonara she'd cooked for supper. She wasn't at all pleased that I was still downtown. By the time we hung up, we were almost in a snit again, and my nerves were on edge all the way home.

When I arrived, Mom was pacing the kitchen, trying to keep food warm and swatting my poor, starving father out of the way as he tried to sneak bites. The table was decked out in more than its usual finery, three places set with the good china, silver, and wineglasses.

"Oh, you're home!" Smoothing her apron as if I were the guest of honor, Mom took my box of school materials and ushered me in the door. I waited for her to ask about the dress, whereby I would have to admit that I'd failed to fully accomplish my mission for the day.

"Special occasion?" I asked.

"Oh, no." Mom's voice jingled like birdsong. "I just wanted us all to have a nice, quiet dinner tonight. There's been so much stress lately. . . ." The sentence trailed off into a bright smile, and she stood motionless, waiting for my reaction.

Making one more sweep of Mom's hopeful face, the table, and my father's bewildered expression as his gaze darted back and forth between us, I had a dawning understanding. This was Mom's attempt at repairing the rift we'd opened this morning.

I instantly felt guilty. "Sorry I'm late," I said, and instead of adding the usual admonishments about how there was no need for her and Dad to wait dinner for me every night, I added, "This looks beautiful. Thanks, Mom. What a treat after sitting in traffic."

Her lips lifted into a warm smile. "Oh, pfff." She waved a dismissive hand. "It's nothing. Just a little pasta."

Dad, who had probably been watching her fuss over the meal all evening, gave her a double take.

Catching his gaze, I winked and he shrugged, as in, *There is no figuring this woman out. I've tried for years, and she still confuses me.*

"I have the perfect finishing touch for that table." Tossing my coat onto the hook, I ducked back into the garage for my purse, briefcase, and Mim's roses. "Just right for wine and pasta," I pronounced, handing Mom the impromptu gift. "These are for you. A peace offering. I'm sorry about this morning."

Mom's eyes teared up as she took the three roses. "Oh, my. Oh, goodness, I just don't . . . You shouldn't have done . . . Where did . . . Well, they're absolutely beautiful. Thank you. I can't remember the last time someone brought me flowers." She glanced pointedly at Dad, who'd just picked a crouton out of the salad. He blanched, swallowing the lump guiltily, and gave me the thumbs-up as Mom went to the cabinet for a vase.

Suddenly, all was right with the world. We sat down to eat, passing around the pasta and making polite chitchat about the on-again-off-again winter weather, and the food. Mom seemed determined to keep mealtime light and happy, avoiding all the taboo subjects, but eventually Dad commented on how perfect the roses were, and that led to a discussion of where I'd gotten them, the cleaner, and the wedding dress.

"I'll pick up the estimate tomorrow," I said vaguely. "She thinks she can come up with the antique lace and seed pearls she'll need. They do a lot of restorations. People send them dresses from everywhere."

"Oh, that's good." Pushing the pasta bowl my way, Mom gave my plate a concerned frown. "Have some more, sweetheart. You must be famished."

"Not really. I had a big lunch." I took a conciliatory second helping, which I would mostly stir around on my plate.

"Oh?" Raised brows indicated the need for more details on the day's intake.

"Yes. I'm tutoring a student during noon hour. We shared her sack lunch."

Lowered brow, look of mild panic. "That couldn't have been much."

Shift to defensive posture. "Oh, no, it was plenty. Her mother packs double so that she can have a snack after school."

"You ate a child's after-school snack for lunch?"

The conversation slid downward from there, proof that the food police were on active duty, even tonight. Finally, Dad hopped up from the table and offered to do the dishes. I didn't argue with him, because I couldn't stand to look at food anymore. My stomach was a tight knot around the pasta, and acid gurgled in my throat. What I really wanted to do was run to the bathroom and be done with it. I couldn't, of course. Mom listened carefully for bathroom sounds and toilet flushes after each meal.

Getting up from the table, I scraped my plate and put it in the dishwasher. "Where's Joujou?" It was unusual to be by the trash can without Joujou hanging around waiting for scraps.

"Oh, I put her outside." Mom glanced casually toward the sliding glass door, where Joujou was huddled in her playhouse, looking wistfully toward us. "I didn't want her bothering us at supper. She can come in now." Walking to the door, she called Joujou in, picking her up and cuddling her, commenting on how chilled her fur was.

I realized again how important the dinner had been to my mother. She'd left Joujou at the mercy of the elements, ostracized to the doggy penthouse so that we could have quiet time as a family without anyone begging for handouts or licking our toes.

Joujou's feelings were hurt. Snorting unhappily, she nestled her head under Mom's chin, and Mom cooed to her like a baby, promising her Italian sausage.

"The dinner was great, Mom, thanks," I said, and started helping Dad with the dishes.

He shooed me away, glancing toward my box of grant-writing materials. "Go on; I'll handle this. Looks like you've got work to do."

"Grant application for a new performing arts center," I said. "It's amazing how much detail they want in these things—everything from blueprints to median income levels of students' families."

"Sounds challenging," Dad replied blandly, more focused on finding the right Tupperware container than on the conversation.

"A little, but I'll get it together eventually." Picking up the box, I turned to leave. "Thanks for doing the dishes, Dad."

"Sure, honey."

Before he could empty the pasta pan, Mom took away his Tupperware bowl and replaced it with a smaller one. "Use this. It's the right size," she said, then started digging through the drawer for the lid. "I can't imagine what's happened to the top. I usually . . ."

Lifting her hands from the drawer, Dad closed it. "Don't worry about it. I'll find something. Why don't you go put your feet up?" he suggested, and she laid her head wearily on his shoulder.

I tiptoed from the room, realizing again how much stress they were under. As hard as my illness was for me, it was harder for them. They had no control over it. Now, there was also Bett's situation, and the fact that our family was changing, whether we were ready for it or not.

Upstairs, I put on sweats, spread the papers on the bed, and worked on the grant application for a couple of hours, until my eyes kept falling shut. Finally, I unearthed Dell's spiral notebook papers tucked in my briefcase with my DayMinder.

Stuffing the grant materials back into the box, I lay back against the pillows and began to read.

I saw Mama in a dream. I was singing at the church in Hindsville. Colored light flowed through the windows, and the room was full of faces. Mama came in and stood in the back, and even with so many people there, I could see her. Her hair was long and shiny golden brown like fall grass, just a little darker than Angelo's baby hair. She was wearing an old denim jacket, and her eyes were that color, too. Like little pieces of faded blue jeans, soft and sad and clear, like something I could curl up inside.

I'm not sure if her eyes were really that color, but that's how I re-member her. She's gone misty in my mind like an old picture, and I paint in the detail when I need to. It's probably better that way. Maybe one day I won't be able to paint her at all. I wonder if she never says anything in my dreams because I've forgotten her voice.

When I see her in the church dream, she's trying to speak, but no sound comes across the room. I move closer, but there are so many peo-ple and they want to keep me from Mama. I wonder what she would tell me, if she could. I wonder if, before she died, she was sorry about Angelo and me. Did she think of us, or did she just fall away with her mind foggy and blank? Nobody ever told me. Granny just came one day after school and said my mama was dead. "That's that," she said, like when they gave Angelo away. I wasn't to talk about it anymore.

"It's OK," I told her. Mama was gone from my heart by then, so I didn't cry about it. It only hurt because it seemed like she should be there, and she wasn't. Grandma Rose says we cause most of our own misery by thinking in should-be's. There's no use in should-be's, she says. We have to find happiness in what is.

I know she's right. There's no sense going on about how things might be different. But then I wonder who I am, where I came from, and why I'm here. Brother Baker says that God is my father, but God didn't make me out of thin air. He knit me together, but what did He use for string?

I think sometimes about the man with the long dark hair and the cowboy hat. I wonder if he was my father. Sometimes when he came to drop Mama off, he would stand at the gate and look at me like he was thinking. When I had the flu, he took me to the doctor because Granny was sick and Mama was too messed up to do it.

The nurse at Dr. Schmidt's office said I might of died, with a temperature like that. He told her it went up all of a sudden, but that wasn't true. The sofa had been swimming under me for days and I saw things in the room that weren't there. Sometimes it felt like I was floating on air.

He filled my prescription at the pharmacy, then handed me a box of ice-cream bars and a little pink stuffed horse. My body melted the ice cream on the way home, but he didn't get mad. He carried me into the house and put what was left of the ice cream in the freezer. For a while, he came around to make sure I got my medicine and got better.

He might of been my father. He never said, and that was probably best. He was as messed up as Mama. He brought the stuff that got her messed up. She'd ask him for it every time he came.

"You got some stuff?" she'd say before she let him in the gate.

"Sure, baby." Then he'd snake his arm around her neck and kiss her like he was going to choke her to death. When he did that, it felt like he was pulling her away from me.

The last time I saw her, he was loading her things in his truck to move to some apartment in Kansas City. He let her overdose there, and I never saw her again.

Why would I want someone like that for a father? If I came from him and Mama, then how could there be anything good in me? How could James and Karen, and Grandma Rose, and Kate and Ben love me? How could anyone love me?

Unless they don't know who I really am.

Setting the paper on the nightstand, I slipped beneath the comforter, turned off the light, and closed my eyes. I lay thinking of Dell's life, of her need to know who she was and where she came from. I understood the desire for answers and the fear of them. Respect for my dad wasn't the only reason I'd never asked why my mom was an unwed mother when my parents met. The truth was that I was afraid of the answer, afraid it might change who I was. Redefine me in some way I couldn't predict.

It was easier not to ask.

Yet those unsaid things were a haunting presence that pervaded my life, a shadow so dark that when I drifted into it, no light followed me. Filmy and thick like tar, it held me in place. Each time I broke free, pieces clung to my feet as I walked away, so that there was always a trail into the past.

If Dell's questions were never answered, if she carried them hidden for as many years as I had, would she eventually find herself where I was now? Twenty-seven years old, lost, having starved herself almost to death because she was afraid she wasn't worthy of real love?

The possibilities swam through my thoughts as I drifted into sleep. I hoped my dreams would take me to the river, where I would dance, but instead, I found myself on Division Street, where the taco stands were lined with cars—dark ones with tinted windows, their drivers shrouded in mystery. At the cleaner's, the parking lot was filled with white dresses on faceless mannequins, their wedding veils floating softly on the breeze. Among the maze of bridal finery, Jumpkids dancers followed Mrs. Mindia in a swaying line, like village children enraptured by the pied piper. As they passed, Mim gave them roses and Granmae dropped tiny angels on their shoulders. The air was filled with miniature celestial beings, their light so bright it pushed back the shadow of Division Street. . . .

I awoke to the feel of something warm and wet bathing my eyelashes, my cheeks, my forehead. It tickled the inside of my nose, and I jerked off the pillow, sneezing.

I smelled liver and onions.

"Joujou!" I croaked, shuddering. *Eskimo-kissed by a dog. Yuck.* Glancing at the clock, I realized I didn't have to be up for another hour yet. The house was still quiet. Mom and Dad weren't even out of bed.

Bounding onto the pillow, Joujou wagged her tail and yipped.

"Go wake up Mom," I urged, and she growled playfully.

From somewhere down the hall, Mom's sleepy voice called, "Jooooujoooou?" and then a little more cheerfully, "Joujou? Sweetie-poo?"

Joujou cocked an ear toward the endearment, but remained on my pillow, wagging her tail expectantly.

"She's in here," I called down the hall. "I think she needs to go out. I'll take her."

"Ohhh-kaaay," Mom's drowsy reply drifted back.

Scooping up Joujou, I headed downstairs, put her out on the patio, and proceeded to search for the old waffle iron. For a change, I could be the one to start breakfast.

While Joujou raced around and around in her doggie dream house, I created waffles, which no one in our house had done in years. By the time Mom came down, I'd stacked several on the breakfast table and consumed two myself—dry, no butter, no syrup. Much less fattening that way.

Mom eyed me skeptically when I told her I'd already eaten and I'd better be heading upstairs to get ready for school, since I had to go by the cleaner's this morning. "Are you sure you've had enough to eat?" she questioned.

"Yes, I did." No matter what, I was not going to get in a tiff with her this morning. My days of adding stress to Mom's life were over. Period. "One thing about cooking waffles—you get plenty of time to nibble."

"Well, there's—" She was about to point out that there was plenty left, but Dad came into the kitchen and gave her a stern head shake.

"Go ahead, sugar," he said benevolently. "We don't want to make you late."

As I left the room, I could hear them arguing. About me, and about food. Again.

When I came back downstairs, I rushed past the kitchen on purpose.

"Thank you for cooking breakfast, sweetheart," Mom called after me.

"You're welcome." I was putting my things in the car when I remembered that I needed a double sack lunch for today's tutoring session with Dell.

Mom glanced up as I hurried back in the door. "I need a sack lunch," I explained. "With tutoring, I don't get any time to go to the cafeteria."

Popping out of her chair, Mom went to the pantry. "That cafeteria food isn't good for you anyway." She started pulling things from the shelves, while I took out the jelly, thinking I'd make sandwiches.

Mom had much grander ideas. "I have some canned chicken salad and cracker kits, some Vienna sausages, Cup-a-Soups, chips, SpaghettiOs. . . ."

"A couple of peanut butter and jelly sandwiches ought to do it." Why in the world did Mom have SpaghettiOs in the pantry? Sometimes, I wondered if she had ever truly faced the fact that there were no longer kids in the house.

"Oh, let me." Snatching the bread from the bread box, Mom inched Dad's newspaper out of the way and set slices on the breakfast table. "I have some deli turkey right there in the meat drawer. Can you pull it out? It's just wonderful. Honey smoked, from the natural-foods market. No phosphates. I think it tastes better."

Taking two sodas and a couple of pudding cups from the fridge, I stood back and let Mom create sandwiches that were fully loaded works of art. As she bagged them up, she glanced at me, smiling. "I haven't made a school lunch in years. This is just like the old days."

I didn't point out that in the old days, Grandma Rice made my school lunches and saw me off in the mornings. Instead, I kissed Mom on the cheek, grabbed the lunch sack, and headed off to school feeling good. On the way, I called Bett to tell her about Mim's roses and discuss the issue of wedding flowers. Bett was afraid that if we used a florist all the way across town, Mom would have a nervous breakdown. When I thought about it, I had to agree. In the cold light of reality the idea seemed slightly insane.

Still, I felt a twinge of guilt. Judging from Mim's faded clothes and old tennis shoes, she could use the money. It probably wasn't easy selling flowers in that neighborhood. Maybe I'd ask her about making some bouquets for the rehearsal night. That way, if the bouquets weren't very good, or Mim failed to come through, it wouldn't be the end of the world. "Her roses really are amazingly beautiful, but you're right: It's probably too risky to have her do the wedding flowers. What if I ask her about some practice bouquets? I know normally on rehearsal night, people use bouquets of ribbons from the bridal shower, but since we don't have time for a shower, real flowers at the rehearsal might be a nice touch. Just something simple. What do you think?"

"That sounds good," Bett agreed, then her call waiting beeped, and we said good-bye as I pulled into the parking lot of the cleaner's.

When I went inside, Mim wasn't there, so I left a note for her with Granmae, inquiring about the cost of some small bouquets and perhaps a table arrangement or two for the rehearsal dinner. When Granmae handed me the estimate for the dress restoration, I wished I had looked at that first. Dad was going to have a coronary. Maybe I would make Mim's flowers my special treat for Bett, and pay for them myself.

Granmae tapped the bill with her fingertip. "Now, I done told ya it would be high. But our work is guaranteed, one hundred percent. That dress'll leave here lookin' like it just come off the runway, and I'll even put an angel on the shoulder of it for free."

I smiled at that idea. "All right then." I hoped Dad didn't flip when he saw the cost. "And you're sure you can have it done in time?"

Granmae eyed me with the shrewd look of an experienced business-woman. "Yes, sugar pie. It'll be ready." Leaning across the counter, her heavy bosom resting on the wood, she picked a scrap of lint off the shoulder of my pantsuit, and winked at me. "You got one too many on there today. Sometimes, they like to congregate, but then they ain't fo-cused on their job."

I realized she was doing the angel-on-the-shoulder thing, so I played along. "Oh, well, maybe someone else can use that one."

"Maybe so." Narrowing her eyes, she set the extra angel atop an old card catalog drawer filled with yellowed invoices. "I'll pass it on to Mim. She'll give it to someone."

"Tell her I said hello," I added, then headed for the door. "Thanks for the shoulder-angel crowd control."

"My pleasure." As the door fell shut, I could hear her chuckling.

Across the street, the two men were sitting in their dark pickup again. They watched me as I exited the cleaner's and walked to my car.

Unlocking my door quickly, I got in and left Division Street behind, trying not to think about who the men were, why they were watching me, or whether any of the cars doing business at the taco stands belonged to Harrington students.

Cameron wasn't in one of the cars, at least not this morning. As I pulled into the faculty parking lot, his father was dropping him off at the front door. He trudged slowly up the steps, bent against the cold, and sat down on the railing, waiting for the doors to open. He looked far less jubilant than he had yesterday, arriving in the back of a high schooler's car.

"Ms. C?" he said, hopping off the railing and following me to the door.

"Yes?"

"I'm sorry about yesterday." Holding open the door, he followed me in. I wondered if the apology was genuine, or merely an attempt at buttering me up so that I would let him come inside. The first bell hadn't sounded yet, and students weren't allowed in the building. Cameron focused on his feet, so that I couldn't see his expression. "I was in kind of a . . . crazy mood."

The apology sounded contrite enough, but who could tell? I knew this routine—the one where you screwed up, almost let yourself be found out, then tried to cover it up by playing the perfect kid for a while, so no further questions would be asked. Every time someone got close to the truth of my eating disorder, I made sure I was good until the heat was off.

"Well, Cameron, yesterday was inappropriate in a number of ways," I replied flatly. "And I tend to wonder why a kid like you would act that way."

Shaking off the chill, he sagged in his oversize jacket, fiddling with the zipper. "It was just a bad day, you know? Things aren't so great at home."

I nodded. I could relate to problems at home with parents. "Anything I can do?"

He shook his head, still studying the floor.

"Anything you want to talk about?"

Another quick head shake. "Nah. Just some days, I don't want to be here, you know?"

Looking at his sad, slouched-over body, I understood more than I could possibly admit to a student. I could relate to not wanting to be here, there, or anywhere. To wishing you could just disappear from your life altogether.

What was going on in his family? It could be anything from serious problems to simple growing pains. "Cameron, you don't have to talk to me, but I'm here anytime you decide to. What you're going to find, sooner or later, is that no matter how many ways you try to avoid it, you keep coming back to the same place. And until you deal with the problem, whatever it is, you always will."

The last part was a direct quote from Sister Margaret. The farther out of recovery I got, the more I was finding that she was right about almost everything.

Cameron only shrugged, glancing back toward the door like he thought it might be easier to sit outside.

"You might as well stay in," I said, resigned to the fact that he wasn't ready to talk to me or anyone else about his problems. Not today, anyway. "I'll find something for you to do. No sense sitting out in the cold."

If Granmae's angel was still with me this morning, I willed it to flit over to Cameron's shoulder. Right now, he looked like he needed it more than I did.

Chapter 13

Since Cameron wasn't in the mood to talk, I gave him a hall pass so that he could get his saxophone and practice in one of the rehearsal rooms until school was officially open. After he was gone, I called the state coordinator with some grant-related questions, and discovered that the application was due a week earlier than Mr. Stafford had told me. Leafing through the booklet, I found an amended time line, still sealed in the envelope, tucked in the back of the book. It confirmed that the due date in the booklet was incorrect. I called Mr. Stafford, and suddenly he remembered having heard something about a change in the due date last semester, before Mrs. Kazinski left. He assumed she'd made a note of it in the book. . . .

I panicked.

As I was hanging up the phone, spiraling downward into grant-writing despair, Mrs. Morris came by to start an argument about my giving Cameron a hall pass, when he wasn't supposed to be in the building yet. She'd intercepted him in the hall, and when she'd tried to send him back outside *where he belonged,* he had produced the hall pass from me. Since it *wasn't proper* to contradict another staff member *in the presence of a student,* she had *let it go,* but she wanted to be certain I knew that allowing students in the building before seven thirty was *against policy,* and it *shouldn't happen again.* She added numerous other backhanded insults, including the fact that having so recently been a student here myself, I should have a firm grasp on the rules.

Her snide comments quickly pushed me the final inch, and I hit the end of my rope with a twang. "You know what, Mrs. Morris?" I snapped, and I mean snapped in more ways than one. "He's just a kid— a child—having a bad day, and apparently going through some problems at home. It's cold outside, and he's huddled out on the steps, because, for whatever reason, his father dropped him off early. How about we show a little compassion?"

She met my question with a cold stare. "If we begin making exceptions, soon there will be no standard to uphold." Raising her chin self-righteously, she sniffed the air, probably trolling for eye of newt and toe of frog for her latest witch's brew.

"Surely, as professionals, we are capable of discerning when exceptions are called for," I countered. *Remain calm, remain calm. Remember, the shoulder angel is watching.* "That is what we're here for, is it not?"

Mrs. Morris's lips pinched together until there was nothing but a thin line of wrinkles, like the navel of an orange left in the bowl three months too long. "I am here to create excellence," she snapped, heading out my door. "Soft treatment creates weaklings." One last glance over her shoulder told me that by "weaklings," she, of course, meant me.

"Rrrrr, I hate the woman," I growled, gripping the side of my desk and thinking, *Breathe, breathe, breathe.* "I hate that woman, I hate that woman. . . ."

I placated myself by doodling a Mrs. Morris stick figure on my Day-Minder, complete with pointy hat and broomstick, while I gave the shoulder angel an earful. Picking up a Sharpie, I obliterated the witchy pictograph, wishing I could get rid of the real thing so easily.

Even though the grant application was crying out for attention, I turned on the computer and went instead to commentary sites for *The Grapes of Wrath*, downloading and printing page after page of brilliant literary analysis. Grant application or no grant application, I'd show Mrs. Morris a thing or two. This week, I was going to tutor Dell like crazy. By the time we were finished, she would be an expert on Stein-

beck's dust-bowl masterpiece. She would know more than any other kid
in the class. Mrs. Morris would be baffled as to how it happened, frustrated because the "wrong kind" of student could suddenly answer all
of her persnickety questions.

If Cameron showed up early tomorrow, I would not only give him
a pass to a rehearsal room, I would walk him there myself, so that Mrs.
Morris couldn't harangue him in the hall. One way or another I was
going to show the wicked witch of English that this school did not belong to her. This was war. . . .

The thing about war is that it eventually takes its toll on both sides, and
sometimes the neutral countries in the middle. By the end of the week,
I was exhausted from arriving early to intercept Cameron, reading *The
Grapes of Wrath* until late at night, tutoring Dell during lunch and
Study Buddy time, working on the grant application every spare moment, and seeing to all the normal counselor duties, including the rapidly growing problem of finding substitute teachers during what was,
apparently, a worsening flu epidemic.

Dell was not nearly as thrilled to see me coming as she had been earlier on. My presence meant hard work, but her daily grades were im-
proving, especially in English. Dell could now read the passages in class
somewhat more fluently and explain the meaning. What Mrs. Morris
didn't know was that Dell and I had bypassed the syllabus and started
reading ahead. Dell read the chapters a second time alone at home, so
that when she arrived at class, she was covering the material for the third
time and had an understanding of the underlying meaning, which
greatly improved her confidence and ability.

Mrs. Morris was perplexed by Dell's sudden improvement, which
made it that much more satisfying. Dell's chances of achieving a passing grade in English were looking more promising, but she would most
likely need some extra-credit points. That, I was afraid, was going to be
a problem. If Dell asked Mrs. Morris for extra-credit work, Morris
would probably tell her to leap off a tall building.

With Dell's needs, the grant application deadline change, and everything else piling up, I lost focus on the drug issue. Cameron came early

every morning, transported to school by his father rather than his high-school friend, Sebastian. Slouched over on the stoop, huddled against the late-winter chill, he seemed sober and sad. I let him in each day and escorted him to a rehearsal room. Since he was in perfect-kid mode for the moment, our conversations were all *Please,* and *Thank you,* and *No, ma'am, Ms. Costell, nothing's wrong. Can I go practice my music now?* But somewhere between the lines I determined that his parents had split up, and he was privy to all the gory details.

On Friday, he wasn't waiting on the stoop, but came wandering in late, carrying a grease-stained lunch sack, looking glassy-eyed, mellow and content. He transferred houses weekly, and this was his week with his mother. She let him ride to school with Sebastian because she was busy at home with his soon-to-be stepfather, who came prepackaged with two young daughters.

After Cameron passed by with his tardy slip, I went to Stafford's office and closed the door. "I know we have random drug testing scheduled for next Friday," I said, "but I have a student I'd like to see tested today. Is that possible?"

Leaning back in his chair, Stafford frowned, his suit jacket falling open as he laced his fingers over the polyester beach ball of his stomach. "The tests are arranged according to a computer-generated list. Completely random, so as to avoid lawsuits or complaints that we're profiling, picking on somebody, things like that. The list comes out every other Thursday; then the kids report for testing on Friday. If they're absent Friday, they know they have to come in first thing Monday morning."

"Do we have the power to put someone on the list, or to test on an *unscheduled* day?" I pressed. What good was a drug test if the kids were warned about it ahead of time? There were stories all over the Internet of kids beating the test by sneaking in clean urine samples. They hid them in the bathrooms ahead of time, concealed them in condoms and Ziploc bags tucked in their underwear. For kids who could afford it, there was even a pill that could reportedly make the urine test yield a false negative.

If Mr. Stafford knew any of that, he wasn't concerned about it.

"Typically we stick to the regular schedule so that we're not pulling kids out of class during something important. . . ." His disinterested expression told me that the answer would be no. Part of me wanted it to be. Cameron had enough problems already, and getting nailed for using drugs would only blow the situation wide-open. On the other hand, not confronting a potential addiction allowed it to take over your life.

"Who is it?" Stafford asked, and I handed him Cameron's name on a sticky note. If the secretary was outside the door, I didn't want her to hear, particularly since Cameron's father was on the school board.

Stafford's eyes widened; then he folded the note in half, sliding his thumb and forefinger crisply along the crease. "I don't think there's a problem here. Just a little teenage rebellion. Dad's got it under control."

"Dad may, but Mom doesn't. This kid needs help."

Stafford met my comment with a patronizing smile. If I'd been close enough, he probably would have patted me on the head. "Don't worry, Ms. Costell. The kid has good parents."

"Parents don't always want to know what's going on."

Tucking the note in his shirt pocket, he flicked a ladybug off his desk. "These situations tend to work themselves out. When you've been in administration as long as I have, you'll realize that," he said pleasantly, then changed the subject. "So how's the grant application coming along?"

A muscle started twitching in the side of my jaw. I wanted to jump up and down and scream, fly into a fit, tear my hair out, and run down the hall like a crazy woman. Anything to get someone to pay attention. Instead, I said, "Fine. I've moved up the timetable with the architect, the permit study, and the district financial officer, so that everything will be complete for the school board to review the application and act on the agenda item in time."

Stafford was delighted. "Wonderful! Good job catching that change in the deadline. Well-done, Ms. Costell." And behind that, there was the unspoken, *Good girl.* Finally, I was keeping my nose where it belonged, quietly writing my little grant applications rather than interfering in the lives of the students. "You've got a ladybug on your shoulder," Stafford pointed out, cheerfully wagging a finger at me.

Clenching my teeth to prevent anything from getting past my lips, I walked out the door with the ladybug taxiing along. To top it off, Mrs. Jorgenson handed me three messages from my mother. Thank God it was Friday.

Back in my office, I called the high school guidance counselor, hoping he could arrange to have this Sebastian kid tested, nipping Cameron's problem at the source. Mr. Fortier sighed into the phone. In addition to counseling, he served as assistant principal, due to recent budget cuts, and had just come back from three days of chaperoning kids at a district music contest. "Not likely," he answered in a tone of emotionless surrender. "I'm sure the Sebastian you're talking about is Sebastian Talford. His dad's a city councilman. No chance he'll turn up on the random drug testing list anytime soon; I can promise you that. Up here, we test only according to the list. Principal's orders."

"Figures," I muttered.

"Yeah. Pretty much does," he agreed wearily. "Welcome to Harrington, kid. It's no place for dreamers."

"Thanks," I bit out, then hung up the phone. Standing there, staring at the mountain of paperwork, the never-ending attendance reports, and substitute teacher requests for Monday, I decided that what I really needed was a trip to Jumpkids land tonight. My brain was on overload, my body was double-knotted like a toddler's shoestring, and I'd had all I could take. I needed a hug, some cheese crackers, and a good workout with Mrs. Mindia.

When I passed Dell in the hall, I told her I'd see her at Jumpkids. "Cool," she replied. She actually had a friend with her this time, a cello player named Darbi, who was a minor misfit and not an outstanding student. She and Dell were talking about Mrs. Morris's latest test on *The Grapes of Wrath*. Dell had apparently done fairly well, and now she was giving Darbi the same advice I'd given her about taking Mrs. Morris's torturous literature exams. It was good to see her laughing and talking with someone her own age.

By the time the afternoon was over, I was counting down the minutes, and I headed for the door at four thirty-one, still calling substitute teachers on my cell phone. Recently, Mr. Stafford had been stopping by my office every day after dismissal. He'd kept me late several evenings in a row, standing over my shoulder reading the performing arts center application and suggesting pointless word changes. Today, I was out of there before he could catch me.

Exiting with the box of grant materials under my arm and my cell phone balanced on my shoulder, I ran into Mr. Verhaden. On the phone, yet another prospective substitute declined the opportunity to teach algebra next week, and said that she wouldn't be available to fill in during a maternity leave in the life sciences department, either.

"No subs, huh?" Verhaden surmised, nodding toward the phone as I tossed it in the box with the grant materials.

"No," I grumbled. "There's no one available, and the algebra teacher is out all next week, at least. Then Mrs. Carter goes on maternity leave the week after next. I still need someone to take her classes for the rest of the year. I don't know what I'm going to do. Most of the noncerti-fied subs have worked their maximum number of days for the year, and most of the certified ones are already on long-term assignments."

"Why are you the one calling subs?" he asked. "The administration office usually does that." The wind lifted flyaway hairs from his evolving comb-over, and he reached up to carefully smooth them back into place. Considering that Verhaden was only about forty, it was strange to see him holding down his hairdo like an old man. When I was a Har-rington middle school student, he was the young and single teacher all the girls dreamed about—an idealistic earth child with a talent for both teaching and music. He had us recycling cans to support the homeless shelter and playing benefit concerts to save the rain forest. Now he was just another guy with dark circles under his eyes and a receding hairline.

"Stafford asked me if I'd take up the slack," I told him. "Mrs. Jorgen-son is busy with arrangements for the eighth-grade graduation banquet and Spring Fling."

"Looks like someone needs to take up the slack for you." He nodded toward my box of papers. "Better watch out, or filling the sub list will be dumped on your plate permanently. The first thing you have to learn around here is how to say no."

"I can handle it."

Verhaden smiled benevolently, winking at me. "They'll drain you dry and spit out the shell," he said, his expression adding, *And you'll end up forty, with no family, no life, and a bad comb-over.* His face turned slowly grave. "Seriously, Julia, you can't take over the office work, adopt every kid who's dropped off too early, and tutor all the ones whose grades are below par. There are too many of them. These kids have to learn to sink or swim on their own."

I recoiled, as much at the Darwinian philosophy as at the fact that Verhaden was the one espousing it. I'd always thought he was one of the good guys. "I have to do what I can. If I don't, why am I here?"

"You'll burn yourself out, Julia." Meeting my eyes, he laid a hand on my shoulder. I had a sudden inkling that he knew why I was now a guidance counselor, rather than a dancer with the KC Metro.

I chose to quickly change the subject. "If Dell Jordan doesn't get some help, she's not going to make it. She's way behind academically."

I could tell I'd struck a nerve. Withdrawing his hand, he stepped back and crossed his arms. "While she's spending time in tutoring, she's not getting the extra practice she needs in instrumental or voice. She has an incredible talent, but she's way behind all the other kids in formal training."

If I hadn't been holding a box filled with my grant-writing blood, sweat, and tears, I would have thrown my hands into the air, and said, *Excuse me? This is a school. Reading, writing, 'rithmetic, remember?* "If she doesn't pick up her grades, she's not going to be here long enough to develop her music. First things first."

"Exactly," he countered, still annoyingly sure of his position. "She's got spring concert with the symphonic coming up, and the Harrington Spring Fling. If the music's good enough, and the long, sad story about the little prodigy from the sticks makes the newspapers, the board will approve her application for next year. She'll be retained in the seventh grade, and that'll give her extra time to develop before she moves on to high school."

"Oh!" I burst out, color flaming into my cheeks. "Oh!" I paced a few steps away, my heart hammering an angry tattoo in my throat. Why was everything always about the performance? Didn't anybody realize there were kids, real people with needs and emotions, involved here? Didn't anybody care?

I pulled in a long breath, then blew out, thinking of Mrs. Mindia. *Relax, breathe deeply, imagine clear water trickling softly along a riverbed.* . . . If I didn't settle down, I was going to have a stroke right here on the steps and be buried under mountains of grant paperwork.

Settling one last breath in my lungs, I turned around, and Verhaden drew back, apparently surprised by the heat in my face. I was on fire. "Have you ever looked at the statistics on retention? Ever? Have you?" He shook his head vaguely, and I rushed on. "I'm not saying that it doesn't work in some cases, but the research is clear that much of the time, it is so detrimental socially that the kid just gives up and falls further behind. Do you know what the dropout rate is for retained students? And you're talking about a kid who already doesn't fit in well socially, who's already one of the older students in her grade. She doesn't feel that she has any right to be here. Have you ever thought about what it might do to her if she's retained? It will only confirm what she already believes about herself—that she's not good enough, that she's destined for failure."

For once, Mr. Verhaden didn't have an answer. Arms hanging slack, he coughed indignantly. "I don't think . . ."

The door opened, and Mr. Stafford stepped out, heading home with his briefcase. Pausing, he looked from me to Verhaden and back. "Everything all right?"

"Yes," we hissed in unison.

Shrugging, the principal continued down the stairs. "All right, then. You get that substitute list filled yet, Costell?"

"I'm trying," I bit out.

If he noticed the frustration in my voice, he didn't respond. "Have a nice weekend," he called back, then waved a little toodle-oo over his shoulder.

Neither of us answered. We just stood there at an impasse. Hiking the box onto my hip, I braced it under one arm. "Look, Mr. Verhaden . . ." I was going to say, *Give me a few weeks and let's see what's possible with Dell,* but he held up a hand to stop me.

"I stand corrected on the retention question, concerning Dell. It's not an issue we deal with very much here," he acquiesced. "But you have to understand that it's a gamble. Dell's here because of the music. She's an experiment, not our normal sort of kid, and plenty of people find that a threat. If she doesn't sparkle during the spring performances, it's not going to matter what her grades are."

"Point taken," I said, thinking that getting kicked out of Harrington might be the best thing that could happen to Dell. This place was like a cancer. On the other hand, failing here might be the straw that would finally break her. "Let's hope she can do both."

Verhaden nodded, looking slightly pessimistic. "I'll see what I can do about getting a decent table and chairs put in the storage room. I assume you'll still be using my storage room?"

I couldn't help smiling at the fact that he knew. Not much at Harrington escaped Verhaden's radar. "It's quiet. She doesn't want the other kids to see her in tutoring sessions. . . . And speaking of the storage room . . ." The next thing I knew, I'd blurted out the question about donating used instruments to the Jumpkids program. Talk about bad timing.

Verhaden dropped his mouth open, as in, *Wow, does this woman have nerve. What's she going to ask for next—the shirt off my back?* "I'll have to give that some thought." Scratching his head, he turned and started down the steps, glancing back over his shoulder, his bemused look adding, *Who is that woman, and what has she done with mousy little Julia Costell?*

Waving with much more confidence than I felt, I started toward the parking lot, satisfied that in some small way I had finally gone against the crippling tide at Harrington. But as I got in my car and drove down the block, the reality of what I'd done set in. I'd signed Dell up for an unspoken gamble she couldn't possibly understand. What if, because of everything else we were working on, her music did fall behind? What if Verhaden was right, and the music was all that mattered? I was meddling in her life, and neither she nor her foster parents knew anything about it.

Guilt fell over me like the shadow of an approaching storm.

To top it all off, when I arrived at Jumpkids, the first thing Dell did was give me an adoring smile, and her foster mother welcomed me with open arms.

"Dell was hoping you would come down to our Jumpkids mini-camp in Hindsville this weekend," Karen said as we stood in the doorway of the gym, waiting for the kids to finish their snacks in the cafeteria.

I had no idea how to respond to the invitation. My instant reaction was to say yes, but then I remembered the grant deadline and *The Grapes of Wrath* waiting in the trunk of my car. I needed to be home working all weekend. I should have been there right now.

"I'll have to see how the weekend progresses," I hedged. "I'd really love to go, but I have a pile of work in my car."

Karen nodded sympathetically. "Well, if things change, we'd love to have you. Hindsville isn't very far, and it's a pretty drive. Feel free to come on down if you find some time."

"I'll try," I answered. Beside me, Dell let out a long sigh, already giving up on me for the weekend. Turning away, she walked across the room, sat down on the bleachers next to a portable keyboard, and tapped out the melody to one of the Jumpkids songs.

"Play something for us," Karen urged, and Dell took a breath, then arched her body over the instrument. Closing her eyes, she swayed slightly, as if the music were silently building inside her, until finally it spilled onto the keys and filled the room with a version of "The Hallelujah Chorus" from Handel's *Messiah,* worthy of the Sistine Chapel. I stood amazed, speechless, watching her lose herself in the melody and transform from a shy girl to an artist, captivated by a magic that was both startling and awe-inspiring. Even though I'd read about her musical ability in her profile and heard about it from other teachers, I'd never fully understood how talented she was until that moment. With nothing but an inexpensive keyboard, she took away the bleakness of the grade school gym, and transformed it into a concert hall, a place of reverence, a sanctuary. Music lifted her from the ordinary in a way that transcended explanation. To allow an ability like hers to go undeveloped because she had difficulty with *The Grapes of Wrath* would be criminal, a denial of an inborn, God-given gift that was meant to be celebrated.

Whether she knew it or not, whether she believed it or not, she was extraordinary.

Chapter 14

Saturday morning, I woke up stiff and sore. The phone was ringing, and for some reason, nobody was answering it. Rolling over, I grabbed it clumsily and croaked, "Hello?"

"Julia?"

It took a minute for my mind to register the voice. My thoughts swam sluggishly through a murky mixture of past and present. "Jonathan?" I murmured, blinking sleep from my eyes, momentarily snuggling into the idea that the past eight months had never happened—that my breakup with Jonathan, rehab, the end of my dance career, moving home with Mom and Dad, the job at Harrington, the scene with Jonathan and his new wife at the mall's gift registry were all part of a long, strange dream, and I was finally waking up.

"Jonathan?" I said again.

"Julia? Are you all right?"

"I just woke up."

He chuckled. "Sleepyhead. It's after eight." Jonathan was always an early riser. He'd never understood those of us who weren't. The tenderness in his voice made me laugh along with him.

"It's quiet here this morning." The words ended in a sigh, and I closed my eyes again, my mind wandering back in time, convincing my body to travel along.

"I just wanted to"—he arrested the sentence with an odd hesitation—"see how you were doing. I figured if I called early, your folks might still be out for their walk." Every Saturday morning, my parents took a walk to the park and back. Jonathan, of course, knew the routine.

"I'm sore from . . ." From what? I dragged my eyes open again. Why was I so sore? I was never sore after a performance . . .

Slowly, the memory of dancing with the Jumpkids wound into my consciousness. I recalled lifting tiny dancers into the air as they practiced *pas de chat* and *changement de pieds* over, and over, and over. Yawning, I surveyed the grant paperwork strewn on the floor, where I'd worked last night after surviving Mrs. Mindia's latest dance class, dinner with the Jumpkids, and countless exuberant hugs.

My mind snapped back to the present like a rubber band with a spit wad of reality attached to it.

Clearing my throat, I sat up, brushing strands of tangled hair out of my face. "Jonathan, why are you calling me?"

"I just . . ." Another trailing sentence, punctuated by a gap, during which I tried to imagine what he was thinking. "I just . . . I've been . . . You've been on my mind this past week. I wanted to know that you're all right."

"I'm all right," I replied flatly, then felt a pang of guilt. His concern was genuine, his voice colored with shades of leftover feelings and latent regrets. It only made talking to him more painful.

"I knew. I knew what you were doing, Julia, and I didn't do anything about it. I just put more pressure on you. I didn't understand how serious it was. I . . . I thought it was something you could control." The words rushed out as if he'd stored them up, practiced them before dialing my number. "But seeing you the other day, and then hearing that news story last week about that girl who's brain-dead because she went too far with diet pills and purging . . . God, Julia, I realized that could have been you. I'm so sorry. I should have done something about it."

A dozen possible responses raced through my mind. I felt myself shrinking and shrinking and shrinking, until the room, the world, seemed too big. "Jonathan, it wasn't your responsibility. It *isn't* your responsibility. I was the only one who could do anything about it. I still am."

"I should have been there for you. Things could have been different. We could have—"

"Jonathan." I stopped him before he could go any further, before he could say something he would regret and I would torture myself with forever, thinking about what might have been. "Things *aren't* different. We are where we are. I drove you away because I knew you were figuring me out. It's part of the addiction—keeping everyone at arm's length, maintaining secrets. It's over, and now I have to move on. *We* have to move on. You have a wife; you're going to have a baby. I have a new job I'm really into right now." Maybe that was becoming true. It sounded convincing, anyway. "It's OK. Things are OK."

He sighed, a long, slow, resigned passage of breath, as if he knew I was right. "Things should have been different."

Tears prickled in my eyes, and I pressed my fingers to my nose to keep from sniffling. "Jonathan, what is . . . is. There's no point thinking in should-bes. It only causes misery." A direct quote from Dell's grandma Rose. Now I understood how true it was. Both Jonathan and I had to accept the truth and move on. "You and Carrie seem really happy together. I wish you the best. I really do."

"Julia—"

"I'd better go. Lots to do today." Even as I said it, I was hobbling stiff-legged to the shower.

"I'm always here if you need anything. I still care about you, even though it didn't work out." Behind the words, there was an unspoken uncertainty: *Maybe I still love you.*

Or maybe he was just unsettled by the collapse of a long-term relationship, finding someone new, getting married, and now becoming a father, all in less than a year.

"Be happy, Jonathan. You and Carrie seem great together. Really." *She's much better for you than I ever could be. She's normal.*

"Take care of yourself, Julia." He hung up without saying good-bye, leaving the conversation feeling unfinished.

I stood in the bathroom trying to decide what to do next. The prospect of hanging around the house all day was unbearable. I had to get out, do something, even if it was only perusing bridal registries or shopping for honeymoon lingerie with Bett.

Showering and dressing quickly, I pulled my hair back into a damp ponytail and left the room, sidestepping the piles of grant papers and promising myself I would work on them this evening and all day tomorrow. Right now, I needed to go . . . somewhere.

Things were quiet downstairs. Joujou was asleep on the sofa, making peaceful little pug-nosed snorts, her legs twitching in some dream. Outside on the patio, Dad was trimming the holly bushes and the crape myrtles, getting them in shape for spring. On the kitchen table, there were scrambled eggs and toast on a plate and a note from Mom. Bett had a touch of food poisoning this morning, and Mom thought she'd better go over there. I pictured poor Bett, pregnant, sick, having both Mom and Jason fussing over her, when what she probably wanted was to sleep or camp out in the bathroom. I considered attempting to lure Mom away from Bett's place with some wedding-related errand, but there wasn't much chance it would work. When Mom took charge of a situation, she hung on with all ten claws.

Standing in the kitchen, I tried to decide what to do next, then finally settled on heating a small portion of the leftover breakfast. Before I realized it, I was hiding the rest of the food under a newspaper in the trash. Old habits die hard. Staring at the contraband, I heard myself telling Jonathan, *"I'm all right."* What a lie that was. Three months out of rehab, and I was still hiding food in the trash. When was I ever going to be all right?

"Focus on the little battles, not the war," Dr. Leland had told me when I was at St. Francis. *"One step at a time—two forward, sometimes one back, then forward again. That's how recovery is done . . ."*

"Fall down nine times; get up ten," Sister Margaret advised. Japanese proverb.

Taking the plate from the microwave, I ate what was left. One step forward.

While I was eating, I focused on the successes of the past week. I had shared more or less regular meals with Mom and Dad all week. I hadn't stood at the mirror loathing my reflection and imagining that I could see every calorie clinging to my body—I hadn't had time. At school, I hadn't skipped lunch or picked through a cafeteria salad, carefully dipping each lettuce leaf in the dressing so I would consume less fat. I'd eaten lunch each day without even thinking about it while tutoring Dell in the storage room. Not once had I stopped to lament the calories or consider how much weight gain might be caused by a bag of Cheetos. I had arranged for the wedding dress to be restored, ordered some nice bouquets for Bett's rehearsal, and given a little business to a sweet old lady who'd treated me to free flowers. Best of all, I had attended Jumpkids on Friday and danced without feeling as if I were tasting the forbidden fruit that would surely bring about my downfall.

Compared to all of those achievements, a few eggs in the trash can didn't mean much. Overall, it had been a successful week. If Mom searched the wastebasket, which she probably would, and found the hidden food, I would tell the truth and move on. One piece at a time, I would put together a life for myself—one that could, perhaps, *include* dance even if dance could no longer *be* my life.

All of a sudden, I knew where I wanted to spend my Saturday. I wanted to dance with various partners, none of whom was over four feet high. Finishing the last bites of breakfast, I put the plate in the dishwasher, left Mom and Dad a note, grabbed my purse, jacket, and briefcase, and headed for the Jumpkids minicamp in Hindsville.

In the driveway, I called Karen's cell phone, hoping she would answer. When she did, the reception was so scratchy I could barely hear her.

"Karen?" I said. "This is Julia Costell. Seems like my day is looking pretty clear, after all. Do you still need help with the minicamp in Hindsville?"

"Oh, don't say that unless you mean it," Karen blurted out. "Mrs. Mindia's got the flu this morning, and James had to leave late last night to fill in for another pilot who had a family crisis. I've got fifty kids coming and so far only myself, Dell, my sister from Hindsville, and some of the local church volunteers to help. One of our counselors from last summer was supposed to be driving up from New Mexico, but he had car trouble and doesn't know if he's going to make it, and . . ." The sentence faded into static, then came back. ". . . stressful morning, sorry. If you can come, we would be thrilled. We're in the car, about thirty minutes out of the city right now. Do you know how to get to Hindsville?"

"Just a minute." Fishing a map from the console, I unfolded it, traced the road south, and found Hindsville in microscopic print along a winding river. "I see it. What do I do when I get there?"

"Just come to the Baptist church. You can't miss it. It's right on the square, next to . . ." Static overtook the line again, and I waited, thinking the connection might be lost for good this time. It didn't matter. I had a destination and an invitation, which was all I needed.

Karen came back on the line, laughing. "Dell's bouncing up and down saying, 'Cool, cool, cool!' Can you hear her? She's had the blues all morning because James had to leave, and Keiler might not make it to minicamp. She looks happy now, though. I think you've got a fan."

"It's a mutual admiration society." It sounded like a lighthearted quip, but it was true. In some strange way, Dell was doing as much for me as I was for her. "She's quite a kid."

"Yes, she is," Karen agreed. "Listen, we're about to go down a hill, so I'll sign off before this thing fuzzes out again."

We said good-bye, and I hung up, then pulled out of the driveway and headed for the interstate as I called Bett's place to see how she was doing. Jason answered and gave me the abridged version of Bett's symptoms. Her nausea was worse than usual, and she couldn't keep food down, but she wasn't running a fever. My mother was the one who had diagnosed food poisoning.

"Listen, just make sure it's not the flu," I said, thinking that Mrs. Mindia had the flu, and several Harrington teachers and students were out with it. "Bett's had her flu shot, hasn't she?"

"Now you sound like your mom," Jason chided. I was reminded again of how lucky Bett was to have him. He could even laugh at Dr. Mom, right in the middle of a family medical crisis. "Yes, Bett has had her flu shot."

"Good, then I'll leave you alone." I was suddenly very, very glad I was leaving town, so that Mom couldn't drag me into the food-poisoning drama. Next, she'd be trying to move Bett out of the apartment and back home, so that Mom and Joujou could look after her properly. "You *three* have a good day, all right?"

Jason groaned, then said good-bye and hung up.

Chuckling, I relaxed against the headrest, thinking that I'd made exactly the right decision today. An adventure was just what I needed. The shadow of gloom and worthlessness that had haunted me all morning flew out the window, and suddenly I was as bright and sunny as the late-winter day.

The drive to Hindsville was quiet and peaceful. Leaving the interstate, I transferred to an old two-lane snaking lazily through the Ozarks, climbing wooded hillsides, plunging into valleys, climbing again. By the time I reached the outskirts of Hindsville, I was far from all my normal reference points. The town itself seemed as unreal as the road that led me there. Comprised of an old-fashioned square with a park and gazebo in the center, it looked like an advertising print on a calendar selling some wholesome, all-American product like baked beans, fresh bread, fruit, or apple-pie filling.

As I pulled into town, the place itself seemed to be yawning and stretching, just waking up as sunlight reached the valley floor where the town was nestled like a tiny diorama tucked within the folds of a thick, winter-brown quilt. At the café, men were standing on the sidewalk next to a pickup truck, laughing and sipping cups of coffee, steam rising from the mugs and dancing near their mouths. In front of the hardware store and the grocery, merchants were setting out their wares, and at the Baptist church, the steeple bell was ringing. I pulled in and parked, feeling like I'd just dropped out of my own life and into someplace that didn't seem quite real.

Climbing out of the car, I stretched, taking a long breath of the clean, fresh air as I slipped on my coat and surveyed the town. What a perfect place to take a short vacation from the stress of ordinary life.

A flock of geese flew overhead as I walked to the front door of the church. Shading my eyes, I stopped to watch them lazily circle the town, sizing up the river as a landing site. Finally, they veered off and headed north again, the change in direction effected when one bird took the lead, in a hurry to move on toward spring nesting grounds.

"Indian legend has it that sometimes they'd circle until they fell out of the sky." An elderly man, balding, with puffy shocks of gray hair on the sides, was standing in the doorway, holding open the door. Portly and modest of stature, he reminded me of Mr. Stafford, except that this man had a quick eye and a kind face. He focused on the geese again. "Of course, what they're really looking for is a leader. All those birds, and they'll just keep circling forever until one breaks the cycle and heads north again." Tapping a finger to his lips, he made a quick notation on a spiral-bound pad taken from his shirt pocket. "I'll have to put that in the Sunday sermon. I'll call it, 'One Bold Bird.' " He waved a hand across the air, as if he were putting the title up in lights. "What do you think?"

"It sounds great," I said, smiling. "I'm a middle school guidance counselor, so I understand the 'one bold bird' theory. Most of the kids want to circle with the flock, unfortunately." Strange how easily *I'm a middle school guidance counselor* rolled off my tongue. I'd never identified myself that way before, even in my own mind.

The man at the doorway nodded in agreement, or recognition. "You must be the one from Dell's school. She's been looking for you ever since she got here. I hear you're our dance teacher for today."

"I think so." Again, strange how quickly and naturally that answer came out. *Julia Costell, guidance counselor, dance teacher.*

He extended his hand as I walked up the steps. He had a warm, two-fisted grip that lingered for a moment. "Brother Baker. Welcome to First Baptist of Hindsville."

"Julia Costell." Taking another breath of the fresh mountain air, I gazed up at the old frontispiece, its peak adorned with stained glass showing a dove landing in Jesus' hands. "What a beautiful old building."

Leaning back, he studied the window with me, then glanced into the building, the lines of his face straightening with concern. "How are things going for Dell in school?" He checked the doorway again, making sure we were alone. "She started the year very excited about the musical opportunities there, but the last few times she's been here, she has seemed somewhat worried and overburdened by it all."

I winced, wondering how much to say. "She's . . . trying," I hedged, tempted to blurt out the whole story. I wanted to talk about Dell with someone who knew her, but I couldn't risk driving her away. In her desperate bid to preserve the ideal family image, she had to fill the role of ideal daughter—talented, smart, helpful, loving, not conflicted in any way, not failing in anything. Especially not failing her classes at school.

"I was afraid of that," Brother Baker said soberly. "It's too much, isn't it?"

Blowing out a long breath, I stared at the sidewalk. "It might be." Ethics or no ethics, my job was about helping kids, and the best thing I could do for this kid was to find out more about her. "We're trying, but she's behind. She doesn't want her foster parents to know."

Brother Baker nodded. "It isn't uncommon for adoptive kids to have a hard time relating honestly to a new family. When life has taught you that you're not worth loving, you either reject the idea of love altogether, or you try to mold yourself into someone good enough to be loved. Kids in Dell's situation are afraid to be real. Experience has taught them that doesn't work. We are all products of our experiences."

I realized he was looking at me very directly, and I was falling into the words, thinking not only of Dell, but of myself, hopelessly convinced that the real me wasn't good enough, that I needed to be a little thinner, a little more talented, a little more successful. "I think a lot of this stems from being abandoned by her father." I blinked, trying to separate the mixture of Dell's life and mine, like egg whites from yolk. "Her biological parents, I mean. She writes often of her mother's reasons for leaving and of wondering about the identity of her father. I think she'll always be seeking the answers to those questions."

Brother Baker rubbed his brow, then his eyes, looking tired. "That's a can of worms."

I wondered if my mother might answer the question about my father the same way, if I asked. *That's a can of worms. . . .* "She has a lot of questions about her past. She's coming to the age of trying to figure out who she is, where she came from."

Brother Baker nodded in a wise way that made me wonder if he knew this was as much about me as it was about Dell. "I can't tell you much about Dell's past," he admitted. "Not beyond what you probably already know from her school files. Her grandparents were agricultural workers down on Mulberry Creek, never had much, never were considered very fine folks, if you know what I mean. The grandfather died in a farming accident when Dell's mother and her brothers were teenagers, and the family went further downhill after that. One of the brothers got killed. The other one, Bobby, was in and out of jail and right now he's back in for DUI. Dell's mother quit school as a teenager, ran off, got involved in drugs and whatnot. Came back a few years later, with Dell just a tiny baby. Never said who the father was, as far as I know. She eventually left again, got pregnant, later gave that baby to its father, and took off a third time. She died in Kansas City. Overdose. Dell was left with no one but a grandmother, who was in declining health and unprepared to raise a little girl."

Shaking his head, he sighed. "One of those stories that never seemed like it would have a happy ending, but here we are. Karen's grandmother, Rose Vongortler, lived across the river from Dell's granny. Rose was lonely and Dell was lonely and the two of them became friends. Eventually, Dell was like a part of the Vongortler family. It seemed a natural thing that when Dell's biological grandmother died last year, Karen and James took her in. They'd never been able to have children of their own, so Dell was a long-awaited gift. God has an amazing way of weaving lives together."

Clearly, he wanted to leave the story at that. Happy ending. No more to be said. I pushed for more, anyway. "Dell has mentioned a boyfriend of her mother's—someone with long dark hair. She thinks he might be her father. Do you know who that could have been?"

Brother Baker squinted upward. "No, I don't believe I do. Dell's family always kept to themselves. They didn't like a lot of people knowing their business—always afraid of the welfare authorities and things like that." Tapping a finger against his chin, he frowned thoughtfully. "I hate to say it, but if Dell has a biological father out there, she's probably better off not knowing him. Dell's mother didn't run with a very sa-vory crowd."

"I suppose not," I muttered, but in the back of my mind, I felt that even if the answers weren't pleasant, Dell still had a right to find them. I'd learned from experience that ignoring the questions wouldn't make them go away.

Chapter 15

*I*nside the main chapel, Karen and another woman were busy setting up rudimentary props for what looked like a production of *Alice in Wonderland*. Karen introduced the other woman as her sister, which was obvious because of the family resemblance.

Even without the physical similarities, I would have quickly determined that Karen and Kate were sisters—only sisters talk to each other that way. Friends require a certain level of politeness, little niceties and conversation makers. Sisters get right to the point. Only half as many words per sentence are necessary. The rest comes from unspoken understanding and common life experience. Watching Kate and Karen laugh and joke with each other as we constructed the theater set, I felt a pang of missing Bett. Standing next to a giant Styrofoam toadstool, I was momentarily overwhelmed by the fact that I was losing her. In two weeks, she would be married and moving away.

Bett would have loved helping with the Jumpkids production of *Alice in Wonderland*. When we were little, she always wanted to play storybook dress-up with my dance costumes. Even though she didn't pursue ballet after the first grade, she still loved the performance outfits. The one from *Alice in Wonderland* was her favorite, but I was always stubborn about letting her wear it. Now, I wished I'd let her be Alice every time she wanted to. Our years as sisters and playmates went by faster than I'd ever imagined. Now we were grown-up, and life was sweeping us into an entirely new phase, taking us to unknown places.

I wanted to speed home, burst into Bett's bedroom, wrap my arms around her, and tell her I loved her and she couldn't move away.

Dell came through the side door, and I wiped my eyes, feeling silly. She frowned as I dabbed my face with the remodeled bathrobe that would soon clothe the Queen of Hearts.

"Sorry," I said, laying the bathrobe over my arm and reaching into the prop box for the queen's crown. I was supposed to be sorting out the costumes, not musing over Bett's life changes. "I was thinking about my sister getting married and moving away. I was having a little *moment*."

"Oh." Dell was still perplexed, the way kids are when they realize that—*oh, my gosh*—schoolteachers have actual human emotions beyond simple anger and irritation. "Well . . . ummm . . . you should get this thing we've got on the computer. You can call each other up and talk and see each other on the screen, and everything, and it's all free. Karen and Kate do it all the time." Before I could stop her, she'd hollered across the stage, "Karen, what's that computer thingy we've got where we can talk on the phone?"

"Phonefamonline," Karen answered, then paused to glance over her shoulder, and added, "Why?"

"Ms. C needs it."

To my horror, everyone turned to look at me, standing there clutching the Queen of Hearts bathrobe, wiping my eyes. "Sorry," I said sheepishly, feeling like a complete moron. Terribly unprofessional, crying in front of a student and a parent. "My sister's getting married in two weeks and moving to Seattle."

Karen and Kate seemed to understand perfectly. Girl thing. Sister thing. They made pouty lips at each other, then lamented, "Aaawww," in unison. Karen got misty eyed, and Kate, whom I didn't even know, came across the stage and gave me a sympathetic hug.

Dell joined in, patting my shoulder and saying, "I'm sorry, Ms. C."

I began to blubber in earnest, babbling on about my sister, and how she was going to be so far away, and of course I was happy for her, and

Jason was a great guy, but I was losing my sister. . . . And so on, and so on. All the things I couldn't say to Mom or Bett.

Karen walked over, and the three of them stood consoling me, while I drenched the queen's gown, vaguely aware that when I finished, I was going to feel so idiotic that I would have to make some excuse and leave. I would never be able to face these people the rest of the day.

"What's this, *Steel Magnolias*?" A man's voice came from the back of the room, and I wanted to turn to vapor and dissipate out the back door.

"Keiler!" Dell squealed, and I registered the fact that Dell's friend Keiler was here, and he wasn't a little kid.

Kate withdrew from our circle of sympathy. "You made it!" she said, as Dell jumped off the stage and ran across the room.

"What happened to the hopelessly broken-down car?" Karen asked. She kept her arm around my shoulder, and I realized I was about to be introduced.

I couldn't remember the last time I'd felt so ridiculous and completely undignified. Fortunately, Dell delayed our meeting by tackling Keiler with a hug. I wiped my eyes furiously with the bathrobe, taking in the guy in the stocking cap with MENTAL embroidered on the front, a RED RIVER SKI STAFF T-shirt, woefully wrinkled khaki hiking pants, a hiking boot on one foot, a multicolored walking cast on the other, and a guitar case slung across his back. He stumbled sideways, catching Dell and bumping the guitar case against one of the pews.

Karen gaped at the cast. "Well, I guess now I know why you're back here helping us before ski season's over," she commented, still keeping her arm over my shoulder, as if she'd forgotten I was there. "What happened to your foot?"

Dell let go, and Keiler righted himself, mussing her hair with a lazy movement that was both playful and sweet. "Tried to catch a kid falling off the ski lift." Holding out his hands with a few feet measured between them, he added ruefully, "Big kid. I did a good job of breaking his fall."

"Oh, my gosh." Dell leaned down to investigate the nylon-and-Velcro cast, and Keiler pulled off his ski hat, dropping it on her head.

"Eeewww!" She squealed, tossing the hat on the pew, then slapping a hand to her mouth. "Oh, my *gosh,* you cut off all your hair!"

I wondered how much hair Keiler had before, because from where I was standing, he looked like he still needed a haircut. The thick brown mass came out of his ski hat, sticking up in all directions, seeming to have a will of its own.

He shook it out, grinning good-naturedly at Dell. "Got bored in the hospital. Did it myself. What do you think?"

"I don't know . . ." Dell mused, standing back to survey the haircut. *It looks like you did it yourself,* I thought.

"That's what the nurse said." Keiler ruffled Dell's hair again, then grinned and winked toward us.

I found myself smiling back. It would have been impossible not to like Keiler. The dusty, silent room came alive the minute he walked into it. He was like Tigger from the Winnie-the-Pooh stories, immersed in a cloud of lovable insanity.

Dell led him, limping, onto the stage, and made the introductions. When Keiler Bradford shook my hand and smiled, I felt like there wasn't anyone else in the room. He had a charisma that was unrelated to looks, fashion sense, or haircutting skills. He was simply authentic— that was the clearest way I could categorize it in my mind. His brown eyes sparkled with a magnetic enthusiasm for life.

"Guidance counselor?" he questioned, lowering a brow at me. "You don't look like a guidance counselor." In any other context, I might have been offended, but Keiler made it sound like a compliment, as if I must be something better than an everyday guidance counselor— Superwoman or Helen of Troy. Someone far too extraordinary to have a regular job.

"Today she's our dance instructor," Karen interjected. "Mrs. Mindia couldn't come."

"Well, that makes more sense," he said as he unstrapped his guitar and set it on a chair. "You look like a dancer."

I could have sprouted wings and floated right off the stage. For the first time in months, I had a sense of being myself again, as if everything I was and everything I'd worked for hadn't died that day on the dressing room floor. Even now, I looked like a dancer. When Keiler Bradford said it, I believed it was true.

Dell jumped in with confirmation. "Ms. Costell studied at *Harrington*. She was, like, with the KC Metro and everything." Lifting her hands, she let them fall against her thighs with a slap. "She helped us with Jumpkids the last two Fridays, and she's, like, such a good dancer. I wish I could learn to be like that. Ms. C is way cooler than the other teachers at Harrington, too—well, except maybe for Mr. Verhaden, because he's cool, too—but Ms. C tutors me at lunchtime, so she's my favorite of all." Dell snapped her lips shut, probably realizing two things. One, all three of us were gaping at her, shocked by the flood of words; and two, she had just slipped up and revealed the fact that she needed tutoring.

Karen met my eyes with a questioning look, and I tried to act nonchalant. If Karen asked about Dell's grades here in front of everyone, I had no idea what I would say.

The back door opened, allowing a spray of light into the chapel, and all three of us turned to look, relieved to have the conversational cloud puffed away by the inflow of fresh air. I suspected that none of us wanted to delve into the weighty subject of grades and tutoring right here on the *Alice in Wonderland* stage.

A teenage African-American girl came in with a toddler on her hip, then kicked the door shut behind her and swaggered up the aisle with copious attitude.

"Hey, Sherita." Dell exited our circle and quickly walked a few steps toward the newcomer.

Nodding in response, the girl surveyed the stage, her gray eyes narrowing skeptically. "So what we doin' this time?"

"*Alice in Wonderland*," Dell replied hesitantly, watching for Sherita's reaction.

Pressing her full lips together, Sherita nodded toward me. "You Alice?"

I chuckled at the joke. "Ummm, no, I'm not, but I could probably arrange for you to be."

Sherita grinned, clearly impressed that I wasn't intimidated by backhanded adolescent humor. "That'd be some sight—a nappy-headed black girl playin' Alice. I don't do that little British schoolgirl accent too good. Anyway, I wanna be the evil queen. I can get with that off-with-their-heads stuff."

"Man, isn't that the truth," Keiler piped up.

Sherita did a quick double take, a broad smile lifting her face. "Keiler Bradford? Where'd you come from?" Taking stock of his rumpled outfit, she stopped when she reached the cast. "What'd you do to your foot?"

Keiler rolled his eyes wearily. "Tried to catch a kid falling off the ski lift. Big kid." He spread his hands farther this time, the rescued kid growing like a trophy bass in a fish story.

Sherita laughed. "Well, you'd think a dude with a education from New York University would know better'n that. You don't never, ever get between a fat boy and the ground. Don't they teach you that stuff at NYU?"

Keiler shook his head, and the rest of us chuckled.

Sobering, Sherita checked out the stage again. "Meleka's gonna be along for day camp in a little bit, but I gotta watch little brother for the day." She hiked the toddler onto her hip like what she really wanted to do was bounce him off into the eaves somewhere. "Can Myrone be a toadstool or somethin' in the play?" She glanced toward Karen for approval.

"Sure," Karen said.

"All right, then. I'll stay."

"Great." Karen seemed completely unaffected by the surly reply. "Kate's kiddos are back in the nursery with some of the church volunteers. Why don't you take Myrone back there for now? Myrone and Joshua can practice being toadstools together, and you can help us with the setup or the registration table, if you want."

Sherita shrugged as if it didn't matter to her either way, then turned on her heel and headed from the room, in a hurry to be rid of her little brother and moving on to something more interesting.

Keiler noticed me watching her go. "Don't worry; she's more lovable than she seems at first."

"Most of them are." That was the guidance counselor in me talking.

Keiler seemed surprised. *Under the blond hair, there is more than just a dancer.*

The idea caught me unprepared. For most of my life the dancer part of me was all that mattered, but standing here talking to Keiler Bradford, NYU grad and fashion-challenged ski resort worker, I liked the concept of being a competent professional.

"Guess you got your car fixed," Dell said, and I realized that both Keiler and I were lingering there watching Sherita carry Myrone away.

"Nope," Keiler answered, reaching into the costume sack and fishing out a pink headband with the White Rabbit's ears on it. "Traded my old ride in for a Harley. It was hard to say good-bye to the green Hornet. She's been a good car, but her time had come." Popping the ears onto his head, he smiled, looking like a cross between a ski bum and a deranged Easter bunny.

Sherita stopped at the door, glancing over her shoulder. "A Harley? You got a Harley?"

"You traded the green Hornet for a *bike*?" Dell breathed, spinning around and heading toward the door. "Cool!"

"I gotta see this." Sherita started after her, with Myrone already making engine sounds in her arms.

Bounding off the stage to follow them, Keiler hit the floor with a thud, then doubled over and gritted his teeth, grabbing his leg.

"You've got a cast on your foot," Karen reminded him cryptically.

"Yeah." He sucked in a breath with one eye squeezed shut.

Karen motioned toward the cast. "How in the world can you ride a motorcycle with a cast on your foot, anyway?"

"Oh, hey, not a problem." With a shrug, Keiler headed up the aisle. "It's a walking cast. Amazing how lightweight these things are now. Keeps my foot warm, too. I'm thinking, since I'm in this thing for four more weeks, maybe I'll paint it black and get that full-blown biker look."

"You don't look like no biker," Sherita observed, giving a sassy chin wiggle as she stopped to hold open the door. "If you're comin' out here with me, you gotta lose them rabbit ears. I ain't bein' seen on the street with no giant Energizer bunny." Keiler grabbed his ears defensively, and she slid out the door, letting it close in his face.

Winking over his shoulder, he grabbed the handle and disappeared into the sunlight, leaving behind the momentary shadow of a very tall White Rabbit with a bum leg.

"I adore him," Kate said, laughing as she began attaching a fake tree to the wall. "I absolutely adore him. If I weren't a married woman and ten years older, I would snap him up."

Karen rolled her eyes. "Yeah, you two could bum around the country, operating ski lifts by day and playing guitar in tourist traps by night." She was teasing, but the comment had a bite to it.

Kate gave her sister a scornful look. "Oh, Karen, leave the boy alone. He's enjoying himself. Might as well do that while you're young."

Shrugging, Karen pulled a clipboard from her briefcase and started checking off items. "I just thought, after working with Jumpkids last summer, he'd be inspired to do something a little more . . . serious. By twenty-six, most people have some idea what they want to be when they grow up."

"He's been working with the Indian school out there in New Mexico, and helping with the Special Olympics. That's serious."

Karen continued checking her list, then finally said, "You know what I mean. It's a shame to take a biochemistry degree and use it to operate ski lifts. He's so smart. Think what he could be doing."

"He wouldn't be happy in some office." Kate glanced toward the door as a Harley roared to life outside, the sound rattling the building. "I can't picture Keiler in a suit and tie. Whatever happened to seminary school, anyway? I thought he was going to seminary in Dallas."

Karen sighed like the parent of an unruly teenager. "Said he decided not to go. Said he didn't feel he was being led in that direction . . . something like that."

"Well, he'll figure it out." Kate went back to work. "There's a special purpose for someone like him. He'll end up being president of the UN or ambassador to Africa, or something."

"He probably will."

"I'm glad he's here, anyway."

"Me, too."

"How long is he staying?"

"He didn't say."

"*Where* is he staying?"

"He didn't tell me that, either."

"I'll call Ben and have him get the guest room ready at the farm."

"That's probably a good idea. Although, knowing Keiler, he might have brought a tent and figured on camping out. In February."

Kate chuckled knowingly. "Once a free spirit, always a free spirit. I'm just glad he's flitted our way for a little while."

"Me, too," Karen agreed.

As Jumpkids camp slowly revved up to full speed, it became clear how much Keiler was truly needed. The building filled with excited kids, and he was the center of their attention. They were fascinated by the tale of the ski lift accident, and by the Harley. When they lost interest in that, Keiler amused them with funny skiing stories.

The day fell into a comfortable, if occasionally frenzied, rhythm as we moved through the process of registering children who came to the camp from Hindsville and surrounding towns, assessing their various talents and interests, then dividing them into groups with Wonderland-appropriate names like the March Hares, the Cheshire Cats, and the Mad Hatters. I began my day with a dozen White Rabbits, who ranged in age from six to nine, and were the wiggliest bunch of dancers I'd ever worked with. Fortunately, their part of the program was uncomplicated, as was the entire production, a one-act *Alice in Wonderland* directed by an on-tape narrator and designed to be learned in a single day, then performed the next day. Dell stayed to help me with the dance class, which was good, considering that I didn't even know the steps.

Keiler poked his head in the door just as the White Rabbits were finally falling in step. "Snack time," he announced. My dancers promptly mutinied. Scampering from the stage, they clustered around him, trying to pull off his rabbit ears and asking when they were going to his station down the hall, where he'd been teaching the March Hares to play simple percussion instruments.

Holding his rabbit ears in place, Keiler shrugged toward the door. "I guess if nobody's hungry, I'll just leave. If these White Rabbits were hungry for some bunny chow, they'd be lined up at the door, ready to go to the fellowship hall." The kids promptly fell into a squirming column. Counting them off in eenie-meanie-miney-mo fashion, Keiler chose a little boy named José as the line leader. "OK, head 'em out, José," he said, and my dancers marched off like the Queen of Heart's playing-card soldiers.

Keiler motioned to Dell and me. "Time for snacks."

Glancing pensively toward the hall, Dell shook her head. "I'm gonna stay here, 'kay? I'm not hungry."

He eyed her sideways. "Dell Jordan, not hungry? Since when?"

"I'm just not, all right?" she returned sharply, and both Keiler and I blinked in surprise. "Sorry," Dell muttered, her eyes hooded.

" 'S all right." After studying her a moment longer, Keiler turned toward the door. "Your next group will be here in about . . . twenty minutes."

"Thanks," I said, then waited for him to leave before speaking to Dell. "Are you sure you're not hungry? It's been kind of a long morning already. A snack and a soda might be just the ticket."

"I don't want anything," she insisted, sounding less than convincing because her stomach was rumbling audibly. In that flicker of an instant, a dozen thoughts ran through my mind. *Why would she deny being hungry when she obviously is? Why does she want to stay here instead of going to the snack room? What if something deeper is involved?* I'd been about her age when I'd started obsessing about food—my body just beginning to develop the curves of a feminine figure.

Don't jump to conclusions, I told myself, but deep inside me was a fear that my problems could be spread like a contagious disease, and just by being around me, someone else might catch it. "Dell, is something wrong?"

Sighing, she focused on her hands. "I've got two nine-week tests on Monday, because this week's the end of the grading period. English and science. The study sheets are huge. I can't learn all that stuff by this weekend."

"How long have you known about these tests?" It occurred to me, of course, that we could have been studying for the past several days during our tutoring sessions.

"I don't know." Crossing her arms, she turned her shoulder to me evasively. "The teachers just told us Friday."

Even though the seventh-grade science teacher was young and inexperienced, and I couldn't stand Mrs. Morris, I knew that probably wasn't true. "Was it on the chalkboard?"

"I dunno . . ." she muttered reluctantly. "I guess so . . . maybe. But we had Jumpkids after school all week. I was gonna study this weekend." Her gaze fluttered upward, caught mine hopefully, then sank again.

"When, exactly?" I asked, trying to sound gentle, nonjudgmental, to lead her to form her own conclusions rather than hammering her over the head, as my parents would have done to me. "Because it sounds like you're tied up with minicamp all day today, then church tomorrow morning, then Jumpkids performance after church. When were you going to study?"

Flyaway strands of dark hair caressed the smooth cinnamon skin of her cheeks as she sighed, despondent at the reality of it all. "In between . . . stuff." Another hopeful glance fluttered my way, saying, *That'll be enough, right?*

I wanted to tell her yes. *Yes, you can spend the weekend singing and dancing in Wonderland, helping underprivileged kids whose schools offer no music classes, and then Monday at Harrington, things will magically work out.* Instead, I dosed up reality like castor oil. "You know that's not going to do it. Come on, Dell. Achieving passing marks this grading period is going to take some serious work, and you've been doing it. You can't whiff on it now just because there are other things you want to do."

"Karen needs me to help with Jumpkids." Uncrossing her arms, she flung her hands into the air, then let them slap to her thighs. "She didn't have anybody this weekend, and—"

"Dell." I cut off the litany of excuses. "Karen would understand, but the fact is that you're not telling her you need more time for your schoolwork. As wonderful as Jumpkids is, you can't spend all day at

Harrington, and all afternoon at Jumpkids, and, I suspect, all evening practicing your instrumental and voice pieces, and expect to pass your classes. Classes come first, and then all of those other things." How many times had teachers told me that—class comes first, then dance? I never believed it. At a place like Harrington, you quickly learn that the performance is what really matters. The rest is just window dressing— everyone assumes you've got the basics down, and nobody wants to hear otherwise.

The problem was that, in Dell's case, the basics were about to bring everything else to a crashing halt.

"You need to tell Karen and James the truth," I said softly, laying a hand on her shoulder.

Her eyes met mine, soulful, pleading. "Can't you just help me? With the tests, I mean? If you help me get through these exams, then the next nine weeks, I'll work harder, I *promise*. Please."

"Of course I'll help you." I sighed. "But you need to tell Karen and James the truth. You need to be honest with—"

"I'll get my backpack." She was gone before I finished the sentence, bolting like a caged rabbit making a dash for the escape hatch.

Chapter 16

*D*ell and I studied intently throughout our breaks, and during the classes, she stayed in the corner with her book as much as possible. She sat there with her head in her hands, making very little progress on her study sheet for English, except when I popped over and helped her find an answer. Her mind was clearly in Wonderland with the Jumpkids. When Karen, Keiler, Brother Baker, or one of the church volunteers came in, she hurriedly set down her book and joined the class, watching nervously to see if I mentioned her schoolwork to anyone else.

By the end of the day, I knew more about transitive verbs, subordinate clauses, and prepositional phrases than I had since high school. Unfortunately, Dell still hadn't memorized everything she needed to know, and there was also a list of forty literary terms to learn. I started mentally calculating percentages, ciphering how many questions she would have to answer correctly on a hundred-question test to achieve a passing grade.

In addition, we hadn't even cracked the science book yet, and science was not my forte. When the final dance group went outside to participate in outdoor recreational activities, Dell and I sat down in one of the church pews with her textbooks, both of us looking like we had to climb Mount Everest in a single day and the fate of the free world hung in the balance.

"Let's concentrate on science for a while." I was trying to sound positive, but the statement fell flat. I was tired from a full day with the Jumpkids, vaguely aware that I had grant writing work to do at home, and surprisingly hungry because we had skipped both snacks and rushed through our lunch to catch a few extra minutes of study time.

"I know the science a lot better." Dell raised her eyebrows hopefully. "Mr. Duncan's a really great teacher. We did most of the study sheet in class."

"Good." *Finally, a bright side.* "Let's see."

Opening the book to a diagram of the universe, she pulled out a study sheet that was at least ten pages long, front and back. I wanted to crawl under the bench, slink out the back door, and never be a guidance counselor again.

I was contemplating the idea when the door opened and Karen came in.

"Hey, you two," she said cheerfully as she crossed the room. "So, how did your day go?"

"Great!" Dell chirped. "It's gonna be a great play tomorrow . . . if the White Rabbits don't go crazy. They're kind of . . . well . . . bouncy."

Standing beside the pew, Karen smoothed a hand over Dell's dark hair, pulling it into a thick ponytail and circling it with her fingers. "Don't you want to go outside and play softball with the other kids?" She tilted her head, giving the textbook a confused look.

Dell's nose crinkled as she squinted upward, shrugging casually. "Nah, I've got some tests to study for." The implication was clear—*No problem, Mom. Walk in the park. Nothing to worry about.*

"Need help?" Karen asked.

"Huh-uh. Ms. C's helping me." Sliding the partially finished study sheet between the pages, she closed the book, as in, *Butt out, Mom. We've got this situation under control. No big deal.*

"All right." Releasing Dell's hair so that it spilled over her shoulders, Karen patted her shoulder. "Let me know if I can help."

"I will," Dell answered, giving Karen a happy-kid smile as she turned and walked away.

I bit my tongue until she'd left the room. What I wanted to do was jump out of my seat and say, *Time out! Wait! Everybody stop what you're doing. We've got a serious miscommunication here.*

But part of me knew that the truth needed to come from Dell, not from me. When Karen was gone, I turned to Dell, waiting for her to say something. Instead, she pulled out the study sheet, a silent cue that we should proceed with schoolwork, no discussion of other issues.

"Dell, you know that was wrong," I admonished, frustrated and at a loss as to how to handle the situation. "You do need help, yet you're telling your foster mother you don't."

"I don't like it when Karen helps me, OK?" Her answer was edgy and impatient. Flipping the science book open so that it clattered against the pew, she picked up the pencil and bent over the pages, pretending to focus on her study sheet. "I hate all these big words." Change of subject.

"No, Dell, it's not OK." Pushing the paper back into the book, I closed the cover and leaned forward with my hand holding it shut. "Karen and James obviously love you very much. It's not all right to lie to the people who care about you. It's little lies, and then it's bigger lies to cover up the little ones, and pretty soon you're so far down the hole, there's no way out." Everything in me wanted to grab her by the shoulders, shake her, and say, *Listen to me. I know this from experience.* "You can't lie about who you are to try to make people love you." Touching her face, I lifted her chin, so that she was looking at me, her eyes dark and desperate. I saw myself at thirteen, afraid of the world. Afraid of being unwanted. "Because then it isn't *you* that they love. It's someone made-up, like a storybook character. That kind of love leaves you empty inside. In your heart, what you really want is for someone to love *you.* The real you. People can't if you won't let them in."

Her face said it all. *How could anybody love me? My real parents didn't.*

The door opened and both of us jerked upright. Dell ducked her head, rubbing her face on her sleeve as Keiler entered the room carrying a plastic storage tub filled with percussion instruments and flutophones. Setting down the box with a groan, he stretched his back and held his injured foot off the floor.

"Looks like you shouldn't be carrying boxes around," I said.

He smiled confidently. Sometime today, he'd lost the rabbit ears and gone back to the ski hat with MENTAL on the front. "Nah, it's fine. I'll be kickin' up fresh powder again in no time."

I chuckled as he hopped closer. "I think you're off the half-pipe for a while, radical dude."

His lips spread into an even white smile. "You like to ski?"

"Love it. My parents used to have a cabin in Durango. We went every Christmas and spring break when I was a kid."

Clearly, Keiler was impressed. "Ski or snowboard?"

"Depends on the snow," I quipped, then felt compelled to admit the truth. "I'm really not that good, but I love the mountains."

"Yeah, me too," he agreed wistfully; then the conversation ran out, and he tipped his head to look at Dell's schoolwork.

"Studying science?"

Dell frowned up at him, opening the book and displaying her worksheet. "There's nine-week tests on Monday in English and science, and I've got to get the rest of this study sheet filled out." Why she'd suddenly decided to tell someone the truth, I couldn't guess. I hoped it was something I'd said.

"Ahhhh." Keiler raised an eyebrow. "I'm no good with English, but you're looking at Mr. Science." Pressing a splay-fingered hand to his chest, he feigned modesty, then grabbed a chair from the *Wonderland* stage, brought it back to the pew, and sat down. "Let me see that review sheet."

Dell handed the paper over as if it were a hot potato and she lacked an oven mitt. "Ms. C is helping me with the English."

Keiler winked at me. "I can see you're in good hands. Did Ms. C happen to ask you why it's two days before the test and you're just now getting the study sheet done?"

Dell's head sagged against her arm. "Yes." She sighed, sensing another lecture coming on. "She already asked me that."

Leafing through the papers, Keiler nodded. "Well, then, I won't bother repeating the question." Laying the paper on the bench, he pointed to an empty line blank. "This one is 'atmosphere,' and the next one is 'hydrosphere.'" He studied the page while she wrote in the answers. "The one at the bottom of the page is probably 'nitrogen,' but let me see the book for a minute. Mmm-hmm, see, read this sentence." He pointed to the book. " 'The most abundant gas in the Earth's atmosphere is . . .' " He let Dell fill in the blank.

"Nitro-gen." Sounding out the word, she wrote it in and pointed to another question. "What about this one? It's, like, an essay question, and I don't know what he means."

"Let's see . . ." Keiler read the question, then started flipping through the chapter and finally pointed to a diagram. "It's asking how and why the atmosphere on Earth is different from other planets. So why is it?"

Dell rolled her eyes. "Because God made it that way."

Keiler chuckled. "True, but how does it work?" Limping over to the instrument box, he pulled out a flutophone and played a few notes. "For instance, would you be able to hear this on . . . say . . . Venus?"

"Well, no, because you'd be dead on Venus." She cocked her chin to one side, silently adding, *Duh*.

"Exactly." Wheeling a finger in the air, he sat down in his chair again. "Why?"

"Because you can't breathe the gases in the atmosphere there." She held her palms up, impatient with the elementary line of questioning.

"And why does Earth have an atmosphere you can breathe?"

"Because the plants make oxygen and the ozone layer keeps out the radiation from the sun."

"Rrrr-ight!" Grinning, Keiler marked an invisible scoreboard hanging between us. "See? You just answered an essay question on why the Earth is different from other planets. So, think about what you know, and then explain it in writing just like you're explaining it to me. The secret to essay questions isn't knowing everything; it's making good use of what you do know." Propping his injured foot on the pew, he rested an elbow on his knee and watched as Dell started writing the answer with more enthusiasm than I would have thought possible. I sat marveling at him, amazed, impressed, and, in an odd way, envious of his ability with kids.

Brown eyes twinkling beneath the MENTAL hat, he grinned at me and made the OK sign behind Dell's head.

"I wish English was this easy," Dell muttered, and my mind went back to the English study sheet. If only she could whip through that as quickly as science.

My mind drifted to the matter of talking to Karen. One way or another, I had to make her aware that Dell needed help, and more study time—whether Dell wanted to admit it or not.

When the science worksheet was finished, Keiler sent Dell outside to get a little exercise before she started in on English again. Sliding over to the pew, he leaned back with his fingers intertwined behind his head. "Long day."

"A little," I agreed. "But it was good."

He motioned to Dell's schoolwork. "So, I take it that classes aren't going so well."

It probably wasn't the right thing to do, but I told him the truth. "No, they're not, and she doesn't want to admit it to her foster parents."

"That's pretty typical." Picking up the flutophone, he moved his fingers over the holes, listening to music I couldn't hear. "When you're a foster kid, there's always this honeymoon period during which you convince yourself that if you're helpful enough, and sweet enough, and charming enough—perfect enough—the new family will love you and let you stay. I was just a little older than Dell when I finally got out of the foster care system, and even though I wanted it, moving into a permanent family was a tough adjustment." His eyes were soft and contemplative, focused on the colored light from the wavy stained-glass windows. "James and Karen love Dell, but it'll take her a while to understand that. Love is like Santa Claus—if you don't believe when you're young and innocent, it's hard to buy in later. But it's not impossible." He shifted his focus until we were tangled in an intertwined gaze. "I believe in Santa Claus."

"You'd think, being Mr. Science, that would be a little hard. Considering the physics of flying reindeer, and so forth."

"I've worked it all out," he said softly.

"I'm not quite there yet," I admitted, suddenly wishing I had the kind of blind faith he was talking about—the ability to trust in things I couldn't see. When I was passed out on the dressing room floor, I dreamed I saw Grandma Rice as an angel. The doctors said it was the result of an electrolyte imbalance—probably true, because I continued to hallucinate everything from angels to jungle animals for days, until my electrolytes leveled off.

"Of course, I have the benefit of having seen a few flying reindeer after surgery a couple years ago," Keiler joked, and I had the odd sense that he'd read my thoughts. "Saw the Easter bunny, Napoleon, the Wicked Witch of the West, and Super Mario chasing Pac-Men around the room, too. But the flying reindeer were real."

"Me, too." My focus narrowed, came inward until I was aware of breath coming in and out of my lungs, and the pulse drumming steadily in my neck. I felt a kinship with Keiler that I couldn't explain. "I had some pretty wild hallucinations when I was in the hospital for . . ." I stopped just short of blurting out the whole truth. "Well, long story, but they said it was caused by my electrolytes being out of whack."

He nodded, and I felt, in the strangest way, validated. "For me, it was a brain tumor, but the principle is the same."

I drew back, surprised, at who he was. Former foster kid looking for love, brain tumor survivor, Santa Claus enthusiast, NYU grad, and Mr. Science, masquerading as a guitar-playing ski bum with a broken foot. There was much more to Keiler Bradford than met the eye.

"I'm sorry," I said, realizing I was staring at him, wondering why he didn't seem like damaged goods. How did he find the strength to lumber through life with a grin on his face and a twinkle in his eye? Why couldn't I do that? Why couldn't I convince myself to drop the load of guilt and self-loathing, let go of the past, and move on with the business of living?

Playing the "Theme to *The Pink Panther*" on the fluteophone, he lightened the moment, then set the instrument aside, rested his head in his hand, and said, "So, how's the skiing in Durango?"

We fell into an easy conversation about ski resorts and wild spring-break trips with busloads of college classmates. I gleaned that he was not always the clean-living, bunny-ear-wearing nice guy he was now. His foster parents, he said, deserved to be nominated for sainthood for taking him in at fifteen, a kid with a hardened heart and a bad attitude, and showing him unyielding patience until he finally grew up. Now they were both retired from professorships at NYU and living in the Upper Peninsula of Michigan—conveniently near skiing, Keiler noted.

He was describing their house on Lake Michigan when Dell came back in with Karen. They crossed the room looking purposeful, and for an instant, I fanned a hope that they'd had a heart-to-heart about the upcoming tests, but Dell seemed much too pleased to have been discussing the issue of school. When they reached us, she stood with her arms clasped behind her back, looking expectantly up at Karen.

"We were hoping you'd come on out to the farm and have supper with us." Karen smiled pleasantly, obviously unaware of Dell's situation. "It really is the least we can do after you saved our lives today. I'm sorry I didn't think of it sooner, but we would love to have you."

"Oh, I don't . . ." Pausing, I caught Dell's hopeful gaze. I was momentarily torn. On the one hand, I really wanted to join her and her family for dinner. On the other hand, I had a pile of work to do at home and so far, no substitute teacher for algebra class next week. If I had to teach algebra again I would go crazy, first of all, and second of all, it would be impossible to finish the grant application in time. "I really shouldn't—"

"Pleeeease?" Dell curled her hands under her chin in a begging-dog imitation.

Karen frowned sideways at her. "Dell, Ms. Costell might have things to do." She turned to me. "We understand, if you do. We can give you a rain check. . . ."

Needling me in the arm, Keiler shrugged toward Dell and mouthed, *C'mon. . . .*

The decision sifted through my mind as everyone watched me. *Maybe I could make substitute teacher calls on my cell phone. . . .* "Are you sure I won't be in the way?"

Keiler gave me the thumbs-up.

"Oh, no, of course not. We'd love to have you," Karen reiterated.

"Yes!" Dell cheered, like her team had just hit a home run in the World Series.

I couldn't remember the last time I'd felt so wanted.

Chapter 17

While the rest of the crew was busy arranging Jumpkids materials for tomorrow's performance, I went to my car to make calls on my cell phone. I started by dialing home to check on Bett and tell Mom and Dad I'd be late. Waiting for Mom to answer, I drafted a mental list of explanations for my all-day trip to some little town she had probably never heard of. Fortunately, Dad picked up. Mom was still over at Bett's, making chicken soup to help my sister along the road to recovery.

Dad was stuck home babysitting Joujou and gathering his income-tax materials for the CPA. When he was finished with that, he had an online meeting with his fantasy baseball club. Every week without fail, Dad gathered with numerous other perfectly sane adults who, as nearly as Mom and I could decipher, pretended to be the managers of Major League Baseball franchises. Before the season started, they drafted teams, and then all summer long they carefully tracked the imaginary progress of their imaginary players, in hopes of eventually winning the pretend World Series. Dad had never even made the division finals, but struggled on through the thrill of victory and the agony of defeat, dreaming of one day achieving fantasy baseball glory.

"How's the baseball draft going?" I asked, after he'd run through his list of evening activities and finished complaining about income taxes and how this year would surely leave him in the poorhouse. "Hope those fantasy baseball players work for fantasy paychecks."

Dad gave a sardonic laugh. "You all can ridicule me now, but when I win the World Series, you'll be sorry. I won't invite you naysayers to the awards ceremony in Las Vegas. Joujou and I'll go alone. Just the two of us." I could tell he was cuddling Joujou close to his face. She was growl-whining into the phone, enjoying her daddy time.

"Be sure you buy her something nice to wear."

"Very funny."

"Just think, you'll fit right in with the high rollers in Vegas, with that fine-looking blonde on your arm, or . . . well . . . in your arms . . . or on a leash. Anyway, she's blond."

Dad scoffed indignantly. "At least Joujou believes in me." No doubt this was one of those times when my father wished he'd been blessed with a houseful of boys, rather than three women and a neurotic Pekingese.

"I believe in you, Dad." It felt good to be joking with him rather than talking about food, or Mom, or what I was doing and when I would be home.

"I know you do, honey," he said tenderly.

I was filled with a rush of warmth that I couldn't put into words. These past months, Dad had been a rock, always solid, always on an even keel when the rest of us were falling apart. I wished I could tell him how much that meant. Instead, I talked about baseball. "Hey, I heard that one of the teachers at school might have a pair of Kansas City Royals season tickets to sell. I thought maybe I'd check into it—what do you say?"

Dad didn't answer at first; then he finally smacked his lips suspiciously and said, "You hate baseball."

"Yeah, but for you, I'd do baseball, Dad." There was a world of unspoken appreciation in the statement. I hoped he understood the things I couldn't say.

"That's my girl." He chuckled softly, then let me off the baseball hook. "Maybe instead of season tickets, we could just do a game or two."

"All right, Dad. I'll see you later on this evening. It might be late."

"Leave your cell phone on, all right? Mom tried to call earlier and got your voice mail. You know she worries."

"Yes, I know, Dad." I could feel us slipping into the same old routine.

"Where did you say you are?"

My body tensed up. Now we would have to go through the litany of explanations. "Helping with an arts minicamp. I'm going to stay for dinner, so it'll be a while."

"All right." And then the sound of papers rustling. His mind was already back to the taxes and fantasy baseball. "Be careful driving. Call us when you're headed home."

"I will. Bye, Dad." Hanging up the phone, I fished the substitute teacher list from my briefcase and began making calls. Once people went out for Saturday night, it would be that much more difficult to fill the vacancies.

Propping the paper on the dashboard, I started down the list. The sad story of the teacherless algebra class netted me three answering machines and four negative replies. The prospect of having to teach math all next week, on top of having been AWOL half of the weekend, loomed large on the horizon. I said a little prayer that one of the answering-machine owners would call back and accept the job.

A knock on the passenger window startled me from my thoughts, and I looked up as Dell opened the door.

"Karen said I could show you the way out to the farm, and they'll be along in a little bit. Kate needs to get some stuff at the grocery store for tomorrow, and Keiler's gotta fill a prescription for pain medicine for his leg. Kate said he's probably not supposed to be riding around on a Harley, and he ought to leave it here tonight and ride out to the farm with her." With an exasperated eye roll that was a perfect imitation of Karen's, she added, "He's such a goofus."

"He seems to be," I agreed, moving my briefcase out of the way so that she could slide in.

She reacted with a look of concern. "But Keiler's, like, real smart and stuff. He only seems like a dope. He's really not."

"I can see that," I agreed, charmed that she felt the need to defend her friend.

"He's, like, really cool and stuff. He does all those silly things on purpose, so the kids will have fun. He calls it the Jumpkids secret—if he's the biggest gooberhead in the room, none of the kids feel too embarrassed to try stuff." Her face brightened with sincere amazement. "It works, too. It's hard to feel stupid when Keiler's around."

I started laughing, and Dell smiled sheepishly as we pulled out of the parking lot. "Turn left here, then right at the next one, then left on the highway," she said, pointing down the road. "It's about ten minutes to the farm."

"All right. Here we go." Piloting the car through the small-town streets to a winding ribbon of highway into the hills, I had a sense of moving farther from my own world and deeper into Dell's. I imagined her growing up in this tiny town, living in some ramshackle house along the riverbank, maybe riding her bike up and down the rocky slopes by the water, like the kids at the edge of town were doing. Far from any house, unsupervised and unrestricted, they glided down the hill with their jackets flapping and their feet spread out like stabilizers. At the bottom, they zipped under the highway bridge, then pumped up the other side.

I slowed to watch, recognizing Sherita among the group, and thinking that where I came from, kids would never be allowed such unstructured folly.

I was struck again by how it must be for Dell, having one foot in this world and one foot in another. It was no surprise that she felt like the shoes would never fit. Beside me, she leaned closer to the window, as if she wanted to be with the other kids, gliding down the riverbank in the late-afternoon sunshine. "Want to go for a walk when we get home?" she asked. "Just for a little while, and then we can study?"

I felt a rush of sympathy. She looked tired, worried, slightly lost—a little girl in mismatched shoes. "Sure. That sounds great. I bet both of us could use a break."

"We could go down to the river."

I pictured the river being like the one in my dream. "That sounds good. I'd like to see it." We fell into silence, Dell lost in her thoughts, while I remembered the sensation of dancing on the current, bathed in sunlight. Before the dream, I'd been empty and useless, ragged as I drifted into sleep. Those emotions seemed far away now, and I realized I hadn't fallen into that pit lately. I was healing in some way, growing stronger, slipping more firmly into the body of this new woman, this guidance counselor who was searching for a mission in life.

When did that happen? How did it happen? I couldn't say, but looking over at Dell, I knew that she was part of the answer. Somehow in helping her, I was finding my way out of the darkness.

"Turn there." She pointed. "That's the road."

I piloted the car into what looked like a long gravel driveway leading lazily through a winter-bare farm field, then uphill toward an old two-story white house, high atop a bluff overlooking the river.

"What a pretty place," I commented as we drifted past an ancient hip-roofed barn and started uphill toward the neatly kept clapboard structure.

"That's Grandma Rose's house." Leaning to peer out the front window, Dell pointed toward it. "Kate and Ben live there now, though. And their kids, Josh and Rose. Grandma moved out and gave them the big house. She said the little house was closer to the river, and she liked it better because she could open the windows and hear the water passing."

I imagined having a river running by my bedroom window, falling asleep to the sounds of the current trickling over rocks. "That must be wonderful."

Dell nodded solemnly. "I used to hear the river from my granny's place. Sometimes I'd lay and listen to it until late at night. It's a good sound. Like music."

"You must miss it."

"Sometimes," she whispered, then lifted her shoulders and let them fall in a gesture of helplessness. "Karen got me a little fountain for my room. It doesn't sound the same, but I like it."

"That's nice." Reaching across the car, I squeezed her hand. "It's OK to miss the way things used to be. It doesn't mean you're not grateful for the way they are now. Both lives are always going to be part of you, Dell. That's the way it should be. The past is always part of who we become."

Her eyes searched mine, as if she knew those words weren't just about her. "Do you miss being a dancer?"

"Sometimes." The word hung in the air between us, barely a whisper. "I miss how it felt. The good parts of it."

Her fingers squeezed mine. "Me too," she said.

Pulling up behind a detached three-car garage, I turned off the ignition. By the yard fence, a dark-haired man was trimming the winterbare branches of a climbing rose and tossing the clippings into a barrel.

Dell waved to him as we got out. "Hey, Uncle Ben. This is my guidance counselor, Ms. Costell." She introduced us from a distance. "I'm going to show her the river before everybody else gets here, OK?"

"Sure, go ahead." Smiling, he lifted the pruners into the air in greeting, and we waved in response.

"Where's Rowdy?" Dell called.

"Not sure." The man returned to his pruning. "Out chasing rabbits or burying bones. You might run into him on your walk. He's missed you."

"My old dog lives here now," Dell explained. "He wasn't happy in the yard in Kansas City." Leading me away from the car, she angled toward a small guest cabin out back. "The trail's behind the little house." She glanced over her shoulder at the driveway as if she were afraid someone would prevent our escape. Skirting the yard fence, we slipped through a seemingly impenetrable wall of barren blackberry brambles to a well-worn forest path. Ahead of me, she moved with a natural grace, her body twisting and curving in and out of overhanging branches and dangling briars, her passage as soundless as a slip of breeze, as if she were as much a part of the landscape as the soil and the trees.

I stumbled along behind her, stopping to push back tree limbs and pry myself from the clutches of marauding brambles. Dell moved farther ahead, seeming to have forgotten I was there. When she disappeared around a bend in the trail, I had the disquieting sensation of being alone in the forest. A moment later, I passed through the last of the dry underbrush and emerged on the riverbank. Dell was standing at the water's edge, mesmerized by the play of light and shadow. I watched, thinking of the girl in the river. Even now, was part of her wishing the current would rise up and carry her away?

She looked over her shoulder at me, her eyes narrowing contemplatively.

"It's beautiful," I said, but my voice seemed out of place.

"I'll be back," she whispered, then turned and crossed the shallows, hopping easily from rock to rock. On the other side, she used a nest of exposed sycamore roots as a ladder and disappeared into the tall brown grasses.

Glancing uncertainly up and down the river, I considered following or waiting, then finally decided to cross the water myself. Other than sliding one toe briefly into the icy current, I made it across relatively unscathed, and climbed the opposite bank to a well-worn path that led through the dry leaves and up the hill. At the edge of the woods, the trail disappeared among thick unmowed weeds and cattails, now clothed in winter brown. A dog barked somewhere nearby as I pushed through the tangle and emerged on a gravel road. Turning toward the sound, I surveyed a row of decaying cracker box houses, the yards strewn with the carcasses of rotting furniture, trash, and discarded bits and pieces of automobiles. In front of one of the homes, a dog was straining at its chain, barking at Dell, who stood motionless in the road. She seemed oblivious, transfixed by something beyond the bend. Moving closer, I followed her line of vision toward a tiny house crouched in an overgrown field where the road turned. The place may have once been painted pale green or white, but was now just a fading relic with weathered wooden siding and a sagging roof partially bare of shingles. The entire structure leaned toward the river, as if it might slide down the slope and float away when the spring rains came.

"That's where we lived." Dell spoke the words with some amazement. Her eyes reflected the road, the decaying houses, the cornucopia of trash in the ditch. "I guess somebody else lives there now."

I was momentarily mute. It was hard to believe that anyone could be living there, or had lived there recently. The distance Dell had come in the months since her grandmother's death suddenly seemed so much more vast, her talent for music that much more amazing.

"I guess so," I whispered, tugging the zipper upward on my jacket as a puff of breeze traveled past, warning of a cold night ahead. I tried to imagine what it would be like surviving the winter in that tiny house, where, as Dell had written, the walls were paper-thin.

Her gaze moved slowly back and forth, scanning the yard, the house, the rotten mattress, box springs, and recliner in the ditch. Watching her, I understood her in a deeper sense, and I realized something important about my job. Dell was coming from a place I couldn't imagine, but so were all of the kids who passed me in the halls at Harrington. Some lived in good places, and some lived in difficult places, and I would never be able to tell the difference just by looking. In order to know who they really were, I had to go below the surface.

"What do you think of when you look at your old house?" I asked.

Shrugging, she turned her shoulder to it and started back the way we had come. "I think it's gross," she said flatly, her lips a thin, determined line. "I can't believe I lived there."

Falling in step beside her, I sighed softly, and she glanced over, surprised. "But there's part of you that misses it," I said.

"No, ma'am." Her steps quickened, as if she couldn't be gone from the place fast enough and wished she hadn't been drawn to return there. "What's there to miss? It's a rat heap, and my granny was out cold on the couch most of the time from all her prescriptions, and I slept on a mattress on the floor, and half the time nobody got me up for school, or all the clothes were dirty, or there wasn't any food in the house and all the food stamps were used up. Who would miss that?"

"Someone who suddenly feels a lot of pressure to keep up," I said, watching my tennis shoes crunch through the dead grass as we crossed the ditch again. "To keep a schedule, keep up with grades, and music practice, and spring performance with the symphonic, and relationships with a new foster family."

She shrugged. "But those are good things."

"Yes, they are, but sometimes we can get so focused on all those outside things that we don't find time for the inside ones." I pointed to my heart, swallowing an unexpected rush of emotion. "And while we're

ntil'ssobigwe

doing all those outside things, the to-do list in here is getting longer and longer and longer until it's so big we can't face starting on it."

Lips twisting into a one-sided smirk, she turned toward the trail again, her hair swinging around her shoulders. "Like when you clean the room by stuffing everything under the bed, and pretty soon you don't want to look under there at all," she interpreted. "Grandma Rose told me always sweep out under the bed and clean the closets; then you'll be happy to have folks over to visit."

I chuckled at the analogy. "Exactly. That's it exactly. We all need time to look through the closet and consider what's in there. We've stored all that stuff for a reason. It's all part of who we are. If we let it stack up, then pretty soon we're afraid to have anybody over, because we're hiding a mess."

Grabbing an overhanging vine, Dell flipped herself onto it like a gymnast, then sat looking down at me from above. The vine was worn smooth, as if she'd completed the maneuver many times before. "You sound like Grandma Rose."

"Thank you," I said, and moved on down the path, feeling surprisingly content with the footsteps I was walking in.

By the time we reached the farm, Karen and Kate were in the kitchen preparing supper, and Keiler was in the yard giving lawn-chair airplane rides to Kate's kids, preschooler Josh and toddler Rose. The afternoon was growing dim, and an evening chill was coming in, so they followed us inside. We sat at the table with Ben as Kate and Karen took prepackaged lasagnas and garlic bread from the oven, and set them on the table with a hastily prepared salad and bottles of dressing.

"Sorry it's nothing fancy," Kate said as she and Karen sat down. "I figured easier was better, considering that there wasn't anyone home to cook."

Coughing indignantly, Ben raised his hand. "Excuse me, what am I—Casper the Friendly Ghost? I'll have you know I slaved away all afternoon putting this together—boiling those noodle . . . things, and putting those other"—he leaned over to examine the concoction in the prefab foil pans—"things in there." Grabbing the spoon, he scooped small portions onto Josh's and Rose's plates to cool. "See? I sliced mushrooms, and made minimeatballs, and put in some kind of white . . . cheese-looking stuff."

Frowning, Rose bent close to her high chair tray, then curled her top lip. "Eeewkie," she said.

"Not eewkie," Ben countered, pilfering a minimeatball and popping it in his mouth. "Good stuff. Daddy made it."

"Eeewkie," Rose insisted, and the rest of us laughed. Then Keiler said grace over us, and Ben began dishing up lasagna. Only when my plate came back with a huge helping and a butter-covered piece of garlic bread did I consider the ramifications of having to eat in front of strangers—especially having to eat something as fattening as lasagna and garlic bread.

As I took a helping of salad, all the old excuses ran through my head—

I'm not feeling well. . . .

I'm on a diet. . . .

I have this food allergy. . . .

I ate a big lunch. . . .

That was delicious. May I use your restroom?

The rest of the table, completely unaware of my insane mental dialog, fell into a conversation about Keiler's road trip from New Mexico.

Taking a deep breath, I started picking at my food, trying to focus on the table talk rather than my plate. Keiler was telling the ski lift story again. The kid who fell on him was up to a hundred and eighty pounds by now.

Dell started laughing. "Sherita told him not to get between a fat boy and the ground."

"That sounds like Sherita," Ben observed. "So where does the Harley come in?"

Keiler began telling the tale of his wild night stranded in a truck stop–slash-Harley-repair-shop, during which he developed an understanding of biker Zen while sitting around a burning trash barrel with a traveling motorcycle gang. By morning, he had traded the broken-down green Hornet and the remainder of his ski resort salary, plus a small injury stipend, for a Harley that probably had more miles on it than the green Hornet. He ended the story with a hand over his heart and a few words of homage to his old car and his lost nest egg, then closed with, "Guess when I get back to the folks' place in Michigan, I'll have to get a job."

Kate pointed a fork at him playfully. "Hopefully, something that doesn't involve ski lifts."

Frowning at his foot, propped on an extra chair beside the table, he nodded. "Not this year, anyway."

"I wish we could keep you on at Jumpkids," Karen said, giving Keiler a weary look. "We're so understaffed, and Mrs. Mindia's daughter just called and told me Mrs. Mindia has a serious case of the flu, and they've taken her to the hospital, so it might be a while before she's back. You could stay at our house, but I don't have any salary money available until summer internships start." Her brows lifted hopefully. "We'd feed you." Kate elbowed her, and she sagged, hatcheting the air with her hand. "I'm sorry; ignore me. Begging has become second nature since I took over Jumpkids. I didn't mean to put you on the spot."

The table fell silent as everyone dived into the food.

An idea struck me, and I jerked upright like a cartoon character with a lightbulb overhead. Everyone, including Keiler, turned toward me. "Are you interested in substitute teaching?" I blurted, and they all sat staring, surprised by the out-of-the-blue question. Keiler leaned forward curiously, and the prospect of having possibly found an algebra teacher for next week sent a tingle of exhilaration through me. "Seriously. It's not *great* money, but it's not horrible. I'm desperate for subs every single day, and there's almost no one on the list who hasn't already subbed the maximum number of days." Raising a finger in a gesture of eureka, I grinned from ear to ear. "But *you* haven't subbed at all, so you'd be good for . . . gosh, almost the whole rest of the year, even without teaching certification. School hours are eight to three thirty, so you'd have afternoons free for Jumpkids, or . . . Harley rides . . . whatever." I realized I was babbling, probably looking as desperate as I felt. The strange thing was that I didn't care. "Please?"

Karen turned to Keiler expectantly. "She's not even going to apologize for begging."

"I have no shame," I admitted. "If I don't get someone, I'll have to teach algebra next week. I hate algebra."

"It'd be so cool if you were at Harrington!" Dell gasped. "C'mon, Keiler. Say yes. You can stay in our guest room and ride to school with us. You and James can play guitars at night, and stuff. It'll be . . ." She searched for a word, then finished with, "Cool."

Tipping his chin back, Keiler pretended to think, his gaze shifting to and fro, as if he were weighing his options. "Sounds cool," he said finally.

"There are no ski lifts involved," Kate chimed in.

"We-hell, sounds like I got me a job offer," Keiler drawled.

"Absolutely," I rushed out, then bit my lip. "You do have to fill out some paperwork and a few things. You don't have a criminal history, do you?"

Grinning, he leaned across the table, his eyes twinkling. "Not that anybody knows about."

"Good enough for me." I was surprisingly excited about the prospect of his coming to Harrington. "You're hired."

"Better get a haircut," Ben interjected, and the rest of us burst into laughter before returning to our lasagna.

We finished dinner with conversation about Jumpkids, and Harrington, and the question of Jumpkids procuring used instruments from the Harrington storage room. When Dell described the number of discards, everyone was amazed. Keiler, it turned out, had worked his way through high school in a music shop, and knew something about fixing instruments. Soon, we were all making plans to save the world. Or at least add a little more music to it.

By the time we cleaned up the dishes, I felt surprisingly comfortable at the farm, as if I'd fallen into the fold of a second family. Looking at my plate, I realized I'd eaten most of my lasagna and wasn't even worried about it. As Keiler and Ben took the kids to the living room, I helped Karen carry some of the leftovers out to the spare refrigerator in the guesthouse. Walking along the path, I took in the myriad stars, my breath floating like smoke on the air. In the farmhouse, I could hear Kate's children squealing and Keiler telling a story that included numerous voice impressions.

"I have to apologize for the mess out here," Karen said as we strolled along the stone path. "Kate and I just recently started cleaning out the little house. It took us a while to bring our minds around to the task, after Grandma Rose passed away."

My focus was still hovering thousands of miles from the earth. "I didn't realize your grandmother had passed away." The comment sounded strange and a bit insensitive, so I quickly explained, "Dell talks about her so often, I just assumed she still lived here, and maybe she happened to be gone today."

Karen shrugged apologetically. "You're not the first one to make that assumption. Grandma Rose passed away over two years ago, but Dell has never really let go. She has a habit of talking about my grandmother in the present tense. She says she has dreams about Grandma and they talk to each other. It's one of the things we've had a little . . . issue over. We've tried not to make a big deal of it. Dell has had so many adjustments in the past few years. I think pretending she can still talk to Grandma Rose is a coping mechanism. They were very close before my grandmother passed away."

"Does Dell talk about her biological grandmother?" I asked, as we walked up the steps to the guesthouse. "The one she was living with, I mean."

Karen opened the door and turned on the lights in the cabin. "Not really. She's never been willing to discuss it, and her caseworker's advice was not to force her. Her grandmother only died last summer, so it's all still pretty fresh." Turning on a floor lamp on the other side of the room, she set the leftover lasagna on a small dining table and regarded me in the uneven amber light. "Has she talked to you about it? About her real family, I mean?"

"Some," I answered.

Looking wounded, Karen searched my face as if she might read Dell's words there. "What does she say?"

I wanted to bridge the self-imposed gap between Dell and her foster mother, but I knew it wasn't the right thing to do. "Give it time. There's a lot she's trying to work out in her head, but it wouldn't be ethical for me to divulge things she has said in confidence."

Karen sighed. "I understand."

We hovered for a moment in uncomfortable silence, and I found myself wishing I hadn't carried the salad bowl out to the little house. Things were easy when the whole family was laughing, talking, joking, and the room was filled with activity, but alone here with Karen, I felt a new kind of pressure.

Flipping on the kitchen light, she came back for the lasagna pan, but stopped instead, facing me. "Is Dell really doing all right in school? I notice that she's been studying a lot lately, and now you're tutoring her. But whenever we ask her about Harrington, she gives us glowing reports. Every day we get some glittering story about rehearsal, or her music for the symphonic, or the new friends she's made in the lunchroom." Karen's brown eyes searched my face with a compelling need. "Is she making those things up?"

I winced, caught between loyalty to Dell, Karen's need to know the truth, and some counseling ethics class I could barely remember. "I think you should talk to her about it. I know she's having a hard time opening up, but that's not a rejection of you. It's a self-defense mechanism."

"I know." Threading her fingers together, she kneaded her hands in frustration. "We understand that—James and I. It's just that we want to give Dell what she needs. We realize that she's struggling with her past, and we want to help her. We love her so much."

I had the overwhelming urge to comfort her, but the counselor voice inside me was saying, *Be professional; remain detached*. . . . "And she loves both of you too. Her deep investment in the relationship makes her desperate to protect you from anything ugly or unpleasant. It's going to take time for her to believe that your love isn't conditional upon her being perfect all the time."

Karen's lips trembled, and she pressed her fingers against them. "What do we do in the meantime? How hard do we push? How can we help?" Tears glittered in her eyes, and she wiped them impatiently. "James and I have never been parents. We don't know exactly what's normal with a girl her age, and on top of that, she's not an ordinary thirteen-year-old. We thought Harrington would be great for her—that the chance to pursue her music would help her open up to the world. Dell really wanted to get into Harrington, and we wanted it for her, but now I have a sense that things aren't right. Maybe we should have encouraged her to go to school out in Prairie Village, near our house. But the thing is, with Jumpkids being headquartered downtown and James gone overnight for work several days each week, she would be latchkey, and her opportunities to pursue music would be limited. . . ." She turned away, then back. "I feel like we're failing her, but I don't know what to change."

I realized she was looking to me for solutions, suggestions, professional advice, and I was woefully underqualified to offer anything. "I think some of those answers are going to have to come with time," I hedged. "But I can tell you that more quiet hours are needed for her studies. As much as she loves Jumpkids, she needs to spend more time on her schoolwork."

Karen blinked at me in complete surprise. "I ask her every day if she has homework, and she either says no, or just a little—that she can do it on the drive home, after Jumpkids."

I couldn't help smiling at Karen's naive reaction. Obviously, she was farther past adolescence than I was. *A teenager, lie about homework?* "Many days it may be true that she doesn't have actual homework, but that doesn't mean she wouldn't benefit from rereading some of the day's lessons. Study time may be something you have to enforce. Her reading comprehension is low, but she is working on it, and the more she reads, the more she will improve. You might think about getting her a tutor a few days each week, maybe a student a few years older than she is."

"I'll talk to James about that. Could you help us find someone?" Karen seemed ready to take the situation in hand—perhaps a little too ready.

I felt the need to put on the brakes. "I'm sure I can help you find a student tutor, but keep in mind that Dell isn't going to be happy about my telling you any of this, so it might be best to progress as naturally as possible into a homework schedule, closer monitoring of her assignments, talking to her teachers. She's working very hard right now to pick up her averages before the nine-week grading period is over and report cards go home. If she feels like the cat's out of the bag, she might give up. My advice is to see where she's at when report cards come out, then slowly begin making adjustments as needed."

Karen frowned at the wait-and-see approach. She seemed like the type who wanted to keep things under control, which was why she was so good at running the Jumpkids program. Chewing her bottom lip, she nodded slowly, then sighed and said, "Thank you for giving Dell special attention. Other than musically, no one at Harrington seems to have much interest in her needs."

"School is a busy place," I replied. At least a dozen other responses ran through my mind, none of which was appropriate to share with a parent.

Karen seemed to sense that there were things I wasn't saying. She waited to see if I would offer anything else, then finally said, "I want you to know we really appreciate it. Dell has needed someone to talk to—someone with counseling experience, I mean. She sees her case-worker, Twana Stevens, here in Hindsville every two weeks, but it hasn't been very productive. Dell associates Twana with the trauma of being placed in emergency foster care last summer when her grandmother died. I don't know if Dell will ever move beyond that issue with Twana. She needs someone else, and we're very grateful she has you. I know you've got a lot of kids to look after." Glancing at her watch, she winced guiltily. "And speaking of that, Dell was counting on some more time with you before you left tonight. I hope we're not keeping you too late." Grabbing the lasagna, she put it in the refrigerator, then came back for the salad bowl.

"No, it's fine." I thought of my cell phone in the car with, no doubt, a dozen voice-mail messages from my mother. "It's a beautiful night for a drive. No rush, but I'd probably better call home, so no one worries."

"Why don't you use the phone out here? There's a lot less racket," she suggested. Flipping off the kitchen light, she crossed the living room and opened the door, letting in a rush of cold air. After our conversation, she looked as pensive as Dell had earlier. I felt sorry for both of them, trying to feel their way through building a family. "Just leave the lights on when you're done. Dell and I are staying out here tonight."

206 · Lisa Wingate

"All right," I replied. "It'll only take a minute." I waited until she descended the porch steps before I called home. To my surprise, Mom still hadn't returned from Bett's, and Dad was in the middle of his online fantasy baseball meeting, so I was off the hook with a "Drive carefully, sweetheart."

Hanging up, I stared at the receiver in amazement. I felt almost like a grown-up, an independent, responsible adult. I'd called home and there wasn't one question about food, or when I'd be back.

A light knock sounded on the door as I sat there marveling at the phone.

Dell came in carrying her English books. "Am I bugging you?"

"No, you're not." I patted the sofa beside me. "How's the studying going?"

Opening the book, she handed me her English papers, some of which she must have worked on while the rest of us were chatting after supper and cleaning up the kitchen. "I think I've got the study sheet done, but can you check it? I know some of the literary terms, too." She measured the amount with a narrow eye. "Maybe about half."

I turned the study sheet around so that I could read it. "You have been working hard." An unexpected burst of pride made me smile. Suddenly all the lunches in the storage room seemed worth it. "Now let's see what we can do about getting you ready for this English test."

Chapter 18

There are occasional Mondays when you awaken with a sense that more than just two days must have passed since Friday—when the world appears new and fresh, and you have a feeling that this week, everything will be different.

Monday morning, I couldn't sleep past five o'clock. I awoke with my thoughts racing through grant ideas, a plan for a community outreach program that would encourage Harrington kids to volunteer with Jumpkids and other organizations serving the neighborhood. Beyond that, there was the thought that, when I arrived at work, Keiler would be there. His application packet had already been filled out online, forwarded for a background check, and sent to Mr. Stafford, who was thrilled with the prospect of fresh meat in the substitute-teaching arena.

All in all, things were coming out rosy, and I looked like a hero. I'd even managed to complete an entire section of the grant proposal on Sunday. When I e-mailed it to Stafford, he responded by saying I was a wonder. The comment smacked of *"Good girl, Costell,"* but I chose to ignore that and just be happy that everyone was . . . well . . . happy.

I dressed and gathered my grant-writing materials with a renewed sense of enthusiasm for my job—for life, actually—then I headed downstairs, beating Mom to the kitchen again. Dad was just making coffee, and Joujou was by the door waiting to be let out. Releasing her into her outdoor playpen, I quickly fried some bacon and made French toast, so Mom wouldn't have to cook. She needed a break, after hovering over Bett all weekend.

When the first batch was off the griddle, I stood at the counter, eating dry French toast while cooking the remainder of breakfast. Surprisingly, Mom didn't come in to see what I was doing. Dad said she was exhausted, and he'd turned off the alarm to let her sleep.

"Breakfast is here when you're ready," I said, then grabbed my purse, briefcase, and the box of grant-writing materials. "I'm heading into work early. I want to swing by the cleaner's and check on Bett's dress, and I have a new substitute teacher coming today, so I can't be late."

"All right, honey." Kissing me on the cheek, Dad returned to his latest listing of fantasy baseball statistics. "Have a good day."

I paused in the doorway, amazed. No *Be careful driving?* No *Did you eat?* No *What time will you be home tonight?* Just a perfectly normal *Have a good day.* "You too, Dad," I said. "See you tonight."

"Julia?"

Stopping with my back to him, I steeled myself. Now would come the well-meaning questions. "Hmmm?" I turned halfway, and his lips were curved slightly, making his eyes smile also.

"You look very pretty this morning—like your old self." His jaw trembled with emotion, and I realized again how much this man, who was my dad but not my father, really loved me. "That color suits you."

I glanced down at my pastel-blue pantsuit, knowing it was nothing special, and it wasn't the pantsuit he was talking about. If I hadn't had my arms full, I would have walked back into the kitchen and hugged him. Instead, I said, "Thanks, Dad." I smiled back at him, and he winked.

"Go get 'em, Tiger."

He hadn't called me Tiger in years.

I headed off to work feeling good about my day. *My day*—that was how it felt, as if I had the world by the tail, and the day belonged expressly to me. Even the traffic seemed to cooperate, and after an easy trip across town, I was waiting outside the cleaner's when Granmae sent

Justin and Shamika off to school. Justin gave me a hug. He must have known it was *my* day.

Releasing me, he peered across the street, said, "There da mens again," and waved at two men who were setting up survey equipment across the street. When they pretended not to notice him, he smiled and waved again, cheerfully calling out, "Hey, cops!"

"Justin!" Grabbing his arm, Granmae yanked him away. "You stop with that, now, and git on off to school."

"But Mim said—"

"Mim shouldn't be tellin' you that stuff. Now git."

"What 'bout my angewl?" he protested, and Granmae went through the motions of plucking invisible cherubs from the air and dropping them on the kids' shoulders. "There you go. Now you two hurry all the way. Don't look left nor right, jus' straight to school. No talkin' to nobody, and stay together."

"Yes, ma'am." Shamika took Justin's hand, and he leaned against her grip, staring cross-eyed at the shoulder of his jacket.

"Did I det a boy angewl today?"

Bracing her hands on her ample hips, Granmae leaned over him. "No, you didn't get no boy angel. You too rowdy for a boy angel. You got that little blond-haired one that don't know the neighborhood." Glancing at me, she winked. "She got a pretty blue suit on, so don't you get her dirty, y'hear?"

"Yes, ma'am," Justin replied, looking disappointed as he turned and followed his sister down the block toward school.

"That boy!" Granmae grumbled good-naturedly, but my attention was fixed on the van across the street. CITY LAND AND SURVEY, the side said in faded lettering. Watching the men as they set up their equipment, I wondered if Justin could be right—if the survey crew could be an undercover police unit. Peering through his lens, the surveyor used sign language to relay letters and numbers to his helper, who returned to the van to operate some sort of ten-key device. Standing up for a moment, the surveyor glanced down the street and refocused his scope, then looked through the lens again and signaled more numbers. I followed his line of vision to the taco stands.

Not the taco stands—the cars.

He signaled another set of numbers and letters: 423, followed by three letters.

License plate numbers. Suddenly, it all made sense—the survey crew this morning, the men sitting outside in the dark pickup truck when I'd come by the cleaner's before. Different disguises, but they were always watching the street. Police surveillance—like something in the movies, only real. This morning, the survey crew was taking down license plate numbers of customers at the taco stands. With the long lens, they could stay far enough away to remain unnoticed.

What if some of those license plates were traced to Harrington students?

My perfect day fell to my feet with a heavy thud.

When I looked up, Mim was walking along the sidewalk with her flower cart, the wheels making a slow *creak, creak, creak* that echoed off the buildings, growing louder as she approached the survey crew. The surveyor jerked away from his scope, surprised when Mim stopped her cart and handed him a single yellow rose. With a wave and a smile, she turned in our direction and proceeded to cross the street.

Sniffing the rose, the man tucked it in the pocket of his coveralls, shaking his head in dismay as Mim wrestled her cart over the drainage tile and into the dry cleaner's parking lot.

"Mim, what're you doin' bothering them police officers?" Granmae asked.

Straightening the hump in her shoulders, Mim peered up at her and smiled as she met us on the stoop. "Oh, they're no bother to me."

Granmae turned her attention to me. "Here's our girl that asked about the weddin' flowers."

Mim squinted at me. I had a feeling she'd forgotten who I was, which didn't bode well for the eventual delivery of Bett's rehearsal bouquets. Finally, she shook a finger in the air, then turned back to her flowers. "I have something for you."

"For me?" What could she possibly have for me? Hopefully not the bouquets, two weeks early. Even Mim's flowers couldn't last that long, although the three roses I'd given to my mother still looked amazingly fresh.

Mim sorted through her flowers, her knobby hands moving from bucket to bucket, parting the blooms, then letting them fall back together again. "I have hidden it somewhere, and now it's so safe, I can't find it." She pushed stray hairs out of her face. "But if folks on the street saw it, they would want it, and it's for you." Finally, she lifted one of the buckets, shoved it into Granmae's hands, and fished something from between two egg crates. "Well, here it is," she said, coming out with a single perfect rose—perhaps the most beautiful I had ever seen, ivory, almost iridescent, with the slightest tinge of pink blushing the edges and tracing the intricate network of veins. "Ask your sister if she would like these in her bouquets. They would be heavenly for a spring bride."

"It's beautiful," I whispered, bringing the bloom to my face and taking in the scent. "Does it have a name?" As soon as I showed Bett this rose, she was going to want them in the bouquets from the floral shop, as well. It was, indeed, the perfect choice for the antique dress.

Mim gave a crafty smile, her pale blue eyes astute, as if she sensed that I might be cutting in on her market. "Oh, who can say?" she replied evasively. "It is from a very old plant. The old ones are not only beautiful, but they carry scent, as roses are meant to. Many of the new ones might as soon be plastic. They are all for show."

I nodded in agreement as the air around me filled with fragrance, pushing away the smell of damp sidewalks, exhaust fumes, and tacos being served up down the road. "I can't wait to give it to Bett."

Mim patted my arm, then turned to Granmae. "Have you shown her the dress yet?"

"Not yet. I was just seeing the children off to school."

Impatient with the answer, Mim circumvented us and tugged her cart up the wheelchair ramp. "Well, let's go. I can't wait for her to see."

Holding open the door, Granmae waited for Mim, then ushered me inside and headed around the end of the counter. "We been puttin' some serious time in on this old thing," she said, but I was watching the survey crew across the street, wondering what they were going to do with those license plate numbers, and how I should react. The idea of Harrington kids being caught in a drug sting was unbearable. The scandal could destroy the school.

Yet, if a pervasive drug problem was being swept under the rug, then the school was neglecting the kids.

Which was worse?

I heard the wedding dress swish onto the counter before I saw it.

"Well," Granmae said, "feast your eyes."

"Of course it is far from finished," Mim added. "We still have more to do on the details."

Breath caught in my throat. There, suspended over the counter, in a spill of ivory satin, French lace, and seed pearls turned golden with age, was the dress from my mother's wedding pictures. It was incredible. What Granmae and Mim had done with our tattered relic was nothing short of miraculous.

"Oh," I whispered, stepping closer, touching the fabric, tracing a finger along the ivory lace, blinking back a mist of tears. "It's perfect. You can't imagine how happy this will make Bethany." Looking up, I caught Granmae's gaze, then Mim's, wishing I could express my gratitude for every careful stitch. "It's her dream."

Mim smiled tenderly. "What a fine thing to be the answer to someone's prayers."

I sniffed and nodded, grateful that with all the ways I had failed Bethany as a sister, I would be able to do this one thing right. I could show her how much I loved her before she left, and our lives moved onto new paths.

Granmae responded to the release of emotion with a grunt. "It's not finished yet. It'll look better when it's done." Drawing the dress back across the counter, she hung it on a hook by the wall. "There's still more work on the train, but we cleaned and despotted it, restitched the seams, did the alterations, matched up the lace that was missin', and Mim is workin' on the seed pearls and addin' on some other antique ones that match. It'll be ready to go by Friday. That way, you'll have a week before the weddin', like you wanted."

"Thank you so much." The words hardly seemed adequate. No matter what the bill was, it wouldn't be enough.

The bell rang behind me, and a man stepped in with an armload of dirty laundry. Saying good-bye to the ladies, I left them and hurried on to work, my thoughts again returning to the question of a police stake-out and whether Harrington kids would be caught in it.

When I walked into the school, the first face I saw was Keiler's. He was standing by the office door with a beaten-up backpack slung over one shoulder, charming Mrs. Jorgenson with the story of his broken leg. The rescued kid had grown to the size of a junior sumo wrestler—the story like something that would be on the cover of *The National Enquirer:* World's Largest Eight-year-old Crashes Ski Lift, Injures Operator . . .

Mrs. Jorgenson was laughing hysterically and fanning her face. "So, then, where did the biker gang come into it?"

Keiler raised a finger astutely. "I thought you might ask that," he said, and Mrs. Jorgenson laced her fingers, resting her chin on them, waiting for the rest of the story. I noticed that Keiler hadn't gotten a haircut, but he had tried to comb it. "You see, that wasn't until after the ski resort, when the green Hornet broke down at a truck stop some-where in Colorado. The foot wasn't in such bad shape until the me-chanic dropped part of a Harley on it. Nice guy, though. He felt so guilty, he traded me a used Harley for the green Hornet and every last dime I had left in the world. So, that, to answer your question, is how a perfectly sane—well, all right, mostly sane—biochemistry grad from NYU ends up here as a substitute algebra teacher."

Mrs. Jorgenson tucked an application packet, undoubtedly Keiler's, into a file, the laugh lines around her eyes deepening. "Thank you for clearing that up. I have to say, I was definitely confused when I saw your résumé."

"It's all right," Keiler replied, taking a step backward into the door-way. "I have that effect on people, but, hey—better to confuse than to be confused, Confucius say. Unless you're a teacher, which, come to think of it, right now I am."

Setting the folder aside, Mrs. Jorgenson gave him a thumbs-up. "You'll do fine," she assured him. "They'll love you."

"That's what Julia said." Keiler motioned to me. "Well, actually, she said she'd pay any amount of money to get out of teaching algebra this week." Catching my glance, he smiled.

I felt as if I'd just walked into an empty house and found an old friend waiting there to help me make the place a home.

Shaking her head, the secretary waved us off as she reached for another stack of papers. "You've brought in a live one here, Costell. Take him down and show him the classroom, will you? Mr. Beaman left lesson plans for the week on the computer. Just log in as Beaman, and they should come up."

"Sure," I said. "Come on, Limpy."

Turning around in the doorway, Keiler waved farewell to the secretary. "I never get the respect I deserve," he complained, then started down the hall without me.

Mrs. Jorgenson motioned covertly for me to come closer. "Where'd you find him?" she asked.

"Volunteering with an after-school arts program this weekend." Leaning back, I glanced out the door. Keiler had reached the end of the entryway and was standing at the T, looking up and down the main hall. He'd just noticed the ladybugs.

"I hope he stays." Jotting something on a sticky note, she stuck it to her phone. "He'll loosen the laces around here a little." Pulling the sticky note off the phone, she wadded it up, tossed it in the trash, and started writing another one. "Cute, too, in a rock-'n'-roll kind of way. Too young for me, though." Tapping the pen on the desk, she blinked at me pointedly. *Not too young for you.* Mrs. Jorgenson was newly single at forty-six and always on the lookout for available men. She had a bad habit of giving me unsolicited dating advice.

I chose to ignore it, as usual. Instead, I glanced toward Stafford's office door—still closed, no light underneath. "Where's Mr. Stafford?" As soon as Keiler was settled in, I wanted to catch Stafford and tell him about the police stakeout. Maybe then he would take the drug issue seriously. The first step would be to reinstate the big, ugly stick-on Harrington parking decals, so that the kids would be recognized wherever they went. The second step was probably to call the drug prevention officers and set up some town hall meetings with parents. There was also the issue of bringing in the drug dog when the kids were present. . . .

"Out sick. The flu again." Mrs. Jorgenson was busy with her sticky notes. "High school principal's gone to the central office all week for budget meetings, and Mr. Fortier will be in and out. He's chaperoning soloists at the district instrumental contest, so I guess we're in charge around here."

I waited for her to say, "April fools," but she didn't. "Will you let me know if Mr. Stafford calls or makes it in? I need to talk to him."

"Sure thing," she replied cheerfully. "Oh, your mom phoned a few minutes ago. She wants you to call her."

Great, I thought, *just great.*

I caught up with Keiler, who was following a trail of ladybugs down the wrong hall. "This way," I said, and we did an about-face.

"That's amazing." He gaped upward at the ladybug jamboree around the light fixture. "There must be thousands of those things."

"Don't mention that to the principal when you meet him," I advised. "It's a sore spot." Keiler gave me a wry sideways grin, and I added, "No ladybug pun intended."

We continued down the hall, taking a quick school tour and talking pleasantly about Jumpkids camp, the weekend, Harrington school, and how I ended up back as a counselor after having attended as a dancer. Making the story sound neater than it was, I quickly moved on to a description of the classes he would be teaching that week. "You'll have all the algebra classes," I said, "so, that's the upper deck of eighth graders and a few high-scoring seventh graders. Those who are mathematically challenged, like I was, take prealgebra in the eighth grade."

Keiler quirked a brow at me. "It's hard to imagine you as mathematically challenged."

"You don't know the half of it." I was flattered enough that I actually blushed. "You should have seen me trying to teach algebra last week. I can't remember any of that stuff—actually, I'm not sure I ever knew it. All I wanted to do in high school was get through my classes so I could keep dancing."

"Guess it worked," he commented with obvious admiration, as we walked into Mr. Beaman's algebra classroom. "Dell says you were with the KC Metro Ballet. That's pretty impressive."

The usual lump formed in my throat, then sat on my lungs like a weight. "It was good," I said, and then a strange thing happened. The lump dissipated, and instead of feeling lost and out-of-body, I felt I was exactly where I was supposed to be. "But eventually you have to grow up and join the real world."

Keiler flinched away from me, his lip curling in distaste. "Whose rule is that?"

"Well, maybe not all of us do, Peter Pan, but for me it was time." I focused on Mr. Beaman's computer and the lesson plans. "Change of seasons, you know—a time to dance, a time to move on. It was time for me to move on. I'm OK with it." And for the first time, I could tell that I really was. Somewhere between passing out on the dressing room floor and showing Keiler the algebra lesson plans, I had grown up and found myself.

It was a good feeling.

"I can see that about you. You're really solid about who you are." When I looked up, he was smiling slightly. "It shows."

I found myself smiling in return—from the inside out. It was the most affirming thing anyone had ever said to me. No compliment about my dancing, or my looks, or a performance in some show could have equaled it.

Chapter 19

By Thursday, I no longer had a handle on the meaning of life, and I was beginning to wonder if school administration was for me. Stafford was still out with the flu. Dr. Lee and Mr. Fortier were busy covering for sick teachers at the high school, attending yearly budget meetings at the central office, and dealing with the fact that the campus maintenance supervisor was out sick for the first time in twelve years. Most of the maintenance crew spoke only Spanish.

At the middle school, things were piling up on Stafford's desk, and I seemed to be the only one available to handle matters that couldn't wait. My days were a blur of minor discipline issues, building tours with prospective parents, a plumbing meltdown in the B Hall boys' restroom, and a health department inspection of the cafeteria. They said, of course, that we needed to get rid of the ladybugs.

I'd had absolutely no time to tutor Dell. She'd managed a "B" on Monday's science test, the English exam grade wasn't back yet, and she still had upcoming nine-week tests in math, history, and music theory, as well as chapter quizzes on *The Grapes of Wrath*. Fortunately, Keiler had stepped in to take up the slack. He'd managed to enlist the help of my hapless office assistant, Barry, who was good in English and writing. After the initial shock of having to actually speak to a girl, Barry had begun to strike up a friendship with Dell. I saw them walking down the hall together on Thursday afternoon, laughing and talking, oblivious to the crush of students around them.

As they passed, Dell pulled some papers from her notebook and waved them in the air. "Mrs. Morris finally graded the English tests." Propping her chin on top of the paper, she blinked at me, trying to keep a straight face to build the suspense. "I passed. I made a 'B,' " she blurted, waiting for me to read Mrs. Morris's grudging 80.5 at the bottom of the paper. "Minus, but it's still a 'B.' "

"Fan-tastic!" I wanted to grab her and give her a bear hug. We had been on pins and needles all week, waiting for the English grade. Mrs. Morris checked tests on Wednesday afternoons, and could not, of course, be bothered to make an exception. "So, a 'B' on the science test and a 'B' on the English test. Not a bad way to end the grading period, right?"

Blushing at the compliment, she lowered the paper and ducked her head. "Well, I still have nine-week tests in history and math."

"But she's good in math," Barry piped up, nodding vigorously in support of his new best friend. "And Keiler . . . errr . . . Mr. Bradford's helping her with history. They've been doing a unit on Indians, and, shoot, she's part Indian. That ought to count for something."

I chuckled. "I don't think you get extra credit for being part Native American. But it is kind of neat to study something that's connected to your own history."

Dell's brows drew together when I said "neat" in reference to her Choctaw heritage. "I don't think this unit's very interesting," she commented blandly.

"Gosh, I wish I was part Indian," Barry interjected with a hopeful smile. Dell's crossed arms conveyed her skepticism, and he added, "Really. I think it would be cool."

Her surprise was obvious. Somebody actually thought she was cool. I had the urge to plant a kiss atop Barry's chubby little head. If there was anyone, anywhere, qualified to be a one-man admiration society for someone who needed it, it was Barry.

"See," I said, leaning closer to Dell. "It's cool."

"I guess."

"But you are studying the material, right?" I pressed. "It's not going to study itself, and you need to pass your nine-week test in history."

"Oh, she's studying." Barry to the rescue, again. "Keiler and I helped her make an outline at lunch yesterday, and then today we went over it, and . . ."

The phone in my office rang, and I tuned out momentarily as Barry ran through a litany of Dell's study plan, while she stood patiently watching him. Only a person as quiet as Dell could tolerate someone who talked as much as Barry did when he was excited.

"That sounds good," I replied. The phone was on its third ring. "You two head on to class. I'd better answer that." Stepping back through the door, I caught Dell's eye and gave her English paper a thumbs-up.

Smiling, she waved it at me, then turned and headed off with Barry, who had started talking again. There was a lightness in her step that, in the past, I had seen only at Jumpkids. She moved down the hall with her shoulders back and her hair swinging in a ponytail, whisking back and forth. By his locker, Cameron stopped to take notice. My phone rang a fourth time, but I hung in the doorway, watching as Barry and Dell passed Cameron's locker. If he said anything to spoil their moment, I was going to forget the phone, launch myself down the hall, and release some stress in his direction. All week long, he'd been showing up for school in Sebastian's car, tardy half of the time, overly mellow and smelling heavily of cologne, which was probably a cover for the smoky-sweet scent of marijuana. By noon, he looked like a sidewalk bum with a hangover, and he couldn't stay awake in class. He didn't want to talk about it, and the way the week was going, I didn't have time to pursue him. As soon as he switched back to his dad's house, which would hopefully mean that he would arrive at school sober, I was going to call him in and at least try to get through to him, perhaps with Keiler's help. Cameron was one of his algebra students, and they seemed to be hitting it off. Two days in a row, I'd passed by Keiler's classroom on my way to after-school door duty, and seen Keiler demonstrating guitar licks to several kids, including Cameron.

Dell and Barry passed Cameron's locker without incident, and I dashed into my office, grabbing the phone from the wrong side of the desk, hoping it was Sergeant Reuper from the drug prevention task force. I'd put in calls twice this week, and so far he hadn't been in touch. I'd begun constructing a conspiracy theory in which Sergeant Reuper was dodging me because he knew that Harrington students were going to be caught in the stakeout of the taco stands, and he was afraid I would question him about it.

The voice on the other end of the line was a woman's. "Hello, Ms. Costell? This is Twana Stevens, with social services down in Hindsville. I'm Dell Jordan's caseworker. Do you have a few minutes to talk?"

A myriad of reasons for the call ran through my mind, none of them good. "Yes . . . uhhh . . . yes, of course. What can I do for you?" Side-stepping around my desk, I slid into my chair.

Her words seemed carefully phrased. "Brother Baker at the Baptist church here mentioned that Dell might have shared with you some information about her father?" She paused, perhaps waiting to see if I would jump into the conversation, then went on. "I don't know to what extent you're aware of Dell's background or home situation. . . ."

The sentence trailed off, and I felt obliged to interject, "She has told me some things about it, and there are various reports in her file." I stopped there, unsure of where the conversation was going, or how much I should reveal. Perhaps this woman, this voice on the other end of the phone, could unlock the secrets to Dell's history. "She is preoccupied with the question of her father's identity, as anyone in her situation would be." The irony of that statement struck me. "I think it's hard for her to move on with those issues unanswered."

She replied with another question. "But she hasn't given you any information about her father—maybe his last known whereabouts, a middle name—anything like that?"

The inquiry made me wonder if Dell really talked to her social worker, or if they just sat in a room looking at each other. "As far as I can cipher, she knows almost nothing about her father's identity, but there may be things she isn't telling me. Her file says that her father is part or all Choctaw Indian, and she seems to be aware of that segment of her heritage. She's resistant to discussing most things face-to-face, but she has been journaling some things about her life. All she's mentioned so far are some vague suppositions about a man her mother dated—someone with long dark hair. I guess that doesn't ring any bells?"

"None. I've only been on the job here for three years. Our dealings with the family during that time have been the usual game of hide-and-seek. As kids grow older, they become adept at playing the game. They see us as the enemy, so it's not surprising that she has been unwilling to reveal any information to me. I thought she might have told you more."

"Not about that. I wish I could be of more help, but to be honest, Dell's school file is somewhat hodgepodge. There's no father's name on any of her paperwork. Come to think of it, there's no copy of the birth certificate in the file at all. That's odd."

"Our files aren't what they should be either," Twana admitted. "Things slip by, especially in instances that don't involve imminent danger to the child. I'm trying to clear up Dell's papwerwork right now, the reason being that her foster parents intend to petition for adoption, and I'm doing everything I can to make that happen. But on her original birth certificate there's a father's name listed. Thomas Clay."

My heart skipped a beat, and I grabbed my notepad, carefully writing down the name, *Thomas Clay*. Dell's father. Did she know there was a name on her birth certificate?

"Does that sound familiar at all?" Twana asked. "Has Dell mentioned anyone by that name, or any relatives on that side of her family?"

"No. Never."

"Is there a reason she believes that this man who was dating her mother might have been her father?"

I thought about the things Dell had revealed to me, wondering how much I should share. On the one hand, there was her privacy. On the other hand, there was the issue of Dell's future with her new family, and her unanswered questions about her past. On the third hand, there was Brother Baker at the church in Hindsville, telling me that none of the men Dell's mother dated were very savory characters. "She only mentioned a feeling she had, and the fact that he took her to the doctor once when she was sick. That could be simple coincidence, or something more."

"All right." Twana paused, as if she were making notes. "Thank you for talking with me."

"Is there a specific reason you're trying to find the identity of her father—other than just clearing up her paperwork, I mean?" I interjected before she could close the conversation.

There was a contemplative pause, and then she lowered her voice in a way that told me we were talking counselor to counselor now. "Confidentially, this person, this Thomas Clay on her birth certificate, may be her father or may not be. Brother Baker says her mother had quite a reputation. But whoever this man is, legally he is her father. Before Dell can be cleared for adoption, he either has to relinquish parental rights, or we have to file to terminate them. We are obligated to attempt to notify him of this process. Considering that he has never had any contact with Dell, the easiest and quickest scenario would be for him to relinquish rights, or for us to determine that he is deceased. The other alternative is more complicated, but it looks like we may have to go that route."

"Do Dell's foster parents know all of this?" The word *custody* sat on my chest like lead. In my internship with social services, I'd learned more about the complicated world of child custody than I ever wanted to know.

"They're aware that we are trying to clear up Dell's file," Twana replied. "They're willing to do whatever it takes. Dell's lucky to have found people who love her so much. So many kids aren't so fortunate, especially kids her age."

"I see." I felt a need to end the conversation. My mind was a sea of what-ifs. What if Dell's father was found, and he decided to petition for custody? My time with social services had taught me that parents can have no interest in their children—right up to the moment someone else asks for permanent custody. Then suddenly, they're interested.

On the other hand, what if social services discovered that Dell's father was deceased? How would she feel about that? The last person who could give her the answers she yearned for would be gone.

The greatest likelihood was that he would never be found at all. *Thomas Clay* wasn't much to go on. Maybe the best thing I could do for Dell was encourage her to forget the past and move on with her future. . . .

Outside in the hall, someone was slamming lockers. Everyone should have been in class, so I probably needed to check on it. "I'm sorry I couldn't be of more help, Mrs. Stevens. Please don't hesitate to contact me if you need to in the future."

"Certainly, we will. Thank you Ms. Costell." She said good-bye, and I slapped the phone into the cradle. In the hall there was yelling, or wailing. Long, mournful sounds echoed through the corridor, and by the time I made it to my door, the hall was filling with chaotic noise as kids spilled out classroom doorways, trying to see what was going on, while teachers hollered for them to get back in their seats. Somewhere, Mrs. Morris was screeching, "Return to your rooms, all of you! Class is still in session! Anyone I see in this hallway will be going to detention!"

Near my office, an art class with a substitute teacher had bolted into the corridor, so that I couldn't see what was happening farther down. "Back in class," I hollered, herding them toward the door. "Back in your seats." They retreated to the doorway as the sub tried in vain to restart the lesson.

Shooing more kids toward their rooms, I cleared the hallway until I could see the source of the commotion. Halfway down, Cameron was standing with his back against his locker, slowly banging his head on the door, moaning something about a history grade, and his father, and how he couldn't take this anymore. "You're such a screwup. You're such a screwup!" he wailed, the words loose and slurred. "You should just kill yourself and get it over with. You're such a screwup. . . ."

Mrs. Morris was standing in front of him, one hand on her hip and the other pointing toward a classroom, saying, "You will stop this right now, young man. Back to your class this instant, or I am calling your parents." Beside her, the eighth-grade history instructor, a quiet, mousy second-year teacher who had constant discipline difficulties, stood dumbfounded, while other staff members delivered questioning glances from their doorways, uncertain whether to interfere, or let the history teacher and Mrs. Morris handle the situation.

"What's going on?" the geography teacher asked as I passed.

"No idea," I admitted. "I'm sure we can handle it, though."

"OK," she replied doubtfully, glancing toward Mr. Stafford's office, probably wishing he were there. "I'm here if you need me."

At the opposite end of the hall, Keiler rounded the corner, hobbling toward Cameron and Mrs. Morris as fast as he could.

"Call 'em. Call my parents. They won't care," Cameron wailed, emitting a string of expletives that set Mrs. Morris on fire. "They don't care." His head fell back with a metallic crash, and he slowly slid down his locker until he landed on the floor with his head in his hands, sobbing.

Mrs. Morris stood over him, her fists braced on her hat-rack hips. "Now, you listen to me, young man. That is enough of this foolishness. . . ."

Keiler reached Cameron just before I did. Sidestepping Mrs. Morris, he squatted down in front of the lockers. "Come on, Cam. You don't want to do this—not here. Let's go to the counselor's office and talk about it, all right?" He laid a hand on Cameron's shoulder, and Cam looked up, his eyes unfocused and dilated, filled with an inner desperation.

"I flunked my test," he cried, his head crashing against the lockers and rolling miserably back and forth. "I forgot it was today. I just . . . forgot. My dad's gonna kill me. He's gonna say it was because I was at my mom's."

Keiler gave Cameron's shoulder a squeeze and a little shake. "It's one history test in the eighth grade, Cam. It's not the end of the world."

"My dad's gonna kill me."

Sitting back on his heels, Keiler rested his hands on his knees, determined to stay there, squatting on the floor, as long as it took. "That doesn't seem real likely, Cam. Your dad's got . . . what . . . fourteen years invested in you? I doubt if he's gonna off you now."

Cameron blinked, his head bobbing as he tried to focus. "You don't . . . know my da-ad." The words were slushy, his eyes falling partway closed.

"You probably don't either, at this point," Keiler said gently. "Messed up like this, you don't have a clue what's real and what's coming out of the purple haze. What are you using today, Cam? You coming down off something?"

"No." Cameron sniffed, wiping his nose on his sleeve. "I'm just havin' a bad day."

"Cameron," I said, squatting down also, aware that kids and teachers were still watching, seeing and hearing everything that was going on. "Why don't we go talk about this in my office? There's no sense sitting out here."

"Darned straight," Keiler agreed, sliding a hand under Cameron's arm. "Why have a bad day in front of everybody? That'll only make it harder to get dates."

Cameron laughed drowsily. "Yeah. Thanks, Mr. Bradford."

Standing up, Keiler dragged Cameron with him. "OK, big guy, let's try to shape up and look good for the girls, now," he joked, and Cameron laughed again, then hung his head, probably aware, somewhere in the fog, that everyone had seen him crash and burn.

Keiler glanced back over his shoulder. "Can someone check on my class? They're supposed to be doing a study sheet."

"I'll handle it," Mrs. Morris barked. "I'm on planning period, anyway."

"Thanks, Ada," Keiler replied, and I could have fallen over from shock. Mrs. Morris had a first name? And Keiler knew it?

Even Cameron, as out of it as he was, didn't miss Keiler's unheard-of slip. "Bore-us Morris's got a name?" he asked, way too loudly. Then he proceeded to sing, "Aaaa-da, Aaaa-da," in a way that made the word echo down the hall.

Glancing sideways at me, Keiler frowned sympathetically. "Doubt if he's going to have a very good day in Accelerated English class tomorrow."

"Probably not," I agreed. After this, Cameron would be on Mrs. Morris's hit list, whether his dad was on the school board or not. Catching my breath as we moved down the hall, I mopped the nervous perspiration from my forehead. *Good God, what a day . . .*

When we reached the administration office, Mrs. Jorgenson was waiting outside the door, repeatedly tapping the tips of her fingers to-

gether, then pressing them against her lips, as if she didn't know what
to do next.

"You'd better call Mr. Stafford," I said as we passed. "He should decide how to handle this."

Mrs. Jorgenson winced. "I tried, but no one was home. Could be
he's gone to the doctor or something."

I vacillated as Keiler led Cameron into my office. I had no idea what
the school's policy was on an issue like this, and if I did the wrong thing,
it would be my head when Stafford found out. A situation of this type
required careful handling, especially with a high-profile kid like
Cameron. "Ask Mr. Verhaden—"

"Gone to that contest with the jazz ensemble," she cut me off.

Isn't anybody in charge here? I wanted to scream. *Think, Julia, think.
What would Stafford do?* I knew the answer to that question, of course.
Stafford would try to minimize the situation. I didn't want to be responsible for letting Cameron off the hook; nor did I want to open a
can of worms while Stafford was gone. "Call the principal's office at the
high school. See if Dr. Lee or Mr. Fortier can come over."

"I can try, but last I heard they were both gone to the district office—budget meetings, again. They're trying to convince the central administration that we need to go back to having a full-time assistant
principal. Mr. Stafford's been calling in every few hours to see how it's
going. I'm sure he'll call again soon"—her brows lifted hopefully—"if
you can just wait."

Wait. And do . . . what? Let the kid pass out in my office? Wrapping
my fingers around my neck, I had the strangest urge to squeeze off the
blood flow to my brain and sink into a peaceful darkness. Only because
Mrs. Jorgenson was looking at me expectantly did I feel forced to come
up with a plan. "Let me know as soon as you find someone. In the
meantime, call the nurse and tell her we're bringing him down there.
She'll need to monitor him to make sure he's all right. Call his parents
to come get him."

Mrs. Jorgenson swallowed visibly, tipping her head to peer at me
over the top of her reading glasses. "You want me to call the *parents?*"

"Yes." Why was she was gaping at me like I'd just blasted off for

Jupiter? "This is definitely a situation in which the parents should be notified. Their kid just went off his rocker in the school hallway."

"But he didn't . . . hurt anyone, or anything," she stammered. "He didn't really even"—raising both hands in a gesture that said, *Whatcha gonna do? Kids will be kids,* she finished with—"break any school rules or anything. Well, maybe not being in the classroom when he was supposed to, and causing a little disruption in the hall, but that's usually something we would just . . . handle." She checked the clock on the wall. "Especially this late in the day. School's out in an hour and a half."

I stared at her with my mouth hanging open. *Let me get this straight—you want me to leave a kid in my office, having a drug-induced meltdown for an hour and a half, so you won't have to make a phone call?* "Mrs. Jorgenson, that kid is coming down off something and he's crashing hard. His emotions are out of control, and he doesn't even realize what's going on."

She clicked her tongue against her teeth sympathetically. "Well, you know, he takes medication for ADD and depression, and once in a while, what with all the confusion with his folks, his mom says he gets his pills confused. I'm sure that's all it is."

What, are you nuts? I thought. *Has the whole world gone crazy but me?* If I let this go, and something happened to Cameron, I would never forgive myself. "Call his parents. Both of them."

"Mr. Stafford should be checking in anytime. . . ."

"Call his parents," I repeated. "Tell them he's had an emotional outburst at school, and we need to talk to them. If Staff . . . Mr. Stafford checks in, make sure he knows what's going on."

"All ri-hight." She sighed, as if I'd just burdened her to the max; then she turned around and headed for her desk.

In my office, Keiler was leaning against the file cabinet, while Cameron sagged in a chair, his eyes glazed over. The storm of high emotion seemed to have dissipated, and now he was sinking into sleep.

"How are you feeling, Cameron?" I asked.

"Not so good." Clamping a hand to his head, he moaned softly. "I'm so . . . I'm so . . ." His eyes fell partway closed; then he pulled them open again. "I'm so stooo-pid."

"You're not stupid, Cameron, but I think you've probably done something stupid. I think there are some things going on in your life you need to deal with, but drugs aren't the way."

His eyes opened, blinking in half-time. "I don't got"—sighing, he looked away—"issues. I just . . . just . . . did some . . . mixed up my ADD med-uhhh-cations. Tha's all."

Bracing his hands on his knees, Keiler leaned closer. "You're on a whole lot more than ADD medications, Cam." The usual easygoing tone was gone. This voice left no room for argument. "You're talking to the guy who's seen it all, dude. Why don't you tell me what your poison is today? Got a pretty good case of the sniffles going on there. You crashing off a little ice, or you been huffing something?"

Cam blinked again, his mood ricocheting from defensive to contrite as his eyes fell closed. "I'm sorry, Mr. Bradford. I didn't . . . did-did-didn't mean to—"

The nurse stepped in the door, and Cameron dragged his eyes open, giving her a lopsided smile. "Hey, Mrs. Harper."

Mrs. Harper, looking no different in her white skirt and bouffant hairdo than she had when I was in school, breezed into the office in her usual no-nonsense manner. "Did ya mess up your medications again, Cameron?" she barked. The question was obviously rhetorical. She'd already made up her mind.

"Yeah," Cameron mumbled. " 'M sorry."

" 'Sall right." Snaking a meaty hand under his armpit, she hoisted him up like a sack of potatoes. "C'mon. You can lie down in my office. Your mom's on her way to getcha."

"Why don't you just leave him here?" I suggested, touching her arm. "Cameron has some things he needs to talk about, and then when his mom comes, the three of us can have a chat."

Glaring at my hand as if she were considering biting it off, Mrs. Harper jerked Cameron toward the door. "Nope. This happened a time or two last semester—didn't it, Cameron? Mom's instructions are to take him to the nurse's office and let him lie down, and not to call Dad. It's just a mix-up with his meds. No point starting a family wrangle over it. Dad doesn't like him on the ADD meds and antidepressants in the first place."

"We've already called both of his parents." *And if we haven't, I'm going to.* "Both of them should be aware of what happened today."

"Nope." Mrs. Harper moved her patient efficiently toward the door. "We only call the custodial parent, unless the custodial parent's not available. Mrs. Jorgenson checked with me to be sure, and that's what I told her. This week his mom is custodial. Cameron doesn't change until Thursday night after supper, so technically he's with Mom until tonight."

"In this case, I think—"

Holding up a hand, she flashed the stop sign. *Talk to the hand.* "We don't get in the middle of disagreements between parents, divorced or whatever, Ms. Costell. Not our job." In a sweep of white fabric and antiseptic odor, they were gone.

I groaned in frustration, falling into my chair so hard it spun completely around. "I hate this place! Oh, God, I hate it, I hate it, I hate it. This place is driving me crazy."

"Only takes one barnyard cat to stir up an entire flock of chickens," Keiler observed wryly.

"I don't want to stir things up." I let my arms fall limp on the desk. "I just want to come to work, do a good job, go home. I don't want to think about Harrington night and day, but I also don't want to shuffle kids along, ignoring everything, as long as they keep it together on the surface." I was on a roll, and the words were tumbling out like high tide crashing over the seawall. "I won't be the one who teaches these kids that there's no room for anything less than perfect—that the way to succeed is to stuff everything down and let it eat you up on the inside. I did that for years here, and I know there were staff members who realized there was something wrong with me, who probably even suspected that I was cultivating an eating disorder. I can't tell you how many times Mrs. Harper found me throwing up in the bathroom, and she ignored it. Geez, not so many years ago, I was the kid passed out in her office, and all she did was pat me on the head and give me Kool-Aid. How can they watch these kids sinking and not throw out a lifeline?" I realized I'd just spilled my whole story to Keiler, and I didn't even care. I was so frustrated, I felt like exploding.

Keiler took it all in, his gaze the warm brown of solid ground. "Because they're treading water themselves," he said softly. "Sooner or later, to be any good to anybody else, you've got to swim for the boat."

His eyes held mine, and I saw an amazing strength, an abiding faith that was obvious, even to me. I understood now how he could drift around the country, living moment by moment with no particular plan. He was solidly in the boat.

Sitting up, I filled my lungs with a long breath, then turned to my computer and opened the student information database. "I'm going to contact Cam's father."

"I would," he replied, then left my office without another word.

Chapter 20

*C*ameron's father was out of town, not expected to return until late that evening, according to his secretary. She suggested that I leave him a message, either by voice mail or e-mail, so I did both. After that, I called the police department again and left yet another message with the drug prevention task force, this one asking if they would be willing to answer questions at a town hall–style forum, which I was planning to hold as soon as I could get it arranged. I didn't mention that I would somehow have to convince Mr. Stafford to go along with this plan. I was hoping that hearing about the police stakeout around the corner, and then Cameron's meltdown in the hall, might finally spur him into action.

I spent the afternoon compiling my drug prevention and intervention research into several pages for the Counselor's Corner of the school Web site. Keiler came by after school, on his way to parking lot duty, and tried to lure me to the afternoon Jumpkids session.

I realized that the final bell had just rung, and I hadn't even noticed. That meant Cameron's mother must have picked him up and left without even bothering to stop at my office.

Keiler didn't seem surprised. "I had a feeling that was going to happen," he said.

Rubbing my forehead, I imagined Cameron going home to his mom's, sleeping it off, then waking up in his usual clear-eyed-but-somber mode, and heading off for his dad's week, during which his father's intense before- and after-school supervision would keep him from hanging out with Sebastian. Probably.

I was glad I'd left the messages for his father. At least now Cameron's situation would be out in the open. "I can't imagine his mother not stopping by here. I really can't. What kind of a parent would do that?"

Crossing his arms over his chest, Keiler gave a knowing look that said, *Come on, Julia, don't be so naive.* "A parent who's busy with her own life. Or a parent who loves her kid and doesn't want to believe the worst. A parent who can't imagine that a bright, talented kid from a good home would be using. A parent who trusts her kid, who thinks he's too young for this issue, who's got blinders on, who doesn't think her baby would lie to her, who doesn't want the scandal . . ." Wheeling a hand in the air, he stretched the options on and on. Take your pick. "It's not hard to understand the science of denial. We defend the people we love, even when it's hurting them."

I nodded, thinking back to all the times my parents had accepted my lies, and how good I'd become at telling them. I was desperate not to be discovered. "You're right. You're right."

He nodded. "It's not hard for a kid to hide a habit, and it's not easy for a parent to stop a kid from using. From the time I went into foster care when I was ten, I was around kids who were using. We weren't into any hard stuff—just the usual recreational drugs kids consider harmless. As a kid, you think you're just taking the edge off, making life a little easier, and you're not hurting anybody. You think it's your own business and everybody ought to stay out of it. You defend it in all kinds of ways. I didn't feel the need to quit, even after I was adopted at fifteen and I knew I was going to be staying in one place and I knew my parents loved me and how disappointed they'd be if they found out I was using. I didn't quit until the day I got sick of myself, and I realized God didn't put me here to be a loser. Ultimately, life has to be a self-commitment, because everyone else you can fool."

I rubbed my eyes, still seeing the glowing white square of the computer screen. When I looked up, Keiler was watching me, perhaps knowing that I was painting an entirely new picture of him in my head.

He was more than the hapless Harley-riding guitar player with the baggy hiking pants and bad haircut. There was a depth of spirit in him that I had only just begun to see. He was light-years ahead of me on the emotional learning curve. "How is it that you know so much?"

"It's the hair," he quipped, pausing to turn an ear toward the door. "Wow, listen to that."

Moving away from the hum of the computer, I heard the faint sound of music. Somewhere down the hall, a chorus was singing what sounded like a medieval hymn. The notes drifted through the empty space, soft and angelic, giving the hallway the aura of an ancient chapel.

"That's Dell," Keiler said, as a soloist rose above the chorus. He started toward the sound, and I followed.

"They must be practicing the music for the Spring Fling," I whispered as we walked down the hall. Ladybugs were clustered around the auditorium doorway, as if they had stopped to listen.

Stepping inside, Keiler and I leaned against the wall, bathed in music as the girls' chorus rose to a crescendo; then the music softened, and Dell moved to the solo microphone again. There was no hint of timidity in her as she sang. Her voice filling the room, she tipped her head back, closed her eyes, and sang with her arms outstretched, like the girl in the river.

When the song finished, Barry, alone in the empty seats, stood up, whistled, and clapped. Dell laughed as the choir director shushed him.

Keiler applauded and shouted, "Bravo," from the back, and the director threw up her hands. Keiler had made inroads with her, also, because she didn't shush him, just shifted her hips impatiently to one side and stood there tapping her baton against her arms until he finished his ovation.

Dell slinked back into the chorus, blushing and grinning.

"She's amazing," I whispered to Keiler as the choir director started into a diatribe about hitting the notes and keeping the tempo.

Leaving the auditorium, Keiler and I walked back down the corridor.

"She's something," he said as he left me at my office door.

"Yes, she is," I agreed. "I knew she was fantastic at the piano, but I've never heard her sing a solo before."

"She has a musical soul." The look in his eyes made it seem as if he were talking about me, as much as about Dell.

"Yes, she does," I agreed, realizing that, no matter what else I did in my life, I couldn't let go my love of music and dance. It was a God-given passion I had to use. Somehow.

In the meantime, a plan was forming in my head. As I said good-bye to Keiler, I was thinking of Bett's wedding. So far, she hadn't been able to find a soloist on such short notice. It looked as if Bett's musical selections might have to be played on tape, which wasn't what she wanted. . . .

I was on the phone before Keiler was halfway down the hall. "I think I might have found a soloist for you," I said, then told her about Dell and how talented she was.

"Really?" Bett sounded interested. "How old did you say she is?"

"Thirteen," I answered, "but trust me, she's really good. Actually, I could probably get a whole chorus for you, if you'd like. I just heard them practicing for the Spring Fling, and they're wonderful. There are some benefits to working at an arts school."

Bett laughed. "As nice as that sounds, I think Mom would have a heart attack if we told her we needed to squeeze choir risers into to the solarium."

"When did we decide to go with the solarium?" Suddenly, I felt like I'd been deleted from the wedding planning loop. "I thought we were having the wedding in the country club's main hall."

Bett grumbled in her throat. "Mom wanted to use the hall, but you know what? I've always wanted a wedding in the garden, and, being as it's only March, the solarium is as close as we can come. It's available on our date, and last weekend I put my foot down, that's all."

"Last weekend?" I repeated. "Geez, where have I been?"

Bett paused to do something, and I heard the *click-click* of computer keys. "Sorry," she said when she came back on. "I'm trying to get all the fall showroom orders done ahead for the store. Saturday's my last day. As of this weekend, I'm unemployed until after the wedding and the move, and then I'll start putting out résumés in Seattle. Anyway, Mom said you'd been really busy with work this week. She said she's hardly seen you."

"The principal has been out sick." I felt like I was making excuses for not being there to discuss matrimonial details. "But, listen, I don't want you to think I'm bailing on the wedding plans. Anything you need, I'm here, OK?"

Bett laughed into the phone—her sweet, little-sister laugh, which I was going to miss. "You're already taking care of the dress, and the rehearsal flowers, and now you've located a potential soloist. I'd say that's enough. You do have your own life, you know."

I do? I thought. The idea came as a surprise. *Julia has her own life.* An important life, filled with important things to do. *Thanks,* I wanted to say. Somehow, Bett's recognizing it made it real. "By the way, the dress is looking wonderful. You are not going to believe how gorgeous it is. I'm supposed to pick it up tomorrow after school, and then I'll take it straight to Mom's. Don't want Jason to see it, after all. Oh, and did you see the sample rose I left with Mom on Monday?" I was suddenly aware of how little I had talked to Bett in the last few days.

There was an audible intake of breath on the other end of the phone. "Oh, my gosh, Julia, that thing is beautiful. I have it in a vase on our table, and it's become more incredible as it has opened up. I told Mom we should use these in all the bouquets, just cancel the wedding florist and have your lady do it, but Mom pretty well had a heart attack about the idea."

I hated to admit it, but I had to. "Mom's probably right. This lady is really sweet, but I think doing all the wedding flowers may be more than she can handle. I don't even know where her shop is or where she grows her flowers, really. I just see her at the cleaner's with her flower cart."

"It's a gorgeous rose, anyway," Bett replied wistfully. "You are really the world's best big sister."

If I could have hugged her through the phone, I would have. Instead, I sighed, like it was all in a day's work, and said, "I know, I know. What can I say?"

"I can't believe rehearsal's a week from tomorrow." There was a flutter of anticipation in Bett's voice.

"I know." I tried to sound equally excited. "One week and two days, and you won't be a Costell anymore."

"Yeah," she said.

"Yeah," I repeated, shoring up the sad sister inside me. "It's going to be a wonderful wedding, Bett."

"Yes, it is," she agreed; then her call waiting beckoned, and we said a hasty good-bye.

I went back to the dismal subject of kids, drugs, and all the bizarre hiding places that could be used to conceal a stash from parents or teachers—lipstick tubes hollowed out, tiny flashlights modified to serve as pipes, breath-freshener strips laced with LSD, AA batteries hollowed out and filled with crack, mechanical pencils refitted to hold illicit contents. The list went on and on. By the time I'd uploaded it all to the Counselor's Corner section of the school Web site, I was more determined than ever that changes had to be made at Harrington. We needed to implement random testing, unannounced searches by the drug dog while the kids and their possessions were in school, swabbing of lockers for drug residue, among other things. There was no way to spot the paraphernalia or the drugs just by looking. Which was why, on the surface, Harrington looked fine.

Outside, the hallway was quiet and growing shadowy by the time I closed my office and left. The Spring Fling rehearsal had finished an hour ago, and most of the teachers had gone home. In the instrumental music room, a single saxophone was playing, and I walked down to tell Verhaden I was leaving. He was sitting in the center of the cavernous room, curled lovingly over the sax with his eyes closed, playing a sad, slow melody. In that position, in the dim light, lost in his music, he looked like the idealistic young teacher who'd come to Harrington when I was Dell's age.

Waiting until he'd finished, I knocked on the door as if I'd just come in. "I wanted you to know I'm out of here. I'll make sure the front door's locked."

"Sounds good." Setting the sax in a chair, he stood up and stretched.

"Hey, I'm working on getting some instruments for your after-school program. I've got some kids who need to get in their community service hours, so Keiler's helping them refit some of the ones in the closet that need only minor repairs. No sense in that stuff sitting around, and it's good for the kids to know how their instruments work. Stafford probably won't be nuts about the idea, but I can push it through the superintendent's office. Pays to know the right people."

"Thanks." I smiled, pleasantly surprised to find Verhaden taking the initiative on my behalf. "You can't imagine how much the instruments will be appreciated. The Jumpkids director says she has plenty of kids interested in instrumental, but they haven't been able to pursue it because of the costs. Hopefully, now she'll be able to find a few volunteers to give lessons." Glancing toward what used to be the flute section in the corner of the room, I remembered my very short career in instrumental music at Harrington. "I could teach flute."

"You were about the worst flute player I ever had," Verhaden scoffed. "I might be able to help out with some tutors. Let me talk to a few people at the high school. It's the kind of community service our kids should be doing."

"I agree completely." I stopped just short of jumping onto my soapbox about Harrington kids being constructive in the community.

Shaking his head, Verhaden picked up the sax again. "You're a hopeless idealist, Costell," he said, then positioned his fingers on the instrument. "Go home, already. Have a good evening."

"You, too." I turned away as soulful notes again filled the room.

On the drive home, I thought about Mr. Verhaden, sitting in the empty band hall. When did he change from rugged idealist to weary music director? Did he surrender little by little, or did he wake up one day and realize the tide at Harrington had turned so far that he could no longer swim against it? Did he think about it when he sat playing soulful notes on his saxophone? Was that why he wanted to help provide instruments and instructors for the Jumpkids program?

Whatever the reason, I was grateful. As I exited the highway in Overland Park, I called Karen on her cell phone to discuss the possibilities and to ask her about Dell singing for Bett's wedding. She seemed excited about both ideas, and Dell was amenable to performing as a wedding soloist, so I made plans to deliver Bett's CD to her the next day at school, so that Dell could practice the music over the weekend, and then next week with her vocal music teacher.

"There will be more time after tomorrow, when the grading period is over," Karen said, lowering her voice in a way that told me she had moved away from Dell. "She and Keiler have been studying like crazy, and then a couple of nights, this friend of hers, Barry, came to Jumpkids with us, and the two of them studied; then he rode home with us. Turns out, he lives not far away from here. It's great to see her with a friend her own age. It never occurred to me that it wasn't normal for her to be hanging around adults and Jumpkids all the time."

I chuckled into the phone. "For a kid with so many life changes this past year, I think Dell's doing really well. She's a tough little nut."

"I hope her grades come out all right." Karen sounded worried. "She's been working so hard. I'm trying not to hover or make too big a deal of it, so that if the report card is a disappointment, she won't think it's the end of the world."

"That's good." I felt a pang of guilt that I hadn't been able to keep up with Dell's situation this week as much as I'd wanted to. "Grades will be in the computer by Monday, so I can check and see how she ended up. I know she did well on all of her tests this week, so that will help. I'm sorry I haven't been able to do more for her the last few days. The principal's been out with the flu all week, and it has turned into a pretty insane week." I wanted to spill the whole story, to unload it on somebody older and wiser, but I knew a parent from the school was not the person to tell. "Thank God Keiler came along when he did."

Karen laughed softly into the receiver. "For a man without a plan, Keiler does a pretty good job of showing up when he's needed. You'll find that out about him."

"I already have."

"Speaking of being needed," Karen went on, "with Mrs. Mindia still out with the flu, we sure have missed you at Jumpkids. I've been having to teach dance, and let me tell you, it's not a pretty sight."

"I bet you're great at it," I joked.

"Hardly. Any chance you'll be back next week?" Her voice rose hopefully, as in, *Please, please, please? Say yes.* "I hate to beg, but I will."

Laughter bubbled in my throat, light and effervescent. Once again, I had that warm feeling of being valued and accepted, of friendship. I realized that other than Bett, I hadn't had a close friend in years. I'd driven them away a bit at a time, slowly increasing the distance between myself and other people as my secret became more dire and harder to hide. "Hopefully, I'll be able to help next week. I've really missed it, and by the time the principal gets back, I'm going to need stress relief." That was true in more ways than one. "I'm sure he'll be back by next week, and I'll be finishing up a big grant proposal this weekend. After that, I'll have more time in the afternoons."

"Sounds good, but seriously, though, no pressure. We're happy to have you whenever you can work it in," Karen replied graciously, letting me off the hook. "Unlike Keiler, you do have a life."

"Thank goodness Keiler doesn't have a life."

Karen paused contemplatively, as if she suspected more than just professional gratitude in the comment. "I think Keiler's glad he came along when he did. He's really enjoying the teaching, or . . . ahem . . . something about that school." Her voice rose with a hint of, *Girlfriend, I've got a secret.* Then she seemed to change her mind and finished with, "It suits him, anyway."

I felt myself blushing in the dark, alone in my car. "I'm glad," was the only reply I could think of.

We said good-bye as I pulled into my parents' driveway. Bett's car was parked in the extra space, and when I went inside, she was sitting in the living room with Mom and Dad, finishing a powwow about catering. All three of them looked as exhausted as I felt.

"Hi, sweetheart!" Mom said. "How was your day?"

I was momentarily stunned. Not one word about whether I'd eaten dinner, or whether I was hungry? Just, *How was your day?* "Strange," I said finally. "Kind of far-side-of-the-moon strange." Setting down my briefcase, I sank onto the sofa.

Dad lowered his *Wall Street Journal,* which he'd no doubt been hiding behind as Mom and Bett hashed out catering details. "Tough day at school?"

All three of them turned to me with expressions of genuine interest, and the need to talk about the week's events welled up so strongly that I couldn't force it down. The next thing I knew, I was spilling the entire story—everything from hiring Keiler as an algebra substitute on Monday, to finding Cameron having a meltdown in the hall on Thursday, and then contacting his parents.

"I hope I did the right thing, calling his father." Leaning my head back, I closed my eyes momentarily. "There's so much potential in that kid—too much to throw away because he's having a tough time with his folks' divorce."

"Of course you did the right thing." Mom's tone was so indignant that I looked at her in surprise. She was sitting forward in her chair, her back stiff, her chin raised defensively. "You did exactly the right thing. The man should know what's going on with his son. That *is* your job—to look after the well-being of the kids." She sounded as if she were ready to pick up a *Just Say No* banner and crusade through the halls of Harrington right along with me. Her eyes met mine, and I realized she had a personal interest in the matter—me. My mother cared about the problems at Harrington because I cared about the problems at Harrington.

"Sounds like that principal hasn't been minding his shop too well," Dad chimed in, and when I glanced at him, he punctuated with a managerial nod. "First sign of a poor manager—more interested in covering up issues than solving them. Not a creative problem solver. Can't think through the solutions, see?" Dad pointed a finger at me. "That's when new blood is needed. That's when a young go-getter with fresh ideas can really make a difference."

"Dad's right," Bett concurred. "There's no way you could turn your back on a situation like that. It would be wrong. You're not the kind of person who settles for halfway. That's what made you so good at dance. You'll do whatever it takes."

"Thanks," I said, swelling with emotion as I looked from Bett, to Dad, to Mom. My family, solidly behind me.

In spite of everything that had happened that day, I felt myself filling with air, catching a new wind, so that it seemed as if I could sail out into the world and take on anything.

Chapter 21

I left for Harrington early on Friday morning, after waking at three a.m., nervous and out of sorts, and then tossing and turning until four thirty. Finally, I gave up and worked on the grant application. By five thirty, I'd come to a standstill related to construction dates, square footage, and seating capacity of the school's existing performance hall. Those facts would be contained in documents somewhere in the school's basement file room, so I packed up the application materials, showered, dressed, ate some toast, left a note for Mom and Dad, and headed for work in a wintry predawn haze.

On the horizon, a thunderstorm rumbled as I traveled downtown. Without the usual stress of rush-hour traffic and cars darting in and out, the drive was peaceful, but my mind was swirling and churning like the early-spring thunderheads on the horizon. A vague sense of unease cast a pall over the morning, as if something had gone wrong overnight, and I just didn't know it yet.

I conjured a haunting vision of Cameron having slipped away from his mom's house and done something stupid. I tried to banish the idea, as if thinking something so awful might make it a reality, but I knew the knot in my stomach wouldn't loosen until Cameron came up the front steps this morning, hopefully with his father.

Stafford's not going to like your contacting a board member to tell him his kid was high at school, a voice in my head warned. *Better be prepared to explain that . . .*

A litany of potential responses and results ran through my head as I role-played the conversation with Stafford. Pulling into the school parking lot and turning off the engine, I stopped to consider the dialog in my head. I was doing exactly what I hated most—trying to modify and mollify, and make the situation less dire than it was. I sounded like Stafford or the school nurse, making excuses, intent on covering my backside in case things got messy.

Stop it, I told myself as I climbed out of my car, waved at the campus security officer near the gate, and walked up the stairs to the front door. *You did the right thing. You did the only thing you could.* Inside, one of the custodians was running the polisher on the hallway floor, so I descended the steps and went in the basement entry to the file room to search for the documentation I needed for the grant. After an hour of digging through old files, scanning school informational brochures, school maps, and construction blueprints, I finally had most of the required information. Outside, the parking lot was filling up with cars, and overhead, the hallway was coming to life.

Glancing at my watch, I hurried up the back stairs to the main hall, put my things in my office, and stationed myself at the front door. If Cameron's father brought him in early, as he usually did, I wanted to catch him. Keiler was making his way up the steps with a box containing paper airplanes. Holding the door open, I frowned quizzically at his cargo.

"Homework." Nodding toward the paper airplanes, he flashed a broad grin. "Math can be fun."

"Pfff," I scoffed. "You'll have to save that line for the students. I can't remember *anything* having to do with math ever being fun."

He leaned close to me. "You've never had Big Bad Bradford for math. Today we're going to calculate the volume, surface area, and linear dimensions of the school, in Jelly Bellies." Pulling a huge sack of jelly beans out of his box, he winked. "Then, of course, we're going to eat them. These kids will do just about anything for candy."

I laughed. "When you figure out all the Jelly Belly totals, let

244 · LISA WINGATE

me know. Maybe I can use some of that information on my grant application."

"You got it," he replied. "Just tell me what you want to know, and we'll figure out a way to convert it to jelly beans. . . . I hope. Some of my ideas work out better than others."

I glanced into the box of assorted paper airplanes, some of which had elaborate designs and complex decorations. Obviously, the kids had put a great deal of time into their projects. "Looks like this one worked out pretty well."

He shrugged, silently saying, *Yeah, what can I say—I'm good.* "The principal liked them."

I frowned, confused. "You've met Mr. Stafford?"

Nodding, he tucked the jelly beans back into his box. "Yeah. Bumped into him a half hour or so ago, on my way in with the first box of paper airplanes. I had to run over to the Jumpkids office and get this box out of Karen's car. Not easy carrying boxes on a Harley. There are some times when I miss the green Hornet."

I suddenly lost all desire to chat about paper airplanes and jelly beans. Looking over my shoulder toward the office, I wondered where Mr. Stafford was now. "I'd better go. Have a great day, Keiler. Good luck with the jelly beans."

"I'll let you know how it turns out." He headed off down the hall, whistling the melody to "Yellow Submarine."

Taking a deep breath, I peeked into the administration office. Mrs. Jorgenson glanced up from her computer, and her expression sent a cold lump down my throat.

"Where's Mr. Stafford?" I asked.

"In his office with someone." She gave a meaningful look over the top of her glasses. "And he does *not* want to be disturbed. I don't know who he went in there with, because I was down getting the coffee machine started, but a minute ago, I tried to put through a call to him, and he bit my head off." Leaning across the desk, she crooked a finger, motioning me closer. "He's still not feeling too well. He didn't look at all well this morning. If I were you, I'd make myself scarce until he either gets better or goes home."

Nodding reluctantly, I turned to leave the office. "All right. If you see Cameron Ansler, will you let me know?"

Mrs. Jorgenson tilted her head to one side, her brows drawing together. "Oh, he's already here. I saw him in the hallway, down by the teachers' lounge. Said he was headed to retake some test from yesterday." Leaning across her desk again, she caught my gaze and whispered, "He looked a lot better."

My mind raced to assimilate the barrage of information. "Cameron's already here?" I repeated, and she nodded. "And he's making up a test from yesterday?" She nodded again, and I stood trying to figure out how all of this could be taking place before school hours, considering that the problem had come up only yesterday afternoon. "Did his parents come in with him?"

She raised both hands, palms up. "Don't know. Didn't see. Like I said, I was down the hall." Picking up a pen, she jotted something on a sticky note. I had a feeling she knew more than she was willing to say.

Glancing at Stafford's door, I wondered what might be happening and whether it had anything to do with the principal's sudden reappearance from sick leave.

The phone rang, and Mrs. Jorgenson seized it, clearly glad to have an excuse to send me on my way. She gave a quick smile and an uncomfortable finger wave before she started into a phone conversation about a student who was absent with the flu.

Outside, the front hall was filling up with kids rushing to their lockers, now that they had finally been allowed through the doors. Somewhere in the main corridor, Mrs. Morris was hollering, "No running! Stop that running! Young man, you go right back down the steps and . . ." Her voice was absorbed by the hum as I made my way around the corner to my office.

Barry passed by and waved. "Hey, Ms. C. Have you seen Dell?"

"Not so far today."

With an impish grin, he hiked up his droopy pants while walking backward. "Don't worry; I'll find her," he said, with more enthusiasm than I'd ever seen him show toward anything. "I bet she's down in the vocal room, practicing. Girls' ensemble was supposed to come in early this morning and work on the Spring Fling music."

"Could be." In spite of the way the day was going, Barry's happy-morning face made me smile. "When you see her, tell her I have a CD to give her—the solo music for my sister's wedding."

He stood blocking traffic, oblivious as other students squeezed by with backpacks and instruments, giving him dirty looks. "Am I gonna get an invitation?"

"To the wedding?" Why in the world would Barry want to go to my sister's wedding?

"Yeah . . . I just wondered." Glancing down at his shoes, he reddened and rolled his shoulders uncomfortably.

Suddenly, I understood. Dell would be at the wedding. I wondered what Bett would say, but, then, knowing her, she probably wouldn't care. "The invitations are kind of informal, but you're welcome to come. Maybe you could ride over with Dell and her parents."

His posture straightened and he took on the joyful glow of a young man with a serious crush. "Cool. I'll ask my mom."

"Sounds good."

He stood smiling at me a moment longer, as if transfixed by dreamy-eyed visions of himself and Dell together. Another eighth grader passed by with a drum, knocking Barry sideways and jolting him from fantasyland. "I could take the CD to Dell for you." His eyebrows rose hopefully. *Ah, a reason to track down Dell . . .*

"All right." Stepping into my office, I took the CD from my briefcase.

Barry was at my door. "Thanks, Ms. C," he said, then cleared his throat and added, "I mean, see you later on."

"See you later." I allowed myself the pleasure of watching him walk away, his shoulders straight and a lightness in his step. A new man, living in a new world, where there was a cute girl who actually knew his name. What could be better than that?

It was almost enough to rub the tarnish off the day. Almost.

The moment Mr. Stafford stepped into my office, halfway through second period, it became clear that the day was more than just tarnished. Stafford looked sick and tired, red faced and ready to bite off someone's head. Mine.

Closing the door, he flung a hand in the air, stabbing a finger toward the front hall. "I've just been in my *office* for *over an hour* trying to calm down Cameron Ansler's mother. She has been calling anyone and everyone, outraged that we have maligned her and made completely unwarranted accusations against Cameron. In her mind, this is all part of a plot to undermine her in the custody battle between herself and Cameron's father. She's talking about suing for slander. She called the superintendent at six a.m., *at home,* saying that because of Mr. Ansler's position on the school board, we were trying to aid him in gaining custody." His hands moved emphatically in the air, then flopped to his sides. "What the h-e-double-l went on around here yesterday?" The speech sent him staggering sideways, and he leaned against the back of a chair, coughing into his sleeve.

Offering him a tissue, I waited for him to catch his breath, and tried to get my head together. *Be calm. Be calm. You did the right thing.* When Stafford had finally regained control, he wheeled toward me with a murderous glare, then caught the back of the chair again. "I want to know what happened yesterday."

"Cameron Ansler had a meltdown in the hall." I hoped my voice sounded self-assured, determined, unwavering. The words felt like Jell-O in my mouth. "Not just a little meltdown, Mr. Stafford. He was out of his head. He didn't know what he was saying, what he was doing. He barely knew where he was. He had no control over himself, and he was so drowsy that we couldn't keep him lucid. He was coming down from something and crashing hard."

Stafford began forming a reply before I'd even finished speaking. "Did he admit this to you?"

"Well, no, but it was obv—"

He held up a hand. "The boy was having a bad day. His mother concurs that he'd been to a birthday party with friends the night before and he forgot to study for a history test. When he got to class and discovered there was a test, he panicked. He got emotional." Stafford's body language added, *All perfectly normal—could happen to anybody.*

"Mr. Stafford"—I half stood from my seat—"this was not just a kid having a bad day. Cameron walked out of class, made it as far as his locker, and went crazy, screaming and crying and banging his head against the door. He was off the deep end."

Lifting his chin, the principal cleared his throat, peering at me through the bottom of his glasses. "There was a mix-up with his ADD medications. His mother admits that occasional—"

"Mr. Stafford." I could feel my temper ratcheting up. I could not believe he was willing to swallow that load of hooey, and now he wanted me to quietly slink off to a corner and agree. "The kid's mother lets him ride to school with some older student—Sebastian . . . something. This is not the first time I've seen Cameron come in looped, hopped up, under the influence, whatever you want to call it. It's not the first time he's stepped over the line. When he stays with his mom, he's out of it. His behavior is bizarre and unpredictable. He's either so hyperactive he can't function, or so drowsy he can't stay awake. When he's with his father, Dad drives him to school and drops him at the door—no time to hang out or run around town with older kids. Cameron shows up sober. What does that say to you?"

"It could mean any number of things. Teenagers are volatile creatures." Stafford pointed a finger at me again. "Your obsession with this drug issue has gone too far. You need to step back and gain perspective. This is a good kid with solid parental involvement. A school board member's kid, for heaven's sake."

Standing up, I slammed my hands on the desk. "This kid is sinking down a well, and nobody's pulling him up!" My voice reverberated around the office. Reining myself in, I pressed a hand to my forehead and closed my eyes momentarily, thinking, *Breathe, breathe, breathe. This isn't doing any good.*

"You're out of line!" Stafford bellowed. "You are a recent college graduate with only two months' experience. I have been in school administration for over thirty years!" His protest filled the room, then died, and we stood in a stalemate.

I stared at my desktop—at the clutter of sticky notes, attendance sheets, grant paperwork. What was any of it worth if we couldn't help these kids when they needed us? "Mr. Stafford." I waited as he staggered sideways, slumping against the chair, exhausted. "I'm sorry if my decision was not the one you would have chosen. You weren't here, and I dealt with the issue in a moment of crisis—"

"I explained to the Anslers that you are inexperienced." He cut me off with a patronizing expression of sympathy. "I explained that, given the heat of the moment, and the fact that other members of the administration were unavailable, you were forced into a position for which you are unqualified, and as a result, made a novice error in judgment." He smiled slightly, and I felt the invisible pat on the head, the silent, *Good girl, now how is the grant paperwork coming along?* "They seem to have calmed down, but they do expect an apology—both to the mother and to Cameron. Your accusations have been very upsetting to him."

Gripping the sides of the desk, I leaned across, feeling myself come close to some boiling point I hadn't approached in years. For so long, my temper had been tamped down by the idea that, since I'd screwed up my own life, I had no business giving advice to anyone else. Now, I was filled with righteous indignation. How dared he sweep this under the rug, smooth it over, and order me to do the same? What was wrong with him? Didn't he care about these kids at all?

I met his eyes—tired, vacant eyes that reminded me of Mr. Verhaden's. If there had ever been passion in Stafford's soul, it was gone now. He looked like a man who wanted to be anywhere else but here. "I will *not*." My fingers tightened, my elbows a shaking brace between my body and the wood. "I will not stand here and tell a student and his parents something I know is not true. Especially when the secret could kill him. I don't have what it takes to do that." *What does it take to do that?* I looked into Stafford's face and tried to figure it out. "I won't. I can't. It's wrong."

Sighing, the principal rubbed his forehead, then drew the hand slowly downward, dragging droopy layers of skin so that his eyes sagged, red rimmed and weary. His stomach billowed with a long, raspy breath, then deflated again, and he coughed into his sleeve. Reaching up, he mopped his brow. "I suggest that you calm down and consider who you are talking to. Convictions are a wonderful thing, Ms. Costell, but the fact is that we can't afford to operate in la-la land, here. In the real world . . ." He paused to cough again, and I took advantage of the conversational gap.

"In the real world, there's a police stakeout just a few blocks from here, Mr. Stafford." I motioned toward the window. "They're taking down license plate numbers at the taco stands on Division Street." The irony of that name suddenly hit me. "The taco stands sell drugs. Probably meth, weed, crack, buzz bombs, who knows? When the police net closes, some of our kids are going to be caught. We'll be the ones who stood by and did nothing to prevent it."

He raised his chin indignantly. "We do everything that is reasonable and customary in terms of drug prevention. We have search dogs; we provide student activities, antidrug curricula." The words sounded rehearsed.

"We can't turn a blind eye when the problem becomes real, Mr. Stafford. We have to do something."

Crossing his arms over his chest, he rocked back on his heels, then lost his balance and braced himself against the door frame like a plastic soldier, slightly melted. "There has never been a drug problem at Harrington, Ms. Costell," he refuted, leveling a determined glare. "And there will not be. Not on my watch."

Therein lay the rub, the heart of the matter, and I knew it. Stafford was only a few months from retirement. He didn't want this problem; he didn't have the energy for it. He wasn't going to have it on his record. Period.

The only trouble was, the problem was coming to us, whether we wanted it or not. "I'm sorry, Mr. Stafford." And in a way, I was. In spite of everything, I had sympathy for him, standing there sick with the flu, confronting such a huge issue at the end of what was probably a long and successful career. "But I won't lie to Cameron or his parents."

Lacing his fingers, the principal brought his hands to his mouth and blew into them, slowly shaking his head. "This isn't the time to get on your high horse, Costell. Next year's contracts, including yours, come up for renewal at the board meeting Monday night." The threat in those words was unmistakable, the implication clear. *Make nice with Cameron's parents, or else.*

Outside in the corridor, the first bell rang, and shadows passed by the door. Glancing over his shoulder, Stafford softened, then turned back to me. "We can't help these kids if we're not here, Ms. Costell. We all have to play the game."

I let my head sag between my shoulders, confronted with the reality of my situation, not knowing what to say. In a twisted, pathetic way, Stafford was right. If I didn't play the game, I could lose my job. If I wasn't here, I was no good to the kids at all.

"I want you to take some time to think things through," Stafford said softly. "Pack up whatever you were going to do today; take it home. Simmer down over the weekend. I'll let everyone know you're out with the flu." Turning away, he put his hand on the doorknob. "Go home, Julia. Consider the implications of what you're doing. You have the makings of a good guidance counselor. It would be a shame to throw it all away in order to stand on principle. This isn't the time for rash decision making."

Opening the door, he stepped into the flow of students, and was gone.

Chapter 22

As I gathered my things, my mind whirled like a leaf caught in the vortex of a tornado. I couldn't focus on any specific thought, on any one action, but wandered numbly between my desk and the file cabinet, trying to decide what to do. Dell came by and poked her head in the door, and I jumped, then caught my breath.

"Ms. Costell?" she said, as if suddenly I were someone she didn't know. "Barry brought me the CD of the wedding music. Mrs. Levorski says she'll help me practice it in my vocal class this week. I was wondering, instead of using the instrumental track off the CD, do you think maybe Keiler could play the guitar? I bet he'd do it, and we could practice at home this week. . . ." She paused as I braced my shaking hands on the desk. Around me, the world was shifting and spinning, moving so fast that everything was a blur. "Are you all right, Ms. C?"

"No . . . yes . . . I'm sorry, what did you say?" *Think, Julia, think. The wedding music . . .* I tried to focus as she repeated the question. "I think . . . that sounds . . . good." The reply was robotic, distracted.

Dell's brows drew together apprehensively. "We don't have to if you don't want—"

"No, it's good. It's fine." My head reeling, I sank into the chair. "I'll check with . . . ummm . . . Bett, but I'm sure it will be fine."

"Is something wrong, Ms. C?"

"Yes." The words trembled. I felt myself cracking. I wanted to tell her everything, as if somehow this thirteen-year-old child, who was almost as lost as I was, could fix the problem. "I just . . . I'm going home . . . sick."

"I'm sorry. I hope you don't have the flu like Mrs. Mindia." Behind the words, there was a thread of concern. *If you get the flu and go to the hospital like Mrs. Mindia, who's going to tutor me?* Leaning against the door frame, she rested her head near the hinge. "We're starting a new book in English on Monday. *Flowers for Algernon.* It looks hard."

"I've read it." *You can't help them if you're not here.* Stafford's words echoed in my mind. "It's a good story. It's about how difficult it can be, sometimes, to know what's right." *What's right . . . ? What is right?*

Chewing a fingernail, Dell studied me narrowly, sensing something wrong, unsure how to react. She pushed off the door frame and hovered there. "Do you think we could start working on it at lunch Monday?"

Stafford's dire warnings repeated in my head. *"Next year's contracts, including yours, come up for renewal at the board meeting Monday night. . . ."* "I hope so."

"Are you sure you're OK, Ms. Costell?"

"Yes. You'd better go on to class now."

" 'Kay." She turned to leave, then came back and stood absently toying with a pen on the corner of my desk. "Keiler went around with me this morning, and we asked my teachers for my grades." Her lips twitched upward. " 'B' in math—I did good on the test Wednesday— 'C' in social studies and science, 'A' in vocal, instrumental, and chorus, and Mrs. Morris doesn't have her grades figured yet, but she told Keiler I was doing better." The smile bloomed fully, like a flower caught in time-lapse photography. "That's not too bad."

A nugget of joy slipped into the oily soup of the morning, glittering out of place in the darkness. "That's not bad at all." Reaching across the desk, I squeezed her hand. "You're on your way, kid. You just keep with the study plan and next nine weeks you'll see even more improvement."

Shifting uncomfortably, she looked away, then back. "I have to do better the next time. To stay in chorus and to have a solo in Spring

Fling, you have to have 'A' and 'B' grades. You're still going to help me, aren't you?"

An invisible vise tightened around my throat. What if I wasn't here? What would happen to Dell? Would she be able to get by with Barry's help, and Keiler's, if he stayed on as a sub? Who would Dell talk to if her adoption became complicated by the appearance of a father, and she didn't feel comfortable confiding in her foster parents? What about all the other kids at Harrington? What about Cameron? If I wasn't here, I couldn't even attempt to convince him to come clean with his parents.

Then again, if I stayed at Harrington under Stafford's terms, I couldn't either.

"I plan to," was the only answer I could come up with. "You'd better head to class now."

" 'Kay," she replied, shooting a final look of concern over her shoulder as she left. "Hope you feel better, Ms. C. See you Monday."

"Have a good weekend." My stomach constricted until I felt hollow inside. This weekend was going to be anything but good.

Packing the rest of the grant materials into a box, I headed for the door without bothering to put on my jacket and without stopping to say a word to anyone. I burst through the front exit and onto the steps, feeling as if I couldn't stand the scent of textbooks and lockers, plaster and aging woodwork a moment longer. A burst of March wind pushed me down the steps to my car, and I left without looking back.

I was almost home when I remembered that I was supposed to pick up Bett's wedding dress today. Exiting the highway, I headed back downtown, perversely relieved by the diversion. I wasn't ready to calmly analyze Stafford's ultimatum yet, and I didn't want to talk to anyone about it. Arriving home so early would only prompt a conversation with Mom. With the extra delay of going back for the dress, I would get home after Mom left for her Friday bridge game. Neither she nor Dad would return until suppertime. I would have the afternoon to sort things out in private.

When I reached the cleaner's, the street was quiet. The undercover police car was nowhere in evidence, and for a split second, I had the

Drenched in Light · 255

perverse thought that I'd imagined the whole thing. Inside the cleaner's, neither Mim nor Granmae was present. I struggled to gain a grip on what was real as the young woman behind the counter brought out the dress and hung it on the counter hook.

"Here it is," she said. She had Granmae's smile. "Granmae's newest masterpiece. She said that if it doesn't fit with the alterations you had marked, have the bride bring it in next week and we can adjust it. Granmae will be sorry she wasn't here to give it to you herself. She had to go to a funeral today."

"Oh, I'm sorry." I had a subtle awareness that in spite of my own cataclysmic day, the world was still turning, life playing all the normal rhythms. "Tell her I'll snap a picture of my sister in the dress and bring it by next Friday, when I pick up the rehearsal flowers."

The young woman found the bill and laid it on the counter, widening her eyes and whistling at the total. "They got you for dress restoration and flowers, huh? I'll tell you what, I don't even know why I'm in nursing school. I just need to hang around Granmae and Mim. They can talk more people into more stuff."

"Actually, I had to talk them into this one," I said, running my finger along the carefully restored lines of golden pearls before pulling out my checkbook. "This dress was almost too far gone to save, but it's going to mean a lot to my sister. She's always wanted to wear it."

The salesgirl smiled, punching the calculator to add tax to the bill, then writing it on the receipt. "Listen, none of them are too far gone for Granmae. I've seen her take half an old dress that got burned in a fire, and rebuild around it. She just likes to make a big deal about how hard it'll be, so that when you get the bill, you're not shocked." Grinning, she turned the slip of paper around and slid it across the counter.

Four hundred and twenty-five dollars seemed a surprisingly small price for a dream, and now, seeing the dress, I knew we would have gladly paid twice as much. "It's worth every penny."

"Granmae's work always is." Craning her neck, she read my check number, leaned across the counter, and wrote it on the bill. "Don't make the payment out for any extra, either, or Granmae will just hang on to it until you come write her a new one. That's the way she is. She doesn't take any charity. Just honest work. I don't know how much the flowers will be. You can pay Mim for them next week."

"All right." Finishing the check, I handed it to her, then waited for her to secure the gown in a zip-up dress bag. She carried it out and hung it in the backseat of my car, then thanked me for the business. As I left, a Lexus pulled in bearing another young bride-to-be, her mother, and a garment bag, undoubtedly containing a wedding dress that had seen better days.

On the way home, I tried to focus on Bett and the wedding, and the whirlwind of last-minute preparations that were to be taken care of this weekend. One thing was for sure: Neither Bett nor my parents needed the added burden of knowing what was happening with my job. Stafford's ultimatum was a decision with which no one could help me, anyway.

"In the end, your life comes down to your own conscience," Sister Margaret had said. *"Only you can choose where you will bend and where you will stand firm."*

Was now the time to bend or the time to stand firm? How was I to know?

I sifted through my options over and over again. None of them felt real. It seemed impossible that I would leave Harrington, yet I could not imagine telling Cameron and his parents that everything was fine, turning a blind eye to drug use at the school, however pervasive it was, and simply waiting until some outside force blew the situation wide-open. There had to be another way.

I tried to imagine what it would be, tried to draw the answer from thin air and a vapor of hope that somehow everything would turn out all right. My mind was a million miles away as I drove home, carried my belongings into the empty house, and cleaned up Joujou's latest protest in the entryway. Bringing in the wedding dress, I took it from the garment bag, and hung it on the curtain rod next to the guest bed, in all its glory. With Joujou in my lap, I settled into a chair in the corner, looking at the dress. Following the curving lines of lace and pearls, I imagined my mother's hands creating it, Granmae's and Mim's bringing it back to life, making it beautiful and whole and allowing it to serve a purpose again.

If such a thing were possible with an old dress, how much more was possible with my life?

Closing my eyes, I let my thoughts drift. In my lap, Joujou was already growling and twitching in her sleep, and I felt myself slipping away also. . . .

When I woke up, Mom and Bett were standing in front of the wedding gown. The fabric rustled softly as Bett took the dress from the hanger and held it against herself, her brown hair spilling over the beadwork.

"Put it on," Mom murmured. "We'll surprise her when she wakes up." I closed my eyes again as Bett turned my way. Beneath the shadow of lashes, I watched as my sister slipped into her dream, and Mom fastened the back. When Bethany turned around, I couldn't pretend any longer. With an audible intake of breath, I sat up, and my sister's eyes met mine.

"It's perfect," she whispered, and in that moment, everything else fell away. There was only my sister and me, and one rare and precious instant in which everything was as it should be. Setting Joujou down, I came across the room and hugged her. Mom wrapped her arms around both of us. From the doorway, Dad smiled at me, flashed the OK sign, and then walked away wiping his eyes.

After that, the weekend descended into a whirlwind of last-minute wedding plans and preparations. The hum of activity and the sheer volume of details helped keep my mind off the problems at Harrington. Both Bett and Mom eventually picked up on the fact that something was not right with me. They knew me well enough to see that, mentally, I was elsewhere.

On Sunday night, Bett hugged me extra hard before she left. "I love you," she said, pressing her lips together in a tender I'm-not-going-to-cry frown. "Thanks for everything you've done for the wedding. I couldn't have a better maid of honor . . . or sister."

"You're welcome," I said, feeling that in some small way, I'd made up for all the times I'd let her down in the past. "I love you, too, Bett."

Giving me a final hug, she went out the door. I was still standing in the entryway, reveling in the glow of sister love, contemplating one of our baby pictures on the wall, when Bett rushed back in.

"There's a guy on a motorcycle out here, and he says he's a friend of yours." Her voice was hushed, so as not to alert Mom, Dad, and Joujou in the living room. Pulling her bottom lip between her teeth, she quirked a brow.

"A guy on a motorcycle . . ." I repeated hesitantly. "I don't know. . . ."

"Kind of tall, brown hair, nice smile." Wheeling her hands in front of herself, Bett glanced toward the crack in the door. "Has a cast on one foot . . ."

"Keiler?" Slipping past my sister, I walked outside. Keiler was next to Bethany's car, leaning casually against his Harley as if it were perfectly natural for him to be in my parents' driveway. "What are you doing here?"

He shrugged, crossing his arms over his chest. "I was in the neighborhood, and . . ."

"James and Karen don't live near here," I countered, vaguely aware that Bett was behind me, watching the interplay and waiting for an introduction.

Keiler grinned mischievously, and my heart bubbled up like soda pop, slightly shaken. "I wanted to see how you were doing. I heard you went home sick Friday."

My sister glanced sideways at me, confused. She knew I wasn't sick on Friday.

I had that old sense of being entangled in a lie, and out of habit, the first thing I did was offer up a diversionary tactic. "How did you know where I lived?"

"Looked it up on the employee database. Want to go get a cup of coffee or something?"

"Sure," I chirped, then blushed, because the word conveyed over-the-top enthusiasm.

Behind me, Bett cleared her throat, and Keiler looked at her like he hadn't realized she was there. Stepping forward, he smiled and extended his hand. "Keiler Bradford."

"Bethany Costell," Bett said, giving him the once-over, then cutting her gaze toward me.

"I'm sorry." Bethany's interested look spurred me into action. "Keiler, this is my sister, Bethany, and Bett, this is Keiler. He's a new substitute teacher at Harrington. Actually, he saved me from having to teach algebra."

"Eeewww." Bett curled her lip.

"Math can be fun." Keiler raised a finger to punctuate his point.

A charmed chuckle twittered past Bett's lips.

"Keiler's the one who's going to play guitar accompaniment for the wedding soloist," I interjected, then swiveled back to him. "Dell did ask you about that, didn't she?"

"Sure. We've already been practicing. That girl can sing, I'll tell you. I'm amazed every time she opens her mouth."

"Sounds wonderful." Taking a step toward her car, Bett gracefully bowed out of the conversation. "Well, listen, I'll leave you to visit. I have about a million things to do at home."

"Nice to meet you." Keiler shook Bett's hand.

I leaned over and hugged her. "Night, Bett."

"Nice smile," she whispered in my ear. "I'll call later—I want the dish."

Having the mortifying feeling Keiler could hear, I yanked the back of her hair, and she came away rubbing her head.

"Talk to you *later,* sis. Nice to meet you, Keiler." Waving good-bye, Bett pulled out of the driveway, and I went into the house to grab a coat and tell Mom and Dad I was going out for a cup of coffee. They assumed I was going out with Bett, so I escaped the usual grilling.

When I came back out, Keiler was waiting on the Harley.

I gave the black beast a wary look. "I don't mind driving. . . ."

He revved the engine. "C'mon, live a little. It's a nice night for a ride. I saw a Starbucks by the highway exit."

Glad that the coffee shop was nearby, I hopped on behind him. As we wound through the twilight-dim neighborhood streets, I discovered that I liked riding a motorcycle much better than I ever thought I would. Keiler's body was warm against mine, and the rush of cool

March breeze filled my ears and cleared my mind, so that when we arrived at Starbucks, I was flushed and invigorated.

"That wasn't so bad," I admitted, as we ordered cappuccinos and took a table in the back.

"Guess I should have asked if you were still sick." Tossing his hair out of his eyes, he looked pointedly at me, gauging my reaction. "A motorcycle ride in the cold might not be the best thing."

"I wasn't sick Friday, Keiler." I stirred my cappuccino, watching the steam rise. "Something happened."

"I gathered as much. It had to do with Cameron's incident in the hall last Thursday, am I right?"

"How did you know?"

He glanced away. "I have my sources," he answered evasively, then looked back at me. "But mostly, I'm just guessing. I saw you Friday morning. I knew you weren't sick. Mrs. Jorgenson mentioned the big powwow with Cameron's mother, and Cameron was seriously lying low all day Friday. Basically, I put two and two together, being the math teacher that I am. I was going to wait and see you Monday, but I was out riding this evening, and I thought about you, and ended up here." Taking a sip of his coffee, he pushed it forward, then rested both hands in his lap and leaned across the table. "So what's going on, Julia?"

I gazed up at the ceiling, exhaling a long breath. "It's bad. It's really bad." I told the story as Keiler sat listening intently. He seemed quick to understand, slow to judge, and as I recounted Friday's happenings, a thousand pounds seemed to drop from my shoulders. "I really don't know what I'm going to do tomorrow," I said finally, then added as an afterthought, "I'm sorry to dump all of this on you."

If Keiler felt staggered by the burden, it didn't show. He frowned thoughtfully into his cappuccino, which was probably growing cold. "That's a serious dilemma." Stretching a hand across the table, he laid it over mine. "I don't know what I'd do. I really don't. But I do know that the kids need you there."

"That's the problem," I admitted. "This job is about more than just what I want or what I think; it's about the kids. I've found the place I'm supposed to be. This is what I'm supposed to be doing at this point in my life—I'm sure of it. I got here by accident, but I'm needed, you know?"

"I don't think anything happens by accident." Keiler's eyes were soft and large, filled with a kinship I couldn't explain. "You understand those kids because of everything you've been through. You can relate to their dreams, you know their fears, you've experienced the kind of pressure they're under." His fingers molded around my hand, and I felt the warmth of the circle, a bond of friendship that told me I wasn't alone. "You're a great dancer, Julia. I have to admit, the first time I saw you at Jumpkids, I thought, *Why is this beautiful girl, with this incredible talent, hanging around some high school, working as a guidance counselor?* But it didn't take me one day at Harrington to see how good you are there. You're the one who can make the difference."

His praise, his belief in me made tears tighten my throat. I swallowed hard, rubbing my forehead, trying to smooth the tangle of conflicting emotions. "I want to be there, Keiler, but I can't imagine telling Cameron and his parents that everything is fine—that nothing went on last Thursday. What if something happens to him? What if he gets in a car with some friend who's as messed up as he was last week, and they have a wreck and kill themselves, or someone else? All of that's in my head, and I can't get past it. I can't do it. I can't lie about what I saw."

Keiler nodded, chewing the side of his lip. "Then I guess you have your answer." As if it were simple. *Go with your conscience. No compromises. No gray areas.*

"But if I leave Harrington, I can't help the kids at all. I can't be there for Dell, or Cameron, or anyone else." The idea seemed as unimaginable as lying to Cameron's parents. Tears welled over and trickled down my cheeks, and I wiped them impatiently. "Sometimes I wonder if Stafford is right—if I'm abandoning the kids so I can sit on my high horse. Maybe I should just play the game—do what I can."

Giving my fingers one last reassuring squeeze, Keiler broke the connection and folded his hands in his lap, leaving me alone on my side of the table.

"I can't tell you which way to go, Julia," he said softly. "That choice has to come from you. You have to decide what you can live with. But beyond that, I'll listen, I'll pray, I'll tell you that all this is happening for a reason."

"I can't imagine the reason," I admitted, wishing I had his faith.

"Give it time," he said with calm assurance. There was an incredible sense of relief in finally having shared the whole story with someone, in not being trapped in this mess alone. "The answers don't always come according to our self-imposed schedule. You ought to know that. You're the professional counselor here. I'm just a substitute algebra teacher."

Sniffling back the tears, I managed a trembling smile. "I'm so glad you're here." In spite of everything, Keiler Bradford could still make me laugh.

Chapter 23

*B*y Monday morning, the answers still weren't clear, and I was running out of time. I left for work early, needing a quiet place to think. When I got there, the administration offices were still dark, and the janitorial staff was sweeping the floors. Down the hall in the auditorium, a girl's ensemble was practicing, and someone was playing "Jesu, Joy of Man's Desiring" on the piano. I listened for a moment before slipping into my office and closing the door behind me, as if that could keep out the realities of the day. It only shut out the music, of course. Everything else came inside with me. I stood looking at the file cabinets, the plaster walls, the cluster of ladybugs in the corner, the piled-up in-box. All of it seemed foreign, as if I'd been gone for a month rather than three days.

I tried to imagine being gone forever.

When I turned to my desk, there were two sheets of spiral notebook paper resting atop my DayMinder, weighted down with a stapler. They fluttered slightly in the draft from the air vent as I picked them up.

As usual, Dell's essay didn't have a title. It was just her thoughts, like an entry in a journal, all of which would have remained locked inside her if Mrs. Morris hadn't brought the first one to my office. *God can make good ends from bad motives*—a quote from Sister Margaret.

Sitting down in my chair, I started to read.

I found out this morning that my father had a name. Thomas Clay. He was somebody real. He signed the paper when I was born, and so he knew about me. He must have cared a little bit to do that, but not enough to stay.

Twana Stevens explained it all to me real slow, like maybe I couldn't understand it, but I do. She says they have looked for him, but they can't find him. Now the courts will do some things, so I can be adopted by James and Karen. She asked if I thought I'd want to change my last name, and I said yes, I would. Jordan isn't a very good name.

So, I'll be Dell Sommerfield. I may put my father's name in the middle. I'll have to think about it. Twana says that his last name should have been my name all along, but Mama and Granny never did use it.

The funny thing is that now I don't feel like I care so much about everything that happened before. It's fading away, like a story you tell about someone who isn't real, and never was. I think the girl in the river will get smaller until she's only a tiny piece inside me. That's good, because it leaves more room for other things.

Karen and I talked for a long time last night. She told me that years ago, she and James were going to have a baby, and they lost it before it was born. She always thought about who that baby would be, if it grew up. What she didn't know, she says, is that her daughter was growing up all that time, only not the way she thought. She never imagined she'd find her daughter living across the river from Grandma Rose's farm.

After Karen left my bedroom, I laid there thinking about what she said. If I didn't have my real mom and dad, I wouldn't be who I am. If I didn't meet Karen and James, I wouldn't be living in the bedroom with the high ceiling and the pretty fan that you don't really need because the place is air conditioned. It's OK how things worked out.

Grandma Rose says the secret to a good life isn't in getting what you want; it's in learning to want what you get. I'm learning to want what I've got and not to think about the rest so much. Maybe the only thing God used my real parents for was thread, so that he could knit me together a certain way for James and Karen. Maybe James and Karen didn't have a baby so they would have room for me.

I hope someday I'll see my baby brother, Angelo, again, so I can tell him about the things we used to do together. He ought to know that I cried when he left, and I always missed him, and when Grandma Rose taught me how to pray, I always said prayers for him. Someday I want to tell him that.

But right now I'm here, and I have a good family. Sometimes, when we're all at the breakfast table, I close my eyes, and I feel just like the girl in the river, like I'm drenched in light from the inside out.

Lots of people don't ever feel that, no matter where they come from.

Looking at the paper, I felt a sense of joy and accomplishment that was out of keeping with the day. Whatever happened from this point on, there would remain this one fact. I had helped the girl in the river begin to take ownership of her new shoes. If I'd turned a blind eye, as Mrs. Morris and Mr. Stafford wanted me to, it wouldn't have happened. Harrington might have been one more failure in a long string of disappointments for Dell. Who could say if this would have been the one that closed her off to the possibility of success? To her own right to happiness?

With that question came my answer to the larger dilemma of my future at Harrington. I knew what was right, the same way I'd known it the day Mrs. Morris sent Dell to my office. If I sold out now, I would be serving only myself. Soon enough, I would begin to loathe who I'd become, and I would be right back where I was all those years with the eating disorder. Sitting in my office, holding Dell's essay, I struck on an epiphany. Dance hadn't ruined me; the instructor who said that ballerinas should be slim like the willow hadn't ruined me; and Harrington hadn't ruined me. Nor had my parents or the question of my biological father. I had ruined myself. I had chosen it. The light comes from the inside out, and so does the darkness. We choose the things that fill us.

It is as simple as that, but it makes all the difference.

It was exactly what Sister Margaret had been trying to tell me in the hospital. I was my own victim. I was poisoning myself, and it was time to stop.

When Mr. Stafford came to my door, I was ready. I was sitting with a packet of Dell's essays in hand, marked, *For Dell Jordan. Personal.* I hoped that someday she would share them with her new parents. It would be her choice.

I turned the envelope over on my desk, quickly tucking in a sticky note—*Checked your grades this morning, all passing, "C" in English. Good work!*—as Stafford came in and slowly closed the door. Smiling hopefully, he took a breath to speak.

I answered without waiting for the question. "I'm not going to do it, Mr. Stafford. It's wrong. I'm sorry." His eyes widened in surprise, then narrowed in condemnation, as I went on. "I won't lie. I know what I saw. I'll be happy to counsel Cameron and his parents. I'll talk with them. I'll help them deal with the issues. I'll do whatever it takes."

Stafford threw his head back, then yanked it forward again, scratching his temple roughly. "If you go this route, you'll never get the chance."

"It's the only route I can go." I felt an amazing sense of peace, a certainty in the words.

"You understand that we're talking nonrenewal of your contract, and most likely either administrative suspension, or immediate dismissal from your job?"

I nodded, feeling far away from Mr. Stafford's fury, as if someone else were sitting in my chair.

He reached out in a gesture that represented either a plea or a desire to strangle me. "I won't even be able to give you a reference, Julia. Think about what you're doing."

"I understand." Laying one hand over the other, I folded them neatly on the desk. "I presume that nothing will happen until tonight's board meeting—that I still have today?"

Nodding vaguely, he crossed his arms over his midsection, glaring around the office, no doubt thinking of all the things I did in a day and who was going to take care of them now.

"I'll do my best to get the grant application in order," I told him. "It's close to being finished."

Shaking his head, he turned away, dismissing me with a wave of his hand. "Stay away from the students," he said, then disappeared, slamming the door behind him.

The sound rang through my office like a funeral bell. It was done.

I left the door closed all morning and worked on the grant. Stafford came by before lunch, looking slightly calmer but with a sheen of perspiration glistening on his neck and forehead. He stared at me for a long moment, as if he were considering trying to change my mind, then finally, he said, "I'll ask the board to accept your resignation. That will look better for you."

"I won't resign. They'll have to fire me. I haven't done anything wrong. I intend to be there at tonight's meeting." The idea had been brewing in the back of my mind all morning. Why just lie down and make this easy for them? Why not show up for the board meeting? Why not sign up for a spot on the public agenda, and use my four minutes of allotted time to say what needed to be said?

Stafford looked mortified. "I . . . I don't think that's advisable," he stammered. "There may still be some chance that I can soothe the board . . . tell them you're inexperienced, that you made a poor judgment call. . . ." His face softened, opened, waiting for a positive response. When I gave none, his expression narrowed again. "Julia, if you show up at the public forum and say anything about Cameron, I guarantee his mother will have you in court before you can say slander. She has her good name to protect, and she can afford high-dollar lawyers."

Maybe she should stop thinking of her good name, and start thinking about her son. "I would never reveal a student's personal information," I said. "I'm not trying to hurt anybody, Mr. Stafford. I'm not trying to send my career up in flames or behave like some irresponsible, impractical hothead. I am concerned about these kids. I'm concerned about Cameron. Whether you want to face it or not, there is a problem here."

Stafford didn't answer, just threw up his hands and walked out.

After he was gone, Dell appeared in the doorway, her gaze darting nervously toward the administration office. Clearly, she'd seen Mr. Stafford's angry exit, and she knew something was wrong.

"Is everything OK?" she asked, picking at one of her fingernails.

"Yeah, Dell, it's OK." The words sounded hollow.

She pursed her lips into a solemn pout. "Keiler said you might not be able to work with me at lunch today."

The comment stung, and as much as I'd thought I was prepared to leave Harrington, the idea quickly became painful. After today, this office might not be mine anymore—*would not* be mine. Barring a miracle, there seemed to be no way out. "I . . . can't today," I admitted, wondering what else to say. It seemed unfair to let her think that tomorrow things would go on as normal. At the same time, I couldn't share confidential school business with a student. As soon as the school board meeting was over, the rumor mill would go wild. I felt the need to explain to Dell. "Dell, I want you to know that the grades this nine-week period came from you, from your hard work. You even earned a 'C' in English—I checked this morning. That didn't happen by magic, and I didn't do it. You did. You need to remember that, if things . . ." I searched for a word, a way to make her understand without telling her what was happening. "If things change, and I can't tutor you every day, I don't want you to quit. You've got Barry, and Keiler, and your folks. They'll work with you anytime you need it."

Her dark brows drew together. "But you're going to help me sometimes, too, aren't you?"

"Of course I will." *Don't make promises you can't keep.* "Don't worry, OK?"

She studied me as if she knew there was more I wasn't saying, then finally turned to leave. " 'Kay." Slanting one last glance over her shoulder, she added, "See you later, Ms. C."

"See you later." I watched her disappear through the partially open door.

After a few minutes Barry showed up, asking if I knew where Dell was. When I told him I thought she was looking for him to study over lunch, he smiled and said, "Cool. Glad you're feeling better, Ms. C." I thanked him, then got up and closed the door.

The rest of the school day ticked by one class period at a time, the halls silent, then filled with noise, then silent again. I tried to finish the grant application and organize things in my office, though it was a fairly feeble effort. My mind was racing forward to the school board meeting, then back to last week's incident with Cameron. I pictured him sitting in my office chair, talking out of his head, his eyes glassy, his reactions slow and drowsy, his neck limp, head resting on the wall, the file cabinet, his shoulder. How could anyone ignore that and then face the mirror the next day?

An eternity seemed to pass before the dismissal bell rang. I sat listening as the hall filled with the sounds of day's end—kids talking, hurried footsteps, lockers slamming, Mrs. Morris screeching above the din. The normal afternoon routine. It was hard to imagine myself somewhere else at this time of day. I wasn't sure when it had happened, but the rhythm of my life had shifted to include this place.

Someone knocked on the office door. *Stafford,* I thought, and my pulse raced with nervous adrenaline. *Stafford wouldn't knock.* Rubbing a hand over the hammer slamming in my chest, I got up and opened the door.

Keiler was on the other side. "You're here." He seemed surprised to have found me in my office. "I saw your door closed this morning and I thought . . ." The look on his face said that he'd assumed I told Stafford to take this job and shove it. Now, he was guessing the opposite—that I'd decided to stay and bend to Stafford's will. Keiler seemed at a loss for words. "Anyway . . . uhhh . . . Barry came by a while ago and said you were in your office."

"Doesn't look like it'll be my office much longer." Glancing into the hall, I made sure no one was listening. Kids were still passing with backpacks, but the corridor was rapidly clearing out. "Stafford won't settle for anything but an apology to Cameron and his parents. He's ready to play hardball about it. He's talking nonrenewal of my contract and suspension or dismissal for the rest of the year. So, barring a miracle, I'm out of here." The tough-career-girl facade fractured momentarily, causing the last sentence to tremble.

"I didn't think you'd cave in." The admiration in Keiler's tone bolstered some sagging part of me.

"I told him I wasn't handing him a convenient resignation, either. They're going to have to fire me, and I intend to be at the school board meeting tonight when they do it. In fact, I've already e-mailed the board clerk and signed up for a spot on the agenda during the open forum, so that I can say what needs to be said. Cameron isn't the only kid in this school with a problem, and not all parents are as blind as the Anslers. Maybe someone will listen."

Keiler smiled slightly, his brown eyes reflecting the resolute face of a woman who surprised even me. "I'll come early and get a front-row seat. In fact, I'll be on the agenda with you, if you want. I haven't been here long, but long enough to have seen some things. I worked one summer at a youth boot camp, so I know what to look for." Raising his brows so that they disappeared under the might-have-been-combed hair, he looked ready to attend the big shoot-out, then move on to his next adventure. "I don't have much to lose. After all, I'm just a sub."

The idea was surprisingly disturbing—not just because I wanted him to be here for Dell, but because the thought of him getting on his Harley and heading for Michigan made me feel lost. "I don't want you to do that." The protest came out too quickly, with too much emotion, and I paused to rein myself in. "Keiler, if I leave, Dell's going to need you—so will the other kids. You're good with them. They need somebody . . . real. Please tell me you'll stay. It would make all of this a little more bearable."

Shifting uncomfortably, he herded a ladybug toward the baseboard with one sneakered foot. "It won't be the same with you gone." He glanced toward the front door, as if he were thinking of making a run for it.

"Please, Keiler. Please don't leave."

Crossing his arms over the CATCHIN' AIR COLORADO logo on his sweatshirt, he deflated. "I'm not leaving," he admitted, like he'd known it all along. "But I will be at that school board meeting."

"It probably isn't a good idea—for you, I mean," I said, checking the hallway again. "You shouldn't be seen here talking to me, either."

If he was worried, it didn't show. "See you at the meeting." With a quick wink, he sauntered off down the hall in his normal unhurried way. I watched him go, then closed the door and finished tidying my office, gathering my personal items on one corner of the desk, and stacking the grant materials on the other. I labeled the piles with sticky notes, in case someone else came to clean out the office. Even as I left and closed the door behind me, it was hard to imagine that reality.

Bett called as I was driving home, and despite the fact that I'd kept my work situation secret all weekend, when my sister asked me if something was wrong, I couldn't hide the truth any longer. I spilled the whole story, and Bett took it all in.

"I'm going to that meeting with you tonight," she said when I'd finished unloading my baggage. "These people don't know who they're dealing with."

My sister's show of bravado made me smile. "Bett, you don't have to do that. You've got so much on your plate right now. You're getting married this weekend, for heaven's sake. The last thing you need is—"

"I'm going," she insisted. "I'll be at the house when you get there. What time does this school board meeting start?"

"Six thirty." I wanted to reach through the phone and pull Bett into a big-sister hug.

"All right, I'll see you at Mom and Dad's. We'll grab something to eat, and I'll help you write the speech on the way to the board meeting. They'll rue the day they ever messed with the Costell sisters." She ended the call before I could ask her not to tell Mom and Dad. When I called back, I got her voice mail—proof that she was now a Costell sister on a single-minded mission. She'd turned off the cell phone.

By the time I got home, Bett had done exactly the thing I didn't want her to do: She'd rallied the entire clan. Bett, Jason, Mom, Dad, and Joujou were waiting in the front entry like a mob of Transylvanians ready to storm Dracula's castle with torches and pitchforks.

They all started talking at once, until finally the chaos was so bad that Joujou threw back her head and wailed like a soprano fire engine.

"Joujou," Mom scolded, as if the dog were the one making all the racket. "Hush!"

Sneezing, Joujou gave her an offended look.

I took advantage of the break in the melee. "Everyone calm down, all right?"

"I'm calm," Dad protested. "I'm as calm as I can be. How dare that principal put you in such a position? I'd like to wrap my hands around his neck."

"And with all the extra time you've put into that job," Mom chimed in with a fire I hadn't seen in her eyes since Bett and I sneaked out of the house and went to a forbidden party back in junior high. "I have half a mind to call our lawyer. They can't fire you just because you won't agree to lie. After all the years of volunteer work I put into that school, they ought to have more respect." In her arms, Joujou growled in agreement.

Bett bit her lip apologetically, and behind her, Jason widened his eyes and clamped both hands into his hair, no doubt wondering what kind of a lunatic fringe he was marrying into.

By the time we'd grabbed a quick sandwich, and I'd gone through all the details, everyone was calming down somewhat, and the protests on my behalf had ebbed to a dull roar. I tried to convince them that there was no need for the whole family to attend the school board meeting, but it was hopeless. With the exception of Jason, who was fairly neutral, everyone was determined to stand beside me in my hour of need. We left the house at five forty-five in a disorganized caravan—me in the front with Bett riding in my car because she was determined to help me write my speech, Jason following in his car, in case Bett got tired later and needed to go home before the meeting was over, and my parents bringing up the rear, fully committed to staying at the school board powwow until the bitter end.

By six thirty, we'd arrived at the Board of Education Building, signed in on the agenda, and were stationed, at my mother's insistence, in the front row, where "everyone will know we have nothing to hide." We looked like the Hatfields ready to take on the McCoys.

As the clock on the back wall struck six thirty, school board members began filing through the doorway behind the board table. I looked around for Stafford in the faculty section, but he was nowhere in evidence. The board members walked to their seats strangely empty-handed—no briefcases, no files, no agenda items. The reason soon became apparent. After calling the meeting to order and waiting for a trio of Girl Scouts to lead the Pledge of Allegiance, the board quickly called an executive session to discuss personnel matters, and adjourned to executive chambers. No doubt Stafford was back there with them. Discussing my future.

Keiler came in and took the last empty seat in the Hatfield row—down at the end beside my mother. Apologizing for being late, he introduced himself to my parents and shook my father's hand. He'd dressed up for the occasion, donning a shirt with actual buttons and a tie printed with beakers, test tubes, and chemistry equations. I never would have guessed that he even owned such a tie, or any tie, for that matter. He'd dampened his hair and combed it back slick. He looked clean-cut and serious, in spite of the cast on his foot.

My mother seemed thoroughly charmed. She politely explained to him that we were waiting for the board to come out of executive session; then she moved on to asking about his broken foot. He told the ski lift story, and for a moment, the entire affair took on the air of a carnival or a family trip to the theater. Then someone in the aisle tapped me on the shoulder.

Chapter 24

I turned to find Mr. Verhaden squatted down beside me, his expression grave. "Stafford's planning to have everything discussed during executive session, before you have a chance to address the board in the public forum," he told me quietly. "I'm sorry, Julia."

I wondered how Verhaden knew what was going on in the confidential executive session, but then, he was adept at keeping an ear to the Harrington wind.

"I didn't suppose my addressing the board would do any good," I admitted. "Stafford made it pretty clear I was out, but before I go, I intend to say what needs to be said."

Verhaden let out a long, frustrated sigh. "Julia, why didn't you tell me all of this was going on?"

"Why didn't *you* tell *me?*" I searched his sad, empty face. "You know exactly what these kids are into. There's no way you could be totally unaware of it, as much time as you spend with them. How can you just sit here and play this"—I waved a hand toward the room, now filled with parents and the obligatory reporter or two in the back row, all chatting pleasantly and glancing occasionally toward the door behind the empty board table—"this game?" I hated to parrot Stafford's words, but the description fit. It was a game. A ridiculous, pompous game with life-altering implications and deadly consequences.

Mr. Verhaden drew back defensively. "I help the ones I can. You see enough kids with enough problems, after a while you realize you have to focus your energies where you can do some good."

"Oh, come on—what happened to *'save the whales, save the rain forest, feed the starving kids in Africa'?*" Did he even remember who he used to be, or had this place lobotomized him to the point that the spark was completely gone? "Come on, Verhaden, you were the biggest dreamer of all. What happened?"

Shaking his head, he looked away. "I realized that you can't solve anything by getting yourself fired from your job. It may feel good, but it's just a grandstand. It's useless. In the end, you have to work within the existing parameters to make a difference." His sincere conviction shifted the ground under my feet. Perhaps I was making the wrong choice. Maybe I was acting out of pride and stubbornness rather than logic. There was still time to reverse my position—ask to speak to the executive session, tell them this was all a mistake, I wanted to keep my job, and I'd seen the light. Except that there was no light. "You can't make a difference working within these parameters—not the way things are now." At the front of the room, the door opened and board members filed to their places at the table. Verhaden went back to his seat, and I turned around in mine. Nearby, Keiler was talking to Karen and James, who had moved into the row behind us. Karen gave me the high sign, a hopeful show of support. I wondered if she thought I should do whatever it took to keep my job, so I could be there for Dell.

Scanning past her and upward, I took in the faces in the room— teachers and parents, most of whom were probably unaware of the issue being discussed in executive session. To them, this was just another board meeting—a time to talk about field trips, budget issues, repaving sidewalks, and textbook adoptions for next year. In the corner, Mrs. Morris sat perched with the librarian, the two of them surveying the crowd like a couple of vultures ready to devour the weak and the wounded. Morris tapped the woman in front of her, an expensive-looking blonde with sunglasses on her head, and motioned that the board was ready to begin. I watched the blonde a moment longer, trying to decide if she could be Cameron's mother. Hard to say. I'd never met Cameron's parents one on one. I knew his father by sight only because he was on the school board. That seemed incredibly wrong, considering where we were now. I should have done something differently, handled things in a better way.

I watched as Cameron's father took his seat behind the board table, calmly separating various papers into tidy stacks. Just before the board president called the meeting back to order, a group of faculty members slipped in the side door and took their seats in a reserved section near the board table. Mr. Stafford was among them, dressed in a freshly pressed suit, carrying an armload of files, and carefully ignoring my presence.

The meeting resumed with no indication of what had been discussed in executive session, and moved quickly through the consent agenda. The board members looked tense and uncomfortable as the routine business came to an end and the public forum loomed ahead. No doubt, they had seen my name on the agenda.

Stafford cast a hooded glance my way, probably hoping some catastrophic act of nature would make me disappear. My pulse accelerated as the board president concluded the consent items and took his time filling his water glass from a pitcher, then pointing out that the forum was, of course, open to anyone who wished to address the board and had signed up on the list, but we should be aware that each person's time was limited to four minutes, and the board would not be expected to respond—merely to listen and take notes. Any items requiring action would be put on the board agenda in the future. . . .

Tuning out momentarily, I tried to recall my speech and came up blank. Bett and I had practiced it a dozen times in the car. Now I couldn't think of a single word. I glanced over at Bett, who was rubbing her forehead with her thumb and forefinger.

"He's giving me a headache," she whispered, then secretly made a fist in her lap. The meaning—*knock 'em dead*.

"You don't have to stay," I said quietly.

Bett responded with an offended chin bobble. "Are you kidding? I wouldn't miss this. If you need muscle, I'm here."

I smiled into the eyes of my sweet, tough, steadfast little sister.

"Thanks, Bett." She shifted uncomfortably in her chair, and I felt a rush of sympathy for her. She'd been on the run all day with wedding plans, and moving preparations, and solving unexpected problems at her former job. She looked dead on her feet, yet here she was when I needed her. "I'm sorry it's taking so long."

The meeting had already dragged on for over ninety minutes, and the Hatfield row was starting to look weary. Beside Bethany, Jason was covertly tapping something into his PalmPilot, hidden behind his knee. My father, next to him, was staring blankly at the wall over the school board president's head, and my mother was scanning the board table with narrowed eyes, daring any of them to say one unkind word about her daughter. Keiler had given his seat to an elderly woman who arrived late, and he was standing against the wall with his arms crossed. Unfolding one hand, he gave me the thumbs-up as the board president reluctantly opened the public forum. With a last admonition that each of us would be timed and asked to step down at the end of four minutes, he read my name from his agenda, and glanced at his watch.

Bett squeezed my arm, her fingers trembling against my skin. It was hard to say which of us was more nervous. Standing up, I gazed down the row at my family, my supporters, my compass pointing true north. Their faces held not the slightest measure of doubt that I could, and would, do what needed to be done. I felt not like one person, but five— an emissary with a tiny but steadfast army behind me. If I'd ever been ungrateful for my family before, I was now fully attuned to how lucky I was to have them.

My heels clicked against the tile floor as I walked to the podium in what seemed like an impossible silence. I didn't know if the rustle of bodies and the hum of voices had stopped, or if I had merely ceased to hear everything but my own thoughts and the rapid drumbeat of blood in my ears.

Gripping the podium, I stared down at the wood, gathering my thoughts. An eternity seemed to pass, and for a moment, I thought surely the board president would say my four minutes were up.

Somewhere behind me, a man cleared his throat, and I jerked at the sound.

What had I planned to say? How did the speech begin? What were the words?

Chair legs screeched against the floor, and my mind whirled into action. I looked at the board president, who was sitting with his hands folded in his lap, watching me with detachment.

"I'll make this brief." My voice was raspy, and I paused to cough into my hand, then began again. "Excuse me. I'll make this brief, as I know the board has a full agenda tonight." Nearby, Stafford was hunched over his notepad as if he'd rather be anywhere than here. "Because there is some doubt as to whether I will be coming back to Harrington's middle school as guidance counselor, I would like to begin by telling the parents here tonight that it has been a pleasure, even for this short time, to have returned to Harrington and worked with so many extraordinary and talented kids. They show the fruits of not only inborn talent, but also the many years of encouragement, chauffeur service, lessons, belief, and love their parents have provided. I've tried to be equally willing to invest in our students—not just the chosen few, but all of them.

"It is my concern for the kids that has prompted me to speak here tonight. These kids, these bright, talented kids, deserve a school that looks not only to their performance skills and their academics, but also to their physical and emotional health as they grow into adults. They deserve a school that communicates honestly with parents, that does not and *will not* sweep problems under the rug in order to keep things smooth on the surface. They deserve an educational environment that, in particular, is free of drugs and substance abuse, or as close to that goal as is humanly possible. I don't believe they have that." A murmur went around the room, and the school board president sat back in his chair, eyes wide. Stafford's face was flame red. He seemed ready to explode out of his seat.

"I know it is difficult to hear, more so because on the surface, our school appears to be a golden example of the magnet concept— exceptional kids given the opportunity to pursue their gifts." I raised my voice as the murmur grew louder. "It is hard to imagine these bright, talented kids throwing away that opportunity, picking up a fix on the way to school so that they can get through the day, or partying in the parking lot before classes begin. It seems a picture far too ugly for a place like Harrington. But to understand it you have only to consider the kind of pressure these children are dealing with. Not only do they confront all the normal teenage issues, but they have the lure of stardom, the threat of failure, the expectations of parents, teachers. They're looking for an escape from the load, a means of fitting in with their peers, a sense of identity, a way to blow off steam, a thrill—you name it. You can fill in the blank with the reasons, but the fact is that just blocks away, the taco stands sell drugs—most likely everything from marijuana, to controlled substance inhalants, to methamphetamine. The kids know it, the police know it, the Harrington administration knows it, and in my opinion, few effective measures are being taken to prevent it from overpowering our school. We're turning our heads when we should be fighting back."

In his seat behind the board table, Mr. Ansler glared at me, then checked his watch. Three chairs down, the school board president did the same, then continued monitoring the passing seconds. My time was nearly up, and it couldn't be too soon for them.

"Please," I said, scanning the board members like opponents in a bad game of poker, "something needs to be done. We're on a collision course with reality. The only question is whether it happens now, or whether we wait until we're attending the funeral of one of these exceptional kids. In my opinion, that's where we're headed. I won't sit back and quietly watch it happen, and if that costs me my job, then it's a price I'm willing to pay." I didn't wait for the school board president to tell me my four minutes were over. There was nothing left to say, except, "Thank you for listening. Please do what is best for our kids."

When I turned around, Bett was walking toward the door with Jason and my father holding her elbows. My mother was halfway out of her seat, gathering their things.

I met Mom at the aisle as Bett left the room. "What's going on?" I was vaguely aware of chaos escalating around us and the board president rapping his hammer, trying to bring the meeting back to order.

"Bett's having a few cramps." Mom's expression was dark with concern. "It's probably just the stuffiness in here. We're going to go on and run by the doctor's, and we'll see you at home." Laying a hand on my arm, she paused to look into my eyes. "I'm so proud of you, honey. Don't let them bully you." Her hand fell away, and she started after my sister.

In the back row, a woman stood up and shouted something about having taken her son to drug rehab and the school acting like he was a leper when he came back.

I was aware of glances shooting my way as I hurried after my mother, catching her at the door. "The doctor? Mom, it's after eight o'clock on a Monday night. Do you mean the emergency room? Are you taking Bett to the emergency room?"

The two of us slipped into the relative quiet of the corridor. Mom sucked air through clenched teeth, glancing toward the crack in the door, then down the hallway toward the women's restroom. My father was pacing a circle under the sign. Jason must have gone in with Bett. "She didn't want you to worry. She thinks she might be bleeding."

"Bleeding?" The seconds stretched out, and I watched in slow motion as Jason rushed out of the restroom with Bett wrapped in his arms.

"Let's go!" my father hollered.

Mom waved him on. "Go ahead with Jason and Bett. I'll get the car and be right behind you."

"I'll drive you." I spun around to go back into the board room for my purse, but Mom caught my arm.

"Bett didn't want you to—"

"Wait for me," I said, then yanked the door open and hurried into the meeting room, where things had quieted somewhat. A frightened-looking woman was making her way to the podium with a milk crate full of school banners and pom-poms. The board president raised his gavel at my hasty entrance, as if he thought I might knock the pom-pom lady down and take the podium again. The entire room fixated on me as I grabbed my things from my chair.

"My sister is having a medical emergency," I told the board president. Letting his gavel fall loosely, he opened his mouth, then closed it, then opened it again, as if he didn't know what the official procedural response should be.

I didn't wait for an answer, just hurried back up the row, looking neither right nor left, suddenly aware of how little any of this mattered. Compared to the idea of Bethany rushing to the hospital, this meeting was nothing.

Keiler jogged up the side aisle and met me at the back door. "Is there anything I can do?" His expression was steadfast and calm, reassuring. "Can I give you a ride?"

"No, I'm driving my mother over." My fingers shook as I grabbed a business card and pen from my purse and scrawled my cell phone number on the back. "Call me later and tell me what happens in the rest of the meeting, all right?"

Nodding, he shrugged toward the podium. "Good speech. I'll be sure to report in."

"Thanks." I rushed out the door, then hurried to the car with Mom.

On the way to the hospital, my mother sat with her eyes closed, her head resting against the seat, and her arms wrapped around her stomach. Tears seeped from beneath her lashes.

"Mom, it's going to be all right." The words held a false confidence, but inside I was afraid that the stress of trying to support me, on top of everything else Bett was dealing with, had somehow caused this to happen.

My mother drew a shuddering breath, then exhaled a faint sob. "I hope so," she whispered. "Oh, I hope so." She looked for answers in the night sky outside the window. "Surely they're at the hospital by now. I hope they went the shortest way." She craned to see around a gasoline delivery truck that was blocking traffic in the intersection ahead.

"They did. You know they did." I'd never seen such a look of pure horror on my mother's face. Pounding her hands in her lap, she tried to peer around the tanker truck again, then wiped her eyes impatiently.

"Mom, it'll be all right," I promised again. "It will."

"I hope so," she repeated, kneading her hands in her lap, then fiddling with the door latch as if she were considering hopping out and running four miles to the hospital.

"Mom, you have to calm down. If you don't, you'll be checking in right alongside Bett." Her cheeks were flushed and trembling.

"I'm sorry. I'm sorry for being such a mess." Digging in her purse, she found wadded Kleenex, then dabbed her eyes and wiped her nose. "This same thing happened when I was pregnant with you—two and a half months, just like Bethany is now. I was so terrified when I saw the blood." Her hand slipped over mine on the gearshift, her fingers a clammy circle, just as Bett's had been in the boardroom. "I was so terrified I'd lose you. I prayed every minute that God would leave you with me. The doctors said it was a miracle that you survived. If I hadn't already been at the hospital for a prenatal appointment when it happened, there would have been no way. I think about that day, and I can't imagine. I can't imagine how I would have gone on if I'd lost you."

I can't imagine how I would have gone on . . . The words replayed in my head as we inched forward, then stopped at the intersection. Slowly, I looked sideways at my mother, now collapsed against the seat with her eyes closed again, her face pinched and drawn. In the red glow of the traffic light, in the pained lines around her mouth, the tears seeping down her cheeks, I found the reality of my life—the one I had been seeking as long as I could remember.

Even before my birth, I was loved, and wanted, and desperately needed. I was not an accident.

"Mom, who was my father?" The words came so quietly, I wasn't sure I'd said them. I'd always imagined that question entering the space between us in a roar of indignation, during an argument sometime, when the mother-daughter pressure built up so high that the cork finally exploded, uncapping all the secrets and unspoken truths.

Instead, it came in a whisper. *Who was my father?*

Turning her hands over in her lap, Mom stared at them like a palm reader. "I wondered when you would ask." Her voice was soft and pensive, as if she'd rehearsed this scene in her mind many times, and the question had transported her into her own thoughts, away from the excitement over Bett's condition.

"I've always been afraid to ask," I admitted, thinking of all the times those words had been on the tip of my tongue, and I pulled them back, certain that I'd be lighting a powder keg and nothing would be the same afterward. "But I need to know. I'm sorry."

Mother glanced sideways at me. "There's nothing to be sorry for." She tucked my hair behind my shoulder like she would have when I was a child.

"I don't want to hurt Dad." The truth choked in my throat, filling me with the old fear that once he knew I'd asked, he would quit the masquerade of being my father, and let himself be replaced by this shadow man of biology, whoever he was.

"Oh, sweetheart." Mom ran a finger along my cheek. "Your father thought we should sit you down years ago and talk about it. He didn't want you to think it was some dark secret. But I didn't want to force that reality on you if you didn't want it."

"I was afraid he wouldn't love me anymore." I felt like a little girl saying those words—as if they were coming from some arrested place inside me that had never grown beyond eight years old.

Mom looked shocked, then sad. "Oh, honey, I never intended for you to feel that way. Your dad loved you from the first moment he saw you. He couldn't have loved you more if you were his own. I think he was more taken with you than with me the day we met."

I knew the story of the day my parents met, only there had never been any mention of me in it. She was reenrolling in college after having dropped out at the end of her second year. He was a graduate student working in the admissions office. He helped her with some complicated paperwork, and then he asked her to share lunch on the lawn outside the student union.

"I was there?" The picture rushed to repaint itself in my mind—my mother, my father, me on a picnic blanket near the reflecting pool. "How old was I?" A car horn honked somewhere behind us, and I realized we were sitting in the intersection, not moving. My ankle quivered, the muscles tense as I moved from the brake to the gas. The world outside the car seemed far away and unreal.

"You were about six months old when we met"—it was startlingly matter-of-fact, as if the story were nothing out of the ordinary—"and about a year old when we married." I glanced over, and she was smiling slightly, looking out the window, her gaze far away. "Of course, back in those days, people thought differently about things. Everyone felt that, with you being so young . . . well . . . we should just go on and make a normal family life, without . . . issues."

I pictured Mom in Bett's wedding dress, me hidden somewhere in the wings, or with a babysitter, because it wasn't proper for me to be there. "Where was my father . . . my biological father?" Behind that, there was the other question—the one that bit and burned. *Didn't he ever want to know me?*

Smile fading, Mom shifted uncomfortably. "We had . . . problems. We were married less than a year—long enough to create you, of course, but we divorced just before you were born."

"Divorced?" I repeated. I'd never imagined that my mother and my biological father were married. By virtue of the fact that I didn't have his name, I'd always assumed I was the result of an unwed pregnancy. "You were married to my biological father?"

Mom craned to look for the emergency parking entrance as we reached St. Francis Hospital. "There's so much to the story, Julia, and it was so long ago. He was young, and I was young. I was going to school and working part-time for the wardrobe mistress at the Kansas City Ballet. Your father was a wonderful dancer. He came with a touring company that was doing a guest production of *The Nutcracker*." Her eyes fell closed, and she sighed, as if she could see him there in front of her. I pulled the car into a parking space, but she didn't move. "He was beautiful to see—tall, with deep blue eyes and blond hair like yours. And his smile, oh, when he smiled . . ." Her lips curved upward, and she laughed in her throat. "I fell so in love, and when the production moved on, we eloped, and I went with him. It never occurred to me that we wouldn't have much of a life. I thought we'd live on love, I guess." Turning her head, she faced me. "Your father wasn't a bad man, Julia. He was just a dreamer, and it's a hard world for dreamers."

Pulling the keys from the ignition, I tucked them into my purse, knowing we needed to go inside and see about Bett. "Where is he now?" Behind that, there was the unspoken question again. *Didn't he wonder about me at all? Ever?*

Mom reached for her door handle, lifting it slowly, so that only a faint click disturbed the silence. "He died when you were three. I never really knew the details, but it was a car accident. He didn't have any family to speak of, so I heard the news from a mutual friend." Frowning sadly, she reached across the space between us and smoothed a hand over my hair. "He came to see you once before that. He was at your third-birthday party, and he brought you a jewelry box with a little ballerina that twirled when you lifted the lid. You know—the white one I've always kept on your dresser? That was from him. He would have been so proud of you, Julia. If he could be here to see, he would be so proud. He loved you enough to want you to have a normal life." Her tears glittered in the dim light, tracing the fine wrinkles around her eyes. Without bothering to wipe them, she turned away and pushed open the door. "We'd better go inside."

I followed her into the hospital, thinking of the past, my father, my mother, and the choices she had made for me. A stable life, a solid family, a father who soothed my broken hearts and chased away the boogey men at night. He was a poor dancer, but a good man, and he loved me from the moment he saw me. My dad.

He was sitting near the emergency room door, wringing his hands in his lap when we walked in. Crossing the hallway, I sat down beside him, slipped an arm around him, and laid my head on his shoulder. Mom sat on the other side of him, looking anxiously around the waiting room.

"They took Bett right in," Dad explained. "Jason's with her. That's all I know so far."

Mom slipped her hand into Dad's, and we sat there waiting, chained together by a thread of desperate hope. Fifteen minutes ticked by, and then thirty.

Dad got up and paced the room, then sat down again. Mom inquired at the emergency desk, but there was no news.

I closed my eyes and prayed until finally Jason appeared in the emergency room doorway. One look at his face told me everything was all right.

"False alarm." His lips parted into a jubilant smile, as he held up a strip of ultrasound images. "The baby's fine. Here are baby's first pictures."

The four of us gathered around the misty photographs, trying to decipher body parts, discussing the possibilities of a niece or nephew, granddaughter or grandson.

Caught in the beauty and mystery of the moment, we were swept from horrible fear to awe-inspiring joy.

Chapter 25

*I*n the rush of getting Bett out of the hospital and ready for her wedding, I was almost able to forget the controversy at Harrington. Stafford fired me via voice mail on my cell phone, expressing his regret and assuring me he'd done everything he could to prevent it. Keiler filled me in on the details of the board meeting. After I'd left, the audience had several times erupted into questions about the drug issue and accusations of a cover-up. The board president had repeatedly tried to redirect the meeting, and had reminded the audience that the board would not respond to comments made during the public forum, or to impromptu questions. Any inquiries or concerns would have to be submitted in writing before the next board meeting. Finally he'd threatened to have disrupters ejected, reminding them that only those signed up for the agenda were allowed to speak.

On Thursday after school, Keiler brought a box of personal items from my office. I hadn't had the heart to go back. I knew when I did, it would really hit me that this was the end. With Bett's scare and the wedding details, I'd felt as if I were on a long weekend or on leave for a family emergency, and I'd be going back to work in a few days. I knew that next week, with the wedding over and Bett gone, Monday morning would be hard.

Reality struck as I opened the box from my office. Sitting on my parents' front steps with Keiler, I started to cry. The top of the box was filled with notes from students. Most of them said *Free Ms. C,* and had pictures of hands in handcuffs or cartoon characters with tape across their mouths. One had Mr. Stafford as Hitler and me as the Statue of Liberty, stuffed in a trash bag up to the neck.

"They've started a protest campaign," Keiler explained as I wiped my eyes. " '*Free Ms. C.*' They sneak by and stick the notes on your office door, like Stafford has you locked in there. It drives him nuts. He keeps pulling the notes down, and every time he turns around, more appear. When there's a crowd in the hall, someone will yell, 'Free Ms. C!' and Stafford goes crazy trying to figure out who said it." Sitting beside me on the step, he motioned to the notes. "I got these from the trash can. I thought you'd like to see." His eyes twinkled, and I found myself staring into them, the bits of paper limp in my hands. I wondered how much he had to do with fueling this protest. "So, you may not be there, but you've started a movement. There are plenty of kids at Harrington who are serious about pursuing their talents, and you've finally helped them find a voice. It doesn't hurt that, as a whole, the kids hate Stafford. Protesting him has become the thing to do. My classroom is a long way from the office, but I've seen parents going in and out of administration every time I've been by this week. People are asking questions."

I felt a twinge of satisfaction, a hope that my time at Harrington wouldn't be in vain. "How is Dell doing?" There was a voice-mail message from Karen on my cell phone, but I hadn't had the heart to return it. "Tell Karen I'm sorry I haven't called her back yet. Things have been busy with Bett."

"Dell misses you." He squinted pensively, his face catching that late-afternoon sunshine. "But, you know, this has been good for her in a sense. She's angry—not at you, but in a righteous kind of way. With all the things that have happened in her life, that's the one thing that has always been missing. She quietly tolerates injustice, like she deserves it. She's never raged against the machine, against the things that are wrong and unfair, and now she's finally doing that. She's learning what it feels like to stand up and be counted."

A sense of pride swelled within me as I set the *Free Ms. C* notes in the box. I thought of Dell sitting in my office just a few weeks ago, trying to disappear into the chair as I read the essay about the girl in the river. *There's nothing to me that anyone would want to read about,* she'd said. "I'm glad she's finally finding herself." Rubbing away the lingering emotions, I tried to gather my thoughts. "But tell her not to get in trouble for me, all right? Tell all the kids that. I'll be all right. I don't want them getting in trouble, especially not Dell. She's on the borderline at Harrington already, and she's worked hard to stay."

"I think at this point you have to let her make her own decisions." He glanced sideways with a slight, knowing smile. "She's doing what she needs to do. Yesterday, she read an essay out loud in English class—Ada requires them to do that at least once per semester. Last time Dell flunked the requirement, but this time she signed up on her own. She even invited me in to listen—shook Mrs. Morris up a bit, but she let me sit in while Dell did her reading."

A sense of amazement drifted through my black mood like a pinch of misplaced glitter. I couldn't imagine Dell volunteering to read in front of the class, or inviting Keiler to come. "What did she read?"

"An essay about her mother's drug use and Just Say No." Picking a fluffy seed head off his sneakers, he tossed it into the breeze, sending it on its way to someplace it could root. "She said you helped her write it."

A new rush of tears prickled in my throat. Happy tears, the kind that come from knowing some things work out the way they're supposed to. "I can't believe she did that." I imagined how she must have felt, standing in front of everyone, finally telling her story.

"She did." He punctuated the sentence with a definitive nod. "She said she wanted the other kids to understand what it's like to live with somebody who's messed up on drugs. After she finished reading, the kids asked her questions for ten minutes until the bell rang. There wasn't a dry eye in the house, I'll tell you. Even Ada looked emotional."

I tried to imagine Mrs. Morris getting emotional. My mind couldn't form the picture. "That must have been something to see."

"It was quite a moment," Keiler admitted. "It wouldn't have happened without you."

"I wish I could have been there."

"I know." Nudging me, he took my hand in his and looked at my fingers. "But you were. You were in that room more than anybody else. You and Dell."

"Thanks for coming, Keiler," I whispered, and rested my head on his shoulder. We sat like that for a long time, until finally the afternoon light grew dim and the air cold. Shivering, I slipped my other hand into my sweatshirt sleeve, and Keiler smiled.

"Guess I'd better go," he said, standing up, then pulling me to my feet. "See you at the wedding rehearsal tomorrow. Dell's had me playing the guitar track over and over until I could do it in my sleep. She doesn't want to let you down. She and Karen went out shopping tonight for a dress to match the wedding colors."

"They didn't have to do that," I said as we walked to his motorcycle.

Putting on his helmet, he straddled the metal-and-leather beast and raised the kickstand. "It's good for them. Mother-daughter bonding and all that stuff, you know."

The thought gave me a warm sense of satisfaction. In some small way, I'd helped to bring them together as a family. Wherever I landed next in my career, I hoped I would have the opportunity to do that again, but Dell would always be the first. "How is Cameron doing, by the way?"

"Still having a rough go, right now. Hard to say how that will turn out. He's in a tough spot."

I didn't trust myself to answer. It was difficult to know how to feel about Cameron. On the one hand, he had cost me my job. On the other hand, he was a kid with a load of problems he didn't have the maturity and life experience to fully understand.

Starting the Harley, Keiler said good-bye, then turned around in the driveway and drove off. I watched man and motorcycle get smaller and smaller until both disappeared. Then I wished he would circle the block and come back. I waited until the rumble had faded completely before I walked inside, set the box on the guest bed, and sorted through it. I'd forgotten to pack some of my personal items—nothing critical, but tomorrow when I went downtown to pick up Bett's bouquets at the cleaner's, I'd stop by Harrington, remove the last few things from my office, and see the *Free Ms. C* campaign for myself. There would be at least some satisfaction in walking into that building with my head held high.

All night, I tried to convince myself that was how I would feel, returning to Harrington—triumphant, indignant, righteous. Securely on the moral high ground.

But when I drove into the Harrington parking lot on Friday morning, even though I was determined not to be, I was filled with a sense of failure. Sitting in the car with my hands sweating and my heart racing, I waited until the lot was clear and the kids would be in Friday-morning assembly, before I walked up the steps. It was far from the triumphant reentry I had envisioned. Breath caught in my throat as I peeked into the administration area. Fortunately, it was empty, so I hurried toward my office. The hallway felt surreal, and as I turned the corner, I stood looking at a half dozen *Free Ms. C* notes taped to my door. They fluttered in silent fanfare as I went inside, leaving the door cracked behind me, so that if anyone came by, I couldn't be accused of doing something covert.

Sitting on the edge of my desk with my arms resting on an empty file box, I gazed around the room, wondering who would fill it next. The question was too painful to consider, so I packed my books from the bookshelf, the wall clock I'd brought from home, the "Daily Inspirations" calendar Bett had given me when I started the job. Taking one last look in the desk drawers, I hoisted the box onto my hip and walked out. A line of ladybugs, marching single file along the ceiling, led me to the front entrance. Pushing open the door, I paused to look back at the corridor, to consider that this was the last time.

When I turned around, Cameron was hurrying up the steps with his backpack and his saxophone. We stood on the landing, staring at each other, neither of us knowing what to say.

Ducking his head, he scrubbed a toe through the coating of silt atop the cement. "I'm, ummm . . . I'm sorry, Ms. C," he muttered, shrugging to hike his backpack higher onto his shoulder.

"Me too, Cameron." I let the door close behind me.

Shifting his weight to balance the instrument, he cast a hopeful glance at me. "I didn't mean for all this to happen . . . like this, I mean. My mom's a witch sometimes."

The counselor in me reared her head at the comment. *Avoidance, denial, shifting of blame.* "Cameron, what happened has little to do with your mom and everything to do with you. Your mom wasn't the one out of control in the hall last week."

Eyes widening indignantly, he drew back, fidgeting with the tail of his backpack strap, wrapping it around his finger, then unwrapping it. "I went to the doctor yesterday, and he changed my medication, so that shouldn't happen again." Blinking innocently, he nodded as he spoke, hoping, I supposed, that I would nod along.

"Cameron, you know and I know that what happened last Thursday had nothing to do with ADD medications." He opened his mouth to protest, but I held a hand up between us. "Don't bother giving me whatever line worked at home. I'm not buying it." He looked young and vulnerable and terrified. I laid a hand on his arm, imagining myself at fourteen, all my carefully hidden secrets revealed. "Cameron, you've got a problem, and the longer you continue to deny it, the worse it's going to get. When you spend this kind of energy maintaining a lie, everything else in your life suffers. Think about what you're giving up— your music, your grades, your self-respect, maybe eventually your life? Come on, Cam, you're a smart kid. I know you've got problems at home, but you aren't going to solve them with weed or huffing, or whatever you've been doing. When you come down, you're still the same kid, in the same place, with the same problems. You need to tell your parents the truth." I didn't wait for an answer, just let go of his arm and left. He stood looking after me until I was almost to the bottom of the steps, then finally turned and went into the building.

The picture of him standing alone on the steps haunted me as I drove to the cleaner's. When I arrived, Mim and Granmae were playing dominoes at a corner table. Bett's flowers were waiting, carefully packaged in three boxes from the grocery store. Mim pulled off the lids, and breath caught in my throat.

"They're beautiful," I gasped, and even though I knew Mim's roses were outstanding, I was amazed anew by the delicate bouquets of buttercream-colored roses with soft pink tips, nestled in fresh greenery and laced with white baby's breath and tiny clusters of periwinkle blue flowers that looked like miniature wine cups. The scent of old-fashioned roses wafted up and reminded me of trellises at Grandma Rice's house, covered each spring with fragrant red blooms.

"I have them in a little water." Mim was obviously pleased with my response to her work. "And there is floral tape in the box, so that when you are ready to use the bouquets, you may take them out and tape the base of the stems." Reaching into the container, she pulled out a small bouquet and illustrated the process. "I know these are to be for the rehearsal, but this one," she said, holding it up, "is for your bride to throw during the reception." Elbowing me in the ribs, she squinted upward, her blue eyes twinkling. "Perhaps someone very special will catch it."

Blushing, I gazed into the box. "My luck hasn't been running that way, lately."

From the corner of my eye, I saw Granmae wink at Mim. Looking at each other, they nodded. "Your luck's about to change," Granmae said, like she knew something I didn't. "That angel there is smilin' ear to ear, and she got a crafty look on her face." Peering at my shoulder, she nodded definitively. "Yup. She got somethin' up her sleeve, for sure."

"I'd say so," Mim concurred, and I felt like I'd stepped into a Disney cartoon. I doubted my fairy god angel was going to *bippity-boppity--boo* my life into shape anytime soon.

"She must know something I don't know." The comment sounded more cynical than I meant it to.

Shaking a finger back and forth, Granmae made a *tsk-tsk-tsk*. "Angels always do."

We stood in silence for a moment, all three of us—all four, if you counted the angel—taking in the subtle mystery of Mim's incredible roses.

"Now you'll see that in each bouquet there is evergreen," Mim said, fingering the flowers and pointing out sprigs of juniper. "Wedding bouquets should always be made with evergreen, to symbolize a love that grows in every season."

"That's beautiful," I said, thinking that once Bett saw these bouquets, she would surely want to use them for the wedding. At the last minute, she and Mom had settled on silk flowers for the ceremony, but nothing made of silk could possibly compare to Mim's roses.

"It will be a beautiful day, a perfect day," Granmae promised, after conferring with the angel on my shoulder again. "Expect a few surprises."

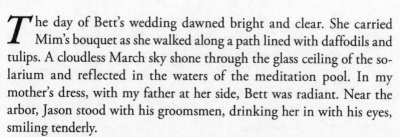

Chapter 26

The day of Bett's wedding dawned bright and clear. She carried Mim's bouquet as she walked along a path lined with daffodils and tulips. A cloudless March sky shone through the glass ceiling of the solarium and reflected in the waters of the meditation pool. In my mother's dress, with my father at her side, Bett was radiant. Near the arbor, Jason stood with his groomsmen, drinking her in with his eyes, smiling tenderly.

Evergreen, I thought. Bett and Jason had found the real thing, the kind of love that would grow through all the seasons. As Dad slipped Bett's hand into Jason's, the solo music started, and I realized it was "Evergreen," originally sung by Barbra Streisand. Bett had chosen it because it was Dad's favorite, but now it seemed incredibly perfect for the moment.

Keiler winked at me as he finished the guitar intro, and Dell began singing along with the music. In the second row, sitting between her husband and Barry, Karen was mouthing along with the words, holding her breath the way mothers do when their children perform.

She needn't have worried. The song was beautiful, as was the ceremony and Dell's final solo as Bett and Jason lit the unity candle.

At the reception, I stood with Keiler and Dell's family as Jason and Bett cut the cake, and then shared their first dance as husband and wife.

Barry was already pestering Dell to dance the next one with him, and Dell was telling him she didn't know how.

"I can teach you," he coaxed. "I'm good."

He wasn't, unfortunately, and as the next song began, they stood on the fringe of the open area, an awkward tangle of arms and legs swaying out of time with the music.

"Guess we'd better fill in, so it doesn't look so bad." James gave Karen a nudge, and the two of them moved onto the dance floor as other guests began to join in.

Keiler cast a rueful look at me. "I'd ask you to dance"—he glanced down at his cast—"but this is a two-step, and right now I only have one left foot."

I chuckled as he held up the cast and did an impromptu hitch kick. "That's all right," I said. After I'd been rushing around with last-minute wedding preparations all day, my entire body felt like wet spaghetti. "To tell you the truth, I'd rather just sit down and enjoy the moment."

The two of us moved to a quiet table near a water garden in the corner, and I waited while Keiler went for some punch and cake, then came back juggling all four items.

"I'm sorry I'm not being a very good hostess," I said, taking the glasses from his hands.

Holding up the two slices of cake, he pretended to weigh them against each other, then handed me the smaller one and sat down. "I thought the maid of honor was officially off the clock after the ceremony."

"I suppose that's true." I couldn't help gazing wistfully toward the dance floor, where Bett was cuddled against Jason's chest, the two of them unaware that there was anyone else in the room. *How would that feel?*

"So are you?" When I turned back to Keiler, he was watching me intently, his eyes a warm, earthy brown with a frame of thick, dark lashes. I lost myself for a moment. The dance music seemed far away.

I was vaguely aware that I was leaning closer to him, resting my chin on my hand, kicking off one satin shoe, so that it hung loose on my toe. "Am I what?"

"Off the clock," he repeated, holding my gaze, as if the question had meaning beyond the words.

I took a sip of champagne punch, and the bubbles floated around in my head. "Yes. I guess I am."

"Then I can tell you now," he replied mysteriously.

"Tell me what?" Drawing back, I frowned at him, then leaned in again, my interest piqued in more ways than one. We seemed to be falling into a strange sort of dance, right there at the table. It wasn't like Keiler to be coy.

He made a show of savoring a bite of his groom's cake, chocolate with white icing. The faintest hint of it remained on his bottom lip.

"Tell me what?" I repeated, growing more insistent. His brows rose playfully, and I slapped the table. "What?"

Turning his attention to the cake, he motioned to it with his fork. "This is good." There was a lilt of laughter in his voice. "Really good."

"Keiler . . ." I ground out between clenched teeth. "Tell . . . me . . . *what?*"

"You should try it." Taking another bite, he added, "The cake, I mean."

"Keiler . . ."

Pushing his plate aside, he grinned at me. "You're kind of cute when you're mad. Anybody ever tell you that?"

Torn between responding to the compliment and threatening to wring his neck, I blushed and settled for playing his game of cat and mouse. Turning my attention to my dessert, I took a bite. "It really is good. You should try the white."

Chuckling, he reached over and stole a hunk of my cake. "Not bad." He pretended to savor it like fine wine, as if he had all the time in the world. Clearly, he knew he could outlast me in the patience game.

Unable to wait a moment longer, I set down my fork, which rang against the china plate like a gong. "All right. Out with it. What's the big secret?"

"Things broke loose at Harrington yesterday." When I reacted with a gasp, he held his hands up defensively. "I was going to tell you last night at the rehearsal, but it looked like you had enough on your mind, so I thought I'd leave it until the wedding hullabaloo was over. Anyway, I really wanted to wait until after I'd talked to Mr. Verhaden today to see what he'd heard. He said the board is going to call an emergency meeting and ask Stafford to take early retirement. By the time it's all over, he thinks they'll be offering you your job back."

"What?" I gasped, the moment slowing down and turning surreal. Any minute, the alarm clock would go off, and I'd be pulled from dreamland. Bett's perfect wedding, and Keiler telling me I might still have a job, would be only figments of my imagination. "That's impossible. . . . How did . . . What happened?"

He responded with a knowing smile. "Cameron went to the office right after morning assembly on Friday and called his dad to come pick him up, sick. I guess it was more of an attack of conscience than an illness, because as soon as they got in the car, the kid spilled the truth about his meltdown in the hall the other day. Mr. Ansler brought him back, and they took it up with Stafford. Apparently, this isn't the first time something like this has happened and Stafford swept it under the rug. Ansler had the superintendent call in a drug dog right then and there on Friday afternoon, and the dog hit on fifteen lockers in the middle school. Marijuana mostly, but there might also be some hard stuff involved. They did some swabbing to test for residues. The high school kids have been having the middle school kids hide their stuff for them, because Stafford doesn't let the drug dog come in while school's in session. When the drug dog does come to the high school, the place is clean, and so is the parking lot because . . . well . . . the stuff is in the middle school, so there you go. By Monday, you can bet there will be parents asking some serious questions."

"Oh, my God." Staring at the tabletop, I tried to take it all in, thinking of those few moments in the entryway Friday morning with Cameron, when he was still so determined to keep his secrets. "I can't believe it."

"Pretty amazing," Keiler agreed. "Either the 'Free Ms. C' campaign worked, or it was Dell's essay. Ada had her read it to the whole school during morning assembly Friday."

"Mrs. Morris?" I repeated, gaping in disbelief. "Mrs. Morris asked her to do that?"

Keiler nodded. "Yeah. She even invited Karen and James to come."

I tried to picture Dell—sweet, quiet, shy Dell—standing up in front of the entire school and her foster parents, reading that essay. "And Dell was willing to do that?"

Taking my hand, Keiler smiled. "She's a tough kid," he said, glancing at the dance floor, where Dell and Barry were finishing up a dance. "She did it for you. In fact, at the end she dedicated it to you. The kids fell into five straight minutes of '*Free Ms. C*'. I thought Stafford was going to pass out. Right after that, Cameron went to the office and called his father to come pick him up."

My lips started to tremble, and I pressed my hand over them, feeling the warm sensation of tears. Everything that had happened in the past months, every painful turn and surprising twist, now seemed worth it. Suddenly they were not disjointed events, but pearls on a string, each painstakingly selected, all perfectly matched to create something wonderful. A life. My life. Not the one I'd planned, yet something larger than I could have ever imagined.

My future hadn't died that day on the dressing room floor at the KC Metro—it had only been washed white and then repainted with something new, something equally amazing. I was just beginning to see the whole picture. I couldn't wait to find out what the next brushstrokes would be.

Sitting back in my chair, I took in everything around me—Bett folded in Jason's arms, slow dancing despite the two-stepping music; and my father, the dad of my heart, stumbling through his usual off-tempo foxtrot while Mom patiently followed; and James and Karen swing dancing in the center while a crowd of Bett's college friends clapped in admiration. In the corner, Dell and Barry were inventing their own step, colliding with each other, then laughing. As the song faded, Barry released her, and she spun away, her dark hair swirling, the diaphanous blue dress floating on an invisible breeze. Throwing her arms out, she sailed through patches of sunlight and shadow, unhindered, unashamed, caught in a moment of careless abandon, of perfect joy. A dancer lost in the music of her own soul, in the featherlight touch of God's fingertip, in the mystery and beauty of herself, as free and light as the girl in the river.

Keiler's hand tugged mine as the song changed. A soft, slow melody filled the air, and he smiled down at me. "I think even I can handle this one," he said, drawing me from my chair. The light caught his eyes as he stepped back into an empty space where golden afternoon sun poured through the veranda doors. "How's this?"

"Not bad," I said, joining him on the impromptu dance floor. Outside the window glass, a ladybug stretched her wings, perhaps catching the scent of the coming spring. As she lifted her lacy black underskirt and took flight, I imagined that she'd come all the way from Harrington, a harbinger of good fortune, a messenger, perhaps reporting to the angel on my shoulder.

Slipping into Keiler's arms, I felt everything else fall away. "It's perfect," I whispered, then stepped into the light, into my life, and was drenched from the inside out.

LISA WINGATE

Drenched in Light

This Conversation Guide is intended to enrich the
individual reading experience, as well as encourage us
to explore these topics together—because books,
and life, are meant for sharing.

A CONVERSATION WITH LISA WINGATE

Q. How do you begin to craft a novel? Does your writing process start with situations or characters?

A. Most often my stories start with a character in a particular situation. Usually, I meet the main character at a point of crisis, when something unexpected and unplanned has occurred, turning the character's life upside down. The remainder of the story is a process of watching the character grow and change, finding a new sense of order in life, a new purpose. I meet my characters as you would meet any new person. At first, I know them only on the surface, but as the story develops, I spend a great deal of time pondering their needs and desires, their secret yearnings and where those deep desires of the soul will ultimately lead them. Following a character through a story is always a growth process. They grow, and I grow right along with them.

Q. Are parts of this book based on real-life experiences?

A. *Drenched in Light* is a combination of fact and fiction. I was never a dancer when I was young—in fact, I flunked out of ballet school before the first recital. This was a great disappointment to me because I desperately wanted the recital costume, so I could play "princesses" with my neighborhood friends. But, like Julia's sister, Bethany, I didn't have the dedication necessary to pursue ballet. I was, however, a fairly serious gymnast in my adolescent years, so I understand Julia's desire to compete, to be the best, and her struggle with body image.

During my first year in college, I had a dormitory friend who was a bright, beautiful girl, but was always melancholy and conflicted about college life. While the rest of us were excited about moving into this new phase, she was very attached to the past and detached from any future plans—almost as if she were walking around in someone else's body. Her parents called often, yet she avoided the calls as often as possible. The relationship was obviously very strained. During parent weekend, it became clear that they were concerned about their daughter's ongoing struggle with an eating disorder, and a bout of depression related to her having to give up a long-held dream of professional ballet, due to health problems. She left college when the semester ended, and I always wondered if she was ever able to overcome her sense of loss and move into a new life.

Q. The stories in your Tending Roses series are connected by common characters. Do you find it hard to leave characters behind when a story ends?

A. Yes. To me, the characters have become very real by the time the book is finished. I find myself thinking of them as friends or relatives who live in another town. I picture them going about their daily lives, changing over time. Often, readers write to me asking what happened to a particular character after the end of the story. Soon enough, I find myself wondering the same thing, and that process of wondering generates another story.

Q. What was the most satisfying part of writing Drenched in Light?

A. As much as I loved seeing Julia find a new sense of purpose in her life, the most satisfying part of writing this story was seeing Dell find her voice. When I wrote the first book in the series, *Tending Roses*, Dell was the character most often asked about in reader letters. The books in the Tending Roses series have since followed her progression from neglected child, through foster care, and now finally into a new family. Throughout her life, she has always been reluctant to speak up, to stand and be counted. In standing up for Julia, she finally begins to take ownership of her own life, and to find her place in the world.

Q. When you begin writing a story, do you know how it will end?

A. I don't know at the beginning exactly how the story will end, which isn't to say that writing is a completely blind journey. Writing each book is a bit like crossing the mountains with a pocket map. On the map, I can see major landmarks, a path from one landmark to the next, and an eventual ending point on the other side of the mountains. Like all climbers, I begin the journey with excitement, enthusiasm, and my lungs full of air. At about six thousand feet, the air gets thin, I'm tired of climbing, and I'm wondering if the map will take me where I need to go. By then, I've encountered a dozen unexpected roadblocks and at least as many wonderful surprises. The story experience is becoming real, and full, and tactile. The characters are taking over, and I want their journeys to end someplace wonderful. I know that if I can just reach the crest of the mountain, I'll be able to see the finish point, and the journey down the other side will be incredibly satisfying. Finally, the characters and I sprint down the other side of the mountain, and celebrate the end of the journey together.

Of course, in reality, this celebration is just me at my computer, surrounded by imaginary people, so all that cheering probably looks ridiculous. Luckily, I'm usually alone when it happens—except for the characters, of course, and they completely understand.

QUESTIONS FOR DISCUSSION

1. Eating disorders are a growing epidemic among women of all ages, particularly young women and teenage girls. In your opinion, what factors in existence today have contributed to this growing trend?

2. Julia says that one comment from a ballet instructor sparked her descent into an eating disorder. Was this the only contributing factor to her obsession with food? What else might have contributed?

3. Before her collapse, do you think Julia thought of herself as having a serious problem? Do women often live in denial of weight and other health problems until they're faced with serious consequences? Why?

4. Now that Julia and Bethany are adults, out of college and moving into lives of their own, they are both struggling to define grown-up relationships with their mother. Do many mothers of young adults have trouble releasing the motherhood role and allowing their children to move into the world? Do many young people have difficulty forming new adult identities and taking on the accompanying responsibilities? To what degree is a parent still a parent, no matter how old the children are?

5. Even though Julia loves her sister, she finds herself jealous of Bethany's new life with Jason. Are our relationships with other people, particularly our siblings, always clouded by envy? How can we overcome this?

6. Often our lives are changed by one chance incident. How does Julia's first meeting with Dell begin to change both of their lives?

7. Julia, while realizing that there are far more problems in the school than she can conquer alone, becomes determined to help Dell. Why? Was there a special teacher in your life who made a difference?

8. Granmae makes a show of putting "angels" on the shoulders of people she meets. Do you believe in guardian angels?

9. Julia finally concludes: "We choose the things that fill us." What things do you choose? How have your choices changed over your lifetime?

10. The Costell family has never discussed the identity of Julia's father. To what degree do families keep painful things beneath the surface in order to protect one another? Is this for the best? Why or why not?

11. Do you think Julia will ever dance again? Should she? Why or why not?

A single ladybug lands featherlight on the teacher's finger, clings there, a living gemstone. A ruby with polka dots and legs. Before a slight breeze beckons the visitor away, an old children's rhyme sifts through the teacher's mind.

> *Ladybug, ladybug, fly away home,*
> *Your house is on fire, and your children are gone.*

The words leave a murky shadow as the teacher touches a student's shoulder, feels the damp warmth beneath the girl's roughly woven calico dress. The hand-stitched neckline hangs askew over smooth amber-brown skin, the garment a little too large for the girl inside it. A single puffy scar protrudes from one loosely buttoned cuff. The teacher wonders briefly about its cause, resists allowing her mind to speculate.

What would be the point? she thinks.

We all have scars.

She glances around the makeshift gathering place under the trees, the rough slabwood benches crowded with girls on the verge of woman-hood, boys seeking to step into the world of men. Leaning over crooked tables littered with nib pens, blotters, and inkwells, they read their papers, mouthing the words, intent upon the important task ahead.

All except this one girl.

"Fully prepared?" the teacher inquires, her head angling toward the girl's work. "You've practiced reading it aloud?"

"I can't do it." The girl sags, defeated in her own mind. "Not . . . not with *these* people looking on." Her young face casts miserably toward the onlookers who have gathered at the fringes of the open-air classroom—moneyed men in well-fitting suits and women in expensive dresses, petulantly waving off the afternoon heat with printed handbills and paper fans left over from the morning's fiery political speeches.

"You never know what you can do until you try," the teacher advises. Oh, how familiar that girlish insecurity is. Not so many years ago, the teacher *was* this girl. Uncertain of herself, overcome with fear. Paralyzed, really.

"I *can't*," the girl moans, clutching her stomach.

Bundling cumbersome skirts and petticoats to keep them from the dust, the teacher lowers herself to catch the girl's gaze. "Where will they hear the story if not from you—the story of being stolen away from family? Of writing an advertisement seeking any word of loved ones, and hoping to save up the fifty cents to have it printed in the *Southwestern* paper, so that it might travel through all the nearby states and territories? How will they understand the desperate need to finally know, *Are my people out there, somewhere?*"

The girl's thin shoulders lift, then wilt. "These folks ain't here because they care what I've got to say. It won't change anything."

"Perhaps it will. The most important endeavors require a risk." The teacher understands this all too well. Someday, she, too, must strike off on a similar journey, one that involves a risk.

Today, however, is for her students and for the "Lost Friends" column of the *Southwestern Christian Advocate* newspaper, and for all it represents. "At the very least, we must tell our stories, mustn't we? Speak the names? You know, there is an old proverb that says, 'We die once when the last breath leaves our bodies. We die a second time when the last person speaks our name.' The first death is beyond our control, but the second one we can strive to prevent."

"If you say so," the girl acquiesces, tenuously drawing a breath. "But I best do it right off, so I don't lose my nerve. Can I go on and give my reading before the rest?"

The teacher nods. "If you start, I'm certain the others will know to follow." Stepping back, she surveys the remainder of her group. *All the stories here,* she thinks. *People separated by impossible distance, by human fallacy, by cruelty. Enduring the terrible torture of not knowing.*

And though she'd rather not—she'd give anything if not—she imagines her own scar. One hidden beneath the skin where no one else can see it. She thinks of her own lost love, out there. Somewhere. Who knows where?

A murmur of thinly veiled impatience stirs among the audience as the girl rises and proceeds along the aisle between the benches, her posture stiffening to a strangely regal bearing. The frenzied motion of paper fans ceases and fluttering handbills go silent when she turns to speak her piece, looking neither left nor right.

"I . . ." Her voice falters. Rimming the crowd with her gaze, she clenches and unclenches her fingers, clutching thick folds of the blue-and-white calico dress. Time seems to hover then, like the ladybug deciding whether it will land or fly on.

Finally, the girl's chin rises with stalwart determination. Her voice carries past the students to the audience, demanding attention as she speaks a name that will not be silenced on this day. "I am Hannie Gossett."

LOST FRIENDS

We make no charge for publishing these letters from subscribers. All others will be charged fifty cents. Pastors will
please read the requests published below from their pulpits,
and report any case where friends are brought together by
means of letters in the *Southwestern*.

*Dear Editor—I wish to inquire for my people. My mother was
named Mittie. I am the middle of nine children and named
Hannie Gossett. The others were named Hardy, Het, Pratt,
Epheme, Addie, Easter, Ike, and Rose and were all my mother
had when separated. My grandmother was Caroline and my
grandfather Pap Ollie. My aunt was Jenny, who was married
to Uncle Clem until he died in the war. Aunt Jenny's children
were four girls, Azelle, Louisa, Martha, and Mary. Our first
owner was William Gossett of Goswood Grove Plantation,
where we were raised and kept until our Marse was in plans to
take us from Louisiana to Texas during the war, to refugee in
Texas and form a new plantation there. During plans, we
encountered the difficulty of being stolen in a group from the
Gossetts by Jeptha Loach, a nephew of Missus Gossett. He
carried us from the Old River Road south of Baton Rouge,
northward and westward across Louisiana, toward Texas. My
brothers and sisters, cousins and aunt were sold and carried
from us in Big Creek, Jatt, Winfield, Saline, Kimballs,
Greenwood, Bethany, and finally Powell town, Texas, where
my mother was taken and never seen by me again. I am now*

grown, being the only one of us who was rejected by my
purchaser in Marshall, Texas, and returned to the Gossetts
after the facts of my true ownership became clear. I am well,
but my mother is greatly missed by me, and any information of
her or any of my people is dearly desired.

I pray that all pastors and friends discovering this plea will
heed the desperate call of a broken heart and send word to me
in care of Goswood Grove Store, Augustine, Louisiana. Any
information will be acceptable and thankfully received.

Chapter 1

Hannie Gossett—Louisiana, 1875

The dream takes me from quiet sleep, same way it's done many a time, sweeps me up like dust. Away I float, a dozen years to the past, and sift from a body that's almost a woman's into a little-girl shape only six years old. Though I don't want to, I see what my little-girl eyes saw then.

I see buyers gather in the trader's yard as I peek through the gaps in the stockade log fence. I stand in winter-cold dirt tramped by so many feet before my own two. Big feet like Mama's and small feet like mine and tiny feet like Mary Angel's. Heels and toes that's left dents in the wet ground.

How many others been here before me? I wonder. How many with hearts rattlin' and muscles knotted up, but with no place to run?

Might be a hundred hundreds. Heels by the doubles and toes by the tens. Can't count high as that. I just turned from five years old to six a few months back. It's Feb'ary right now, a word I can't say right, ever. My mouth twists up and makes Feb-ba-ba-ba-bary, like a sheep. My brothers and sisters've always pestered me hard over it, all eight, even the ones that's younger. Usually, we'd tussle if Mama was off at work with the field gangs or gone to the spinnin' house, cording wool and weaving the homespun.

Our slabwood cabin would rock and rattle till finally somebody fell out the door or the window and went to howlin'. That'd bring Ol' Tati, cane switch ready, and her saying, "Gonna give you a breshin' with this switch if you don't shesh now." She'd swat butts and legs, just play-like, and we'd scamper one over top the other like baby goats scooting through the gate. We'd crawl up under them beds and try to hide, knees and elbows poking everywhere.

Can't do that no more. All my mama's children been carried off one by one and two by two. Aunt Jenny Angel and three of her four girls, gone, too. Sold away in trader yards like this one, from south Louisiana almost to Texas. My mind works hard to keep account of where all we been, our numbers dwindling by the day, as we tramp behind Jep Loach's wagon, slave chains pulling the grown folk by the wrist, and us children left with no other choice but to follow on.

But the nights been worst of all. We just hope Jep Loach falls to sleep quick from whiskey and the day's travel. It's when he don't that the bad things happen—to Mama and Aunt Jenny both, and now just to Mama, with Aunt Jenny sold off. Only Mama and me left now. Us two and Aunt Jenny's baby girl, li'l Mary Angel.

Every chance there is, Mama says them words in my ear—who's been carried away from us, and what's the names of the buyers that took them from the auction block and where're they gone to. We start with Aunt Jenny, her three oldest girls. Then come my brothers and sisters, oldest to youngest, Hardy at Big Creek, to a man name LeBas from Woodville. Het at Jatt carried off by a man name Palmer from Big Woods. . . .

Prat, Epheme, Addie, Easter, Ike, and Baby Rose tore from my mama's arms in a place called Bethany. Baby Rose wailed and Mama fought and begged and said, "We gotta be kept as one. The baby ain't weaned! Baby ain't . . ."

It shames me now, but I clung on Mama's skirts and cried, "Mama, no! Mama, no! Don't!" My body shook and my mind ran wild circles. I was afraid they'd take my mama, too, and it'd be just me and little cousin Mary Angel left when the wagon rolled on.

Jep Loach means to put all us in his pocket before he's done, but he sells just one or two at each place, so's to get out quick. Says his uncle give him the permissions for all this, but that ain't true. Old Marse and Old Missus meant for him to do what folks all over south Louisiana been doing since the Yankee gunboats pushed on upriver from New Orleans—take their slaves west so the Federals can't set us free. Go refugee on the Gossett land in Texas till the war is over. That's why they sent us with Jep Loach, but he's stole us away, instead.

"Marse Gossett gonna come for us soon's he learns of bein' crossed by Jep Loach," Mama's promised over and over. "Won't matter about Jep bein' nephew to Old Missus then. Marse gonna send Jep off to the army for the warfaring then. Only reason Jep ain't wearin' that gray uniform a'ready is Marse been paying Jep's way out. This be the end of that, and all us be shed of Jep for good. You wait and see. And that's why we chant the names, so's we know where to gather the lost when Old Marse comes. You put it deep in your rememberings, so's you can tell it if you're the one gets found first."

But now hope comes as thin as the winter light through them East Texas piney woods, as I squat inside that log pen in the trader's yard. Just Mama and me and Mary Angel here, and one goes today. One, at least. More coins in the pocket, and whoever don't get sold tramps on with Jep Loach's wagon. He'll hit the liquor right off, happy he got away with it one more time, thieving from his own kin. All Old Missus's people—all the Loach family—just bad apples, but Jep is the rottenest, worse as Old Missus herself. She's the devil, and he is, too.

"Come 'way from there, Hannie," Mama tells me. "Come here, close."

Of a sudden, the door's open, and a man's got Mary Angel's little arm, and Mama clings on, tears making a flood river while she whispers to the trader's man, who's big as a mountain and dark as a deer's eye, "We ain't his. We been stole away from Marse William Gossett of Goswood Grove plantation, down by the River Road south from Baton Rouge. We been carried off. We . . . been . . . We . . ."

She goes to her knees, folds over Mary Angel like she'd take that baby girl up inside of her if she could. "Please. Please! My sister, Jenny, been sold by this man already. And all her children but this li'l one, and all my children 'cept my Hannie. Fetch us last three out together. Fetch us out, all three. Tell your marse this baby girl, she sickly. Say we gotta be sold off in one lot. All three together. Have mercy. Please! Tell your marse we been stole from Marse William Gossett at Goswood Grove, down off the River Road. We stole property. We been stole."

The man's groan comes old and tired. "Can't do nothin'. Can't nobody do nothin' 'bout it all. You just make it go hard on the child. You just make it go hard. Two gotta go today. In two dif'ernt lots. One at a time."

"No." Mama's eyes close hard, then open again. She looks up at the man, coughs out words and tears and spit all together. "Tell my marse William Gossett—when he comes here seeking after us—at least give word of where we gone to. Name who carries us away and where they strikes off for. Old Marse Gossett's gonna find us, take us to refugee in Texas, all us together."

The man don't answer, and Mama turns to Mary Angel, slips out a scrap of brown homespun cut from the hem of Aunt Jenny Angel's heavy winter petticoat while we camped with the wagon. By their own hands, Mama and Aunt Jenny Angel made fifteen tiny poke sacks, hung with jute strings they stole out of the wagon.

Inside each bag went three blue glass beads off the string Grandmama always kept special. Them beads was her most precious thing, come all the way from Africa. That where my grandmama and grandpoppy's cotched from. She'd tell that tale by the tallow candle on winter nights, all us gathered round her lap in that ring of light. Then she'd share about Africa, where our people been before here. Where they was queens and princes.

Blue mean all us walk in the true way. The fam'ly be loyal, each to the other, always and ever, she'd say, and then her eyes would gather at the corners and she'd take out that string of beads and let all us pass it in the circle, hold its weight in our hands. Feel a tiny piece of that far-off place . . . and the meanin' of blue.

Three beads been made ready to go with my li'l cousin, now.

Mama holds tight to Mary Angel's chin. "This a promise." Mama tucks that pouch down Mary Angel's dress and ties the strings round a skinny little baby neck that's still too small for the head on it. "You hold it close by, li'l pea. If that's the only thing you do, you keep it. This the sign of your people. We lay our eyes on each other again in this life, no matter how long it be from now, this how we, each of us, knows the other one. If long time pass, and you get up big, by the beads we still gonna know you. Listen at me. You hear Aunt Mittie, now?" She makes a motion with her hands. A needle and thread. Beads on a string. "We put this string back together someday, all us. In this world, God willing, or in the next."

Li'l Mary Angel don't nod nor blink nor speak. Used to, she'd chatter the ears off your head, but not no more. A big ol' tear spills down her brown skin as the man carries her out the door, her arms and legs stiff as a carved wood doll's.

Time jumps round then. Don't know how, but I'm back at the wall, watching betwixt the logs while Mary Angel gets brung 'cross the yard. Her little brown shoes dangle in the air, same brogans all us got in our Christmas boxes just two month ago, special made right there on Goswood by Uncle Ira, who kept the tanner shop, and mended the harness, and sewed up all them new Christmas shoes.

I think of him and home while I watch Mary Angel's little shoes up on the auction block. Cold wind snakes over her skinny legs when her dress gets pulled up and the man says she's got good, straight knees. Mama just weeps. But somebody's got to listen for who takes Mary Angel. Somebody's got to add her to the chant.

So I do.

Seems like just a minute goes by before a big hand circles my arm, and it's me getting dragged 'cross the floor. My shoulder wrenches loose with a pop. The heels of my Christmas shoes furrow the dirt like plow blades.

"No! Mama! Help me!" My blood runs wild. I fight and scream, catch Mama's arm, and she catches mine.

Don't let go, my eyes tell hers. Of a sudden, I understand the big man's words and how come they broke Mama down. Two gotta go today. In two dif'ernt lots. One at a time.

This is the day the worse happens. Last day for me and Mama. Two gets sold here and one goes on with Jep Loach, to get sold at the next place down the road. My stomach heaves and burns in my throat, but ain't nothing there to retch up. I make water down my leg, and it fills up my shoe and soaks over to the dirt.

"Please! Please! Us two, together!" Mama begs.

The man kicks her hard, and our hands rip apart at the weave. Mama's head hits the logs, and she crumples in the little dents from all them other feet, her face quiet like she's gone asleep. A tiny brown poke dangles in her hand. Three blue beads roll loose in the dust.

"You give me any trouble, and I'll shoot her dead where she lies." The voice runs over me on spider legs. Ain't the trader's man that's got me. It's Jep Loach. I ain't being carried to the block. I'm being took to the devil wagon. I'm the one he means to sell at the someplace farther on.

I tear loose, try to run back to Mama, but my knees go soft as wet grass. I topple and stretch my fingers toward the beads, toward my mother.

"Mama! Mama!" I scream and scream and scream. . . .

It's my own voice that wakes me from the dream of that terrible day, just like always. I hear the sound of the scream, feel the raw of it in my throat. I come to, fighting off Jep Loach's big hands and crying out for the mother I ain't laid eyes on in twelve years now, since I was a six-year-old child.

"Mama! Mama! Mama!" The word spills from me three times more, travels out 'cross the night-quiet fields of Goswood Grove before I clamp my mouth closed and look back over my shoulder toward the sharecrop cabin, hoping they didn't hear me. No sense to wake everybody with my sleep-wanderings. Hard day's work ahead for me and Ol' Tati and what's left of the stray young ones she's raised these long years since the war was over and we had no mamas or papas to claim us.

Of all my brothers and sisters, of all my family stole away by Jep Loach, I was the only one Marse Gossett got back, and that was just by luck when folks at the next auction sale figured out I was stole property and called the sheriff to hold me until Marse could come. With the war on, and folks running everywhere to get away from it, and us trying to scratch a living from the wild Texas land, there wasn't any going back to look for the rest. I was a child with nobody of my own when the Federal soldiers finally made their way to our refugee place in Texas and forced the Gossetts to read the free papers out loud and say the war was over, even in Texas. Slaves could go where they pleased, now.

Old Missus warned all us we wouldn't make it five miles before we starved or got killed by road agents or scalped by Indians, and she hoped we did, if we'd be ungrateful and foolish enough to do such a thing as leave. With the war over, there wasn't no more need to refugee in Texas, and we'd best come back to Louisiana with her and Marse Gossett— who we was now to call Mister, not Marse, so's not to bring down the wrath of Federal soldiers who'd be crawling over everything like lice for a while yet. Back on the old place at Goswood Grove, we would at least have Old Mister and Missus to keep us safe and fed and put clothes on our miserable bodies.

"Now, you young children have no choice in the matter," she told the ones of us with no folk. "You are in our charge, and of course we will give you the benefit of transporting you away from this godforsaken Texas wilderness, back to Goswood Grove until you are of age or a parent comes to claim you."

Much as I hated Old Missus and working in the house as keeper and plaything to Little Missy Lavinia, who was a trial of her own, I rested in the promise Mama had spoke just two years before at the trader's yard. She'd come to find me, soon's she could. She'd find all us, and we'd string Grandmama's beads together again.

And so I was biddable but also restless with hope. It was the restless part that spurred me to wander at night, that conjured evil dreams of Jep Loach, and watching my people get stole away, and seeing Mama laid out on the floor of the trader's pen. Dead, for all I could know then.

For all I still do know.

I look down and see that I been walking in my sleep again. I'm standing out on the old cutoff pecan stump. A field of fresh soil spreads out, the season's new-planted crop still too wispy and fine to cover it. Moon ribbons fall over the row tips, so the land is a giant loom, the warp threads strung but waiting on the weaving woman to slide the shuttle back and forth, back and forth, making cloth the way the women slaves did before the war. Spinning houses sit empty now that store-bought calico comes cheap from mills in the North. But back in the old days when I was a little child, it was card the cotton, card the wool. Spin a broach of thread every night after tromping in from the field. That was Mama's life at Goswood Grove. Had to be or she'd have Old Missus to deal with.

This stump—this very one—was where the slave driver stood to watch the gangs work the field, cowhide whip dangling down like a snake ready to bite, keep everybody picking the cotton rows. Somebody lag behind, try to rest a minute, the driver would find them out. If Old Marse Gossett was home, they'd only get a little breshin' with the whip. But if Marse Gossett was off in New Orleans, where he kept his other family everybody knew about but didn't dare to speak of, then look out. The whipping would be bad, because Old Missus was in charge. Missus didn't like it that her husband had him a plaçage woman and a fawn-pale child down in New Orleans. Neighborhoods like Faubourg Marigny and Tremé—the rich planter men kept their mistresses and children there. Fancy girls, quadroons and octoroons. Women with dainty bones and olive-brown skin, living in fine houses with slaves to look after them, too.

Old ways like that been almost gone in these years since Mr. Lincoln's war ended. The slave driver and his whip, Mama and the field gangs working from see to can't see, leg irons, and auction sales like the ones that took my people—all that's a thing in the barely back of my mind.

Sometimes when I wake, I think all my people were just somethin' I pretended, never real at all. But then I touch the three glass beads on the cord at my neck, and I tell their names in the chant. Hardy gone at Big Creek to a man from Woodville, Het at Jatt . . .

All the way down to Baby Rose and Mary Angel. And Mama. It was real. We were real. A family together.

I look off in the distant, wobble twixt a six-year-old body and one that's eighteen years growed, but not so much different. Still skinny as if I was carved out of sticks.

Mama always did say, Hannie, you stand behind the broom handle, I can't even see you there. Then she'd smile and touch my face and whisper, But you a beautiful child. Always been pretty. I hear it like she's there beside of me, a white oak basket on her arm, bound for the garden patch out behind our little cabin, last one down the end of the old quarters.

Just as quick as I feel her there, she's gone again.

"Why didn't you come?" My words hang in the night air. "Why didn't you come for your child? You never come." I sink down on the stump's edge and look out toward the trees by the road, their thick trunks hid in sifts of moon and fog.

I think I see something in it. A haint, could be. Too many folk buried under Goswood soil, Ol' Tati says when she tells us tales in the cropper cabin at night. Too much blood and sufferin' been left here. This place always gonna have ghosts.

A horse nickers low. I see a rider on the road. A dark cloak covers the head and sweeps out, light as smoke.

That my mama, come to find me? Come to say, You almost eighteen years old, Hannie. Why you still settin' on that same ol' stump? I want to go to her. Go away with her.

That Old Mister, come home from fetching his wicked son out of trouble again?

That a haint, come to drag me off and drown me in the river?

I close my eyes, shake my head clear, look again. Nothing there but a drift of fog.

"Child?" Tati's whisper comes from a ways off, worried, careful-like. "Child?" Don't matter your age, if Tati raised you, you stay child to her. Even the strays that've growed up and moved on, they're still child, if they come to visit.

I cock my ear, open my mouth to answer her, but then I can't. Somebody is there—a woman by the high white pillars at the Goswood gate, afoot now. The oaks whisper overhead, like it's worried their old bones to have her come to the drive. A low-hung branch grabs her hood and her long, dark hair floats free.

"M-mama?" I say.

"Child?" Tati whispers again. "You there?" I hear her hurry along, her walking stick tapping faster till she's found me.

"I see Mama coming."

"You dreamin', sugar." Tati's knobby fingers wrap my wrist, gentle-like, but she keeps a distant. Sometimes, my dreams let go with a fight. I wake kicking and clawing to get Jep Loach's hand off my arm. "Child, you all right. You just walkin' in the dream. Wake up, now. Mama ain't here, but Ol' Tati, she right here. You safe."

I glance away from the gates, then back. The woman's gone, and no matter how hard I look, I can't see her.

"Wake up, now, child." In moonglow, Tati's face is the red-brown of cypress wood pulled up from the deep water, dark against the sack-muslin cap over her silvery hair. She slides a shawl off her arm, reaches it round me. "Out here in the field in all the wetness! Get a pleurisy. Where all us be with that kind of troublement? Who Jason gonna settle in with, then?"

Tati nudges me with the cane stick, pestering. The thing she wants most is for Jason and me to marry. Once the ten years on the sharecrop contract with Old Mister is done and the land is hers, Tati needs some-body to hand it down to. Me and the twins, Jason and John, are the last of her strays. One more growing season is all that's left for the contract, but Jason and me? We been raised in Tati's house like brother and sister. Hard to see things any other way, but Jason is a good boy. Honest worker, even if both him and John did come into this world a shade slower minded than most.

"I ain't dreamin'," I say when Tati tugs me from the stump.

"Devil, you ain't. Come on back, now. We got work waitin' in the mornin'. Gonna tie your ankle to the bed, you don't stop dealing me this night misery. You been worser lately. Worser in these walkin' dreams than when you was a li'l thing."

I jerk against Tati's arm, remembering all the times as a child I wan-dered from my sleep pallet by Missy Lavinia's crib, and woke up to Old Missus whipping me with the kitchen spoon or a riding whip or a iron pot hook from the fireplace. Whatever was close by.

"Hesh, now. You can't help it." Tati scoops down for a pinch of dirt to throw over her shoulder. "Put it behind you. New day comin' and plenty to do. C'mon now, throw you a pinch your own self, to be safe."

I do what she says and then make the cross over my chest, and Tati does, too. "Father, Son, Holy Ghost," we whisper together. "Guide us and protect us. Keep us ahead and behind. Ever and ever. Amen."

I hadn't ought to, then—bad business to look back for a haint once you throwed ground twixt you and it—but I do. I glance at the road.

I'm cold all over.

"What you doin'?" Tati near trips when I stop so sudden.

"I wasn't dreamin'," I whisper, and I don't just look. I point, but my hand shakes. "I was lookin' at her."

LOST FRIENDS

We make no charge for publishing these letters from subscribers. All others will be charged fifty cents. Pastors will please read the requests published below from their pulpits, and report any case where friends are brought together by means of letters in the *Southwestern*.

Dear Editor—I wish to inquire for a woman named Caroline, who belonged to a man in the Cherokee Nation, Indian Territory, named John Hawkins, or "Google-eyed" Smith, as he was commonly called. Smith took her from the Nation to Texas, and sold her again. The whole family belonged to Delanos before they were scattered and sold. Her mother's name was Letta; father's name Samuel Melton; children's names, Amerietta, Susan, Esau, Angeline, Jacob, Oliver, Emeline, and Isaac. If any of your readers hear of such a person, they will confer a favor on a dear sister, Amerietta Gibson, by addressing me at Independence, Kans., P.O. Box 94.

Wm. B. Avery, Pastor

—"Lost Friends" column of the *Southwestern*
August 24, 1880